"I . . . I can't move," white lab coat looking

"We had to use the stra "You've had periods of intense violence over the last several weeks." He hesitated, then asked, "Peter, do you know what happened to you?"

Peter shook his head.

"Well, you've been through what we call ingentisization. That is, your body has fully expressed its genotype. It seems you looked like a *homo sapiens sapiens* up until now—but you are actually a *homo sapiens ingentis.*"

"Ingentis?" Peter asked.

"The common term, the media term, for what you are is . . . troll."

Suddenly enraged and frantic, Peter pulled himself up. He saw that his arms were massive, as thick as the thighs of a normal man. The flesh was grayish-green, layered with red heat, and it was rough, with thick horny knobs. The long fingers attached to his huge hands were tipped with hard, sharp nails. And his body . . . although covered in hospital whites, he could tell he was now nearly three meters tall.

But now Peter was getting groggy again, things began to blur. And then all went black. . . .

SHADOWRUN 5: CHANGELING

SHADOWRUN 5:

CHANGELING

CHRIS KUBASIK

A ROC BOOK

ROC
Published by the Penguin Group
Penguin Books USA Inc., 375 Hudson Street,
New York, New York 10014, U.S.A.
Penguin Books Ltd, 27 Wrights Lane, London W8 5TZ, England
Penguin Books Australia Ltd, Ringwood, Victoria, Australia
Penguin Books Canada Ltd, 10 Alcorn Avenue, Toronto, Ontario,
Canada M4V 3B2
Penguin Books (N.Z.) Ltd, 182-190 Wairau Road, Auckland 10,
New Zealand

Penguin Books Ltd, Registered Offices:
Harmondsworth, Middlesex, England

First published by Roc, an imprint of New American Library,
a division of Penguin Books USA Inc.

First Printing, June, 1992
10 9 8 7 6 5 4 3 2 1

For my father, who kept the house well-stocked with books.

PART 1

CHANGING

September 2039

change (chānj). *v.*, **changed, changing, changes.**—*v.t.* **1.** To make different; alter in condition, appearance, etc. <*changing* one's habits>. **2.** To substitute another or others for; exchange for something else <*change* shuttle-craft>. **3.** To give and take reciprocally; interchange <*change* places with someone>.—*vi.* **4.** To become different; alter (fol by *to* or *into*). *n.* **5.** Variation; alteration; modification; transformation. **6.** Passing from one place, state, form, or phase to another <*changing* of the moon>.—syn: **1.** TRANSMUTE, TRANSFORM. **7.** Awakening (slang, North America)

1

A room.

A white room.

A pungent smell of sterility.

He tried to remember his name, and could not.

A sheet covered his body. Across the sheet thick, taut straps held him down, disappearing over the edge of the bed. Brief images of abandonment in the woods, Hansel and Gretel, danced in his thoughts, then vanished. Before him was a door. Who was behind it?

He felt straps holding down his wrists as well, but could not see them, for the sheet covered every part of his body but his head.

Part of the sheet glowed red, a warm red, where the cloth rested over his legs and chest and the rest of his body. The redness dissipated and faded where the sheet was not in such close contact with his body. At the edge of the bed it was the usual white.

"Hello?" he tried to say, but the word came out as only a dry croak. The effort tore a white pain through his throat, and he swallowed to soothe it.

He turned his head, looking to the left. On one side of the room was a window with blinds. It was dark outside, though across the street he saw the bright red lights of a tall building. A memory came to him. A small bedroom viewed from the doorway. Near the room's single window, a crib. The room was dimly lit by the yellow light of street lamps. Inside the room was nothing but the crib. This was where he was put at night. His cries went unanswered.

He turned from the memory and saw machinery to his right. Metal boxes that he could make out clearly enough, but, like the sheet, their sides were tinted by warm redness. On a small round screen a red dot blipped up and down.

He realized that tubes ran from another machine under the sheets—perhaps into his arms.

Was he was supposed to do something? Was there someone he should talk to? How did he get here? He caught another quick glimpse of a memory—a bedroom, getting out of bed, sticky sweat thick on his body, falling to the ground, darkness. . . . But no more.

He tried to move his arms, and could not. The straps.

Everything was wrong. That much he knew. The world was too red. His thoughts too slow. Something had happened.

He was very tired. He wanted to speak to someone, find out specifics, but there was no one to talk to.

He closed his eyes.

He woke up.

He remembered right away he was in a hospital. He remembered he's already woken up in the hospital several times.

He remembered his name was Peter.

Peter remembered he had a father.

He remembered that he and his father lived in Chicago. But where was his father? Peter couldn't remember what he looked like. He wasn't even sure if his father knew where he was.

He heard movement on the other side of the room. He looked and saw a woman, her flesh iridescent with the glow of heat. Her uniform was white, mixed with warmer patches where her body met cloth. She heard him move and turned to look at him. Her face astounded him; an angel of light.

Her face became brighter, a fear tugging at the corners of her cheeks. She tried to hide it, but her half-step back revealed all.

She formed a weak smile and, then, still facing him, she backed up to the door and let herself out.

What had she seen? He tried to raise his hands to his face, but the straps around his wrists still held his hands down.

He tried to think of what he was. A person. Fifteen years old. Yes, that. But something had happened.

He remembered his father.

The two of them were riding in a plated limousine, back from a party somewhere. Peter felt the weight of the car in its movements around turns and when it stopped. His father looked patiently out the window.

A pane of plastic separated the driver from the two of them, and Peter said, "I met someone at the party."

His father turned to him, and said, "Hmmm." His eyes were large and unfocused and frightening. They hovered over Peter like the magnifying lenses of a microscope.

"Her name's Denise. Denise Lewis."

"Well, she was there with her parents. It's not that unreasonable that you'd meet."

"We talked, and we thought we'd get together."

His father turned back toward the window. "Hmmm."

"You know, go out." Wouldn't his father at least smile for him?

His father remained silent.

"I really liked her. She's sharp."

Still nothing.

"I think she liked me, too."

They rode in silence a while longer. Peter decided to give his father plenty of time to say something, but many minutes passed without a response. "This is my first date, dad," he said finally. "I'm pretty excited."

His father continued to look away from Peter. "Just don't expect anything," he said.

"What?"

His father's voice carried something new, a bit of emotional weight that Peter had never heard from him before. "I can hear it in your voice. You're getting your hopes up."

"I'm just happy I met her, and I'm looking forward to seeing her again."

"That's what I mean. You're happy. You have expectations. You don't have to listen to me. I don't think you will. You're young. But happiness isn't . . . You're better off not trying to get it." His father's words resonated with a pitiable wisdom.

For a moment Peter thought he'd stop breathing. How could his father say such a thing? Peter couldn't remember ever being so excited before, and now his father was telling him to have no hope.

He sat back in his seat and clenched his hands together. He wanted to shout at his father, to seize him, to spin him away from his placid position of staring out the window. The impulse building in him was tremendous, both unexpected and dangerous. He wanted to flail his fists at his father's back, anything to get his attention, to show how angry and hurt his father's word made him. But Peter did nothing, for deep within his heart, he feared that his father might be right. "Happiness isn't . . .," his father had said. True? Peter's mother had died at the moment of his birth.

He realized that his father had swallowed the pain of his wife's death and kept it tight in his throat, and now he was suggesting that Peter do the same.

He opened his eyes.

A man stood over Peter. His body glowed, the white lab coat lit from within by the heat of his body.

His father?

No.

Peter turned his head. His father stood on the other side of the bed, looking down at him. A bright, warm glow emanated from his flesh. The clinical and indifferent expression of his eyes turned the face into something demonic.

"Dad?" The word came out dry and nearly silent. His father did not respond, but continued to stare down at him. The dark smudges under his eyes told Peter his father was very tired.

The man in the lab coat cleared his throat. "Peter?"

Peter turned to him. He realized the man was a doctor. The doctor smiled. Peter was relieved for a moment, then realized it was a lie. The man was only forcing the smile.

"Yes?"

"Peter, you've been through a lot in the last month. . . ."

Month?

". . . and I don't want to exhaust you. But you're past the worst now. I want you to understand that."

Peter looked back to his father. He tried to raise his hand, to hold it out so his father would take it, but it was still tied down.

"I'm . . . I can't move."

"We've had to strap you down," said the doctor. "You've had periods of intense violence over the last several weeks. For your own safety, we had to make sure you couldn't do harm to anyone."

Peter ignored the doctor. "Dad, am I going to be all right?"

His father remained silent, then looked away. "I don't know."

Peter heard the doctor gasp. "Dr. Clarris . . ."

"I don't!" his father snapped.

It was as if William Clarris didn't even know his son was in the room. "Dad . . ."

"Excuse me," said his father, who then abruptly turned and left the room.

The doctor rushed after Peter's father. "I'll be right back," he threw out over his shoulder.

"No, it's all right," Peter began to say, but the doctor was already gone.

Peter stared up at the ceiling. He felt his chin begin to tremble, but he didn't want to cry, so he tried to remember things from his past. He remembered he liked to drink milk, and for a moment he thought some was available, sitting on top of one of the machines, but then nothing was there. He remembered too that he went to school. He saw an image of a teacher by a flatscreen, displaying notes for a lecture. But he couldn't remember what he did in school. He learned, he knew that much. But what did he learn about? Words, numbers, frogs, cells. All he could remember were pictures. The rest was gone.

It was while Peter was remembering that his father talked with him about schoolwork that the doctor returned. He'd slapped a fresh, new false smile across his face.

"Well, Peter, I think it's time you and I had a talk."

"My father?" He kept his words simple, for it hurt to speak.

The doctor raised his hands to dismiss Peter's worries. "He went for a walk. He's been very concerned about you, and he just needed some air. He'll be back later."

Peter believed the doctor, and then he didn't, and then he decided he couldn't do anything about it either way, so he said nothing.

"Peter, do you know what's happened to you?"

Peter shook his head.

"How much do you remember about . . . the world,

Peter? Many people who've been through what you have often lose a bit of memory."

Peter tried to remember what kinds of things the doctor might be referring to. "I remember my father. A party. Waking up in the middle of the night."

"Hmmm. Well, Peter, you've been through what we in the medical world call ingentisization. That is, your body has fully expressed its genotype, and it turns out that although you looked like a *homo sapiens sapiens* all your life, you actually are a *homo sapiens ingentis.*" He smiled reassuringly, but Peter was not reassured. He had no idea what the doctor was talking about.

"Ingentis?" Peter asked.

The doctor folded his hands before him and paused before answering. "The common term, the media term, for what you are is troll, Peter. Do you remember that word?"

He thought hard, and then images came to him. Huge people, gray and green, with massive teeth and large red eyes. He nodded.

"Do you remember anything about the history of Unexplained Genetic Expression?"

Snippets. "It surprised people. Before I was born." Magic?

"The UGE cases started just before the Indians used shamanistic magic to get portions of the western American states ceded to them. Magic, for lack of a better word, was altering much of the world. Some children, born of human parents, suddenly began to transform into another species. Some were short and stocky, others tall and thin, with long ears. The media started calling them dwarfs and elves, as if they were living embodiments of mythical creatures. But, of course, they weren't. They just happened to match the image of dwarfs and elves from children's stories. They were *homo sapiens*, just a new subspecies. What the media called dwarfs were *homo sapiens pumillonis,* and what the people called elves were *homo sapiens nobilis.*''

Peter vaguely remembered some of this. "And there are *homo sapiens robustus* and *homo sapiens ingentis.*''

"Yes. And all are human. All are human beings. The media calls them metahumans.''

But something caught in Peter's thoughts. "Why different names?''

"What?''

"Why not 'elves'? Why not 'dwarfs'?''

The doctor's voice raised in pitch. "Because they're not elves! They're not dwarfs! Those things don't exist!''

The doctor's excitement made Peter nervous, so he remained quiet. He perceived a flaw in the doctor's argument, but his thoughts were too confused for him to successfully point it out. Peter's silence made the doctor smile. "There. You see? You'll get better. Right now, your memories are confused. When your body changed, so did your brain. It rebuilt itself. And during that process, you lost some of your memory because memories are stored in the patterns of the brain. But some of it is still there. Some of it you'll have to re-learn. But you can do it.''

Peter ignored the words. "What am I? I'm a *sapiens ingentis?*'' A prickling ran up his spine. Only now did he put the doctor's words together.

"Well, the first thing you have to keep in mind is that you are still you. You must hold this very close, Peter, because this is where most people in your condition get lost. And these days a case like yours is very rare. Spontaneous UG-Expressions haven't been common since 2021. In the last two decades most people are born as their genotype directs. People like you, who live all the way to adolescence as one phenotype, and then radically change to another phenotype . . .

often think they have become someone else—*some-thing* else. They have not. You *are* not.''

"I feel like someone else. My head. Like . . . slow."

The doctor looked down. "Yes. There will be differences."

"Everything is red."

The doctor nodded. "Yes, your eyes are seeing differently. My eyes are sensitive only to normal light, the visible-light spectrum. Your eyes are also sensitive to the infrared wavelengths, to heat energy. In conjunction with your normal vision, you also see heat expressed as a red-coloration shift. . . ." The doctor trailed off. "It will be strange at first, but you'll grow used to it."

Peter remembered the nurse's reaction to him. What had been hazy for the last few minutes became clear. "I'm a troll."

"No! You are a human being."

"I'm ugly."

"Beauty changes, Peter."

He thought of his father's departure. His own father could not bear to be near him. A scream rushed up from deep inside and ripped through his throat. He had to get out, do something. Move. He twisted from side to side, rocking the bed back and forth. He howled. He wanted to break free and slam his hands into his head. He wanted to die. He wanted to feel so much pain that he could just die.

The doctor drew a hypodermic needle from his coat pocket and raised it toward Peter, the needle looking huge and dangerous. Peter lifted his head and tried to bite the doctor's hand. The doctor pulled back and ran for the door. "Orderlies!"

Peter felt the strap around his right hand begin to stretch. He focused on that hand.

A clatter of footsteps at the door caught his attention. The doctor was back, bringing with him two big men. Taking positions on either side of Peter, the orderlies forced his shoulders down. But at that moment Peter finally broke the right-hand strap, and swung his fist up toward the orderly on that side. His fist slammed into the man's belly, the impact lifting the orderly up off the floor and throwing him against the wall.

Peter turned wildly toward the second orderly. He didn't have a plan, he just wanted to hurt someone. But before he could swing his fist to the left, he felt the hypo needle sting his left shoulder. Turning his head, he saw the second orderly and the doctor jump back.

Still enraged and frantic, Peter pulled himself up and grabbed for the strap around his left hand, then froze, transfixed by the image of his right arm.

The arm was massive, as thick as the thigh of a normal man. The flesh was grayish-green, layered with red heat, and it was rough, with thick, horny knobs growing along it. The hand was huge, the long fingers tipped with hard, sharp nails.

Then Peter looked down at his enormous body. Although covered in hospital whites, he could tell he was now nearly three meters tall.

But he was getting groggy again. Things were starting to blur.

He turned his head again to look at his hand. He raised the hand up before his face, both horrified and fascinated that the hand could be his.

And then all went black and a dream washed over him.

2

He dreamed he was back in his house.

The cramps had started in the middle of the night, waking him up doubled-over in pain. It felt like nails or pins inside him, inside his stomach, trying to pierce their way out.

He shivered, thinking for a moment it was winter and that someone had left the window open. Then he remembered the party and that it was the end of summer and not very cold at all.

The sheets of his bed were soaked with sweat. It felt awful and he wanted to get out of bed, but feared he'd be even colder out from under his blanket.

"Dad?" he said weakly. He had wanted to shout it, but discovered he couldn't.

He pushed the sheets off the bed, feeling his muscles sore and stiff. He touched his fingertips to his chest, then pulled back his hand in horror. Something was very wrong. His skin felt hard and rough. He looked down at his body, which was illuminated by the street lamps outside his window.

He looked normal . . . except for the calluses covering his chest and stomach. Slight, barely visible, but there. He pressed his palms together. The same. He'd grown up hearing stories of the plagues that killed millions at the start of the century. Was this another one?

He stepped out of bed. He had to get to his father; he had to get help.

A dizziness grabbed hold of his vision. He took only three steps before falling to the ground. His legs felt as though they weren't his. "Dad?" he said weakly, dragging himself toward the bedroom door. When a light went on in the hall, accompanied by the sound of footsteps, he stopped.

A fuzzy silhouette appeared in the doorway. "Peter?"

His father came and knelt beside him, beginning to probe and poke at Peter's skin with his hands.

Peter heard his father mutter something under his breath—"Goblinization." Then he heard him say out loud, "I'll be right back. I've got to call an ambulance."

His father left him.

Peter woke with a violent gasp, confused for a moment, and then aware of his surroundings. He looked around. An orderly sat in a chair in one corner of the room, watching the flatscreen on the wall. The screen showed an image of buildings on fire. The words "LIVE from Seattle" and "Racial Violence" floated over the pictures. In front of the buildings crowds of pure humans were throwing bottles and rocks at the elves and dwarfs and trolls and orks who were trying to escape the fires. Police in riot gear shot tear gas into the crowds. The gas dispersed groups of pure humans, but blocked the escape of the metahumans.

"What's happening?"

The orderly turned to look at Peter, then stood up slowly and walked to the bed.

A warning clicked in Peter's head. The man was dangerous. He didn't know how he knew, only that the danger was real. With subtle tugs he checked his straps. All were back in place.

The orderly stood over Peter. "Don't know for sure. Looks like the city of Seattle rounded up all its metahumans to send them off to camps, but the fragging pintips lit themselves up. There are riots all over the city now."

"Oh."

"By the way, you really nailed a buddy of mine yesterday."

"I didn't . . ."

The orderly slammed his hand down into Peter's right cheek, which stung with pain. Peter decided that since he couldn't take action, he wouldn't say anything. He'd let things blow over. Let the man get it out of his system.

The orderly punched him again, the pain digging deeper this time.

When the orderly pulled back for the third blow, Peter tried to jerk his head away, but the other man compensated and hit him in the same spot for a third time.

"Stop. . . . Please."

"Why should I, you stupid trog."

"You don't understand. I just changed into a troll. I used to be normal."

The orderly raised his fist. Peter jerked away and the orderly grinned down at him, proud of his trick. "Don't make no difference to me, chummer. You're a troll and you act like a troll."

Peter wanted to ask, "And what are you acting like?" but kept his mouth shut.

The doctor appeared in the doorway, where he'd stopped, startled by the scene in Peter's room. "I told you to call me as soon as he woke up."

"Sorry, Doc."

"Is everything all right?"

"Oh, sure. Me and the patient . . ."

"I wasn't talking to you."

"Yes," said Peter. "Everything is fine."

The orderly walked to the flatscreen and turned it off.

"Please leave us alone," the doctor said wearily.

Moving obediently toward the door, the orderly stepped behind the doctor and caught Peter's eye. He held a finger before his lips and then mimed a punch into his open palm. Then he was gone. Again, Peter decided to hold his tongue.

"Peter, we must talk," said the doctor.

"All right."

"What happened yesterday . . . It does happen in cases like yours. But you must control your anger. You are much stronger than you realize. You cannot afford to lose your temper.

"Now, I understand you're under a lot of stress, but that can't be an excuse. The world still fears people like you. It will take time for things to work themselves out."

"There are riots in Seattle."

"Yes."

"What makes you think it will work itself out?"

The doctor smiled down at Peter. "You're probably wiser than I, but I cling to my faith."

"When can I go home?"

"That's what I wanted to talk to you about, Peter. You're being discharged tomorrow. Your father has secured an out-patient therapist who will help you get used to your body. He's one of the best in the world, actually—"

"What do you mean, get used to my body?"

"Peter, you're hundreds of kilos heavier than when you arrived. You're head and shoulders taller. You haven't used your muscles for weeks. It will take time."

"What about how I think?"

"Think?"

"What about how I think?" He remembered the orderly punching him. "And my anger. You said I can't afford to get angry. But what if I am angry? What if I'm angry about being a troll? Because I'm not a troll, and it makes me angry that I look like one."

"Listen to me! This is very important. Do you remember about DNA—about genetics?"

Peter searched his memory, becoming more and more frustrated. It was bad enough knowing he had forgotten so much. It was even worse to be quizzed so that his lost memories could be catalogued.

But then he did remember something about DNA.

"It's like a code, isn't it? Letters all strung together. They spell a person, right?" Then he felt very stupid, for he knew there were no letters in a person; a person wasn't spelled out like a sentence. "I'm sorry. I'm not sure where . . ."

"No, no. That's good. It's inaccurate, but you're on the right track. We think of DNA as a code. A code with four letters. The letters are based on the four nitrogenous bases that are in the DNA: A for adenine, G for guanine, C for cytosine, and T for thymine. The four letters are arranged in different combinations and different lengths to make up a gene. There might be tens of thousands, or hundreds of thousands, or even millions of these letters defining a single gene. It goes like this: GCATGTATCCTGTA and so on."

Peter got excited. He could taste the memory of the idea, and wanted to swallow it down whole. "And genes, what are they again?"

"Genes are . . . They define the aspects of a person. They define the color of your hair, the size of your skull. They make sure you have blood in your body. They define your skin color."

"Yes! I remember some of it now. And the genes are scattered along chromosomes."

"Exactly."

In his excitement, Peter tried to get up on his elbows, but the straps held him down. He fell back against the pillow and said, "And?"

The doctor tried to pick the energy back up. "Well, at the end of the twentieth century we started mapping the code sequences of DNA. Up until then we knew about DNA, but we didn't know which genes along the code sequence did what. It was called the Genome

Project. It was a worldwide effort though much of the work was done by the old United States government. Scientists all over the world studied portions of many human DNA sequences, then compared the results. They found common patterns, and eventually labeled certain parts of the sequence for certain tasks.

"For example—oh, what was his name? Fajans, at the U. of Michigan, spent thirty-two years following five generations of one family. Several dozen of the hundreds of people he studied had a form of maturity-onset diabetes. Then a geneticist, Bell, waded through the family gene pool, searching for similar areas on chromosomes shared by the family members with diabetes. He found some markers for the diabetes genes, but it was only a beginning. After three and a half years of work, they narrowed the choice of three billion base pairs down to ten million. Good, but not good enough.

"That's just one example. Research like this was happening all over the country. I only know about the Bell project because I studied it in school.

"But when the country broke up, most of the new nations held information back from scientists in other countries. And now corporations hold the information, and they're even more loathe to share it. It became more difficult to double-check patterns. The Genome Project slowed considerably until just recently."

"But they did get a good map of humans, right? Pure humans?"

"Well, they got a pretty good map. The problem was that even when the genes were being 'read,' there were many genes we didn't understand. We mapped them, but ignored them. Some we thought were irrelevant by-products of evolution. Others we thought served some function, such as regulating the expression of the genes, in a way we didn't understand."

"And some of these were the metahuman genes," Peter said, remembering.

"Yes. We used to believe that the magic genes were extraneous. Which, in fact, they were, until the magic returned. Or whatever . . . We don't really know, but we suspect it was the magic that activated the genes. They were always there, but were inactive, invisible."

"So you're saying that the genes are a part of me. I'm a troll because that's what my genes read, and I should just accept it."

"Yes. This is how the universe wrote you."

"But diabetes is a disease, right?"

The doctor paused, uncertain where Peter's words were leading. "Yes."

"And the reason people investigated it genetically was to find a cure for it, right?"

"Yes."

"To change what had been written . . ."

"But diabetes is a disease, Peter. As far as I can tell, you are completely healthy."

"What about the rioting in Seattle? Everyone else in the world wouldn't see me as healthy."

"That's a problem with the world. Not with your body."

Peter turned his head away. He couldn't find the words for what he wanted to say. But his body felt tight, trapped.

No, something else. He felt tight and trapped *inside* an alien body. He looked down at the sheet covering him. That form could not be his body. It was too big, too bulky, too long. Inside the troll body, which was larger than the body of a full-grown pure human, was a fifteen-year-old boy.

"There's a thing on me," he said. "And I want it off."

"Peter. We don't know how to do that. We can't manipulate genes yet."

A fiery idea warmed him. "I'll figure it out."

"Maybe you will," the doctor said somewhat sadly, but Peter sensed he wanted to say exactly the opposite. "I have to go now. Your father will be back to pick you up in the morning. Your therapist, too."

The doctor turned and left.

Peter relaxed and settled himself as comfortably as possible while strapped to the bed. It wasn't for much longer. When morning came, his father would be here to take him home.

The next morning the doctor bustled into the room, trailed by another man who Peter assumed was the therapist. "Good morning, Peter," he said, then gestured to the other man. "Peter, this is Thomas. Thomas, Peter."

Thomas was a huge man with a broad, round, innocent-looking face, but Peter ignored him, glancing impatiently toward the door, expecting his father to appear next. When that didn't happen, he waited for someone to tell him why. Maybe his father was merely running a little late. But neither man spoke, apparently waiting for Peter to return the doctor's greeting. His disappointment was bitter, but Peter buried it deep.

"Good morning."

Thomas stepped over to the bed. "I've got it," he said to the doctor. "Thanks a lot." With a nod the doctor left the room.

"How are you doing?" Thomas asked, looking down at Peter.

"Fine."

"Really? I'd expect someone who's been through what you have to still be a bit off balance."

Peter couldn't decide if he liked the man or not, so he said nothing.

Thomas leaned down and gently undid Peter's straps, as if sorry people had treated him in such a manner. After freeing the final strap, he said, "Wait," then picked up Peter's right wrist, whose gray-green flesh showed a wide band of blue-gray discoloration where the strap had cut into it. Thomas rubbed the flesh with the heels of his palms. Uncomfortable at being touched, Peter tried to pull away, but he lacked full control of his muscles and so ended up jerking his hand so hard it slammed into the rail on the other side of the bed.

"Relax, relax," said Thomas. He took Peter's wrist again and massaged it. The flesh, where Thomas touched it, was growing warmer.

Peter still felt uncomfortable, but was afraid to move his arm away. Within seconds, however, he gave up all thought of trying to get away from Thomas because the touch of the man's hands was so soothing. He gave in and let Thomas do his work.

Thomas raised each of Peter's limbs and carefully massaged the places where the straps had cut into his flesh. He then pulled back the sheet and began to massage the rest of Peter's body, working from the neck down.

Thomas worked quietly, and Peter's furtive glance at the man showed the therapist completely lost in his task. With sure movements, he forced the tension and pressure further and further down Peter's body. Peter couldn't but help close his eyes and savor the feeling.

Then Thomas asked Peter to roll onto his stomach, but had to help him accomplish the awkward motion. Again, Thomas began at the neck and worked his way down. By the time his hands reached the base of Peter's spine, Peter was almost purring with pleasure.

When he was done, Thomas clapped his hands together and said, "All right? Ready to go home?"

Peter thought he'd rather stay here in the hospital with Thomas' magic hands than return home. He was angry at his father for not coming, and was afraid of the anger. But he knew he had no choice.

"You're coming with me, right?"

"Yes. Your father set aside a room for me. I'll be living there with you."

Peter felt good about that, but he tried not to reveal his pleasure.

"So, then, let's go," said Thomas. "Time to sit up." First Peter rolled over onto his back and then he pushed up with his arms. From the other side of the bed, Thomas pushed on Peter's back, helping to prop him up. Peter felt like a sack of fertilizer.

When he was finally sitting up, he felt unbalanced. Thomas put out a hand to help steady him.

"I'm really tall."

"You sure are. Put your arms out. Time for you to become an outpatient."

Peter raised his arms awkwardly while Thomas undid the ties of the hospital gown and slipped it off. Thomas then opened a green plastic bag and produced a massive T-shirt, underwear, and a pair of shorts. "Special troll size?" Peter asked.

"Yup. Your father got you a whole wardrobe. The rest of it's down in my van. Arms up."

Thomas slid the shirt over Peter's head, then said, "Now, roll back."

Peter did so, certain he'd never be able to get up again. Thomas slid the underwear and shorts up his legs.

"All right. Back up."

Peter rocked back and forth, but he couldn't get his stomach muscles to contract hard enough to lift his chest. Thomas crossed around behind the bed and gave a hefty push, and Peter was quickly sitting up again. A shame passed through Peter for being so like a baby, helpless and needy. A fearful idea entered his head: he had no life before him except one thrown to him by others.

"Wait a minute." Thomas crossed to the door and stepped out into the hall. When he returned, he was pushing a large wheelchair built of polished silver metal.

"That for me?" Peter heard fear in his voice.

"Hospital policy. Until you get outside. You can walk, Peter, but it will be a little hard at first. That's why I'm here, though. By the time we're done working together, you'll be in better shape than before your transformation."

The word "transformation" came out of Thomas' mouth without any awkward inflection. Peter realized that Thomas had been through all this before. He had helped other people who had been pure human one week and another race the next. To Thomas, it was just another part of life. Peter couldn't imagine seeing it that way.

Thomas wheeled the chair up to the bed and said, "All right, stand up."

Peter slid off the edge of the bed. Sooner than expected, his feet touched the floor. He tried to raise himself to a standing position, but was afraid. He didn't know where his balance was; his limbs felt like they belonged to someone else. "I can't. I can't move."

"Yes. Relax. Yes, you can." Thomas came over and put his arm around Peter's shoulders. "All right, here we go. Ready? One . . . two . . . three." Thomas pushed on Peter's back again, and Peter tried once more to lift himself. With Thomas' help, he got to his feet.

Peter looked down at Thomas, who looked up at him and smiled. "Hey, big fella."

"I'm huge."

"And still not fully grown yet."

"No?"

"Trolls can reach three meters."

Peter laughed in spite of himself. "The doctor says I'm not a troll," he said.

"Some people can't see the truth if they can't measure it. When it's all done, Peter, you'll figure out what to call yourself. But, me, I'm going to call you a troll. All right, into the chair.''

Thomas helped Peter pivot his back to the chair, and Peter placed his hands on the armrests. As he started to sit down, however, he felt the floor slide to the left. Suddenly, without warning, his body leaned forward, desperately overcompensating. Looking down, he saw the gray tiles of the floor rushing up toward his face. His mind locked in despair as the floor filled his vision. The next moment he smacked into the ground.

Thomas knelt beside him, one hand on Peter's back. ''Are you all right?''

Peter wanted Thomas out of the room. He didn't want anybody to see him like this, unable to move, to walk. ''I don't want to go,'' he said quietly.

''What?''

''I don't want to go home. I don't want my father to see me like this. I don't want the world to see me like this. I don't want to leave.'' Peter spread his fingers across the floor as if he might dig his strong nails into it if Thomas tried to make him leave.

''Peter, you fell. That's going to happen. Gravity's always pulling everyone down. That's part of the contract. You get to stay on the planet, full of air, food, and water, and it drags you down.''

Peter turned his face up toward Thomas. ''What the hell's that?''

''I'm not saying it's brilliantly insightful. Just one way of looking at it. Now come on, you're not going to live out your life clinging to the floor.''

''Why not? I can't fall if I don't get up.''

''Your logic's impeccable. But you can't do *anything* if you don't get back up.''

Peter remained motionless, uncertain of what to do. He didn't really want to get up, but knew that his demand to stay on the floor was ridiculous. Pulling his arms in and bending his elbows, he began to lift himself from the floor. Thomas straddled Peter from the back and helped lift him. Then Peter made his way to the wheelchair.

"That wasn't so bad," said Thomas.

Peter gave him a look. "I want to be able to move like I used to."

Thomas got behind the chair and wheeled it around toward the door. "That's impossible," he said matter-of-factly.

"What do you mean?"

"Peter, you don't have the same body anymore. How can you move the same way?"

They left the room and the sounds of the hall assaulted Peter.

In the privacy of his hospital room he'd forgotten how loud the world was. Out here doctors walked down the corridor talking to and listening to their clipboards. Automated stretchers beeped as they slid along color-coded tracks. At the nurse's station, staff members spoke into little microphones to record patient-data. Everyone was talking into voice-activated machinery, and, from practice, no one was listening to anyone else.

He saw three other trolls, four orks, and three elves also variously being wheeled down the corridor. Some had arms or legs in casts, others were on stretchers. "Did they transform, like me?"

"No. They've been in the metahuman wing. They came in for more mundane healing."

"But it looks like everyone is leaving."

"That's right. They are. The rioting has spread out of Seattle. Right now there are riots all over UCAS, the Confederate states, California. Even in some of the Indian nations. I even heard about riots in London just this morning. There have been a lot of bomb threats demanding that all the metahumans be cleared out of the hospital. And it's the same story all over the continent."

"Why?"

"Stupidity? I don't know. Some people still think you can become a metahuman simply by being around them, like catching a disease. They remember all the problems with AIDS and the VITAS plagues. . . . I don't know. I really don't know."

"So the hospital is sending us all out? Is that why I'm being sent home?"

"No. You were scheduled to go home before the riots last night. Everyone else is being moved out to secret locations. They'll be cared for. Or so I've been told. But the administration believed they couldn't put the other patients at risk of being killed by fanatics."

"So they're dumping us out into the street."

"Not quite. But your anger is valid."

"I'm not angry," Peter said reflexively, though he knew he was.

"Whatever you say."

Thomas' reply made him angrier. "I'm not."

"And the orderly you kidney-punched yesterday isn't going to be on disability for the next three weeks."

"What?"

"Relax," Thomas said with a hand on Peter's shoulder. "I mention him only to illustrate that something *is* going on inside you. And you're not doing anyone any favors by denying it. As for the orderly, he'll be fine. Things like that happen in this ward. It's part of the job."

They came up to the elevator bank. Arrows on the buttons pointed up and down. A map hanging on the wall next to the elevators showed each floor of the hospital, with small icons for the various wards. The third floor was highlighted, so Peter assumed they were on that floor.

He saw four small faces at one end of the map. Two broad faces with big teeth for an ork and a troll, respectively, a narrow face with long, pointed ears, representing an elf, and a face with a beard, meaning a dwarf. The pictures looked ridiculous, simplistic to the point of childishness, but without the energy a child would bring to the enterprise.

The elevator door opened. Standing inside was an attractive woman with a little boy in her arms. She eyed Peter with suspicion as Thomas wheeled him in, but tried to conceal her fear. Then just as the door was about to shut, she rushed off the elevator still carrying her son. Peter's chest tightened.

"Don't worry about it," said Thomas. "It's just fear."

3

Thomas wheeled Peter out across the parking lot up to a large black Volkswagen Superkombi III van. When they reached the door on the passenger side, Thomas stepped around and opened it. Peter stood up carefully, but he still didn't have his balance and fell forward. Grabbing frantically for the heavy door jamb, he managed to steady himself.

Then he turned his head suddenly, catching his reflection in the door window. No one at the hospital had shown him a mirror, and now he knew why.

His teeth were huge—two massive canines protruded from his lower gums and overlapped his upper lip. He had enormous yellow eyes and a monstrous head with large, pointed ears. Peter's mind could not accept that he was looking at himself. Try as he might, he couldn't get past the notion that the glass was some sort of optical trick.

"Well," said Thomas, beside him. "There it is. You ready? Let's get going." They worked together for several minutes, and soon Peter was inside the van. It immediately struck him that few cars were spacious enough to comfortably seat someone like him.

Thomas loaded the wheelchair into the back of the van, then climbed into the driver's seat and started up the engine. He said nothing, and Peter was content to remain transfixed by his reflection in the glass. He was pulled out of his thoughts only twice, when groups of people spotted him and threw bottles and plasticans at the van.

"I think I was safer in the hospital."

"Well, this is why nature gave you such a thick hide. So you can take it."

"Why should I have to take it?"

"Maybe you shouldn't *have* to take it. But you will. You're in this world, you play by the world's rules. World says there are stupid people. There it is."

"Don't we make our own rules?" A word came back to him: laws. "I thought that was the point of laws."

"Well . . . First, who makes the laws, Peter? People. People make the laws. So you don't escape the world hiding behind the laws of men. Nature's still there. She said, 'I'll let there be stupid people,' and the stupid people can make a law just as well as a kind person.

"Second, even good laws can be ignored. You can't legislate intelligence. You can't legislate kindness. There have always been stupid people, and I think there will always be stupid people."

"My doctor said he thinks people will get smarter."

"He may be right. I might believe the same thing someday. I'm only as old as I am. I'll change, I'll learn more. Who knows?"

The van pulled into a driveway, which led up to a small, old-fashioned house, built of wood and ornate metal. Peter didn't recognize it. "Is this where I live?"

"I think so. . . ." Thomas pulled out a book whose

many worn pages were covered with notes written in a tiny scrawl. "This is the address they gave me. It doesn't look right?"

"No, I'm sorry. This is where I live. I forgot. We only moved here three weeks ago. Or, I guess, seven weeks ago. For my father's job at the U. of C." He raised his hand to his head. "I'm so stupid now. It's like thinking through cotton."

Thomas turned to Peter and narrowed his eyes. "You don't sound stupid to me. What makes you say that?"

"Well, I'm a troll. I'm stupider than I was before."

"Peter, your brain rebuilt itself along with your body. It's different. And yes, to put it bluntly, trolls do tend to be mentally slower than pure humans. But when you were a human, you"—he flipped open the book again—"you pulled an IQ score of 184 and a GPH of 18. We don't know what you're like yet. You won't be as smart as you were, but we still don't know the whole story."

Thomas' words disturbed Peter. He had begun to take comfort in the notion of his stupid mind; he wouldn't have to expect much from his life or his future, and this matched his father's outlook. Unpleasant, perhaps, but certain.

"Now, you've got two choices. You can *think* you know everything there is to know about yourself. Or you can live, observe, and discover." Peter remained silent. "It's not a decision you have to make right now. It's one of those life things." Thomas winked.

As Thomas helped Peter up to the house, a few of the neighbors came out to stare in awe at the troll walking up the front path.

Once inside, Peter looked around while Thomas went back out to the van. He noticed some new furniture—heavy stuff with sturdy metal frames. Cold and hard. Furniture just for him.

Thomas returned with a stack of clothing Peter's father had bought—shirts and pants and shoes all tailored for a troll. Peter guessed that such clothes cost a lot of money. He felt bad that his father had to pay out such expenses, but also wondered what trolls who had little money did for clothes. He asked Thomas.

"Good question. There's not a huge market for clothes the size of orks and trolls, so manufacturers don't produce it. The bigger metahumans end up having to stitch lots of clothes together. The colors and fabrics don't always match. Looks sloppy." Peter cocked his head to one side, surprised by the comment. It seemed uncharacteristically critical. "Hey, I'm not saying they *are* sloppy," Thomas told him. "Most of them are doing the best they can to survive. But in a country like UCAS, where the average citizen does pretty well, someone who looks like he's just barely surviving appears sloppy."

After Peter and Thomas had stowed the clothes away, Thomas said, "So, do you want to rest or do you want to get to work?"

"Work," said Peter.

They worked. Peter walked and walked and walked. He walked from the front of the house to the back of the house. He walked up the stairs and down the stairs. He found Thomas kind, but disturbing, as if he expected a great deal from Peter. More than Peter had expected from himself *before* he became a troll. The sooner Peter could walk without Thomas' help, the sooner Thomas would leave, and the sooner Peter could relax.

They continued until late into the night. The walking tired Peter, but every time he thought he couldn't go on, he discovered still more strength than he thought he had, and went on.

After the fourth hour he realized he wanted his father to come home from the university to find him

putting enormous effort into his rehabilitation. But
when his father had not returned by midnight, Peter
guessed that he wouldn't come home anymore that
night. He remembered that it was commonplace for
William Clarris to work late on his researches.

"I'm tired, Thomas," Peter said, his face revealing
the disappointment over his father. "I'm ready for
bed." Thomas looked into Peter's face, searching.
"Sure," he said, amiably. After helping Peter into
bed, Thomas began to massage him again.

Outside Peter heard sirens and glass breaking, but
the sounds came only sporadically. The citizens of
Hyde Park paid well for tight security, and they got it.
The riots barely touched the borders of their neighborhood.

But it wasn't the security guards outside that made
Peter feel so safe. It was Thomas, whose touch somehow made it all right to have the skin of a troll.

When Peter opened his eyes, he was greeted by the
sight of shelves full of optical chips facing him across
the room. It took a moment to recognize them and
remember they were his. Chips about cells and DNA
and literature and history. But he couldn't remember in detail what they were about. He couldn't remember
reading any of them.

Someone knocked on the door.

"Come in," Peter said expectantly, thinking it must
be his father.

It was Thomas who entered. "Good morning," he
said.

"Morning." Again Peter didn't hide his disappointment.

"What is it?" asked Thomas.

"Where's my father?"

"He left very early. He said he didn't want to wake
you."

"Hmmm." Peter glanced at the shelf.

"You read a lot."

"I guess. I can't remember any of it, though."

Thomas nodded, but apparently decided to let the matter drop. "Most people don't read much at all these days."

Yes, Peter remembered that now. Kids had made fun of him in elementary school because his father wanted him to be literate, not just functionally literate, or "iconerate," the new term for those who went through life using only symbols and key words for written communication.

"I wonder if I liked reading?"

"From the number of opticals, I'd say you did."

"I might have been doing it just to please my father."

"Oh." Thomas stepped over to the shelf and looked at the titles printed on the plastic casings. "Well, I bet you liked some of these . . . *Treasure Island* . . . *The Wizard of Oz.*"

"Kids called me a lit-dip for reading so much. They said flats and trid were better."

"Different."

"I don't remember."

"Think you'll try reading again?"

Peter hesitated, afraid to say the words. Then, "Thomas. I don't think I can read. I think I forgot how." As soon as the words left his mouth, his chin began to tremble. He didn't remember much about his reading, but he knew it had set him apart from most other people, from other kids, who were content to be consumers of information, not makers of it. It was bad to be so different, but it had also made him special. It was something that he knew was his.

"You can learn again if you want."

"What if I can't?"

"I know you can learn to read. Any troll can do that, and I suspect you're brighter than most trolls because you were a genius as a pure human."

"But what if I can't?"

"If it'll make you feel better, you don't have to. You can learn a few key words, a few symbols. Few people choose to read these days. They watch the trid and flat for news and entertainment. They use icon and voice-based computers to move data around for their employers. Programmers are literate in the comp language, but not much else. The only people who have to worry about *reading* are the ones who make it all work. They have to know how to read to keep things going, to improve the tech. But it's rare. You can get by without reading if you want. You'll learn a few words, like STOP, and you'll see them just like icons, and that'll be that."

"You're tricky."

Thomas smiled. "What do you mean?"

"Your words are . . . reassuring, but there's something in . . . the way you speak, underneath it all . . . that's saying I shouldn't simply become iconerate."

"True, true, true. I'm a firm believer in everyone reading. Years ago, when the corps took over primary support of the public school system, all the reading programs—well, the entire curriculum—was changed to a more 'vocational' approach. To get a return on their money, the corps decided they wanted people to learn only as much as they needed to carry out a job.

"But what the corps didn't know, or didn't care about, is that perspective only comes from knowing more than you *need* to know. People are taught a word these days, and that's it. No context. 'Why do pure humans throw rocks at orks and trolls?' and the answer is, 'Racism.' A single-word definition like 'Racism' might as well be an icon. Icons give brief, quick, incomplete ideas. They pack a punch—but that's all. That's what you see on the news. They just flash nouns on the screen. 'Racism' says the sign, and then the footage rolls, showing people attacking one another. But no one knows anymore than they did before."

"But some people read. I did. You do."

"Both our parents are from the upper class, Peter. They could afford the better schools, and because of that we were singled out for broader educations. Society still needs some people who are active readers. We're it."

Peter became lost in thought, and Thomas said, "Sorry, for the lecture. I have this thing about the importance of education." He stepped up to the bed. "Ready for the tensions to be rolled away?"

Peter settled deeper into the bed, the memory of yesterday's massage already calming him.

Peter sighed deeply as Thomas rubbed his back. When he reached Peter's feet, Thomas said, "Roll over."

Peter did so, this time by himself, his eyes comfortably closed. He opened them briefly when Thomas' hands began to knead his shoulders, and what he saw stunned Peter. Thomas' eyes were a deep yellow, the pupils vertical and black. His face was expressionless, but his skin had a cool green pallor, looking more like scales than flesh. Peter experienced an instant repulsion and gasped, then slid away from Thomas.

Thomas remained in his dazed state for a moment, then the green faded from his flesh and his eyes returned to normal.

"Peter? What is it, Peter?"

"What are you?"

Thomas blinked twice. "I'm a shaman," he said. "Of the Snake totem. Didn't your father or the doctor tell you?"

Peter was still breathing fast, but not so much as a moment ago. He remembered something about that—shamans taking on the characteristics of their totem when using magic. "My father. I haven't spoken with him for days."

Thomas closed his eyes. "I'm sorry. I would have

told you. When he called me to say he wouldn't be able to pick you up, he said you knew all the details.''

''I only knew you were coming to get me.''

Thomas studied Peter carefully with the same curious look he'd given him the day before. ''Did he tell you he wouldn't be there?''

''Sure. Yes.''

''Hmmm. Well, I'm sorry for frightening you. I can see why you'd be spooked.''

''I wasn't spooked.''

Thomas smiled. ''You don't let much out, do you?''

''No.''

''Listen. I was drawing on magic when I massaged you. It . . . It's a ritual I built myself, for people who have gone through what you have. It soothes the muscles, strengthens them without tightening them.''

''Why did you look like that?''

''My totem is Snake. Snake is a healer. When I use the magic, I take on aspects of Snake, because, well, I'm drawing on Snake for my magic. I look different because, at that moment, when using magic, I *am* different.'' He looked embarrassed. ''It's hard to understand unless you actually do it.''

Peter began to relax. He'd never dealt with a shaman before, but Thomas seemed nice enough. The idea of them had always frightened him. Shamans seemed even stranger than mages, who at least had a semblance of scientific rigidity about them.

Scientific rigidity. Now where had that idea come from?

He remembered that shamans all had totems, and that all totems were animals. Each had different qualities. Coyote is the trickster. Dog is fiercely loyal. He remembered a question he'd often thought about, but had never gotten around to researching. ''Why is Snake a healer? A lot of snakes are dangerous.''

''So they are,'' said Thomas, taking a seat on the edge of the bed. ''And healing is dangerous as well.

Today, most people think that all they have to do is take this pill or that treatment. They don't realize that there are always risks. We don't know everything. We'll never know everything. But people don't want to hear that. They want simple answers for everything.

"An obvious example. You have a cold. The doctor prescribes an antibiotic. You take it. You're allergic to it. You get a whole new problem. Perhaps you die. Or let's say you go to the hospital for surgery—open heart surgery. Routine today, but never, ever, completely safe. Something can always go wrong."

Peter sat up on the bed. He liked the way Thomas spoke: somewhat disturbing, but open and direct.

"At the end of the last century things were very bad with medicine. Patients expected miracles, and doctors, in their pride, fanned those expectations." He turned and smiled at Peter. "It was the only way to justify charging exorbitant fees. Everyone wanted everything controlled and perfect. When something went wrong, it represented a disaster for the entire medical profession, but it was simply a normal phenomenon. Normal bad. I'm not saying healers should be sloppy, mind you. But the snake bite, it's always there."

"Even with magic?"

Thomas looked down at the floor. "Especially with magic." He looked to see how interested Peter actually was before continuing. "Magic, especially the shamanistic tradition—well, it's weird. It requires that you look deep inside. Especially Snake. Snake lives in the cracks in the walls of an old building. Snake lives in small caves in the desert. Snake gets in everywhere and wants to know everything. Snake doesn't want any secrets kept away from her. So if you're going to follow Snake, then you've got to go within." He tapped his chest. "That's some serious healing, too, and if there's one place where the venom is very scary, it's when you have to learn about yourself."

Peter thought of what made him most afraid, and

then suddenly he thought of . . . Denise! The girl he'd met at the party. "Oh, no!" He fell back down onto the bed.

"What is it?"

"I forgot that I was supposed to call somebody. I was too busy turning into a troll."

Thomas laughed. "Well, I'm sure he'll understand."

"She."

"Ah. Well, even so."

"No."

"No what?"

"No, I won't call her."

"Because you stood her up?"

"Because I'm a troll."

"Hmmm."

"You know, Peter . . ."

"What?" he said irritably. Suddenly he found Thomas' simple wisdom annoying.

"Nothing. Why don't we get to work?"

They did.

When they broke for lunch, Thomas turned on the trideo to find the local stations abuzz with the effects of the previous night's rioting. A newscaster reported LIVE from State Street in the Loop, the heart of Chicago's downtown district, bounded by the elevated train lines that carried the city's commuters north, south, and west.

She recapped: Pure humans had raced through the streets, searching out metahumans, dragging them out of doorways, even breaking into homes, then pummeling them to death.

In turn, metahumans had killed pure humans. *Pure humans:* she used the term casually.

The city's security forces, both private and public, had, for the most part, turned their weapons against the metahumans. City Hall had already announced an investigation into the excessive force used by the security teams.

Peter's mouth was dry. He set his sandwich down on the table.

"Peter?"

"That could be me. I could have died."

"No doubt about it," said Thomas, who then calmly took another bite. He seemed to relish the taste of the roast beef, but Peter had suddenly lost his appetite.

The house rattled, slowly at first, more like a deep rumbling, and then with more force. It lasted only moments, but then they heard the screams coming from the trideo. On the screen, they could see that the camera was shaking wildly as the reporter looked around for the source of the loud explosions. Then she turned her back to the camera and looked up, her hands falling suddenly to her sides. It must have been her lapel mike picking up her strained voice: "Oh, spirits." The camera operator swung the camera in the direction of the reporter's gaze.

Fiery red explosions billowed through the walls of the IBM Tower, once called the Sears Tower. The skyscraper rocked and shook, then it began to disintegrate, toppling to the ground.

Its collapse was almost pure. The nine sections that made up the tower began to slide away from one another. First the eight subtowers around the central tower began to fall, slowly at first, then picking up speed as the central subtower followed. All nine fell faster and faster and faster, until the whole structure vanished behind the buildings along State Street.

A moment later flames erupted from the spot where the towers had fallen. Then explosions ripped through one building after another along State Street.

The reporter whirled toward the camera. Her face betrayed panic, but she fought to keep her voice under control. "Explosions are ripping—"

Then the camera fell to the ground, where it lay on

its side, still soaking up the disaster. The sound was cut off.

"The gas lines," Thomas said. Peter looked at him. Thomas' flesh had become almost gray. "The gas lines will rip through the whole area."

When Peter looked back to the trideo, he saw the Loop awash in flames. People were falling out of windows, rushing out of doors, running every which way, their clothes and flesh on fire. Then the image turned to static. Turning his head to look north through the kitchen window, Peter saw that already a thick cloud of black smoke was gathering above downtown Chicago.

"I have to go," said Thomas.

"What?"

Thomas stood. "I have to go. I'm needed."

"Please, Thomas, don't leave me alone."

"You'll be all right. Lock the doors." He walked out of the kitchen.

Peter stumbled as he chased after him. "You're supposed to be here! This is your job!"

"I have a clause in my contract that allows me to leave under just such circumstances," Thomas said grimly. "This is what I do. I make sure to build it into the laws that bind me. Stay here. Lock the doors. Stay calm. I'll be back."

4

Peter returned to the trideo, which had switched back to the news studio. "The anti-metahuman organizations known as the Hand of Five, the Knights of Humanity, and MetaWatch, have each claimed responsibility for the destruction of the IBM Building, citing IBM's practice of hiring metahumans as the reason for the terrorist attack. They demand that corporations across North America fire their metahuman employees or else suffer similar acts.''

The reporter paused, placed a hand to his ear, and then said, ''Humanity One, another anti-metahuman group, has claimed responsibility, as well as the Elven Support Coalition, which claims to be protesting the lack of IBM support for metahuman hiring. We'll have a full list by the end of the day, but now we take you live to a helicopter over the Loop, where fires rage out of control.'' A fancy computer graphic swirled out from the center of the trideo: THE SECOND CHICAGO FIRE!

Peter flipped from trideo to telecom mode. Selecting voice-only he keyed in the telecom code for his father's office at the university. When he asked for his father, the receptionist inquired whether she could take a message. Peter told her it was very important, and she told him she'd see what she could do. A minute later she came back on, saying Dr. Clarris was unavailable, but he'd call back as soon as he could. Peter briefly considered pleading with her to get his father on the line, but gave up.

Peter didn't know what to do with himself. There was always the trid, but he didn't want any more of that, nor did he have anyone else to call. Except maybe Dr. Landsgate.

At the thought of the man, Peter instantly relaxed. Landsgate was the only person in the sciences with whom Peter felt comfortable—and since he only knew people in the sciences . . .

He went up to his room, and punched in Landsgate's code, keeping the telecom in voice-only.

It was Laura who answered.

''Hello?''

''Um, hello, Mrs. Landsgate? This is Peter. Peter Clarris.''

She remained silent for a moment. "Hello, Peter," she said finally. "How are you?"

He knew she knew, and he decided not to go into it. "Fine. Is Dr. Landsgate there, please?"

Another pause. "I'll get him."

A few minutes later Landsgate was on the line. "Hello? Peter?"

"Hello, Dr. Landsgate."

"Peter, it's good to hear from you." Before Peter could respond with the appropriate pleasantry, Landsgate added, "I heard what happened. I want you to know I'm sorry your life is more difficult. But I also want you to know that I'm with you. You can count on me."

Peter stood silent for a moment and sucked in the comfort of the words. "Thank you."

"How are you?"

"I'm frightened."

"Are you in danger?"

"No, but the IBM Tower . . ."

"I know. It's on the trid. Where's your father?"

"At work."

Peter heard Landsgate sigh.

Peter felt his chin tremble. "Dr. Landsgate. Why is my father . . . why does he . . . why doesn't he love me?"

Landsgate's voice dropped low. Peter guessed he didn't want Laura to hear. "Peter, I don't know that he doesn't love you. I think he does, in his own way."

"He ignores me."

"Yes, I know."

"I just want someone I can . . . I don't know."

"Yes, I know."

They remained silent for some time.

"Peter, I'd like to see you."

"I don't think so."

"I really would. It feels like you're hiding from me."

"I am."

"Well, I don't want you to."

Peter wanted to refuse again, then decided he had to know how someone other than his father and a hired therapist would respond. He reached out and tapped a key that switched on the screen, which flickered to life with the image of Landsgate's face. Landsgate looked apprehensive at first, but then smiled warmly. He was young, and carried his enthusiasm around like a hobby.

"I didn't think you'd look at all the same."

Peter touched his hands to his face. "I don't look the same."

"Of course you don't. But there's part of you still there that I remember. You're different, but you're still Peter."

"Thank you," Peter said with relief. No one knew what to say like Dr. Landsgate.

"Is anybody with you?"

"No. I have a therapist, a physical therapist, a shaman, but he went to help with the fire."

"A shaman! Well, never let it be said your father didn't lavish cash on you. But the shaman left?"

"I'll be all right."

In the background, Peter heard Laura shout out the news that mages and shamans were casting spells to put out the fire.

"I'll try to come out and visit you. Maybe next week."

"Really?"

Landsgate laughed. "Yes, really."

"All right."

"I'll let you go now. But it was good seeing you again."

"Yeah. Same here."

"I'll call tomorrow. To check in."

"All right."

"But if you need anything before then, just give me a call."

"All right."

"Bye."

"Bye."

The screen went blank.

With a sigh, Peter selected trideo mode once more. The explosions from the gas lines and the damage from the collapse of the IBM Tower had turned the Loop into something out of a war. Some blocks burned so hot no one could get near then. Working in teams, mages had joined forces, summoning air and water elementals to help put out the fire. Meanwhile, rescue workers struggled to dig trapped office workers out of buildings.

The announcer said, "Already the death toll is expected to be in the thousands. . . ."

Thomas did not return that night.

Peter made dinner—a frozen synth meat dish he flashed through the micro—and ate while watching the trid. The fire was out, but the rescue work would continue for days. So absorbed was he that he didn't hear his father come in until he looked up and saw him standing in the doorway. Peter and his father looked at one another silently. Please say something, Peter thought.

"How are you?" his father said.

"Fine. Thomas went to help at the fire. In the Loop. He hasn't come back."

"Hmmm. Well, he'll either come back or he won't. We can get you someone else."

"I like Thomas."

"I can't do anything about that."

Peter slammed his hand down on the table. "I'm not asking you to do anything about it! I'm just telling you I hope nothing happened to him."

His father remained silent. ''They told me this might happen.''

''What?'' asked Peter, exasperated.

''That you would have outbursts.''

''I'm upset. Why is that bad?''

''It doesn't matter to me. You're the one who's upset.''

Peter slumped down in the chair. He wanted to shout at his father for turning his anger around on him. But he knew that would only make his father's case stronger. He said nothing.

''Good night,'' said his father.

''Good night.''

Peter stayed at the kitchen table, completely motionless, for another half hour. Then he rose, the meal forgotten, and went up to bed.

Three days passed and still Thomas did not return. Peter called the hospitals, but the body had not turned up either dead or alive. He also spoke to Dr. Landsgate each day, and felt better for awhile after each conversation.

Each night Peter's father came back from the U. of C. and greeted Peter with little more than a nod. He never asked about Thomas, and Peter volunteered nothing. Peter's body ached, but he kept telling himself he would give Thomas one more day to come back before finding a replacement.

Meanwhile, he continued to practice his walking.

On the third night after Thomas left, Peter pulled his portable computer from the shelf. The plastic material of the case irritated his hands, so he placed it on his bed and carefully used his fingernails to start it up. The machine seemed pitifully small against his new, large body.

Returning to the shelf, he looked at the racks of optical chips. Some of the words—the short words—

he recognized, but many others he did not remember. He tried to sound out some of the longer words, but it was hard, as if his memories were hidden behind gauze curtains. "Biology," he eventually said. It meant nothing to him, no more than a group of sounds. He suddenly realized only too clearly what iconerate meant. If someone had said to him, "Peter, go get all the chips with the word biology on them," he could have done so. He didn't have to know what the word meant; he didn't have to know the word's implications.

And that's what bothered him as he looked at the seven letters strung out in sequence. He recognized the word now, but behind it was a wealth of meaning to which he'd lost access. Maybe it was enough to see the letters and to grasp the image of the word, the single sound that they represented—but he knew there was more, and he longed to have access to that part of language.

He knew that it wasn't just a matter of memory. His thought process had changed and Peter could actually feel the difference now. His thinking was slower. Whatever he had been, however smart as a pure human, as a *homo sapiens sapiens,* that was gone now. His own body had betrayed him.

He sensed someone watching him, and turned to see his father in the doorway.

"What are you doing?" his father asked.

"Looking at my opticals."

"Why?"

"I want to learn them. To re-read them."

His father pursed his lips together. He stepped into the room, as if to have a lengthy conversation, then stopped in his tracks. "Peter . . . why?"

Peter thought about explaining his plan to find a genetic cure, but was too embarrassed to do so. His father would put him down. "I just . . . I want to . . ."

His father's face took on an expression of infinite sadness. "Peter, you . . . I'm sorry. Do as you wish." He turned to leave, then stopped in the doorway, his shoulders impossibly tired. With his back still to his son, William Clarris gave a deep sigh before turning around once more. He rubbed his hands over his face. When he took his hands away, his flesh looked cool and corpse-white before warmth and color flowed back in. His mouth looked pinched taut and old, though he was no more than forty.

"Maybe you don't understand what has happened to you. . . ."

A fury bubbled up through Peter. "Dad, it happened to me! How could I not understand?"

"You're young, that's why. And because . . . I don't even know what you do understand. You're a troll, Peter. You used to be exceptionally bright. You had that. No matter what else, you could depend on that. You had something that made you *wanted*. Now what do you have?"

Peter wanted to say, Me, dad, what about me? but he didn't know if that was enough. So he said, "That's why I was looking at the opticals. I want to learn it again."

"Peter, you're not what you were. You can't."

"Why not?"

His father shook his head. "Do what you want." He turned to leave once more.

"I'm going to find a cure!" Peter shouted. "I'm looking at the opticals because I'm going to find out how to be human again!"

Peter's father rested his hand against the door jamb. "Now, *that,* Peter, is impossible. *That* is completely beyond our reach right now. No one knows if it's possible at all."

"But it's not impossible."

"That!" his father said and whirled, a finger pointed at Peter. "That right there is the youth I'm talking about. 'Not impossible.' What kind of statement is that? And yes, it might happen someday. But it won't be you. Do you understand me? It won't be *you.*" He walked quickly out of the bedroom.

Peter chased his father into the hall. He could feel the pressure of tears in his eyes, and the words tumbled out so fast he thought they might be unintelligible. "What do you expect me to do? What am I going to do for the rest of my life?"

His father turned on the stairs and looked at him with some surprise. "I expect you to live here. To stay here and be safe."

"Just stay here?" Peter sputtered out. "Just stay here? And do what?"

"Peter, what can you do? Corporations all over the continent are cutting back their metahuman employees. They're afraid of people like you. They don't like you. The *world* doesn't want you. I know I haven't been the best father, but I will do what I can. I will take care of you."

He continued down the stairs.

Peter watched him go, then rushed back into his room and slammed the door shut. The handle snapped off from the impact and clattered to the floor. He stared at his gray-green hands and arms, his fury growing. He wanted to show his father. . . . He had to show his father. He wouldn't sit around his whole life.

The thought of that, waiting to die . . . ? He imagined the years passing by, one year after another ticking away, while he sat in the house, waiting, waiting, waiting for death. But each year wouldn't be the same, one after another. No, they would gather an oppressive momentum.

Would he wait for it to happen?

No.

He would prove his father wrong.

From the closet he pulled out an old gym bag, a

gift from Landsgate to encourage him to exercise more, and began to pack. He threw in a few of his new troll-size clothes and, at the last minute, decided to take a few chips and his portable computer.

Later that night Peter stood before the kitchen telecom screen.

Carefully he typed out a message to his father: "When you see me again, I will be human."

He looked at it, and thought the words sounded cold. It was exactly the kind of phrase his father might write. He wanted to give something more. He added, "I love you. I will make you proud."

Then he left his father's house and stepped into the night.

5

Peter rode the Rail, the elevated train line, north to Uptown and got off at the Wilson Avenue stop. He'd heard that the area was run-down, which he figured was the only kind of place where anyone would give him any lodging.

He stepped onto the platform and descended the stairs to street level. Although it was two in the morning and the street looked empty, he sensed the vitality of it, as if the dark, cool asphalt, the graffitied girders of the Metrorail tracks, the closed krill dog shops, the entire environment, had a life of its own. He felt as if he'd stepped *into* the belly of a creature—a still, sleeping, monster that might wake up at any moment.

He spotted a sign that blinked on and off irregularly with the word Hotel. It looked decrepit enough to be just the sort of place he sought.

Walking toward it, Peter realized he was not the only creature alive in the belly of the street. First he spotted the warmth of an unwashed pure human dressed in rags and huddled carefully in a doorway. Then he saw a man and a woman talking quietly to one another in the shadows under the tracks of the Rail. The woman was dressed in a halter top and torn shorts, the man in a blotch-stained leather duster. They noticed him, but paid him little attention. Or so it seemed. They made him nervous because it was the first time in his short life that he'd encountered what looked like a prostitute and a pimp, but then it occurred to him that he probably made them more nervous. He was, after all, a 2.7 meter-tall troll.

As he walked along he noticed more people. An old woman sitting on a door stoop smoking a cigarette. Two teenage boys laughing quietly together. It wasn't that the people he passed were hidden, but somehow he never really perceived their presence until up close. They had camouflaged themselves to move through the street, and it was almost as if the street offered them protection.

Peter thought there was a word. . . . What was it? Symbiotic.

They were all smaller organisms living on the street, which gave them shadows, shelter, a place to belong. In return, the people kept the street alive, giving it a reason for being.

Reaching the hotel, he pushed open the doors covered in plastisheet boards in place of glass. Seated among the worn tables and chairs of the lobby were two old men. Their eyes glassy, they sat without speaking, staring at the yellow cracks in the wall.

Peter walked up to the desk and rang the bell, which prompted a bit of clatter from a door behind the desk. A moment later the door opened and a teenage boy, who could not have been any older than Peter, opened the door. He was dark-haired and swarthy-skinned.

The boy took one look at Peter, then his mouth dropped open in fear. With all possible speed, he was back in his room and slamming the door shut. "What you want?" the boy shouted from behind the door.

Peter looked around the lobby, unsure of what was happening. The two men had not budged from their overstuffed chairs, oblivious as ever.

"A room," he answered.

"No. No rooms. Sorry," came the shouted reply.

"The sign outside says you have rooms."

"Not for you."

Despair welled up in Peter. "Because I'm a troll?"

"You got it. Look at the sign."

Peter glanced around. A sign above the desk said, "NO METAHUMANS."

Peter lowered his voice. "I have money. I can pay. I just need a place to stay tonight. I'll leave in the morning."

. "Go away," the boy said, his tone a mixture of menace and pleading.

"Look," said Peter, loudly again, "I can pay. I've got the money. I just want a place to stay."

The door opened, and the boy reemerged, this time with a shotgun in his hands. Terror had control of his face, and his hands shook.

Peter had never seen a gun before, not in real life, not up close. And the twin barrels of the weapon were very close. The light of the lobby glinted off their circular ends. He focused on them and imagined a spray of metal pellets rushing out. . . .

"It's a rule. Even if you were the greatest chummer in the world and I liked you, I couldn't let you stay here, yes? The boss says your kind makes too much trouble."

Afraid the boy would panic and fire, Peter raised his hands very carefully, still clutching his bag in one hand, and slowly began to back away. "All right. Yes. Thanks for your time."

The boy kept the gun trained on Peter. A bead of sweat rolled down his right temple and along his cheek.

Peter backed up part way through the lobby, then turned, walked quickly toward the door, and rushed outside.

He stepped out and breathed heavily, leaning against the stone facade of the building.

Had he really come that close to death? Death from fear? A ridiculously stupid death?

Yup.

He walked slowly down the street, afraid of jostling anyone or anything too hard, lest the inhabitants of Wilson Avenue pull out more instruments of destruction and train them on him.

Reaching Clark Street he saw the lights in a chicken shack called the C&E Grill. According to the sign, the C&E was open twenty-four hours a day.

White tiles covered the walls, floor, and ceilings. Someone kept them spotlessly clean. The customers packed themselves loudly into the booths, tables, and counter stools. Everyone seemed to know everyone else, but their conversations had the overblown friendliness of some corporate cocktail party. It took Peter a moment to realize that most of the people were talking to no one in particular. They shmoozed with invisible friends only they could see.

He felt completely out of place, out of his league. He sensed that he'd wandered into a world with its own rules, a world where a single misstep could easily get him killed. But with nowhere else to go, he decided his best bet was to stay here and lay low as much as possible.

Rushing around taking orders was an Oriental man in a white apron. He, too, seemed to know everyone, but Peter believed he really did. With the briefest of nods he acknowledged a customer's order. He had a smile for everyone, always asked, "How are you," waited for a reply, but then didn't wait long enough for anyone to feel obliged to return the gesture.

Pure humans were the majority, but Peter spotted a few elves in one corner, huddled together like anarchists. Sitting alone at another table, his back purposely to the wall, was an ork. He wore heavy boots and something akin to combat fatigues, but patched together, so they didn't really look like a uniform. Peter realized that he, too, could probably benefit from a paramilitary look. But he didn't think he'd successfully carry off the mean-edged glare the ork had mastered. The man, Peter guessed, was a shadowrunner, though he'd only read about such people or seen stories about them on the trideo. Shadowrunners were the invisible agents of the corps, government, and private citizens. Each had erased his or her System Identification Number, which meant they were non-existent in the eyes of the databanks.

Peter caught several people looking at him, like a sales staff scanning to see if a customer needs help. Seeing their eyes run down the length of his arm and settling on his gym bag, he tightened his fists around the handles. One wiry little fellow smiled at the action, as if he thought it were cute.

Peter glanced around for a table and chose one with a large chair, which he identified as suitable for trolls.

The Oriental man came around. "Want a menu?" he asked briskly.

"Yes. Please."

Peter looked around. An old woman stood by the window, looking out, talking to no one. Peter could not hear what she said. Then she moved away from the window and went to look through the garbage can by the door. She picked through a few of the napkins and paper plates and pushed them into a pile to one side.

Another old woman watched the first very carefully, like a security guard eyeing a tour group through a bioplant.

Sitting ahead of Peter was a woman he considered a kind of "in-between." She wore silver earrings, which he thought would be sold soon, and a white lace blouse. Her hair was unwashed. She seemed on the cusp of once having something close to what Peter had just left—clothes, a home, possessions, maybe a family—and having nothing but her own life. Every once in a while she said something softly to herself and then turned to see if anyone was listening.

Was that how he'd end up?

A man walked briskly up to her table and sat down without asking permission. Drawing a pack of cigarettes from his pocket, he offered her one. She took it so casually that Peter thought they must know one another. But when they started to speak, leaning in and trying to be nonchalant, it was with an air of bargaining. Was she a prostitute?

Someone called out, "Rich!" and the cigarette-man turned toward the door. Peter followed his gaze, and saw the four young men who had just entered. Draped over their arms were stacks of brightly colored shirts. Saying a quick good-bye to the in-between, the cigarette-man got up and sauntered over to the young men.

The in-between also got up and left the diner.

Three tables down a man wearing a turban was working carefully at taking apart cigarette butts and dumping the remaining tobacco onto a sheet of rolling paper on his table.

Meanwhile, a man as gorgeous as any trid star came in, looking perfect in white shirt, red bow tie, and black trousers. What was he doing here? Gorgeous walked up to the counter and sat on a stool.

"Sorry," said the Oriental man, suddenly standing before Peter. He set a menu on the table. "How are you?"

Still startled, Peter said, "Fine."

"Good. I'll be right back." He ran off to another table.

A terrible reek forced itself into Peter's senses, and he glanced toward the man in the turban. He had finished making his cigarette, and was now smoking it gleefully.

Peter noticed that a woman in a green vest craned her neck continually to peer at the door. When a tall, thin gentleman entered and walked toward her, she began to smile. The man had grandfather-white hair swept back and cut flat on the top and both sides, which Peter recognized as a formerly fashionable style. Time had passed the man by, but he seemed unaware that things had changed or that he had gotten older. The Oriental man suddenly appeared at the couple's table and deposited two cups of soykaf. The man placed a brown bag on the table and the woman contributed a box of crackers. From out of the bag the man produced individually wrapped slices of cheese. Peter found the moment so simple and yet incongruous that it disturbed him.

At that moment, another man rushed in. "The kids don't believe anymore!" he shouted as the crowd actually quieted down and took notice of him. "But on Halloween! The ghosts will come out on Halloween. They don't believe anymore, but they'll see! You know what'll be funny? When they have to suck their great-great-great-grandfather. They'll think he's just some guy standing on a street corner, but then he'll tell 'em they gotta suck it. They'll have to suck up some ancient history!" The patrons looked askance at one another, obviously distressed by this outburst. Peter saw that everyone wanted the man to stop, but no one wanted to get involved. "You know, you know, that's funny. In England the ghosts don't come out till nine, in Wales at midnight, in Scotland not until two in the morning. But in Chicago''—and here the man's voice dropped almost to a whisper—''we can have ghosts all night.''

In unison the guys carrying the shirts shouted, ''Shut up!''

A woman with too-white skin, fire-red hair, and dressed in boots and a flattering short skirt took a seat across the aisle from a dark-skinned man with perfect, chiseled features.

The Oriental man reappeared before Peter, order pad in hand. ''What can I do for you?''

''Uh,'' began Peter, once again caught off-guard. ''Cheeseburger. Fizzle Coke.''

The man tapped two keys onto his order pad and sailed off.

Peter looked back to the woman and the black man, who had by now moved to sit at her table. From snippets of their conversation, Peter could make out the woman was named Alice, the man was from Québec. They discussed the pronunciation of the word ''France,'' then moved on to how prostitution operated the world over.

Watching and listening to Alice, Peter realized that she was ''off-duty,'' and wondered what it would be like to have someone so attractive *want* to talk to him, as she obviously did want to talk to the man from Québec.

When Alice suddenly noticed Peter staring, she got up and changed seats, taking a chair that put her back to him.

Peter was ashamed for making her feel that he was intruding on her break. If he wanted her attention, money would have to change hands first.

The Oriental slapped a plate of food down before Peter and was gone almost before he knew what had happened. Just was Peter was about to take his first bite, the small man who earlier had smiled when Peter had clutched his bag tighter came up, pulled out the other chair at Peter's table, and sat down.

"Hoi!" he said brightly. Then an elaborate shudder ran down his body; his head twitched twice and he said "Hoi" two more times.

"Hello," said Peter, unsure of how to proceed and not certain that he wanted to.

"Eddy, Fast Eddy," the other man said, thrusting his hand toward Peter. Eddy sounded like a disk that skipped. Peter put out his hand and took Eddy's lightly, afraid of hurting him. Long bulges showed under Eddy's skin—like thick veins. The bulges ran along his arms and wrists, his neck, and even up to his temples.

"Name?" he asked.

"Peter."

"Ah, you're straight. Straight."

"Straight?"

"Straight. You know. . . . Clean. Legal."

"Well. . . ."

"You have a job, a place to live. You're not on the outside, scraping by."

The woman with the silver earrings returned and took a seat next to Peter's table. She began talking loudly and said, "Bill, remember when you were in the coffin?"

Eddy turned to glance at the woman, twitched, then shrugged his shoulders when he turned back to Peter. "Mirium."

"I love you, Bill," the woman was saying, the conviction in her voice astounding. She was definitely talking *to* somebody. "You know what happiness is, Bill? When you die, you go to the Evergreen. It's so beautiful."

"What's wrong with her?"

"I don't know. I don't know. I just know what I hear."

Her voice suddenly changed, and she shouted with
great fear. "Shut the door! Make him go!" Then she
quieted down. "We're all dying," she said. "Our
whole family is dying. And we're going to have a
funeral. We're all dying. I'm dying next." Her tone
changed again, and she seemed to be talking to someone else—a child. "You're my toilet baby? You
dropped out of me into the toilet? And I wrapped you
in wax paper and kept you in the refrigerator for a
long time?"

Peter felt cold and wanted to leave.

"Mirium's got it bad."

"What bad?"

"Whatever. No names. Names. Just listen to her.
There it is."

"Did she really put . . . a baby . . . ?"

"What can I say? She says she did. Whether she
did or not, it's sure there, in her head."

"How?"

"How does it happen? Why's she talking to
herself? Don't know. Chips. Slotted wrong from
birth. Loneliness . . ."

"Loneliness?"

"Sure. You ever been really alone?"

"Yeah," said Peter. He spoke the single word
slowly. He had the strong feeling Eddy wanted to
draw him into something.

"And did you ever start talking to yourself? To
yourself? Not like Mirium, like, but just speaking out
loud. To hear a voice. To test your ideas. To talk?"

"Yes."

"Speed. Now imagine that no one ever comes back
to talk with you. At least you've got yourself. You get
kind of used to talking without people around. You
get better at it. Until finally, finally, you don't even
think it's strange. It's the way you talk. During that
time you're driving people away from you. You're
talking to yourself, they don't want to talk to you,

you're strange. Your habit is a liability. Liability. Liability. People, all people start to ignore you. They don't want to hear your ranting. They don't want to see see see you. They don't want to notice you're there. They don't know how to deal with you so they don't. Then what have you got left?''

Peter didn't want to think about this line of thought anymore. "Do you know a place where I can stay?"

"Well, I've got a doss, a little nook in an alley. . . ."

"No. A hotel."

"You got cash?"

"Some," Peter lied.

"No hotel here's going to take you. Everyone's afraid."

"I know." He glanced over at the woman. Would he end up like her? Isn't that why he'd left home? To avoid being alone?

Should he go back to his father?

No. Not like this. Not after that bold proclamation he'd left on the telecom screen. He couldn't run back, tail between his legs, the very same night.

Dr. Landsgate?

No. Peter had to do it himself. He didn't want to be weak. Or, at least, he didn't want his father or Dr. Landsgate to see him as weak.

"Listen, kid," said Fast Eddy. "You're new to the scene? Right? Right? You don't know the score. Score. I do. I do. I know it. I can help you, but I need your help, see?" Eddy's body rattled wildly for a moment, then settled down. "You're big, you got the bod. I need someone around to handle the muscle—"

"I don't think—"

"You may have noticed noticed my condition. Bad wiring. Reflexes. Wired reflexes. I got one of the first sets. A black-market prototype. Back in thirty. I was twenty years old and I was red-hot. For eight years I was amazing. No one ever knew I was around. I was fast. Quiet. Someone coming? Phht! I was gone. Gone, gone, gone. A ghost. But last year the wiring started going bad. Neural connections wearing away or something. Hey, I'm not a lit, you know. I don't know this stuff. I just want to use it. Use it. Actually, it was going before that. And, people would say, Eddy, what's with the twitch? Just every once in a while, I didn't even notice it. I'd say, Nothing, nothing. What're you talking about, and I'd ignore it. But last last last year, sonny, I got slammed, slammed hard by some guards at Ares security. I just lost it, right there on the job. My body started to flop like a fish all over the floor. These guards find me like a water spirit trapped in a concrete block, you know, slamming my head against the floor trying to get out. I didn't know what the frag FRAG was going on.

"I'm telling you all this up front so you know what you're getting into. But but but I also got to tell you I think we'd make a great team.

"I don't go bad often, and if I had someone like you around, I bet it wouldn't happen so much. It's my nerves, see? It's my nerves, see? I get nervous if something's going to go wrong, and the nerves cycle through my cyberware, and it makes me react fast, gets my adrenaline whizzing, even though there's nothing to panic about. And since I know there's nothing to panic about, I panic that I'm out of control. It feeds my cyberware another cycle of trouble, and there's this adrenaline feedback that keeps looping back on itself. This ain't a fact, by the way. It's my own own own theory." Fast Eddy smiled proudly.

"I don't think so," said Peter. "I'm not . . . looking to steal. I have some work to do."

"Work? After the IBM Tower went down? Where?"

"It's my own work. Research."

Eddy eyed him curiously. "Research?"

"Yes."

Eddy lifted his hands as if surrendering. "Whatever. Whatever. Whatever."

"What's that mean?"

"Nothing. I just just didn't know they were taking trolls on at corps now. For scientists. I mean, that's what I, what I, what I thought you meant." His eyes widened and his head jerked once left and then right. "Oh! You mean they're experimenting on you. Good biz. As long as the tech doesn't go too deep."

Peter placed his hands carefully on the table. "No. I'm doing my own research. Now, please, go away. I want to eat my dinner."

Eddy looked Peter up and down. "You got it, Profezzur. I'll get out of here. But I'm all over the place. If you think you want a partner, just look me up."

Fast Eddy rose from the table and headed toward the door. As he opened it, he turned to give Peter one last look, then shuddered wildly. The next moment, he was gone, vanished into the warm autumn night.

Peter didn't sleep for fear of having his bag stolen or being killed while unconscious. He stayed in the C&E all night, and when dawn broke he was back on the street. A flock of birds flew dark against a pale purple sky. They cried out, guiding each other and giving purpose to their flight.

He walked to the lake front, having nowhere else to go until the employment agencies opened. There he stood, watching as the top of the bloated sun was just coming over the flat horizon of Lake Michigan. The impossibly orange sun was blinding as it cut the low clouds hanging over the lake into patterns of gold and deep shadow.

Peter stayed in Uptown, walking the streets all day as he looked for work. On several street corners he noticed groups of men and women gathered for day labor, waiting to be picked up by trucks. But large signs stated that no metahumans would be hired. Although some of the workers eyed Peter with suspicion as he passed by, many more were frightened. Anyone who got too near a troll these days risked getting a bomb thrown at him.

He passed some stores whose windows displayed yellowed help-wanted signs. Metahumans weren't being excluded from the work force when the signs had gone up, but when Peter walked through the door of such establishments, the strained expressions of the store owners clearly indicated that times had changed.

He walked and walked, and found nothing.

After two days he was exhausted enough, even though fearful, to fall asleep in any doorway. After five days the fear dissipated and sleeping on the street felt normal.

After his long days of looking for work, Peter would go to the lake front, find a tree to sit under, and start up his portable. He started with the basics of reading. The lessons went slowly, for it seemed that as soon as he turned to a new section of a chip, he'd forget what he'd just learned. The vocabulary just didn't stick.

One night he had chosen a young elm for his sitting place while he doggedly reviewed the primer. The sun had traveled far to the west. Behind him the lights of the city were coming on, their glow like an oppressive, unnatural sunset.

The light of the portable's screen was pale blue, but blurred to black because of Peter's thermographic vision. The portable quickly radiated red over the screen, as if it were an arcane device of magic.

He knew there was magic in the world. Magic such as Thomas healing him with shamanistic methods and magicians casting balls of fire. As he sounded the letters formed of pixels on the screen, he felt that he, too, had entered into a kind of magical communion. The pixels formed letters, the letters words, the words sentences, the sentences paragraphs, the paragraphs pages. Twenty-six letters, doubled for capital and small letters, mixed with eight punctuation symbols, letting him tap into an entire universe of ideas. Sixty symbols total, and he could learn about almost anything and someday use the same symbols to write his own research, his own cure to become human, pure human, again.

Peter felt oddly content. If nothing else, he could learn. He still had enough money to survive a while longer. He had his chips. He had the night. For hours he read happily sounding out the words carefully.

Then a beam of light fell upon him. He turned around to seek the source, the light blinding him.

As Peter shielded his eyes, he made out the dark outlines of two cops in metro uniforms standing a few meters away. Each man held a small box, and one was shining the power flashlight on Peter.

"And what have we here?" one of them said in a deep, amused voice. "A lit-dip troll? What are you doing there, troggie? Playing with someone else's toys?"

6

"Reading anything interesting?" one cop said sarcastically. Peter sensed something bad was about to happen, but he didn't know what. It was as if he'd wandered into the scene of a trideo show, for which no one had given him the script. When he didn't answer, the two guards lost their sense of humor at the same instant, as if disappointed that Peter didn't know how to play along. "Enough yakkety," said the first. "Put the portable down and get your hands up."

"Why?" Peter said, knowing he was making things worse, but so dazed by events that he couldn't stop himself.

The first cop raised the hand holding the small box and an arc of sea blue lightning slammed into Peter.

For one horrible moment he was blinded.

When the moment ended, he was sprawled on the ground, the muscles of his neck seeming to squeeze up against one another. His right arm was shivering, as if very cold, and his face rested against the ground. He saw the comfortable glow of the screen a short distance away.

"No more trouble, right?" the second cop said.

The pain receded and Peter raised his head. "Why are you doing this?"

The cops were laughing again, and one of them picked up his bag and began to rifle through the optical chips inside. "Must've rolled a student," the cop said matter-of-factly.

"Hey, keep down," said the second cop to Peter. Silhouetted against the dark sky in their stiff, armored uniforms, the cops looked almost mythically large from Peter's prone angle of vision. Instead of two bullies, they might have been living embodiments of the protectors of the innocent that Peter had always imagined policemen to be.

"I didn't steal the. . . . It's mine. The portable and the chips are mine."

The cops laughed again. "You know, any trog just a bit brighter than you would at least have been smart enough to say that someone paid you to pick them up from a store."

"Hey, here's an ID," the other one said, "Peter Clarris. Poor son of a bitch."

"That's me. I'm Peter Clarris."

"Sure you are."

"I am."

No sooner did he speak than brilliant blue static filled his vision. A warm buzz shot through his muscles, and suddenly he was flat on his back. Peter gulped in air, unable to stop.

"Shut up. Just shut up," one of the cops said.

The fit of hyperventilation passed, and it occurred to Peter that the weapons these cops were using on him could surely kill a pure human. Did the weapons have different settings, or was he just lucky? Or did they have special ones just for trolls?

As his breathing calmed, he made out the two men muttering to one another.

"Should we take him in?"

"Ah, frag it. How about he tries to escape?"

"Sounds like a hum to me."

Peter realized the cops intended to kill him. He could make a run for it, but he didn't trust his still-stiff muscles to move fast enough to escape. "My DNA scan will show you . . .," he began, careful not to move a muscle, not to be a threat.

"Looks like he's making a break for it."

Peter didn't know what to do. All the rules had fallen away and he was standing only on thin air. "I'm not really a troll . . .," he said weakly.

The next moment Peter's muscles felt ripped by countless sharp pins. He rolled wildly to escape the pain, but it followed him everywhere. It started and stopped over and over again. Soon he lost all sense of time, and it seemed that he had lived his whole life under this blade of agony.

Then just as suddenly the pain vanished.

He couldn't move, but he knew he was lying on his back, his fingers curled tightly. A loud hum filled his ears so that he could hear nothing else. He waited, paralyzed, for the next attack to come. But it did not.

Daring only to move his eyes, he let them search around for the cops.

First his eyes found the tree he had been leaning against, still lit softly by the portable's screen. He also saw dark holes in the bark that hadn't been there before. It looked as if the bark had been chewed off.

Then he saw the cops. Their hands were in the air, both of them turning their heads slightly, but seeming fearful of turning fully around to look behind them.

From somewhere Peter heard shouts. At first he couldn't make out the words. But as the buzz in his ears finally cleared, he heard a voice say,". . . . so just take the bag and let's call it square." He recognized the voice, but could not place it.

"Sure, sure," said one cop.

"Now move it. Take the bag and the portable and *get*. Quick!" This was followed by a loud burst of gunshots and a spray of bullets that slammed into the tree.

"We're gone!" shouted the other cop, stooping over to grab the portable and Peter's bag. Then the two were off and running.

For the third time that night Peter's breathing returned to a normal pace.

A warm shadow ran to him, then a face hovered over him. It twitched wildly, then settled down into a grin.

Fast Eddy.

"Hey, Prof, howzitgoin'?"

Peter had expected somebody . . . better. Angry frustration bit into him. "You gave away everything I own." He struggled to get up, but found his muscles still beyond his control.

Eddy pulled back, hurt. "I just saved your life. What's with you, chummer."

"Why didn't you just shoot them?" Peter settled onto his back, unhappily resigned to his helplessness.

"You don't shoot cops, you don't shoot cops. It's part of the deal."

"Deal?"

"Yeah," Eddy snapped, obviously annoyed, "the deal. And if you knew about the deals, or had just just just the tiniest bit of thinking, you'd know that if you're a troll you don't wander around with a portable computer and expect the cops to leave you alone."

"But it's mine."

Eddy dropped to his knees and brought his face to within centimeters of Peter's.

"You are a blood clot! You know that? You are blood clot. A little thing that gets caught up in the system and brings the whole thing to a crashing halt. Let me tell you what happens to a blood clot. All the blood gets stuck and jams up behind it, until there's enough pressure to just shove the clot out of the vein. And then it's dead!"

Peter knew Eddy was wrong, but couldn't remember the specifics so he just kept his mouth shut.

"Now I put my my my neck out on the line for you. I'm not expecting lifelong gratitude, but I'm not expecting face!"

"Sorry," Peter said softly.

"If you're so hot, why didn't you just take them on? Spirits, you're a troll! Why didn't you just nail them?"

Embarrassment made him speak awkwardly. "I don't know how to fight."

"What?"

"I don't . . ."

"I heard, I heard, I heard you. A baby! You're just a little baby dropped out of the sky into the sprawl."

Peter resented the image, but he knew it was absolutely accurate.

"I'm sorry," Peter shouted.

"Come on, let's get out of here."

"Why are you doing this?"

"I saw what was going on. I remembered you. I'm hoping it will endear endear endear me to you. I do want to work with you. Let's go, they might come back. And bring friends."

Finding he could move a bit, Peter rolled over onto to his hands and knees. Then a dizziness gripped him, and he had to pause to get his balance.

"You all right?"

"No."

"Dumb question. Question. Sorry."

Peter stood up, slowly. It seemed an hour passed as he did so, and then, suddenly, he was on his feet.

Eddy shoved a small gun, a small machine gun, its barrel still hot, into his leather jacket. "Let's go."

The whole scene was no more than a shadowy blur as Peter let Eddy lead him along the asphalt path away from the lake front and back onto the streets of Chicago.

7

Peter picked through a garbage can behind the night club. Here on the far Westside people could afford not to finish their meals. Pushing aside a few empty vodka containers, he discovered a small plastic bag full of something soft and squishy. When he looked inside, he saw it was full of meat scraps. A feast.

Looking down the alley to make sure no one had seen him, Peter smiled in delight at his find.

He stuffed the plastic bag into a large canvas sack he'd stolen from another gutter rat a few months back. For just a moment he tried to place the bum's face, but couldn't. As far as he knew the man was dead.

As far as that went, everyone Peter had met since he'd taken to the street was dead. Everyone except Fast Eddy. Street people seemed to have a habit of vanishing and never appearing again.

He made his way out onto the snow-covered street, where he passed a few other pedestrians. Probably wage slaves who'd gone to sandwich shacks for lunch and were on their way back to their offices.

Peter knew they paid too much money for their food. He'd seen the prices. And they paid simply for the convenience of someone else slicing the bread and spreading the soy paste for them. Even if Peter had had enough money for a sandwich at a Westside restaurant, he wouldn't buy one. He'd go purchase the bread and the soy meat and the paste and make it himself. He could dine for days on the food.

When he passed these wage slaves on the street, they looked away, pretending not to see him. He could tell because they worked so hard at it. They had to work at it because he was a huge, muscular, gray-green troll with large teeth and yellow eyes.

Once they'd passed him by, Peter chuckled to himself at the strangeness of other people going to such lengths to ignore him. The change back to indifference had been slow. Immediately following the Night of Rage, which was the media's tag for the wave of rioting that had begun in Seattle and spread to the rest of the world, people on the street used to regard him with fear. And then, slowly, the fear had shifted to an apparent total lack of awareness. If the metahumans couldn't be killed off, then they just wouldn't exist. Fine for the pure humans, drek for the metahumans. Peter had to live with nonexistence.

He paused to look up and down the street for any sign of a patrol car. Nothing. He moved again. It was better to move when no cops were around.

He'd be safer from them in another area. Somewhere like the Noose, which is what people had started calling the Loop ever since it went up in flames during the Night of Rage. Thousands of squatters had moved into the ruined buildings, and the city hadn't lifted a finger to remove them. It looked like the local government was going to wait until all the real estate deals on the south side were in full swing before they turned to rebuilding the Loop.

So the Noose was a great place to live if you didn't have anywhere else to go and didn't mind competing with the gangs for space and thought you could defend yourself against the ghouls that had moved into the Shattergraves, the four-square-block area destroyed when the IBM Tower had collapsed. But pickings were scarce in the Noose. Peter preferred to live where rich people were, because they could afford to waste, discard, or simply lose plenty of stuff for scavenging.

That's why Peter always had an eye out for the cops. Seeing a patrol car coming, he ducked into an alleyway. The street had taught him that it was smarter to stay put and try to act invisible rather than attract attention by running away. If he ran, they'd think he was guilty of something. If he didn't run, they hardly ever suspected him of any wrongdoing. He didn't get thrown in jail too much anymore, and when he did, he usually relished spending the night in a nice, warm cell. They chained him up, but that was all right. He never gave his name, and when they wanted to run a DNA ID check, Peter insisted he'd always been a troll and wasn't a runaway. Invariably, they believed him. Nobody cared much what the trolls did, after all.

Inside a cell he was safe from the pure human gangers who liked to hunt trolls to prove their coolness. On the street Peter wasn't so afraid of the gangs. It was more a fear that a big group would catch him asleep some night, freaking Fast Eddy and leaving him dead.

It was dark by the time he got back to the construction site they called home, which was good. The workers had left for the day, so he and Eddy were free to set up in a little alcove in the open basement. Down there they were safe from the cold and wind, and nobody could see their fire.

Fast Eddy wasn't in the alcove when Peter arrived. That meant his friend was either still scrounging for food or else was dead. Peter never knew which it would be.

He took some wood from a pile he'd collected from an abandoned house a few weeks back, and dumped it into a large trash can. He lit the wood with some oil, and soon a lovely orange fire was burning. Deciding to wait until Eddy returned before cooking dinner, he put the meat aside. He sat down on the ground near the fire. The warmth spread over him, and for a moment he thought he was dreaming, back in his bed in his father's house.

The instant he thought of his father, a sad feeling overcame him and chased away the dream. Peter didn't want to see him or speak to him, only just to know he was around. Like a totem. Something he could focus on and hold close to himself.

Then he thought of his mother, and she was wonderful because he'd never known her. "Mom, Mom, Mom, Mom," he said over and over. By the fiftieth time he'd worn the word out. It had lost its meaning, was just a syllable, a dollop of sound.

The scraping sound of a shoe against cement broke his reverie. Maybe it was Fast Eddy, maybe somebody else. He never knew.

He jumped up and flattened himself against the wall of the alcove, his right hand tightened into a fist. Eddy had taught him how to fight since the night he'd saved his life. Now Peter even liked it. "Just remember what the cops did to you," Eddy had said over and over.

The sound of footsteps slowed, then there was only silence before Eddy appeared around the corner.

"I . . . I . . . didn't know if it was you. Was you, was you," he said. "Got some got some some some meat."

Peter smiled proudly and raised his plastic bag high. "Me, too."

Eddy smiled when Peter smiled.

Peter pulled out his meat scraps and pierced them on an antenna he'd snapped off a car. Peter had quickly learned that his heat-sensitive vision made cooking easy. Soon they were eating, contented to feel their bellies full.

"Tell me a story," Eddy said, chewing off a piece of fat. "Tell me your stuff."

Peter sometimes remembered bits and pieces of his education, and Eddy loved to hear about it. They weren't really stories, but Eddy always called them that.

Peter searched his mind to find something new to talk about.

"Did I tell you about atoms?"

"Nope," Eddy always said nope. Peter knew that either Eddy was lying, or he always forgot, and so he wondered why he bothered to check with Eddy anymore. But he did, and Eddy always said nope.

"You and I are made of atoms."

"Uh-huh," Eddy said, nodding his head up and down.

"Atoms are the things that make up everything." Peter said, scooping up some snow from the ground to show Eddy. "Everything is made of atoms. But not everything is made up of the same atoms. And atoms can be combined in different ways. So it's the kind of atoms and the combinations that make a thing what it is."

He picked a bit of meat out from between his large teeth, placed it on his tongue, and swallowed it.

"When atoms get together, they're called molecules. You and me, we're made of . . ." Peter got stuck. He forget what he and Eddy were made of.

Eddy said, "Proteins, nucleic acids, carbohydrates, lipids. Lip . . . Lip . . . Lipids."

"I thought you said I didn't tell you about this?"

Eddy shrugged expressively.

Peter went on anyway. "But you and I are very different." Eddy laughed, laughed like a little boy. "Right. We're very different. And what makes us different are acids." No, that was wrong. *"Nucleic* acids. Nucleic acids. Little molecules." Or were they big molecules? "The same molecules in each of us. The same . . . the same *four* acids, but it's how they're arranged in us that makes us different."

Eddy laughed again, this time as if he'd heard a tall tale he couldn't believe.

"What's so funny?"

"How could four of anything make you and me and everyone else?"

"No. No. There are four kinds of nucleic acids. I can't remember what they are, but there are four *kinds.* But there are . . . billions of combinations," he guessed. "Billions. And how they are arranged is what we are. It's like a pass code. If you have 'one,' 'two,' 'three,' 'four,' and the pass code has fifteen slots, then you get to arrange the numbers in those slots. That's the combination for that lock. You and me, we've got these billions of slots, and how our four acids are arranged, those are our combinations. That's who we are."

Peter remembered that the doctor in the hospital had told him this, and was disappointed suddenly that he hadn't remembered it from when he was a pure human.

Eddy's jaw was slightly open and he looked at Peter with amazement. "Really?"

"Really."

"You're telling the truth?"

"Yeah."

"You're so smart. Why aren't you a teacher or something?"

"I was going to be a teacher. I think. I might have been a teacher. But I became a troll instead."

"Oh. I was a thief."

"Yes."

They sat silently for a moment before resuming their meal. Then Eddy said, "I thought you said you were gonna cure yourself."

"Yes."

"How's it going?"

"It's going."

Eddy looked Peter up and down. "You don't look much different."

They laughed.

"I'm not working on it right now. I need research chips. I need to be able to read about the stuff. Biology."

"Oh." Eddy looked at Peter, waiting for him to go on. "And . . . ?"

"And I don't have them."

"When are you going to get them?"

"I don't know. I wasn't able to get a job. How would I get the money to buy them?"

"What about libraries? Don't they have the chips?"

"Yeah, but they cost money, too. My father told me that when the continent was the U.S.A., libraries were free. But now they cost money. Everything costs money."

"Why not steal steal steal them?"

"I can't steal them."

"Why not?"

"Because," Peter began firmly, then faltered. Why not? He'd stolen food. He'd stolen a winter coat (which someone had later stolen from him). Why not chips?

There was something about chips, though. You don't steal knowledge.

"You don't steal knowledge," he said gravely, feeling a moral fortitude that he hadn't experienced in some time.

"Yeah, you do. If you know what's worth stealing stealing stealing. You steal knowledge. Data."

"What?"

"What do . . . do . . . do . . . you think is on the black market? Market. Data. That's what you steal. In North America, America you steal steal steal data. Jewels is for babies."

"Oh. I don't want to talk about it. . . ."

"You wouldn't even have to do nothing tough. You don't have to find the stuff. It's there there there waiting for you. You just want chips, right?" Eddy didn't wait for an answer. "Sure. This'd be simple. We could do this, Profezzur!"

"What?"

"We just hit a bookstore. For crying." Eddy took a bite of food, looked around for a moment, swallowed, and then, as if he hadn't interrupted himself, said, "Crying out. Loud."

"I don't know, Eddy. I mean. You know. You're pretty messed up."

Eddy looked away. "Yeah. Yeah. Yeah. I know. Pretty messed, messed up. But, you know, I could still do it. With you, I mean, I mean, you and me. We could."

He looked up at Peter, a hint of slyness in his eyes. Was Eddy scamming him? Had he planned this all along, waiting for the right moment to suggest that he and Peter enter the biz together.

"You want those chips? Well? Do you want them?"

"Yeah."

"Okay. Okay. Okay. Tomorrow we'll case case case out a bookstore."

"Case out a bookstore?"

"Yeah. Unless you want to hit Northwestern or the U. of, U. of, U. of C."

The thought of knocking over a university appalled Peter. "No. I think a bookstore will be a good warm-up."

"Great. Great. Great."

They stood on a roof looking down and across the street onto Hirshfield's Science Unlimited. The wind whipped the snow around them, Eddy, as usual, jerked spasmodically every so often, his shoulders twitching and his head snapping a few degrees to the right.

"So, what do we do? How do you 'case' a place?"

"We watch it. See when they lock up. Go inside and take take take what you need."

"That's casing it?"

"It's only a bookstore, Profezzur. You want to hit Aztechnology, you have to put in a bit more more more work."

"We could have just walked by the door and read the hours on the display."

Eddy turned to Peter and gave him a fixed, annoyed stared.

"O.K., O.K.," Peter said placatingly. "I'm new to this. I'm sorry. I trust you."

Eddy shrugged his shoulders and looked back toward the bookstore, squinting slightly. His features took on the appearance of a rat waiting for a smaller rat to poke its nose out of a hole.

An old man and a young woman were standing by a small plate at the front door of the store. The man tapped some buttons on the plate, and, one by one, steel slats slid down the tops of the windows and snapped into place.

"This looks tough."

Eddy sighed, but continued to watch the man.

"It does!" Peter whispered harshly.

"Relax, relax, relax, relax, relax, relax, relax, relax, relax—" Peter gave Eddy a sharp knock on the shoulder. "Thanks," his friend said after a moment. "All right. As soon as they're gone, we'll sneak around to the back."

Peter wondered again why the "casing" was such an important part of the process, but he was no expert on stealing and decided to let the matter drop.

They went down the fire escape at the back of their lookout building, walked down to the corner, went around the block, crossed the street, and then headed into the alley behind the bookstore.

The back door of Hirshfield's was blanketed with a sheet of thick metal slats.

"I suppose you'll want me to rip the metal apart, or something," Peter said wearily. "People will hear."

"Nothing, nothing so crude. Or so loud." Eddy walked up to the door and leaned down to examine a plate with nine buttons on it, just like the one in the front. He began to press the buttons. Peter was certain he was making random guesses, that the area was about to be surrounded by cops called in by a silent alarm of some sort. "Most people use one combination for all locks," Eddy said under his breath, "even though the corps that sell them the locks say they shouldn't."

He stepped away from the plate and the slats began to rise. Peter looked down at him, his mouth agape. Eddy put his right hand up to his face and placed a finger under each eye. "Binoculars." Peter peered into Eddy's eyes. They looked real, yet Eddy had obviously gotten the combination while the man was locking up.

"You never told me about them."

"Surprise is the thief's greatest asset."

Eddy stepped up to the door and tried the handle.

He turned it, but it was locked. "If you would?" He stepped back to let Peter into the doorway.

Peter grabbed the handle and crushed it in his grip. Then he turned his wrist. The lock cracked in half, the handle snapped off.

It was dark inside the store, the only light coming from the exit signs, which spilled onto the shelves.

Peter thought the place looked like a treasure trove. The dim light glinted off thousands of plastic cases containing optical chips.

"Let's get get get inside."

Peter wandered in and Eddy pulled the door shut behind them. He grabbed a few chip cases off a shelf and jammed then under the door to keep it shut.

"Hey," said Peter, shocked.

"What?"

"Why are you ruining the chips?"

"What's it it it matter?"

Peter wasn't certain he could explain the nearly mystical awe in which he held recorded information. "Well . . .," he began. Then he *knew* he couldn't express mystical awe. So he said, "The chips. They're valuable."

"And you're about to steal them. What's it matter if we just take them or we crush them?"

"I'm going to use them!"

A spasm shot down Eddy's body from his head to his feet, then he flung his hands toward the base of the door and said, "I'm *using* these!"

Peter's big eyes blinked twice. "Never mind." He realized he could be arguing with Eddy until long after the store opened the next morning.

He strode down the aisle, looking for the biology section while Eddy went off toward the hardware section. Peter heard a crash, but decided to ignore it.

It didn't take long to find the chips he needed. It wasn't everything he'd left home with, but it would be enough to let him recapture the basics of biology.

He grabbed Hodgeson's *Correlative Neuroanatomy,* Perkins' *Functional Neurology of Metahumans,* Louer's *Chaos Theory and the Brain: A Critique.* He stuffed his pockets with them. He was trying to find chips he'd already read, figuring that would be the best way to begin.

Eddy appeared next to him carrying a case of portable computers in each arm.

"What are you doing?"

"You're going to need a portable to read them, right?"

He'd forgotten about that. "Yes. Yes I will."

"Well, one of these is for you."

"What are you doing with two *cases?*"

"We're robbing this place, aren't we?"

"We came in here to get my chips."

"No, *you* came in here to get your chips. I came in here to get enough stuff so I could eat well for a while."

"You're not going to share the food with me?"

"Sure I will. Will. Will. You helped me get the stuff, right?"

"So this is robbing?"

"This is it, kid. What do you think?"

Peter looked around the dark empty store. There was something very comforting about the situation. Something *right.* He couldn't quite put his finger on it, but all in all, it was a far cry from digging food out of garbage cans in cold back alleys.

"It's good. I like it."

"There we are. Let's go. The cops'll, cops'll, cops'll be here soon. Soon."

"What?"

"That door you popped. I'm sure it was wired."

"What?"

"Don't worry? This is Chicago. The owner of the store wasn't well-dressed enough to be paying off the force. The heat won't be here for another two minutes.''

8

They got a room in a small hotel in Uptown, paying the owner a special bonus to let Peter stay in his hole.

When Peter first saw the room, it seemed wonderful. The floor might be dirty, the walls cracked, and the sound of mice crawling around in the walls often woke him, but it was theirs. For months he'd lived on the street. Now he and Eddy had their own little haven.

He could have gotten something at one of the new Chicago Housing Authority metahuman projects, but that would have meant having to admit he was a metahuman, that he was truly a troll, and Peter was not prepared to do that. Every day, the moment he woke up, he said aloud, "I'm human, pure human, I'm really human, and I'm going to be pure human again." He feared that if he didn't remind himself every day, he might forget his dream. And then where would he be?

Once he'd mentioned this to Eddy, who shrugged and said, "Well, if you just forgot about it, then it wouldn't bother you anymore. What would it matter if you were a troll?" He wasn't sure if Eddy was joking, but decided not to bring up the subject again.

But now that didn't matter anymore. Peter had his portable and his chips and he was learning about biology.

It was slow going, however. Anytime he read something, he had to re-read it again the next day, and then read it a third time later on to be certain it was firmly in his head.

One day Eddy was out fencing some monitors they'd stolen the previous week, and Peter had the place to himself. He sat on the floor of the hotel room, his massive shoulders hunched over the small portable as he tapped out commands very carefully with the tips of his strong fingernails.

Coming across an interesting item in a chip on basic genetis, he opened a file he'd named My Cure. The file was a collection of notes that intrigued him.

He typed:

> Humans, pure and metahuman, have forty-six chromosomes in their bodies. During reproduction one of the chromosomes of each pair from the mother and the father form the genetic code for a new person. Independent assortment produces 2^{23} kinds of sex cells. The potential number of DNA combinations is even larger than this, because genes on the chromosomes may be exchanged during meiosis.
>
> That's 2,000,000,000,000,000,000,000,000,000,000 possible people all from the same act of sex.
>
> Imagine that.

He picked up his big gnarled hand and looked at it. Inside his flesh, he knew, were his genes. And somehow, out of 2,000,000,000,000,000,000,000,000,000,000 possible combinations, his mom and dad had passed on the genes to become a troll.

Peter stood up and crossed to the window. Outside he saw a man walking up and down the street. He'd been there all morning. Every so often some ragged-looking pure human or ork showed up and talked with the man for a few minutes. Chip deals on a fine spring morning. Two years ago Peter wouldn't have guessed what was going on. Chip dealers and chipheads wouldn't have been part of his field of thoughts. Now he'd forgotten almost everything he'd once learned in school, and he was alert to the scoop on the streets.

He felt his rage rising again. He didn't want to know about hallucinogenic sense-chips and prostitutes and the conditions of prison cells throughout Cook County. He wanted to be the old Peter Clarris again, contemplating abstract theories of molecular biology in the safe, pristine classrooms of a well-respected university.

These thoughts made him want to hit something.

But what was there to hit? It was his own body that had betrayed him, dumped him into the minorities known as metahumans.

So he punched himself.

He balled his hands into fists, slamming himself in the face over and over.

He hit himself so many times that his face began to go numb, and through the stinging numbness, he felt a kind of pleasure, a sense of, "Well, at least I can still feel."

He smiled, as he always did after one of these assaults on himself. He invariably felt better afterward, and usually couldn't remember at all the reason, the deep, non-verbal reason, why he'd wanted to punch himself in the first place. He heard the door open, and turned quickly toward the window so Eddy wouldn't see his face.

"We, we, we, made out like bandits."

"We are bandits," Peter said without turning.

"What is it?" Eddy and Peter had been together too long for the other man not to know the signs.

"Nothing."

"Yes, yes, yes. Something. You're not upset with the work, with the work, with the work, are you?"

Peter turned. "No." He gestured to the portable

on the floor. "It's going fine. I was just thinking about it when you came in."

Eddy laughed, a hissing kind of noise. "No, no. 'The Work.' Our work. When we go out and gather things. It's not bothering you, is it?"

"No."

"Good, 'cause today I spoke to someone about expanding our operations."

"You what!"

Eddy rushed over to Peter. "Hey, hey, hey, take it easy. I just wanted to see if we might—"

"No. No one else." Peter rubbed his hands over his face. Things were moving too quickly. A flood of regret washed over him, and he wondered, not for the first time, how Eddy had talked him into the business of stealing in the first place.

"We can make more money. We we we can get access to better fences. Better connections. Safer operations. They can pay better."

"No, Eddy," Peter growled.

Eddy jumped back in surprise. He rubbed his hands together and licked his lips. "Now, Peter. Peter. No need. . . . I think you're not quite seeing. Seeing. Seeing the opportunity. Here." He gestured to the portable. "What you have here, this is fine. But tell me honest. Aren't you going to need more? For your research project. You're you're bright. . . . smartest troll I ever met, truth, truth, but no one's going to take you in. You're on your own, aren't you? And nothing's going to change that. Except me. *I* make you not alone. And I can help you get what you need. I may not understand what you're up to. Up to. I don't. I don't understand what you're up to. But I know that it's going to take more than a few hundred dollars a week. Right? Right?"

Eddy was right. Peter needed access to expensive computer time, research papers that only a few people had. "Who?" he asked quietly. "Who did you talk to?"

Eddy raised his hands and clapped them together. "Now, that's that's that's more like it."

They walked down the street.

Eddy had bought a new leather jacket for the occasion. He said he wanted to come off as someone who was used to action, moving in and out of places quickly. Peter wore some beat-up fatigues he'd found in a used-clothing store, just like the kind he'd once seen the ork wear. He felt awkward in these clothes, as though they labeled him the wrong way, but he couldn't think of any other style to wear, any other way of presenting himself. And Eddy had made it clear that on the streets you needed a front, an image that would tag you as someone with power and someone who should be left alone.

"Now remember, don't let on that you're smart. . . ."

"I'm not smart."

"Whatever. Don't let on. You come off smart at all, and the deal's off. People like things simple. A guy is like this. A woman is like that. He's a boxer, so he's stupid. She's beautiful, so she's selfish. Selfish." Eddy gestured to his head. "People people people don't like to think. They don't want to have to carry carry too much in their heads. Cops. Cops ain't all bad, but they bust on you because it's easier to bust on you than worry about whether you deserve it. They see you, a troll, you're strong, you're scary, you're stupid." He quickly raised his hand. "That's what they want to see. You come off smart, that's too much for them to handle. They don't trust you 'cause they don't know what you're going to do next."

Peter thought about it and saw that it made sense. Kind of. He'd go along with Eddy. For a while.

Up ahead a pink marquee with green letters proclaimed The Crew. As Peter and Eddy entered the club in the mid-afternoon, they saw orks on their hands and knees, scrubbing up spilled liquor from the previous night's revelries. Their broad, round faces reminded Peter of something . . . a Flemish painting gone awry. He almost connected with them, with their pain and frustration; with their lack of hope of being anything more than near-slaves scrubbing floors and living in roach-infested city housing projects. But he killed the impulse immediately.

Two young punks, Orientals, dressed in expensive silk suits, sat by double doors leading into the dance area. One of them had a portable flatscreen in his lap. The other touched his companion on the arm when he noticed Peter and Eddy. The two men got up, their faces like stone, so similar in their immobility that Peter thought they were brothers.

"We're here to see Billy," Eddy said. One of the punks nodded and pointed to stairs leading up to the right.

"Thanks," said Eddy, and he and Peter went up the stairs.

At the top of the stairs they came to a waiting area with chairs set along one wall. Across the room from the chairs was a frosted glass window.

A man sat in one of the chairs, and he stood when they entered the room. He was middle-aged, with a potbelly and the jowls of a bulldog. When he moved, his leather jacket opened slightly and Peter glimpsed a pistol in a holster. The man eyed Peter suspiciously.

Eddy stopped walking and raised his arms overhead. The man stepped up to him and patted Eddy down. He nodded, then turned to Peter.

Peter didn't raise his arms right away. The thought of someone searching him was offensive, reminding him too much of run-ins with cops. But seeing Eddy's pleading, desperate glance, he relented.

The man did a thorough job on Peter, taking much

more time than he had with Eddy. He pressed hard, prodded, and Peter was certain the man was trying to provoke him.

After patting a pocket of Peter's jacket, he suddenly stopped and said, "Hold it."

Peter froze, unsure what was going on. He looked to Eddy, but Eddy's glance showed equal bafflement.

The man reached into Peter's pocket and pulled out three chips. Peter rolled his eyes up, furious at himself. He'd slipped the chips into his pocket when he'd been working earlier. "What the hell's this?" the man said. "Meta . . .," he said, sounding out the words. "Metahuman Correlative Neuroanatomy? You reading this stuff?" Peter saw a thick layer of ignorance over the man's red face. He probably hadn't read much past fifth grade. Today maybe he read the sports pages and perhaps a menu at a restaurant.

Peter smiled weakly. "No."

"Then what are you doing with these?"

"He was holding holding holding them for me. I rolled some guy yesterday. He had them on him," said Eddy.

"But why does he have them?"

"I like the pictures," said Peter.

"What?"

"I like the pictures."

"The diagrams," Eddy added. "He likes to read chips on science, because he likes the pictures. I call him the Profezzur." Eddy laughed, and the man joined in. Peter decided to play the man for a fool, looked from Eddy to the man with an expression of utter bafflement, then laughed also, as if he didn't get the joke but felt obliged to pretend he did. This made the potbellied man laugh even harder.

A strange good humor filled Peter's chest. If Eddy was right and he had to appear stupid, at least he could take comfort in knowing that he was really only playing on the stupidity of others.

The man dropped the chips back into Peter's pocket and soon the laughter died away. He quickly finished patting Peter down, and opened the door for them.

"Billy, the guy and the *Profezzur* are here." The man laughed once again as Peter and Eddy passed by him. Once they were in, Peter heard the man's idiot laugh even through the closed door.

Billy was in his late twenties, a man with the eyes of a hustler, but the face of an angel. He was beautiful, his features sleek and gentle, a face women loved. Even Peter felt drawn to it. It was a face of the blessed. Peter discovered that he wanted to please Billy, just so someone so good-looking would favor him with approval.

Not only that, Billy wore a beautiful suit. It caught the light and changed colors when he moved. Dressed in his own baggy fatigues, Peter felt ridiculous in the other man's presence.

"Profezzur?" Billy said, his head cocked to one side.

"Yeah," said Eddy. "That's what I call him. He likes to make pretend he can read chips about science. Show him, Prof."

Peter reached into his pockets and pulled out his chips and placed them on Billy's desk. As he leaned toward Billy, he put on his foolish grin. He added a bit of bashfulness, too, quickly looking away when Billy caught his eye. Throwing a quick glance at Eddy, Peter saw that his friend had covered his mouth with one hand, hiding a smile brought on by Peter's act. Peter felt very proud of himself and very clever.

Billy picked up the chips and smiled. "Well. Well, well, well. You read a lot of science?"

"I like the pictures."

Billy turned to Eddy and he and Eddy shared a laugh.

"Hmmm. That's very interesting. But what I've asked you and Eddy here for . . . It's come to my organization's attention that you two seem to know how to work merchandise.''

"Your organization?" Peter asked innocently. He didn't know if it was prudent to take control of the conversation, but he guessed his assumed naiveté allowed him some latitude.

"Itami's gang. We're just beginning to expand. We've heard good things about you chummers.''

"When do we start?" Peter asked, full of innocence. He had a good feeling about the setup. Room for growth. More money. More chips.

"Well, frankly, I hadn't decided yet. How about if we take you on for a while? Give us time to get used to each other.''

"I've got a job I think you'd like,'' put in Eddy.

"Really?''

"Really. Listen. . . .''

Eddy outlined the job.

He wanted to knock over a shipment coming in to the University of Chicago. The shipment consisted of the hides of three griffins. Eddy had gotten a lead on a group of mages who would pay eighty thousand apiece for the hides. "We can sell sell sell to this group for a clean two hundred and forty grand, or we can bid out, with a base bid of two hundred and fifty. It'll take about fifty grand to set up the whole deal. Not a lot compared to what Itami wants to make . . . But it'll be good seed cash. Cash.''

"They want that stuff?" asked Billy, amused and interested.

"Oh, yeah. It's got magic in it. It. It. It focuses whatever it is they do or something. Look. Look. I really don't know why they want it. They're all mages, *neh?*'' He laughed, and Billy politely joined in. "But they want it. And we can get it for them.''

"All right,'' Billy said, his hustler's eyes shining. "I like this. What do you need?''

9

When they got a block away from The Crew, Peter began shouting, "What was that? What was that? Robbing a shipment of magic hides? There'll be guards. Guns. Big, *big* guns. If it's worth a quarter of a million dollars, there'll be enough protection to guard a quarter of a million dollars' worth of merchandise. This isn't our league. We shouldn't be doing this! What are you doing?"

Eddy looked up at him, incredulous and somewhat hurt. "We're switching leagues, Prof. That's the whole point. Point. I mean . . . I don't know what to say. I don't know what to say. I put in a lot of time just finding out about this shipment. And then more more more time into making sure there was a buyer. I thought you wanted to do this."

"I did. I mean. I thought we'd do the same thing for the gang. I didn't think we'd try something like this."

"But, Peter, this is just some flash to kick us off. Off. Off. If we do it, we'll be in tight on the ground level of their operation. More money, more power. And things'll be easier. The guys at the top, they tell people people what to do. That's what we want."

"Eddy, nobody will ever let me tell them what to do."

Eddy grinned up at Peter. "You don't know how it works yet, sonny. Stick with me. I'll get you there."

They had two weeks to get everything ready. The whole thing made Peter nervous, and he didn't want any part of setting it up. "Just tell me where to go," he said.

Eddy smiled at him and said, "Running."

So Eddy went out every day to case the site of the heist. He came back at night and reported who he had bribed. Because he knew some of the guards couldn't be bribed, he hired a decker to break into the airport computer system in order to shuffle the security shifts to place only Eddy's men on duty the night of the heist.

"See," Eddy said, "no guns. No killing."

"I don't want to hear about it. Just tell me what *I* have to *do*."

Two days before the heist, on a Wednesday, Eddy came home early, his arms full of Japanese take-out.

"So, how's the research going?"

"Fine," Peter said, glancing up from his portable. He was certain Eddy was about to tell him all the things he'd done that day to set up the job.

Instead Eddy began laying out food on the table and said, "No, really. Really. How's it going? Tell me more stories. Hungry?"

The smell of the food drew Peter—sushi and noodles and spiced rice and fish. It made his mouth water. He still thought Eddy was leading him on, but as long as he could eat . . .

He saved his work and shut down the portable. Then he got up off the floor and pulled out the troll-strength chair he'd bought the week before. He knew he probably should start working at the table, but the habit of working on the floor was too ingrained in him now.

Eddy pulled down the cheap plates they'd swiped from a fast food place and placed one before Peter.

Peter eyed him suspiciously.

"What?" Eddy asked. "What? What?"

"You're being awfully nice."

"I can be nice."

"I'm not denying that. I'm just saying you usually keep it hidden."

"Ouch."

Peter looked at the food. Six different dishes waited his approval. "Thanks for dinner."

"You're welcome. Now, why are you a troll? Why are there trolls? Why trolls? Why not talking rabbits?"

"Talking rabbits?"

"I saw an old flat cartoon once. Flat cartoon. It had a talking rabbit. Once trolls and talking rabbits didn't exist. Now we got at least one of them. One. Why?"

Peter scooped a spoonful of octopus onto his plate. "That I can't tell you. My guess is, my guess is that once a lot of the monsters did exist. A long, long time ago. And then the magic went down. . . ."

"The magic went down?"

"Yeah. I've been reading about magic. I figure, I'm a troll, and I better know about magic."

"You know, you're talking better."

"I am?"

"Maybe not better. But stronger, more confidence."

"Huh." Peter opened his mouth to take a bite of octopus. It tasted meaty and of the sea. He continued talking while he chewed. "Anyway. This guy, a mage, Harry Mason, he guessed that what happened in 2011, when all the magic started occurring . . . that was the start of magic's rise. First the elves and dwarfs started being born. Then the Indians got their shamanistic powers. Then people started tapping into hermetic magic. And then, in 2021, some people just spontaneously began to change into metahumans—orks and trolls—one out of ten—it just happens. So the magic built in power."

"Yeah. I see."

"So he postulates that the magic, before 2011, was slowly growing back in strength after being down for a long time. It fell from a great height a long, long time ago. Like Atlantis—that might be a true story. A powerful place based on a time when magic was even stronger than it is today."

"Atlantis? You mean Atlanta?"

"No, I mean Atlantis." Peter looked carefully at Eddy to see if he was joking. "You've never heard of Atlantis?"

"No. What is it?"

"It was a place. An island that supposedly sank. . . ."

"Oh! Right! There's that foundation that's looking for clues about Atlantis."

"You never heard the stories about it?"

"No. Should I have?" Eddy seemed a bit defensive.

"I don't know. When I was growing up I read lots of stories like that. Atlantis. King Arthur. Alice in Wonderland. They weren't supposed to be true. But, fantasy. You know. Childhood."

"Profezzur, you remember how you and me used to live on the streets when we first met?"

"Yeah."

"My parents died in the plagues. That's how I grew up."

"Oh."

A silence formed, and the two of them tried to ignore it as they scooped more food onto their plates.

"So those were people you read about," Eddy said finally, "that King and Alice? Or are they flatscreen and trids?"

"I read about them. But people made flatscreens and trids about them, too."

"Hmmm. Yeah. I never read."

"Would you like to learn?" Peter offered. He really wanted to help Eddy do that if he wanted to.

"Naw. That's for profs like you. I know you all think reading is power or somesuch, but, if you haven't noticed, I'm getting by just fine without it." Peter thought he heard regret in Eddy's response, but he decided to ignore it.

"Well. That's the magic. Maybe it was here once before, and maybe it's back now. And the way I see it, the magic is something in the environment that caused my body to change from what it was."

"What? Like getting a tan?" Eddy laughed, and Peter joined him. But then Peter added, "Yes! Kind of. Like a suntan. The sun influences the body to react a certain way.

"See, the genotype . . . the genetic sequence . . . it determines what the body will be like. And the brain, too. But it isn't set in stone. It isn't as if, at conception, a person's body and mind are completely determined.

"What the body and brain end up as, those are the phenotypes. The genotype determines which phenotypes can arise in any given sequence of environments in which the individual who carries that genotype lives and develops."

"Huh?" Eddy asked, and laughed.

"It's like a kid growing up. He's given a genotype at birth. But how he ends up . . . Well, if he gets enough food to eat, he develops one way. He's healthy. He's got muscles that support him. If he doesn't get enough food, his limbs get thin, his belly bloats. Both bodies are consistent within the range of possibilities dictated by his genotype. But only the genotype's interaction with the environment can fully determine what the phenotype will be."

"So you're saying you had the range of genetic possibilities to become a troll, and by interacting with the environment, an environment with magic, you became a troll. Became a troll. Became a troll."

"That's my guess. I don't know. Nobody knows.

Another theory is that people have been subconsciously using magic since it rose in power. The mages know how to use it on purpose, but the rest of us just sometimes tap into it without much control. Maybe parents back in 2011 made their kids into elves and dwarfs, then later, people transformed themselves into orks and trolls. The idea is that it's kind of like . . ." He searched his head for the magic terms he'd recently reviewed. "A kind of physical manifestation of a person's true nature, just like a mage in astral space has a true nature."

"So you turned into a troll because you thought you were a troll?"

"Yeah. Maybe. I guess."

"But you hate being a troll."

Peter thought back through the haze of memory before his transformation. He remembered that he'd felt only loneliness, a longing. He felt himself ugly and socially inept. He couldn't remember the specifics, but the sensations filled his chest, hollowed out his lungs, replaced them with a thick chill. Could he have believed himself into being a troll? Maybe.

"Anyway," he said, shaking off the feeling, "how it happened is almost a religious debate at this point. There's no way to prove the past now. No archaeological records. No one knows. What matters is that my DNA is really different now. That's all I've got to work with. Whether it was passed down to me or whether I did it myself doesn't matter. This is just the way it is.

"The research on this has only been around for thirty years, and since the corps gained power and the U.S.A. fell apart, information isn't developed or shared too well. Somebody might be working on a means of identifying and manipulating metahuman genes right now, and I'd never know about it."

"But you could find out."

"What do you mean?"

"There are ways of getting data out of corps. Like I used to do."

"But that takes money."

"Exactly, Profezzur. Exactly."

Eddy shoved a forkful of rice into his mouth and the mouth shaped into a huge grin. And Peter could see now that even though Eddy had not once brought up the heist, and that even though the conversation was all about genetics, their life of crime rested at the center of the subject matter, like a nucleus floating in the middle of a cell.

10

Peter stood beside a hangar, along with Eddy and three mobsters from the Itami gang. The way the men's muscles rolled under their coats when they moved frightened Peter. These slags were another league.

The five of them looked out toward one of O'Hare's runways. The lights of the O'Hare Subsprawl were even brighter than those of Chicago, changing the night sky into the pale white of early dawn. In the cold, Peter saw their breaths roll out as a thick mist of red, then dissipate to pink, and then nothing.

Everybody but Peter held Uzis. His weapon was a Predator II heavy pistol, specially fitted for his hand. After practicing with it all week, he could use it well enough now. The recoil felt light in his hand, but he knew the gun packed a terrible punch.

Seeing a small, private plane roll to a stop on the runway, Peter felt his breathing become rapid. As planned an armored truck waited to meet the plane.

Perhaps Eddy had been right when he assured Peter that everything was in place, nothing could go wrong, no shots need be fired. But the gun in his hand, the metal cold in the winter air, bit into his flesh. "I'm here," the metal said, "and if I wasn't needed, I wouldn't be around."

Peter's mind swirled as he tried not to think about the problems that might arise.

Watching the guards move with clean precision, shifting the crates to the truck, Peter saw a beauty in their motions. He had been spending so much time crammed into his chip, learning about the smallest elements of human life. But now, watching it all come together, watching how DNA allowed the guards to move . . .

. . . To move the cargo that a man had gone out and hunted. To allow a pilot to fly the hides into Chicago. To allow someone to design the plane that the pilot flew . . .

And Peter and his cohorts. All five of them thieves, all capable of stealing the hides away . . . All because their DNA gave them the urge to want more and the ability to take.

And the guards, they could try to keep the hides.

But they wouldn't. Down through the generations, the capacity to be bribed.

All this coming together on the tarmac.

A genotype determined which phenotypes arose in a given environment. The body as well as the mind. And part of the environment was made up of other people, other phenotypes. And since it was nearly impossible these days for someone to interact with an environment that wasn't manmade, almost everything was controlled by the phenotypes of other people. Life was made up of phenotypes turning genotypes into phenotypes over and over again.

"Hey, Profezzur?" Eddy said with an edge of harshness in his voice.

"Yeah?"

Peter came out of his daze and saw the truck moving down the runway. The plane's flight lights flashed on as it began to taxi in the other direction.

"You're not going to shut down on me, are you?"

"No. I was just thinking."

"You should watch that. Crime isn't crime isn't crime isn't an introspective profession." Eddy smiled up at Peter, who smiled back.

The mobsters became shadowed blurs as they ran for cover behind a pile of crates.

Eddy tugged on his arm. "We're up. Stash the metal. Metal."

Peter slipped his gun into his holster and followed Eddy out into the road leading off the tarmac. The truck drove up and slowed to a stop. The cab doors opened, and two laughing guards climbed out. Against the cold night air their faces glowed a bright red. "Well, it's all yours," said one of them. "Let me just get the guys out of the back." Peter's muscles relaxed. It was going to work.

Eddy followed the guard around to the other side of the truck, and Peter followed Eddy. "And now we just drive away with the hides?" he said.

"That's that's that's right." Off to the right the lights of a van switched on, and Go-Mo, an old friend of Eddy's brought the van around to the truck. "They continue down to the U. of C., go through the whole rigmarole with the boxes, sign in and out. Next day, the boxes are opened and the hides are gone. They think they were stolen from the U. of C., and we weren't anywhere near the scene of the crime."

The guard slipped his lock into the back door of the truck and opened it. The lights of the van illuminated the interior of the truck, revealing two men, one in his late twenties, the other in his early forties. The older man's jaw trembled, his face a mask of fear.

"We've got a problem," said the young guard.

"What's that?" asked Eddy.

"Jenkins isn't on your payroll."

"Jenkins? Jenkins? There's no no no Jenkins."

The young guard hopped out the back of the truck. "Oh, yeah there is." He jerked his thumb at the man inside. "Jenkins, welcome to a robbery."

Everyone fell silent, staring stupidly at the guard.

Eddy whirled around and stamped his foot on the ground. "The stupid decker shorted it."

"Jenkins isn't in on it?" said the guard who opened the door.

"He asked me why we were slowing down," the young guard told him. "He didn't have a clue."

Peter looked at Jenkins, his heart going out in sympathy to the man. Jenkins sat on a crate, silent, confused not only at the robbery, but at a robbery in which his partners were in on the heist.

"What do we do?" asked the young guard.

Eddy turned to Jenkins. "Listen. Listen. We've got a problem problem here. I'd like to make you an offer."

The man's mouth moved, but he was too terrified to speak.

Go-Mo got out of the van and came over to Eddy. "We can't trust this guy. Look at him."

Eddy glanced first at Jenkins and then at the three other guards, obviously trying to gauge the expressions on their faces. Peter saw only a hardening of some kind of loyalty with Jenkins.

"How about we call it off," Peter said. Eddy gave him a look. The other guards looked at Jenkins.

Then Peter realized there was no way to call it off, not if Jenkins didn't go along—he could tag the other guards. And if he did go along, there was no reason to call it off. The fear from earlier crawled up the inside of his skin to his chest, where it came to rest and gently fingered his heart.

Eddy stepped toward the three guards and ignored Jenkins fiercely; he cut Jenkins out of the universe.

Peter glanced at Jenkins and saw that the man had lost his place in the world. He took a half-step back into the harshly lit truck. He fingered his gun, but didn't draw it. Behind him were the crates with the hides. Peter realized the man might well soon die so that Eddy could get those crates. In his mind Peter saw thick slugs ripping through flesh and muscle, the impact startling Jenkins' body so much that it ceased to function.

As Eddy talked to the guards, Go-Mo pulled out his Uzi. "Drop the gun," he told Jenkins. His face going slack, Jenkins placed his gun carefully on the floor of the truck.

Peter wondered why Jenkins' just didn't fake it. Why didn't he just say he'd take some money and be quiet, and if he wanted to fink, he could do it later?

Maybe he couldn't lie well and was afraid everyone would know it was phony. Maybe he couldn't bring himself to lie. Maybe on the verge of death he didn't want his last words to be a desperate act of cowardice.

"What do you want to do about this?" Eddy asked the guards. They didn't look at each other. Peter sensed that in Jenkins presence they felt shamed. Eddy took a step closer and lowered his voice. "Listen. There are are are only a couple of choices here, none of them pleasant. Pleasant. I'll outline them so we can get on with it. We shut this guy down or else the whole thing turns bloody." His neck twitched violently.

Peter wondered if Eddy's body was about to betray him. So many things all interacting, so many things that could wrong.

"I don't know about killing Jenkins," said the first guard.

"Do we have a choice?" said a second.

The third glared at Jenkins, as if the man had purposely hosed everything up. Then he said, "I don't know . . ."

"I think your indecision speaks megabytes," Go-Mo said, then suddenly his gun was up, a roar filling

the air as blood sprayed up from the third guard's
chest. Peter felt a warm wave rush up his body. His
face tightened and he thought he might scream.

"Down! Down!" Eddy shouted and he dove for
the asphalt and worked his gun free. Peter found
himself wanting to move, but unable to. Then the
mobsters behind the crates started shooting wild automatic fire. Bullets slammed into the truck's armored sides, their impact clattering harshly in Peter's
ears. Out of instinct he dove for the ground on the
opposite side of the truck from the guards. Then he
rolled under the vehicle, desperate for safety.

To his right Peter saw the feet of the two remaining
guards outside the truck. They stood, the truck momentarily sheltering them from the thugs. Turning
his head, he saw Go-Mo and Eddy on the ground,
crawling for the van. Then one of the guards took
two steps toward the back edge of the truck. Peter
heard the rapid fire of gunshots and then saw Eddy's
right leg twitch violently.

Peter felt very warm and excited and angry. And
he was so giddy with fear that a cry almost escaped
his lips. He didn't want to see Eddy in pain. Fighting his better judgement, he rolled to the edge of
the truck, where he was suddenly looking up at the
guards. Neither saw him—one was shooting, the
other looking across the tarmac, searching for shelter, thinking about what to do next.

Peter raised his Predator II and fired twice at the
guard shooting at Eddy. The gun sent a soft motion
through his arm. The bullets pierced the guard's pel-
vis just beneath his chest armor and ran up through
his lungs. The man looked down at Peter for a moment, clearly surprised that his life would end this
way, and then toppled over.

The second guard, startled for only a moment by
the loud gunshots, turned his gun down toward Peter. With a frightened gasp Peter rolled back under

the truck. Slugs slammed the asphalt centimeters behind him. He just wanted to be home. Home with
his father. Home with Eddy. Any home. Just home.

Then a roar of submachine gunfire went off. Peter
turned his head and saw the last of the guards outside
the truck fall to the ground, the man's body twitching rapidly. Bullets had turned his face into a land-
scape of torn flesh and blood. Peter looked right and
saw Go-Mo beside the van, his head pointed forward, a big smile on his face.

A silence fell over the scene, but Peter could not
bring himself to crawl out from under the truck. He
shook wildly, and it brought a flash-memory of waking up in a sweat the night his transformation had
begun. He didn't want to hear anymore shooting.

But it started again, this time from just above him.
Jenkins was making his last stand.

Peter saw Go-Mo's body hit the pavement, cut in
half at the waist by intense automatic fire.

A panic gripped his stomach. Death didn't seem
as bad as the terrible violence that accompanied it.

He saw Eddy, his right leg bleeding, rolled under the
van, safe for the moment.

The mobsters tried to move up, but Jenkins kept
them back with a storm of bullets from the rear of
the truck. One hood cried out in pain, and fell to the
ground. When he tried to crawl back to the shelter
of the crates, Jenkins fired into him again. The man
uttered a terrible scream, then fell motionless. The
other two hoods remained pinned down behind low
rises in the ground.

Peter knew security might arrive soon. He also
knew that as long as the guard lived, he himself
might die. Eddy was down, the hoods trapped. He
had to do something. His breathing increased in
pace, and as soon as he noticed it, it got even faster.
He really didn't want to leave the safety beneath the
truck, but he knew he had no choice. To make sure

he didn't get caught in random fire by the mobsters, he rolled out from under the van on the side with corpses. His hand accidentally touched the men's blood, now thick on the pavement. A dizziness passed over him, but he shut his thoughts down and inched his way along the truck until he got to the back, his gun held out before him.

He peered around the back of the truck.

Nothing.

And then Jenkins put his head out the door and looked in the direction of the mobsters, the back of his head to Peter. Peter knew he should shoot now, but he couldn't bring himself to do it.

Jenkins apparently sensed something, for he turned his head suddenly and came face to face with Peter. Peter saw a thought in Jenkins' eyes: he wanted to bring his gun around to shoot at Peter. He knew it was too late, but he would try.

Peter pulled the trigger of his pistol.

The Predator's bullet slammed into Jenkins' skull, shattering it, splattering the repository of the man's personality and knowledge against the metal walls of the truck.

A white hot flush of victory streamed through Peter. He looked at what had once been a man named Jenkins. He had *won*. Though he'd almost died, he'd fought and won.

Then Peter fell to his knees and, despite all his adrenaline-driven good cheer, became quite sick.

11

Billy sat behind his desk and laughed, tears running down his cheeks. Eddy joined in the mirth. Peter sat by, smiling weakly but he was certainly not jovial.

In telling Billy how the heist had gone, Eddy had, thankfully, left out the fact that Peter had gotten sick.

"Security heard the shots and were on their way, but we took the van and made our break through the gate we'd left open, just like like like we planned. That was it."

Billy nodded approvingly. "Well, all hell broke loose, but you two came through. You got the bodies, you got the hides. Slick. Very slick." He stood and held out his hand to Eddy. "Well done. Mr. Itami will be quite impressed. And you," he said to Peter, "the men I sent you with won't shut up about you. You are a true warrior." He thrust out his hand, and Peter touched the fingertips, as he had decided would be his manner when asked to shake hands.

No, no, I'm not, Peter thought. But he kept quiet, because Billy's smile made him want to let Billy think whatever Billy wanted to about him.

"And your leg?" Billy asked Eddy.

"Your magician fixed it right up. Up."

Billy started to laugh again. "He wasn't bribed!" he cried out. Eddy tittered, and then broke out into a full-blown guffaw.

Still laughing, Billy said, "He's dead now."

"Who?" asked Eddy, startled.

"The decker. We tracked him down."

The two of them laughed loudly all over again.

Billy looked up at Peter. "You are so serious. I like that. I have a job for you. How'd you like to be my bodyguard?"

What?

"And you," he said, turning to Eddy, "my lieutenant. Mr. Itami is letting me expand my crew, and I want you by my side. You're crafty, you know the streets. I like you. And now! Let's go celebrate."

* * *

First they went to buy a suit for Peter, at Billy's insistence. After piling into Billy's big Nightsky limo, they sped off to a department store whose owner Billy knew well. A salesman and a tailor were waiting for them, but otherwise the place was empty of customers. In fact, the store was closed.

"You are more than a muscleboy," Billy said to Peter. "I know that much." While he talked Billy paced a circle around Peter, eyeing him up and down. Peter knew that might have made other people nervous, but compared to his father's indifferent, clinical eyes, this scrutiny was like being massaged by Thomas' hands. "I don't want a bodyguard who merely knows how to fight. If a fight breaks out next to me, I'm already too near death. Anyone who would let that happen would be useless as a guard. No, your job is to protect me, but that means keeping anything from happening in the first place. A lot of this has to do with attitude. You shouldn't have to pull a gun or throw a punch. You see anyone look at me the wrong way, you stare him back down. Got it?"

Peter looked into Billy's face and saw that Billy really wanted to know if he got it. It wasn't condescension, thinking that Peter was too stupid to understand. He just wanted to check in with Peter. To connect. Peter smiled. He couldn't help himself. "Yes."

The tailor said, "Give us half an hour. Please."

Billy turned to Peter. "All right with you?"

Peter smiled again, and looked down at the little tailor, a pure human. The man looked up at him, subtly pleading for Peter's good grace. "Yes. All right."

The man let out a sigh.

Peter decided he liked the way things were going.

When the suit was finished, Peter looked at himself in the mirror. He was still massive, but now, somehow legitimate. Adult. Human. Suddenly realizing he'd been slumping for months, he stood up taller and straighter. He wanted to show off his body in his new suit. His massive hands protruded from the dark sleeves, his toothy face rose from the collar, but it was all right. In a nearly perverse way there was something intriguing about him.

They piled back into a limo—a huge limo in which Peter could sit without having his knees up to his chin.

Billy gave instructions to the driver, and they were off.

Compared to the day's earlier ill-events, riding in the car seemed like heaven. Peter settled deep into the soft upholstery. Billy opened a bar and offered him a drink, and Peter asked for a beer. He'd had only two drinks in his life, and he knew he had to be careful of losing control. But he wanted so much to relax, to just forget, just for a little while. Just a little bit.

The music was soft—something very old, classical, it was called, and it smacked of class. After living on the streets and then in a roach-infested apartment for so long, Peter found Billy's invitation into the lap of mobile luxury a tonic.

He closed his eyes, and for an instant he saw Jenkins' ruined head. Then he opened his eyes, and everything was all right. Eddy was laughing with Billy, and even Peter found himself slipping into a smile.

"Ah, so the Profezzur can be happy!" Billy exclaimed. "Terrific."

A thought slid through his mind, tentative at first, and then it nestled comfortably: He was finally safe because he'd killed Jenkins, and since Jenkins was dead, there was nothing to be done about it now. He would enjoy it all however he could.

The limo pulled up before a posh nightclub west of The Crew. Swirling arc lamps lit the sky and formed churning pillars of light. "Just opened," Billy said. "Caters to the new simsense technicians they're housing out here." He leaned forward to Peter. "Tonight's your test. Let's see how well you handle yourself."

Peter slipped on his dopey grin. "Yes, sir, Billy."

"Terrific. Spirits, you're cute. But let me see a *look*. Something that will keep me safe."

Peter tried to focus a threatening gaze. He knew he wasn't quite pulling it off, and then he remembered how he'd felt knowing it was either Jenkins or him.

Billy smiled. "Very good. Let's go."

A long line of people stood outside the door. Eddy walked alongside Peter while Billy remained in the Nightsky. "Get the boss through. He's important. Make the crowd know that." Peter smirked at the line of small people waiting to get in. Suddenly his size and strength didn't seem like clumsy liabilities. Billy had given him the authority to use his natural assets.

He walked briskly up to the line. The material of the suit felt wonderful against his skin; it was a uniform of respectability. The people in the line didn't take long noticing the troll striding up to them. Fear jumped from one face to the next as people nudged one another. The crowd quickly parted. . . .

. . . And revealed two heavy-set guards armed with stun batons. One of them spoke into the small headmike that wound around to his mouth, asking for heavy back-up. The men eyed him, smiled at him, ready for a fight, and Peter remembered the police. He didn't want to fight, he just wanted to be frightening. Suddenly the magic Billy had given him was gone. Fear ran through his body to his arms and into fingers. He wanted to make a fist, but couldn't.

And Billy was beside him, bringing the magic back

again. "These are my associates," he said. "The Profezzur and Fast Eddy."

The demeanor of the guards changed instantly. "Mr. Shaw! A pleasure. We didn't know."

"No problem!" And he shoved some bucks into their breast pockets. Both guards looked up at Peter, smiling and nodding. "Good evening, Profezzur! Sorry about the confusion. But you know, can't be too careful."

Was he blessed? Was Billy an angel from the Christian heaven, come down to surround him with holy comfort? Peter couldn't remember being so well-treated.

Billy strode into the lobby of the club, with Peter staying close. He realized that he was holding his head high, swinging his arms confidently. Glaring, he scanned the crowd, warning all that Billy was under his protection.

And he under Billy's.

They entered the dance area. Tables and booths ringed the dance floor at various levels. Colored lights spun around. They flashed. The music pounded. Somehow the deep tones rumbled through Peter's flesh, pressing hard against the beat of his heart. It was almost like being on the verge of death, but more like living a different way.

A man in a leather jacket spotted Billy and rushed over. "Mr. Shaw! A pleasure. This way, please!" he shouted over the music.

The man led them up a flight of stairs and over to a circular table. The table offered perfect sightlines to everywhere in the club.

Billy and Eddy sat down. Peter thought that as a troll and bodyguard, he would spend the night standing. But then he saw two men struggling with a troll-sized reinforced chair. "Get out of the way," they shouted at patrons whose tables were between them and Billy's table.

Soon the chair was in place and Peter slumped down into it.

"How's it feel?" Billy shouted.

What could Peter say? It was a heavy metal chair, not particularly comfortable. But the fact that Billy asked him how it felt? That made the moment a treasured holo, an image he would carry around forever and savor whenever he needed to lift his spirits.

"Wiz!" Peter shouted back. "Wonderful!" He laughed joyously.

When had he last laughed like that—not because something was funny, but because the very act of being alive thrilled him so? Maybe he never had.

Peter looked to Billy and Eddy, who grinned wildly at one another and then looked back at Peter. His happiness amused them. And that was all right, too.

Months passed.

Policemen quickly learned Peter's name and treated him with respect. Women at nightclubs winked at him, and sometimes even brushed up against him. He knew it was all because of Billy, but he didn't mind. It was better than the streets. It was better than his father's house.

Peter got his own place, and Eddy got his.

Sometimes Peter was so enjoying being important that he let his research slip from his daily routine. But Eddy turned Wednesday night into Story Night, and every week he would show up with an armful of take-out Japanese and insist that Peter tell him the things he had learned. Knowing that Eddy would show up on Wednesday night kept Peter working. Without ever mentioning it directly, Eddy reminded Peter of his claim that he would become human again.

"Some genes are pleiotropic," Peter began one night. "That is, one gene may affect many traits. I think the metahuman gene might be a pleiotropic. It would make sense. If the gene is there in the body, and the 'magical environment' activates it, then it could trigger subtler genetic shifts throughout the body. This way you wouldn't have hundreds of thousands of triggers all waiting to go off in a person. In fact, many people who aren't metahuman might have many metahuman genes, but over the centuries, their genetic branches lost the pleiotropic metahuman trigger. Even when the environment changed, they didn't have the one gene needed to activate all the other genes.''

Eddy nodded his head, greedily slipping fried rice into his mouth.

''The idea, then, is that I've still got the same genes for eyes as when I was human, the same genes for arms, fingers . . . but the pleiotropic metahuman gene alters all of them just a bit. Still have eyes, but now they're bigger and yellow. Still have skin, but now it's gray-green and hard.

''The problem is, there's no way to check this now. It'll be years before work is finished on the metahuman genome.''

''Any way you can do it yourself?''

''Nope. No way. Way too big. I'm talking big machines, huge staffs. I'll have to wait for other people to do it. Like I said, it'll be years.''

Years passed.

The Itami gang's power grew, and so did Billy's position. As he rose, so did Eddy and Peter along with him.

''Peter, I need some wetwork done,'' said Billy one afternoon.

Peter had had to kill three people in his job of defending Billy, but he'd never been ordered out to kill in cold blood. Each of those three deaths he'd justified as part of the game among mobsters. Everyone knew the rules going in and everyone took his chances.

"Who?" Peter asked.

Peter thought he saw a glint of annoyance in Billy's eyes, and then Billy became beatific and generous all over again. "Does it make a difference who?"

It did, or at least Peter thought it might, but all he said was, "No, Billy."

"Good."

It was early evening when Peter walked into Mick's, a bar located in the midst of the Southside in an area under massive redevelopment. Mick's was a hangout for pure-human construction workers. Crude four leaf clovers carved from sheet metal hung on the walls.

O'Malley sat in the middle of the bar, surrounded by his mobster cronies. He controlled the construction industry in Chicago. There were no unions anymore, but workers could still stage slow-downs, still arrange accidents. Itami was tired of slow-downs, tired of accidents. He needed the construction finished in certain neighborhoods so that he could start dumping some of the expensive illegal simsense chips he'd invested in. He wanted the rich to have new homes.

A couple of thick, stocky men slid off their stools and stared at Peter. One or two grinned. They thought they were about to have a good time with a stupid troll.

Nope. Billy was on Peter's side.

Peter whipped out his Uzi and shot it down the length of the bar into O'Malley. The fat Irishman's belly ripped open and his face betrayed surprise for just a moment.

Men rushed at Peter, guns were drawn, but Peter was suddenly invisible, vanished into thin air.

He rushed for the door, leaving mass confusion behind.

Eddy had the Tornado running. He popped the back

door open and Peter jumped inside, spreading out flat along the passenger seat.

The mage sitting in the front seat next to Eddy leaned back as Eddy peeled the Tornado out into the street. Peter caught a reflection of himself in the mage's silver eyes; cybernetic eyes containing microtronics that mimicked the heat-sensing capabilities of Peter's own, natural eyes. Through the window, the dimness of the bar held no secrets from a mage who could see in the dark. "How'd it go?"

The question caught Peter off guard. Yes, O'Malley was dead. So it went well. But another life stopped? Good?

He remembered Eddy's warning: Crime isn't an introspective profession.

"He's dead."

Meanwhile, Peter was following the research. Markel found the metahuman gene sequence in unborn fetuses. Theories supporting the idea that metahuman genes had always been in people were strengthened.

His father was hired away from the U. of C. by a prominent biotech firm based in Chicago. Landsgate was hired by Northwestern University. Peter thought about calling Dr. Landsgate, but couldn't think of what he would say. He simply wanted contact with his childhood friend, like an open channel with neither party talking.

Peter passed through his mid-twenties. He was studying and learning about the secrets of the body and how it lived. He was also learning how to kill it. His life continued along his twin path, a double helix of biology and murder twining inextricably together.

* * *

Wednesday night.

"You you you all right?" Eddy was chewing a mouthful of squid.

"Yeah. I was just thinking . . ."

"That's the Profezzur."

"I was just . . . When a sperm and an egg meet—that's just two cells. Two little cells. But they've got all the information for a lifetime packed into them.

"The sperm's got twenty-three chromosomes. The egg has twenty-three. Each set of chromosomes was randomly picked for each egg and each sperm.

"And then, when the egg and the sperm meet, their meeting is also random. The egg the woman is carrying—each month with a new egg is available for fertilization. What will the chromosome set be for the moment of conception? And the sperm that propel themselves to the egg—there are countless possibilities contained in all the sperm a man produces. Which set will reach the egg?"

Eddy waited a moment, then asked, "And?"

"It's just so random. There's no control."

"And?"

"It bothers me. That's all."

Eddy chewed his food slowly. Peter traced a figure on the table with his finger.

"And killing somebody," Peter said suddenly, softly. "That's control. I walk in with a gun and suddenly I'm master of that man's life. I *stop* his life. I do that. I choose to do that. It's like clockwork. You're in the car. We kill one man after another, and it's all so planned, precise."

"That's why we're still alive."

"But that's what bothers me. Why is the taking of life more comprehensible than the making of it? We go to kill a man . . . or two corps send in strike teams against each other. They sit around with maps and diagrams and figure out who will do what. They make a plan, then they implement the plan, and they go."

"But things can still go wrong. Things *do* go wrong. The hide job at O'Hare . . ."

"But . . . ," began Peter, and then he stopped. "No. You're right. It is all so . . . But killing feels more in control."

"More in control than what?"

"Than . . . I don't know . . . Just living . . ."

Peter hired people to gather research from corps and universities. Dozens of sources followed the trail of the metahuman genes, and Peter had illegal feelers out to all of them. He took the research and rolled it around in his mind.

His own notes grew more and more extensive. He had boxes stuffed with optical chips, generating enough material to keep a team of grad slaves busy for years.

He tried not to learn anything about his father.

It wasn't hard to avoid William Clarris. As the years passed, corporations had become more and more like armed camps, often hidden away, often as secretive as lone, mad, hermetic mages.

It was Wednesday and Eddy arrived.

"Good." Peter rushed to the table and cleared away some space. "I just got some work in from Cal Tech. Spectacular." He cracked open one of the carry-out cartons. "There are some genes called operator genes. They make the structural genes attached to them go 'on.'

"These genes can be blocked by repressor proteins. These repressors are always in the cell, and if they attach to the operator gene, the operator is turned off. Then the structural genes are turned off. The DNA can't transcribe to the RNA anymore, and it's as if the DNA sequence wasn't there."

"Uh-huh," said Eddy. "If the stuff, the repressor, is always in the cell, how can the gene be 'on'?"

"Wonderful question. Like this: the repressor gene can be bound by other chemicals. If the repressor is bound, it can't bind the operator.

"About eighty years ago some French biologists did some work with *Escherichia coli*, a bacteria. Lactose is what controlled the genes, and the gene operator worked the production of digestive enzymes.

"When the cell digested lactose, it reduced the amount of lactose in the cell. When the amount of lactose was too small to inactivate the repressor, the repressor bound to the operator and switched it off. The transcription of the genes stopped, and the cell stopped making digestive enzymes, which was good, since the enzymes weren't needed. If you were to dump one of these Escherichia things into a vat of lactose . . ."

"All of the genes would go on. . . ."

"And stay on. . . ."

"As if the environment had changed."

"Like the magic."

"Exactly. But that was a bacterial cell. A eucaryotic cell, like the ones we have, with nuclei and many chromosomes, is much more complicated. Researchers have been working for decades to get a better understanding of the controllers.

"But I hear that Simpson at Cal Tech has come up with a model of muscle growth based on operator and regulator genes. How muscle growth changes according to the foods given to it."

"Going to get the chips?"

Peter grinned with embarrassment. "Yeah."

At The Crew, Billy told Peter, "I've got another job," and his smile said he knew Peter would do the job and do it wonderfully.

At Billy's office, he never thought of people as full-blown expressions of amazingly long strings of deoxyribonucleic acid. They were packages of self-contained meat; things to be taken care of.

"Who?" Peter asked, as always with Billy, happy for the approval and a chance to belong.

And one day, never thinking it would happen so quickly, Peter was twenty-eight years old.

BECOMING

December 2052

Becoming (bǐ kǔm ǐng), *adj*. **1.** Attractive <a *becoming* dress> **2.** Suitable; proper <a *becoming* sentiment>—n. **3.** Any process of change. **4.** *Aristotelian Metaphys.* Any change involving realization of potentialities, as a movement from the lower level of potentiality to the higher level of actuality.

12

Peter peered at his face in the mirror over his bureau. His troll flesh was like a well-loved sweater now. Comfortable, but somewhat ragged.

He seemed, more and more often, to be himself.

He shook his head, and saw the image shake sadly as well. No, he was not himself. Somewhere, buried inside him, was a boy who'd been tricked by the universe, forced to become a brute, a murderer.

How had it all happened?

More than anything else, he was lonely. Some days the loneliness was boundless. Every day, he cast his loneliness out into the world, waiting for someone, something, anything, to fill the emptiness within him, but nothing ever came back.

I must become human again, he thought.

And then the face in the mirror smiled a big, toothy grin, for he'd accomplished the work he'd set out to do all those years ago.

His portable sat atop the table where he labored over the research, the theories, the clues. A stack of three chips rested beside it, each chip called My Cure, all back-ups of the work he'd finished the night before.

Finally, mercifully, his work was done.

Or he believed he was. He needed someone to read his work and confirm it.

He showered, then slipped into his best suit. Over that he put on a long, tan duster—a gift from Eddy. Armor lined the inside, which made it heavy, but for Peter it was no problem. He called Eddy to ask for a ride.

Downstairs, the cold air chilled the gun resting against his chest. His breath curled up out of his mouth and swirled for a moment before his face, the warmth bleeding out of it in seconds.

Up the street he heard the squeal of wheels, and turned to see Eddy's Westwind zip around the corner from Broadway. He was doing the speed limit as he cut around two other cars, then drove up onto the sidewalk across the street to get out of the way of oncoming traffic. Then he leaped the Westwind off the curb and cut back over to the right side of the road.

For a moment Peter pondered the wisdom of getting into a car with Fast Eddy. In the past several years his friend's nervous system had taken a sharp dive for the worse, if worse were possible. The only time he seemed content was when moving around like a bat out of hell. But somehow Eddy never had an accident. He just kept on moving.

The Westwind came to a screeching halt as Eddy stopped the car just in front of Peter. The window rolled down. "Ready? Ready? Ready?"

Peter opened the door and settled into the back seat. He folded himself up to fit, his knees jammed into his chin.

"Where to? Where to? Where to?"

"The Crew."

"Meeting? Meeting with Itami? Meeting with Itami?" Eddy kicked the Westwind into gear. As it peeled out and made a sweeping U-turn, Peter was thrown first to the right and then to the left. The maneuver also brought the car within centimeters of clipping a metro cop car.

Out the back window Peter saw the cop's mercury lamps go on for a moment, then immediately go dark again.

My connections are powerful and numerous, Peter thought.

The Westwind continued on, careening through the streets that were still snow-free even though Chicago's weather could change from one moment to the next. People bundled up tightly in overcoats made their way to Rail and bus stops. Peter and Eddy made it to the Westside in just under an hour—the Westside, where the houses were large and the simsense dollars flowed thick.

Eddy brought the car to a screeching halt in front of The Crew. "Thanks, chummer." Peter said, unfolding himself and working his way out of the car.

"No problem, no problem, no problem," answered Eddy, shaking his head vigorously. "I like to drive. I like it a lot. I love it."

"Yes, I've noticed." They both laughed. Over the past few years Peter and Eddy had become somewhat distant, probably because Eddy's role in the gang had diminished as Peter's position of trust had increased. Peter couldn't ignore the sadness in Eddy's eyes. He'd been the one to get Peter started, and Peter would never leave him.

As he walked into The Crew, Peter thought how different the place was since the day he and Eddy had first interviewed with Billy. Much fancier. More glitz. With the blossoming of the simsense industry in Chicago, the place where the tech had first been invented, the city experienced a period of relative boom. Simsense had since spread out into the world, of course, creating a kind of revolution in the way people lived. Now people everywhere could jack into pre-recorded sensory experiences—feel what it was like to fall out of an airplane, kiss a beautiful woman, be romanced by a dashingly handsome man, live through a scripted, outlandish adventure story. Itami had invested his cash wisely, dividing it among illegal operations and straight business deals. As Chicago grew stronger, so did he.

The stench of alcohol and cigarette smoke hung in the air of The Crew. Some of it would be aired out by evening, the rest to be covered over by the sweet smells of perfume and other scents when members of the simsense industry mobbed the place to blow their salaries on ambience, bright lights, and watered-down drinks.

"Hey! It's the Profezzur!" shouted Max, the beer-bellied bag runner who delighted in taunting Peter. He was quite old and fat now, and behaved as though his only purpose in life was sitting around and waiting for people to come through the doors of The Crew.

"Hi, Max," Peter said with a foolish grin. He took grim amusement in making Max believe he considered him one of his best friends in the world.

Max stood outside the closed doors of the dance area. With him was a pinched-looking gentleman who Peter had never seen before.

"Mr. Garner," Max said with a broad sweep of the arm, "I'd like you to meet the Profezzur here."

Mr. Garner smiled perfunctorily, obviously uncomfortable. First he'd been trapped waiting with the likes of Max and now he had to deal with a troll.

"It's a . . . it's a . . . uh . . . pleasure . . . to meet you, Mr. Garner.

"Isn't he great!" Max laughed.

Mr. Garner smiled politely for Max's benefit.

The door swung open, and Billy poked his head out into the lobby. "Mr. Garner, would you step in, please?" Relief spread over Garner's face, and he passed through the open door. "Prof, you too."

"*So ka*, Billy."

Billy smiled at the troll's use of Japanese. He seemed

to relish Peter's clumsy attempts to get through life, but Peter didn't mind because Billy's amusement never showed the least trace of mockery. Billy, who Peter admired more than ever, had grown even more handsome with the passing years. Peter envied him the many women, beautiful women, who often shared his bed. On several occasions Billy had tried to set Peter up, but Peter had always refused. He didn't say it aloud, but his thought was, "Not in this body. Not until I'm human."

Mr. Itami sat at a table positioned in the center of the dance floor. His sons, Arinori and Yoake, stood behind him, one on each side. Their faces were stone masks. Like Peter, they packed pistols under their jackets.

Peter took up position about two meters from the table, close enough to hear what was said, but not so close as to impose himself on the proceedings.

Billy offered a chair to Mr. Garner, who took it nervously and gratefully.

Now that Peter's scrutiny wasn't as likely to be returned, he looked Garner over again. The man seemed an average spook, a high-level manager from some corp. He was new at this game, that was certain. A thin sheen of sweat on his forehead caught the colored spots that lit the area.

Billy's chosen meeting spot put Garner right in the center of an open dance floor, which had its desired effect. Peter could almost read the man's thoughts: "There's nowhere to hide."

Nervousness filled Peter, too. He'd never before been invited to attend a meeting presided over by the gang's venerable leader. He'd met Itami before, spoken to him twice, but had never participated in his court. Itami was born in Chicago, but he carried a few watered-down Japanese sensibilities. Peter often had trouble figuring out what the man was up to.

Mr. Itami, his old hands folded on his lap, waited.

The silence continued for a full minute before Mr. Garner said, "Well . . ."

Mr. Itami's broad, wrinkled face seemed to suggest an acknowledgement of the statement. Peter sometimes wondered how the Japanese got anything done. It seemed that their natural inclination was to spend all their time staring everyone else down.

"I think that Amij should be killed," continued Mr. Garner.

Amij? Peter thought. The name was familiar, but he couldn't place it.

Itami remained silent.

"Katherine Amij," said Mr. Garner.

Ah, thought Peter, now he had it. CEO of Cell Works. The company that employed his father.

"Your reason," said Mr. Itami.

Garner breathed a visible sigh of relief, so pleased to get a response. "She helped one of our key scientists escape to another corporation," he said. "She helped him break his contract and leave. And I recently discovered that she is tracking down this man, Dr. William Clarris, while feeding false leads to our own security team."

His father gone?

Peter's heart plummeted. He'd hoped to send his research to his father. His father could confirm it. And also . . . Peter couldn't find the right words. He glanced at Billy, who gave Peter a smile full of confidence.

But what.

He wanted his father to read the research and smile at him that way.

"Mr. Garner," Mr. Itami said, "Katherine Amij is the granddaughter of the Cell Works' founder. She was five years old when the family moved the firm from Amsterdam to Chicago. She grew up working for Cell Works, but it was by her own choice. Her loyalty to the company is a matter of pride among your staff."

He let the words sink in, and then said, "You have, I take it, evidence to back up these charges?"

"Of course, Mr. Itami. Our security has determined that Amij has made contact with a fixer named Zero-One-Zero. She would need a fixer to fence the information, because as far as we know, she is inexperienced in such matters."

"Exactly my point, Mr. Garner. She is inexperienced in such matters. I believe most of your executives have, at one time or another, had occasion to call on the services of a fixer to serve as go-between in some business matter or other."

"Yes, Mr. Itami. Which is why we have a fixer on retainer for Cell Works. He handles all our needs, personal and business. Zero-One-Zero is not a Cell Works man. Amij has gone to an outsider."

Peter glanced at Mr. Itami. The crime lord raised his right eyebrow. "Hmmm. What else?"

"Two things," Garner said with a touch of excitement, happy to have engaged Mr. Itami's interest. "First, she has behaved erratically ever since her fiance's death. Her reputation around the office, and her family ties, protect her, but in any other situation she'd have been fired."

"Fired?" asked Mr. Itami.

"Fired. She performs her functions, but listlessly. At her salary . . ."

"She is in mourning, perhaps?" suggested Mr.Itami, his tone hinting impatience.

Garner moved on to his last point. "Finally, because of her position, she is nearly untouchable. If she is stealing files, as I believe she is, we will never be able to prove it from within the company, nor be able to act on it. She is simply too powerful and too well-connected. This means that Cell Works, which is a major source of revenue for you, might quickly find itself out of the market."

"That is a reason to kill her, Mr. Garner. Not evidence of guilt. In fact, you have no evidence. You have only made allegations.

"I believe that the prime motivation for these suggestions is that you would stand the best chance to become CEO if Katherine Amij were no longer alive. And, as you have just pointed out, because of the family situation, that is the only way the position would ever open up to anyone else. However, before you contacted Billy, we had already become intrigued with Miss Amij. We do, after all, always take a personal interest in our investments, and so we, too, had begun to notice her strange behavior. When we investigated the matter, we found conclusive proof of her misconduct."

Itami nodded at Garner. "The matter will be taken care of. And we will use our influence to ensure that you step into Amij's job." Peter felt his chest tighten. He suddenly knew why he was at the meeting. Everyone he'd killed while working for Billy had been part of the game, *their* game, the crime gang game. For all he knew, this Katherine Amij was completely innocent. But he was sure Itami was about to ask Peter to kill her.

Garner let out a small gasp, then said, "Thank you. Thank you, Itami-*san.*"

"There is one more thing," said Mr. Itami, holding up one hand to indicate that Garner would hear him out. "You will sell us half your shares in Cell Works at a price of one-third their value."

Garner's joy drained from his expression. "What?"

"Did you not hear, or not understand?"

"Mr. Itami?"

"Do you accept?"

Garner looked around, his eyes finally coming to rest on Peter. "I accept."

"Very good. Our business is finished. Billy will escort you out."

Garner stood, and Billy gestured to a door at the

back of the club. Peter knew that everyone came in the front and went out the back.

When the rear door had closed again, Mr. Itami spoke to Peter, though he did not look at him.

"Well, what did you think, Profezzur?"

"The guy didn't seem to know what he was talking about, until you said you knew."

"Yes. And what did you think about being here?"

"I like it here, Mr. Itami-*sama.*"

Mr. Itami smiled. "No, I meant what did you think about being here at the meeting? This is the first time you have been present at such an interview."

"Yes. It was good."

"You will kill Katherine Amij."

Peter didn't know what to say, so he went with the truth.

"But, Itami-*san*, I cannot do that. She . . . is a civilian. She's not part of our war."

A stillness flowed across the room as everyone seemed to freeze in place. A few seconds passed, and Peter thought that he might not leave the room alive.

Billy was the most visibly disturbed. He held up his hand to Mr. Itami, silently asking for a minute to rectify the situation.

He crossed over to Peter, put his hand on his arm and led him off to one side. Though still handsome, Billy had grown fuller and a bit weary-looking. It made Peter wonder suddenly what his father looked like now.

"Listen, Profezzur," Billy whispered. "This isn't a joke, and it's not an option. You've got to do this, or you're going to get into trouble, and *I'm* going to get into trouble."

Peter glanced away. He hadn't denied Billy anything for years. "I can't do it."

Billy lifted his eyebrows, head cocked to one side, as he stared at Peter. He was more than stunned. He was hurt. "Maybe I didn't make myself clear. Maybe you don't know what the word option means. No choice. Got it? When Mr. Itami asks someone to do something, it's done.''

"I didn't hear the proof."

"What?"

"The proof. That the woman helped the man break his contract." Peter knew he was pushing the bounds of his fictional stupidity, but felt he had to stall.

"That's not your problem, Prof," Billy said quietly. "But Garner is right. We checked Amij out. It's all true. And just as important, we want her dead so we can put Garner in her place." Billy clasped his hands together. "Listen, this is how it works. A man who doesn't earn what he got, he doesn't know what he's worth. It's like a gambler. He hits the jackpot, but he can't take the money and use it intelligently. It was luck that got him the money in the first place. So he has to go back to the tables. He doesn't trust himself, so he has to trust fate.

"Mr. Itami is like the hand of fate coming in and making things happen for Garner. It's great at first, but after the thrill is gone, Garner knows he didn't earn his position, he didn't make it happen for himself. Because he doesn't trust himself, and he knows what fate did to his predecessor, he's got no will of his own. He's in the palm of Mr. Itami's hand. That's what we want at Cell Works. We want to control the place. And we will. We've already got people out looking for this Clarris. When we find him, we give him to Garner, who turns him in. Garner's a hero. You kill Katherine Amij. That's it. We win."

Peter hesitated.

Billy saw it. "You'll die." The relaxed good nature flowed out of his face. "Do you understand, Peter? There will be nothing I can do to help you."

Peter thought of Jenkins, the guard at the O'Hare heist who had refused to lie. Peter decided that, unlike Jenkins, he'd try to manipulate fate more to his liking. "Yes, Billy," he said. "I'll do it."

13

Eddy drove Peter down to the Elevated, the massive gentrification project that had transformed the Southside into the new haven for businesses and the rich after the Loop had collapsed years earlier. The real estate developers had abandoned the Loop only weeks after the terrorist destruction of the IBM Tower, and ghouls from all over the city had rushed into the area, turning it into a haven for their kind. The national guard and several corporate security teams had made a total of three attempts to clear the area out. By the time the papers started calling these efforts "A Marshal Plan with a Morbid Twist," everyone decided that the neighborhood was ruined. The developers turned their eyes toward the Southside and investors with land there became rich.

Outside the windows of the Westwind Peter saw the towering monorail tracks that looped around and through the Elevated in a clover pattern. The pylons that held up the tracks, the tracks themselves, and the monorail Skytrack trains all glittered with silver lights that spoke of enchantment and wealth. The lights could be seen from kilometers away—a distant carnival that most inhabitants of Chicago could glimpse but not enter.

Peter looked at the imposing homes along the snow-covered streets. His father probably had a house around here somewhere. Or used to. He'd jumped contract. In 2052 that was close to a capital crime. Perhaps he was hidden away in some underground base.

The homes lining the streets were elegant multi-story buildings with large, heat-inefficient windows that let their owners look out onto grass lawns. Peter would probably have lived with his father in such a house if he hadn't become a troll. Golden rectangles of light spilled out the windows into the night, illuminating white snow and plastic, pure human Jesuses in plastic-molded crèches.

"Sure sure sure sure is nice around here."

"Yeah."

They pulled up to the address Billy had given Peter. "Come on, let's get going. I want to get inside before she gets home."

They parked the Westwind as far as possible from the golden glow of the powerful lamps that bathed the street in lights, hustled out of the car, and up to the back door of the house. Eddy pulled out a security kit and used the skills he'd picked up over the years to open the door in mere minutes. Good, but not as good as some of the young gutterpunks Billy could hire off the street. Expecting praise, Eddy turned to look up at Peter, a huge grin on his twitching face. "Good work," Peter said. "You're still the best. Now get down the street, out of sight, and wait for me there."

Eddy ran off, muttering under his breath, "Right right right."

Peter watched his friend go, for a moment startled by the paradox of their relative competences. Eddy, a pure human, wired to be more than human, slowly falling apart over time. He, a troll, less than human in so many eyes, on the verge of a tremendous scientific breakthrough.

He stepped into the doorway and found himself in the kitchen of the house. Dim white-blue light-strips created pools of illumination and pockets of darkness. Peter saw quickly that everything had its place—a knife rack of finished wood held a dozen blades so shiny he wondered if they'd ever been used, plastic flowers (they gave off no heat) rested in a well-polished vase, The color scheme looked black to Peter's thermographic eyes, but he guessed it was, in fact, blue—the chairs, the tiles on the floor, the paper on the wall, all designed to complement one another. In its own way the room seemed as barren as the bare white apartment Peter lived in.

He left the kitchen and entered a central hall by the front door. One doorway led to the dining room, which also had a door directly to the kitchen, and another led to an office. Wide stairs ascended to the second floor. Everything from the wooden chairs in the dining room to the chandelier in the hall gave Peter a hollow feeling; none of the furnishing radiated a sense of invitation. They were merely carved wood and elaborate shards of glass, and no more.

He noticed the walls of the hall had glass panes built into them, set about a meter and a half off the floor. He stepped up to one and spotted a small switch underneath the pane. When he flicked it, a light came on behind the glass, revealing a miniature room within a box-like shelf set into the wall. He leaned down, fascinated.

Behind the glass was a miniature of an old-fashioned drawing room. There was a fireplace with a mantel over it, wooden chairs with tiny patterns sewn into small cushions, fingernail-size paintings on the walls, small statues and busts resting on top of tiny pillars, and little framed mirrors. A jade Buddha sat on the mantelpiece. The detail delighted him.

Peter leaned in closer, looking for miniature people. He thought perhaps he'd find the figure of a woman reading a book on one of the chairs or a man standing by a false, curtain window. With so much fine detail put into making the room he thought there should also be people there.

But no miniature people were present. Not even a dog on the rug. Despite the fact that the tiny room called out for life, it was empty. The lack of human figures disappointed him. And yet, he realized, if little people were in the rooms, they wouldn't work. The room was perfect because of its stillness, a frozen moment, a tableau that could be real because all the objects portrayed *would* be still. People, thought Peter, are not still, and someone in the room would draw focus away from the detail of the rest, would break the illusion.

He switched off the light and examined two other glass panes, turning on their lights one after another. One shelf contained a miniature cathedral, another an old English kitchen. Their stillness and precision calmed him, drew him in as if they were enchanted items—the lotuses from the Odyssey. Then he remembered the task at hand and clicked off the lights. He stepped up to the front door and looked through the window. Nothing. He checked his watch. She wouldn't be back for at least twenty or thirty minutes, if Billy's information was accurate.

He decided to wait for her in the office. He'd learned the best way to keep wetwork quiet was to pick a spot and sit in it. Meet a target by the door, he bolts back outside. Come up on him after he closes the door behind him, and it's too much like an assault. His instincts kick in, he puts up a struggle.

But let him find you sitting calmly in one of his chairs, like an unannounced guest . . . Well, that changes things. He's thrown off guard. Should he be polite? Should he scream for help? Should he run away? Unsure what to do, he surrenders control of the situation, waits for the killer to explain. It made it all so much easier.

Peter entered the office and turned on a small desk lamp. A Fuchi Nova computer sat on the desk, and several shelves of chip cases and antique books lined the walls. The books were histories of Europe. The chips were recent economic theory tracts, shareholder reports for Cell Works, and other business matters. The word that came to Peter was "functional."

He stepped over to a closet and opened the door.

The mess within startled him. Compared to the order of the rest of the house, the scattered boxes and holo cards caught him off guard. It was like an ancient, secret tomb ransacked by robbers. His curiosity was piqued. He knelt down and found a holo display unit. He took it, along with a stack of holo cards, and carried them to a couch set opposite the desk. He sat down and slipped a card marked 7/18/30 into the unit.

The holo-image of a little girl with bright red hair sitting behind a computer terminal floated before his face. Kathryn Amij, he guessed, for Billy had described her as a redhead. She·was about seven or eight years old. She smiled into the camera—a beautiful smile. Her fingers rested on the keys, but because she looked into the camera, she was obviously playing at typing.

He slid the card out and put in one from 2035. Kathryn on a horse leaping over a fence—proud, face set, in control. She wasn't the cute girl of five years earlier, but a girl on the verge of turning into a very attractive adolescent.

Then he found a card from 2039 and put it in. The change in her appearance startled him. Now fifteen, she was very thin, almost gaunt. The scene showed her at a birthday celebration with other teenage girls. A white-frosted cake sat in the center of the table. The other girls smiled into the camera, some with cake in their mouths. Kathryn looked toward the camera, her expression listless. Peter looked closer and saw that her cake had been mashed up, but looked as though none had been eaten.

He found a card from the following year. Still very thin, she stood on the deck of a boat with a man and woman, also with red hair, probably her parents. She showed a smile now, but her look was more surprised than happy. At the edge of the holo Peter saw a woman seated on the bow of the boat, looking down into the water. Something about her reminded Peter of Thomas.

He felt as if he were watching a story unfold before him in holos, and was curious to find out what would happen next. He seemed to have stumbled onto a kind of arc in Kathryn Amij's life. The next card he slipped in was from '41. A nearly supernatural image appeared: Kathryn in a hospital bed, surrounded by flowers. She smiled for the camera, almost as winningly as when she'd been a little girl. In fact, she seemed genuinely happy. But her face was a death mask, a skeleton frame with skin stretched taut over the bone. The holo transfixed him. He stared into her eyes, wondering what illness had made her waste away.

He would never know, for he heard the sound of a car pulling up, then a mechanical garage door opening. He fumbled with the holo unit, surprised and embarrassed. For reasons he couldn't fathom, he didn't want her to find him prying into the holos. He gathered up the cards and the display unit, rushed over to the closet, and dumped everything back into the secret mess.

When all was as he had found it—the door closed, the desk lamp off—he sat down again on the couch, pulled out his gun, and placed it on his lap.

He heard a door open somewhere in the house. No voices. She was alone.

A few moments later the lights in the front hall went on. He glanced at the computer on the desk. She would probably come in here to check her mail.

She pushed the door open, turned on the light, saw Peter, and froze in mid-step. Her mouth opened a bit, as if to speak, but no sound emerged. She put her hand on the door handle for support.

She was gorgeous. Whatever happened in her teens had been taken care of. She wasn't the industrial standard of beauty that Billy liked to drape over his arm, but something else. . . . Her red hair grew down almost to the small of her back, and she kept it tied in a thick pony tail. She was tall—as tall and strong as a beauty queen from Texas. Solid.

She wore a green jacket and a skirt that came down below her knees. The flesh of her calves . . .

Photons bounce of her body, pass into my aqueous humors, through my pupils and lenses, careen into my retinas, which turn the image into neural impulses, which then slide down the optic nerve into my brain, which, almost magically, turn the original photons into lust.

Amazing. Peter thought he'd killed passion in his flesh years ago.

He also noticed, out of habit, that she didn't seem to be armed.

"Hello . . . ," she said uncomfortably. "Can I help you?"

"Miss Amij," he said, smiling, trying to put her at ease. "Would you sit down please? I must speak with you."

"What is this about?"

Peter uncrossed his legs and revealed the gun. "Please. It will be easier if you sit."

She drew in a sharp breath, then placed her hand on her stomach. "Oh."

"Please."

She moved to the chair by the desk. Watching her move only made the intoxication of Peter's lust increase. He needed to focus. "Miss Amij, I was sent here to kill you." His jaw tightened. Not the best opening.

"Yes?" Her face was a mask that revealed nothing, but he saw something flicker in her eyes. He knew her mind was whirring, making plans, looking for angles. He liked her.

"There was a man who worked for you. . . . a Dr. Clarris."

"Oh."

"Oh?"

"Oh. As in surprise."

He smiled. "Dr. Clarris was extracted from Cell Works a few weeks ago, by mercenaries working for an unknown employer."

"Yes," she said, and cocked her head expectantly to one side. She placed her hand on her stomach again.

"Your security forces are at a loss to explain how it happened, and believe that the mercs must have received information to help them, information that Clarris would not have had access to."

"Yes."

"They are, of course, doing what they can to find Dr. Clarris. It is still not known if he was kidnapped from Cell Works, or if he wanted to break his contract with your company."

"Yes."

"And you helped him?"

"Yes."

Peter was surprised. No denial. She gave him nothing he could use to twist around her later. "Why?"

"I had my reasons."

"Since I'm here to kill you, would you mind sharing them with me?"

"Yes."

Peter drew in a breath. "You have betrayed your own corporation, a company founded by your grandfather. My employer, a man with a great deal of stock in Cell Works, has very traditional, and Eastern, values. Such behavior rubs him the wrong way. And, if I'm not mistaken, if you die, a man named Garner has a very good chance of becoming Cell Works' CEO. . . ."

That caught her off guard. "Garner." She looked away, disoriented, and then her eyes opened and she nodded once, as if the final piece of a mental puzzle had just slid into place. "Garner," she said again, but this time with a firmer voice.

"Yes. Garner. My employer is helping him find Clarris, to bring him back to Cell Works as a trophy. And since my employer is helping Garner get your job, my employer would, in effect, be the boss of Cell Works' boss."

Kathryn stared down at the ground and gripped the side of her chair with her right hand. He saw that things were finally moving too fast for her to keep up. "Who are you?"

"I can't tell you that," Peter said, getting to his feet. "Now, since you've let all my statements slide by without protest, I'm going to assume all are correct. And I'll level with you. I want to find Clarris myself. For my own reasons. Miss Amij, I will help you escape if you will tell me where he is."

She sat quietly for a moment, apparently weighing the offer, then she said plainly, "I don't know. I don't know where he is."

Peter's body went a bit slack, and the barrel of the gun slipped down toward the floor. "You don't know?"

"No."

"You helped him escape from Cell Works and you don't know where he is?"

"I was double-crossed. . . . I don't know where he is."

"Wait a minute. . . ."

"I said I don't know!"

Peter drew back. It was as though his goals, his dreams, all his choices for the last fourteen years were withering away. "Please, you must have a clue," he said softly. "You must have something."

She looked at him carefully. "What is this to you? This doesn't sound like work."

"It isn't."

"Oh."

"Oh," he repeated. "Please, something. You helped him escape. . . . You must know something."

"No, really, I . . ." She raised her hands to her forehead as if a headache were coming on. "I thought he was going to Fuchi Genetics. The people I contacted crashed the plan. He's . . . gone. They got me."

"You contacted someone? To get Clarris out? You weren't approached?"

She stared at the gun for a moment. "Are you going to kill me? I mean right now, because if you're not, could you just . . . not point that at me?"

Peter glanced at the gun. He felt that this was the moment. To not kill Kathryn Amij meant to leave the gang, to leave Billy, to leave everything he'd built over fourteen years. The safety and power he'd attained. He looked at her and knew that he couldn't do it—he couldn't take another Jenkins. He lowered the gun. "I won't kill you. If you help me find him, I'll let you go. I'll help you escape."

She sat silently for a moment, then said, "I wanted him to continue a line of research that he'd been working on for years. My board wanted it cut. I was going to get secret reports back from him."

"And you hired people to track him down. Your own freelancers, shadowrunners from outside your own corporation?"

"Yes."

"Have they found anything?"

She remained silent for a moment. "Whoever got him, it wasn't Fuchi. They laughed—said they'd have loved to end up with him. . . ."

"Anything positive?"

She shook her head. "That's the problem with hiring shadowrunners. They're basically outlaws without legal IDs—no accountability."

"All right." Peter searched his thoughts, looking for questions that might uncover other information. "What he was working on . . . ?" A thought slammed into his head. "Was it . . . Was it on halting genetic transformation? Goblinization? Was Cell Works working on that?''

She stared at him, curious. ''Yes. We were, but it was canceled.'' She paused. ''Who are you?''

''Just a troll with a peculiar hobby.''

Peter's mind raced to come up with a plan. His work was done. He wanted out of the gang. He wanted to get to his father. A rich CEO also wanted to find him. She could come in handy. He decided to take her into his confidence. She might say no—and then the options would narrow quickly. He could kill her, after all, stay in the gang, look for his father on the side. His mind bucked at the plan, but everything was moving quickly.

''I know that Clarris might have been working on a project like that because . . . I think I've got it. I think I know how to do it. Or, at least, I'm very close.'' He put the gun into his holster under his jacket. ''I want to compare notes with Clarris. I think he'd be able to tell me where I'm right and where I'm wrong.''

''You?''

He grinned. ''I'm an exceptional troll.''

''But . . .''

He stepped closer to her. ''I think we can work together. If I don't kill you, I'm in trouble. I'm willing to accept that trouble if I get your help in looking for Clarris. You've got resources. You also set up the deal for Clarris.''

''I really don't know what to say. . . .''

''Think about this: someone at Cell Works has dug up enough goods on you to get you kicked out of your own troop. A contract is on your head now. If you want Clarris, it won't be any use to you to show up for work tomorrow. How bad do you want him? Now's the time to choose.''

He saw her eyes glaze over as she started thinking again. It was palpable activity—the air felt heavier in the room as her mind sorted through her options. She shook her head slightly. "I don't know. I don't know. I'll tell you this, however. If you have found the cure, I won't need Clarris anymore."

"But I need him."

"I'll help you find him if you have what I want."

"We'll need him anyway. He'll have to confirm my work. He's the most qualified, *neh?* That's why you sent him out to continue the research."

"Yes, we should find him." She looked up. "But I don't even know if you've really found the cure. Why should I believe you?" She sighed and leaned back in the chair, her eyes closed.

"You'll read it," Peter said as soon as he had the idea. "My research. I want you to look it over. I think I've done it. I've been working on it for over a decade. You'll at least be able to see that I'm serious."

"Do you have it on you?" He could tell she was trying to humor him. Furious, he pulled the gun out again. "Get up!" She gasped and stood, her eyes shut tight, hands on her belly. "You're coming with me. Back to my place. You're going to read my work."

She didn't move. "Your boss doesn't know about this."

"Nobody does. Nobody knows about my research."

She tilted her head to one side and looked at him carefully. "This is very strange."

"Yes."

"He'll still want me dead. Your boss."

"Yes."

"Why should I go with you? You can just kill me later, when you've gotten what you want from me."

"I could kill you now."

"Don't threaten me."

He stared at her, fascinated. It wasn't a ploy, just a direct command. She was telling him simply how she negotiated. "All right. No threats. When I shoot, I'll just shoot. But the truth is, my life would be simpler if I killed you.''

She stood before him, breathing heavily. Spots of sweat began to show on her expensive suit. "Don't."

"You're not helping."

"Please, just don't. Don't."

"Just read what I've written. That's all I ask."

"And then . . . ?"

"We'll . . . I . . . don't know . . . I know this is . . . Your life is on the line. I know that. But in a way my life, too. I need you at this point." He dropped all pretense of toughness. "Miss Amij, I need to find Dr. Clarris. I'd like your help."

She weighed the statement. Peter saw her reach the same decision he had made only a few hours earlier. "You've got the gun. Lead on."

14

Peter called Eddy on his wristcom, saying to meet him out front. Stepping out of the door, he saw his old friend driving up the street at a speed usually reserved for a raceway. Suddenly Eddy hit the Westwind's brakes *just so,* and the car slid on the snowy ground for some six meters, then came to a perfect stop directly in front of the path to Kathryn's door.

When Peter opened the car's front door, Eddy turned in surprise, for Peter always sat in the back. Then he saw Kathryn, and his face ran the gamut from concern to sadness to fear. Fear eventually won out.

Kathryn took a seat beside Eddy, and Peter climbed into the back.

"Profezzur Profezzur Profezzur," Eddy stuttered angrily, "What gives? Gives? Gives?"

Kathryn looked back at Peter, obviously curious about Eddy. Peter gave her a slight shrug. To Eddy, he said, "Never mind. Just get us back to my place, quick."

"I don't know, I don't know, Profezzur," Eddy raised his hands high, then waved them around like someone doing semaphore. "I don't know. I don't know. I saw her go in. Go in." He held up a photo of Kathryn. "Saw her go in. Long time, Prof, long time. And now she's not dead. Not *even* dead."

"Eddy, go."

"What's up, Prof? What's up? This is your science stuff? Is there some science going on here?"

"Yes."

"FRAG! I knew this would happen. I knew this would happen. Happen. Give you your biology, and the next thing you know, you're trying to pick up the stiffs."

"Eddy, she's not dead. . . ."

"YOU THINK I DON'T KNOW THAT! What do you think I'm worried about? You think Itami's going to like it when I have to tell him, 'Yeah, well, my buddy the Prof, he lays off the slots, I've never seen him with a woman, even though I told him he better get some action, cause it'll drive him crazy, and I was right right right, 'cause he just picked up the slot he was supposed to ice!" He turned to Kathryn. "No offense."

Peter knew that if his flesh could blush, it would have done so. Instead he reached over and placed his frighteningly large hand on Eddy's shoulder. "You don't have to tell him, Eddy."

Eddy's face exploded with surprise, as if Peter had presented him with a new and astounding possibility. "You're right!"

"Yes. Let's go."

When Kathryn looked at Peter again, he opened his

mouth to explain, then realized the world was far too complicated for that.

The car's momentum threw them all back against their seats, and they were off.

Peter's studio apartment was a monk's cell; a mattress lay in one corner, a shelf packed with chips stood against a wall. In the center of the room was a large kitchen table with his portable on it, as well as some dirty dishes. The My Cure chips sat beside the computer, where he had left them that morning.

No pictures decorated the walls. Peter had decided years ago that he would only introduce colors when he was pure human again. But now, with Kathryn in the room, he was embarrassed at how the place revealed the sparseness of his existence.

He wanted to say something, to fill up the emptiness of the room with words and excuses—"I move around a lot, so I keep my possessions to a minimum," or "As soon as I'm back to my life, then you'll see, I'll fill this place with colors. I'm not really like this, this isn't my life. . . ." But he knew such phrases would come out sounding as pale and lifeless as the walls. He said nothing.

"You like to read," Kathryn said, walking over to the bookshelf.

"Yes."

She leaned down to study the titles on the chip casings, her hands folded behind her back, safe from accidental contact with anything in the room. She pulled back sharply and stared at him with complete surprise.

"The Cal Tech Metahuman Genome Appendices! Where did you get those?"

"Stolen," he said sheepishly, but inside very happy, for he could tell she was impressed.

"Cal Tech said it wasn't releasing them for years, if at all."

"I've built contacts . . . over the years."

"Contacts?"

"Never mind. I need you to read something I've been working on."

Her face revealed nothing. "All right."

Peter swept his arm toward the personal computer. The gesture was harsh, lacking either the politeness or the awkwardness of his movements when he'd opened his apartment door for Kathryn. She noticed the difference and moved quickly to sit down at the table.

"Open the file labeled My Cure."

She looked up at him. "My Cure?"

"Yes." He picked up one of the chips from the table and slipped it into the portable.

"You'll know if I'm on the right track. I've never shown this to anyone. I want to bring it to . . . Dr. Clarris. We have him in common."

Her expression softened as she continued to look up at him. Peter discovered he was flattered, though he didn't know why. He didn't want to be flattered by her. Being with her at all was becoming very confusing. She threatened too many of his habits.

She powered up the portable. "All right. I'll read."

An hour passed. Kathryn read and Peter paced. At first his insistent fidgeting bothered her, but soon she seemed totally unaware of his presence. She leaned in toward the screen, her gaze glued to it. Once in a while her eyes would open wide and she would smile, while other times she would shake her head in silent disagreement. Either way, Peter knew his text had captivated her.

When he was assured of her interest, he relaxed and took a position next to the door to his apartment, leaning against the wall. From here he could study her freely. With her attention so focused on the screen, it was almost as if the real Kathryn was not present. Peter could view her almost as an image, an image that couldn't look back and judge him.

He found that he loved the way she read. It reminded him of a sniper waiting for his target to come around the corner; her eyes always alert, on the move, her body poised, ready for any action that might become necessary. She was an active reader. Her eyes seemed to virtually eat up the ideas.

Hearing footsteps on the stairs, Peter whipped out his gun, then saw Eddy top the landing, his arms full of Japanese take-out.

Peter's shoulder's sagged as he relaxed. "What took you so long?"

Eddy twitched a bit and then said, "Got stuck stuck stuck in traffic traffic."

"You?" Peter said with a deep, bellowing laugh.

Eddy laughed too. "Yeah, well well well." Before he could say more, Peter raised his finger to his lips to silence his friend. Kathryn must have heard their voices out in the hall, but was already back to her reading.

As quietly as possible, Peter took a cup of coffee and an order of fried fish over to the table. The floorboards creaked loudly.

Kathryn looked up at him when he reached the table, her lips pursed into a smile.

She thought he was cute. Or so he thought she thought. He couldn't be sure.

Ignoring the food Peter set down for her, she went back to the screen.

Taking Eddy by the arm, Peter escorted him out into the hall and closed the door behind them.

"Think it's a good idea to leave her alone like that?" Eddy said.

"She can't go anywhere. The door's locked. And I don't think she wants to leave just yet, anyway."

"What you mean? What you mean? And what's she reading? She an AI like you? You showing off your library?"

"No. She's reading something I wrote."

"That stuff you're always talking about?"

"Yes." Peter smiled down at his friend. Over the years, Eddy's interest in Peter's "stories" had waned. Except for trying to stay useful enough to maintain his place on the Itami gang payroll, Eddy wasn't interested in much of anything but simsense ever since the technology had come on the scene. Like most people, he was content to "experience" life through other people's recorded sensations.

"You know, I still don't understand why you spend so much time reading."

"Eddy, when you read . . . I get to understand things."

"I'd rather just feel it. And besides. I understand things."

'But words give you perspective. You can step outside a situation and see what it's about. You can find the shades of meaning. . . ."

A creak came from the stairs, followed by a faint shadow poking up from the landing below.

"Peter listen to me. . . ."

Peter clamped his hand over the lower half of Eddy's face to shut him up.

Eddy struggled to speak, and Peter finally removed his hand. "Peter," he said in a harsh whisper, "You can't go against the gang. We got to finish her."

Peter couldn't believe his ears. "You. . . .," he said, but he knew he could never be truly angry at Eddy.

He had to get Kathryn and get out.

Peter opened the door, then shut it quickly behind him, leaving Eddy out in the hall.

Turning around, he saw Kathryn by the window, trying to force its heavy latch. She was going to try an escape after all.

"Get down!" Peter shouted, but the warning came too late. A bullet punched through the glass, sending shards flying across the room. Kathryn screamed and fell back.

"Frag! Frag!" Another detail popped into Peter's brain. Without needing to ponder the situation, his mind produced the hard facts—both exits were blocked, and that was that. Moving with Kathryn in tow would make getting out the window the weaker of the two options. Although they might run into more firepower on the stairs, it was the way to go.

"Come on!" he shouted.

"What!" she screamed. "What is going on?" She wasn't speaking to him, it was a shout of fear to the world.

Peter was frightened, too. He'd protected people before. But nearly everyone he'd dealt with in the business was *in* the business. When the bullets started to fly, everyone always knew what it meant. He watched Kathryn on the floor, her fingers pressed tight against the wood as if it might drop out from under her.

He bolted the door, then went over to her. "Listen," he said softly. "We're in a lot of trouble. Those people who wanted me to kill you . . . they're here now. They're here to ice both of us."

She said, "Don't talk to me like a child. Bullets frighten me, but I think they should." Despite her tough tone, fear shone in her eyes.

"We're going out the front door, down the hall. At the stairway turn right and keep going down the hall. You'll come to another stairway that leads to the laundry room. There's an exit. . . ."

Someone slammed against the door. Peter drew his pistol from its holster and jumped across the room, throwing himself prone before the door. He fired three shots up into the door, cracking the wood. From outside came a short shriek.

With a start, he wondered if it was Eddy. If so, Peter knew he couldn't allow himself to care.

Shots penetrated the door. They flew over Peter's body and slammed into the wall behind him.

Peter crawled on his belly to the door, then flopped over on his back and spun around so he was feet-first toward it. Shifting slightly, he was just a bit to the side of the door.

Everything fell silent as the combatants on either side of the door waited for the other to make a move. Peter's breath rolled in and out of his body. He tried to calm down, telling himself he wasn't nervous, but he didn't buy it.

Soft footsteps moved around outside the door.

Someone touched the door knob; its metal conducted the body heat and turned a dim pink. Peter knew whoever it was would be more careful now—the man was crouched low or tucked off to the side.

Any second. Any second.

The door shattered open.

Through the shards of wood came Bub, a thick-muscled ork from The Crew. Regret filled Peter even as he raised his foot and slammed it into Bub's forward-falling knee. The knee snapped with a horrible crack and Bub fell to the ground with a shrill scream.

Outside the door Peter saw blood splattered along the wall from the shots he'd taken earlier.

Yoake stepped into the doorway, his eyes scanning the room while the submachine gun gripped in his hands followed the path of his eyes. It was only the slightest movement on Peter's part, but it caught the man's attention. By that time it was too late, for Peter had his gun up and had fired three times into Yoake's chest.

The gangster's body went tight, his finger pulling on the trigger as he fell back out into the hall. A spray of bullets ripped into the ceiling, and then the gun went silent.

Peter tried breathing and found his body still

worked. Amazing. There had been such a racket in the last few seconds that he almost thought he'd died somewhere in there.

His next-door neighbor pounded on the wall and screamed, "Shut that racket up!"

Peter looked over at Kathryn and shrugged. "My neighbors don't understand my work."

"Neither do I." She got up off the floor, making sure to avoid a line-of-sight through the window. "Do we run and get shot at now?"

"As a matter of fact, yes." He smiled and slapped a new mag in his pistol His discomfort around her had evaporated. He was doing what he'd spent a dozen years doing. She was out of her league. She needed him.

He stepped over to the table and scooped up his My Cure chips and slipped them into one pocket. Then he went to peek through the door out into the hall.

Eddy's head poked out from the top of the stairs at the landing down the hall. Drops of blood covered his face. He held a gun in his hand, but it shook terribly.

"Eddy. I don't have time to frag around now!" Peter shouted. "Understand?"

15

"You shouldn't have taken shouldn't have taken shouldn't have taken the slot, Profezzur. You know? Shouldn't have."

Peter stepped into the doorway. With his left hand he motioned for Kathryn to join him. Eddy raised the gun higher, but didn't point it at Peter.

"Just kill her, Prof. Geek her and everything'll be

all right. I'll make up a lie. Just like before. We'll make up a shag together.''

When Kathryn was behind him, Peter shouted, "No, Eddy. I'm getting out now. I think I've got it figured out. This is what I've been doing all this for. To become a human again. I think I've got it. I'm going to get out.''

"No. Peter. No. Please, don't. They . . . they don't need me anymore. I'm shot. They know it. I know it. They know it. There's nothing left. Look.'' He raised his arm. It shook wildly. "They're only keeping me around 'cause of you. If you go . . . Peter . . .''

What Eddy said was undoubtedly true. Peter had heard some of the thugs at The Crew wondering aloud about Eddy, though Peter had, of course, feigned ignorance and disinterest.

But he couldn't stay in the biz just for Eddy. "Get out with me.''

"No. No. What am I gonna do?''

Peter heard the glass shatter on the lobby door down the stairs. Behind him, through the window, came the sound of creaking metal: someone was climbing up the fire escape.

Kathryn was at Peter's back, hidden around the corner of the doorway. "Stay behind me,'' he told her. Masked by his massive frame and long duster, she would be nearly invisible to anyone in front of them.

Walking carefully down the hall, he moved toward Eddy.

"Come with me. Come with me or run. But Eddy, I don't want to be in this anymore. This isn't what I was supposed to be doing. I hate it. And I'm only doing it because I'm a troll. The only reason I didn't slit my wrists with a can opener was because I thought I could figure out how to stop being a troll. This is what my whole life is about.''

"That's very depressing,'' said Kathryn.

"Try being a troll," he retorted. "That'll get you down. . . ."

"What are you whispering about!" screamed Eddy. He pointed the gun as best he could at Peter, who was now only about three meters away. An accidental pull of the trigger at just the right moment could slam the lead home.

Peter let himself look down the corridor, which turned right a few steps from where he stood, leading to the back stairs and the laundry room.

"What the frag are you looking at!" Eddy screamed. He stood up, his entire body shaking. Blood soaked his right shoulder, where Peter's bullet had hit him through the door. Beads of sweat rolled down his face. "Where's the bitch?"

"I really don't like this guy," Peter heard Kathryn whisper, while someone from downstairs called out, "Eddy?"

When Eddy turned to glance down the stairs, Peter shouted, "NOW!"

Kathryn broke for the corridor.

Howling like a banshee, Eddy brought up his gun, squeezing off two shots that slammed into the hall's cheap plaster wall behind Kathryn.

With no thought for the consequences, Peter jumped forward and slammed his hand into Eddy's wrist to knock away the gun. When the blow hit, it was with a sharp, cracking sound.

Eddy screamed wildly and brought his hand up to his chest. The blood gushed wildly. With his good arm he cradled the damaged hand like a baby. Peter could see the white of bone piercing the torn and ragged flesh of Eddy's wrist.

"Eddy," Peter stammered, "I'm . . ."

"Shut the frag up! I never did anything to you. I just wanted the slot! I'm your friend!"

Gun shots sounded behind Peter. He whirled and saw the gunman, some kid he'd seen around but had yet to meet till now. Peter decided it wasn't worth firing back. Without a look back at Eddy, he raced down the corridor after Kathryn.

"Peter!" Eddy shouted after him. "Peter, please!"

As Peter passed through the doorway to the stairs, he turned and squeezed off three random shots to hold everyone back. Then he bounded down the stairs, jumping from one landing to the next, his duster flapping wildly behind him. The old floorboards creaked terribly under his weight.

Hitting the first floor, he saw Kathryn entering the laundry room down the hall. He followed her in, then quietly closed the door behind him.

The dim red light of the exit sign over the door to the alley illuminated Kathryn. She stood supporting herself with one hand on the wall, breathing heavily, the heat of her body shimmering in Peter's vision.

"Are you all right?"

"Well, I'm a slightly out-of-shape executive who's not used to running from bullets. And I'm pregnant, so you might say I'm feeling the strain right now."

Peter did a double-take. "You're what?"

"I'm a slightly out-of-shape—"

"No, no, no. The . . . You're pregnant?"

She looked up into his face, her tough edge gone. "Yes. I'm carrying my son."

"Your son . . ."

"Look, aren't they going to come kill us or something?"

"I was going to kill you. You didn't tell me."

"Would it have made a difference?"

Peter paused, flummoxed.

"Strange criteria. You'll kill an innocent woman, but not if she's carrying a fetus."

"You're not innocent. You let my . . . Dr. Clarris leave Cell Works and you're throwing your own people off the trail."

She smiled. "True. But, really, aren't we going to die if we don't move?"

"Yes. But I wanted to wait long enough for everyone outside the building to get fidgety." Peter crossed to the door. "With any luck they'll all have rushed in before we rush out."

He tried to open the door carefully, but it stuck, and he had to force it. The door made a great grinding noise as he forced it open.

He peeked out.

Arinori stood just next to the door, his gun pointed into Peter's face.

Peter's heart sank. So close . . .

Suddenly he had become Jenkins.

Peter put on his stupid face. "Hello, Arinori."

"Hey, Profezzur. Word is you're even dumber than we thought. Where's the meat?"

"I don't know. She ran away."

"Drek. Out of the way. And drop your piece on the floor."

Out of the corner of his eye, Peter spotted Kathryn moving around to the doorway, carefully keeping out of Arinori's line-of-sight. Peter put on an expression of great embarrassment and said, "I'm sorry, Arinori. She was just so pretty. I just thought, you know . . ."

"That ain't your concern, trog."

Peter dropped his gun to the floor and backed up. "Don't call me trog, Arinori. It ain't nice."

Arinori entered the room cautiously, looking first right then left. As he turned in Kathryn's direction, he caught a glimpse of her and brought his gun to bear. Peter leaped forward and slammed his hand down on Arinori's arm. The gun fired and a bullet slammed into a dryer. Arinori whirled toward Peter, but Peter slammed him in the rib cage. As the man doubled over with a loud cry, Peter brought his knee up into his face. Arinori's nose turned into a fleshy smear of blood.

Arinori fell over, unconscious. Peter saw Kathryn staring down at the man, then look up with an expression of horror. She stared at his face, and Peter imagined how he must look through her eyes: a terrible creature . . . rough flesh . . . long, heavy teeth.

For an instant Peter almost wanted to apologize. Then he realized he'd done what he had to. Let her think him a monster. "Come on. Let's go."

He wiped his bloodied hand on his duster and picked up his gun. Taking a look out into the alley way, he saw it was clear.

"You got anyplace that's safe?" Peter asked Kathryn as they took the alley at a brisk walk toward Wilson Avenue.

"Not if the people at Cell Works are hiring hit men. The corporation's always been my home."

"Same with the Itami gang for me," he said with emphasis. He wanted to make it clear that he, too, was now cut loose from his people. "What about the slags you've got tracking Dr. Clarris? Who are they?"

Reaching the street, they picked up their pace even more.

"I don't know who they are. Shadowrunners. I contacted them through a fixer named Zero-One-Zero."

"Do you think you can trust him?"

"Won't he do what I ask if I pay him enough?"

"Usually. Where is he?"

"I've only spoken to him by phone, but he did tell me he was based in the Noose."

A cab was driving down the street. "Flag it," Peter said. "It won't stop for me."

Kathryn stepped to the curb and waved at the cab, which came to a stop in front of her. "This doesn't look like your part of town, missy," the cabbie shouted out the window.

She opened the cab's front door and started to climb in. "Hey, folks usually ride in the back."

"I know. I'm saving that seat for my friend."

No sooner said, Peter opened the back door.

"Hey!" cried the cabbie.

"Shut up," Peter said coldly, mustering his deepest tone. "We've got to get to the Noose. Now."

The cabbie seemed more afraid of the destination than of Peter. "Not in this cab."

Peter pulled his gun up from behind the seat. "Look. We're in a hurry."

"I'm not going in there. I'll take you up to the edge. But not inside." He paused. "I've got a wife and kids. Please don't shoot."

Kathryn glared at Peter, as if to say, "You better not."

"All right, all right. To the edge of the Noose."

The cabbie sighed heavily and tapped the car into drive.

He let them off just north of the Chicago River.

A light snow fell. As they stepped out of the cab Kathryn looked north, briefly drinking in the glitter of the snow against the city lights. She smiled, and Peter found himself enchanted by a woman who could regard snow with the wonder of a child. Especially at a moment like this.

The moment they were out of the cab, the cabbie wheeled his vehicle around and peeled back north with a loud screech of tires.

"Nervous," said Kathryn, watching him leave.

Peter looked south. "He's got reason to be." Across the river stood the ruined skyscrapers of Chicago's old Loop, once the city's downtown. Now it was known as the Noose, home only to squatters, criminals, and— living among the massive rubble of the fallen IBM Tower—ghouls. He spotted some bright orange flames burning through the windows of buildings; warmth for squatters. Aside from those burning dots of light, the Noose was a sea of impenetrable blackness.

Kathryn followed Peter's gaze.

"Maybe we should wait until morning. Daylight."

"No time."

"No time for what? I don't mean to be—"

"But you will be."

". . . .But what are we doing? Why are we together? Thank you for saving my life. Thank you for not killing me. But why don't we just call it a night? I've got my own way of doing things, and it doesn't involve so much lead."

"Well, too bad, because the people you're playing against love lead. Now we're both looking for Clarris. . . ."

"Got some bullets lying around with his name on them?"

"No . . . I told you . . . Kathryn . . . I want to find him before my boss does. Listen . . . ," He took a deep breath, then plunged in. "William Clarris is my father."

It took a moment for the statement to sink in.

"What?"

"Dr. Clarris is my father."

Her jaw lowered slowly until her mouth settled into a perfect O. Peter looked away, not knowing what to say next, afraid she was going to say, "What?"

"What?"

"He's my father. I don't want to kill him. I want to find him. I want to show him my research and have him confirm it. Get it published if it's good enough."

"I didn't even know he had a son."

A cold dagger slid between Peter's ribs and his heart. "I transformed into a troll fourteen years ago. Now, I'll keep you alive, but you have to help me track him down."

She glanced down at the ground and then up into his eyes. "All right. I want to find him, too." He glanced at the dark towers beyond the river. Kathryn followed his gaze and asked, "Did you ever see the *Wizard of Oz* when you were a kid?"

"Oh, yeah. One of my favorite books."

"You read it?"

"Yeah."

"I saw the flat. And a niece of mine had the sim-sense. I watched part of it. It was one of my favorites." She paused, then said, "I feel like Dorothy going into some dark Oz."

"And I'm everybody else?

"From your research, I can tell you already have a brain. And you already have courage. I'll give you that."

"And believe me, buried under all this thick protection against bullets, I've also got a heart. That leaves you. What are you looking for, Dorothy?"

Kathryn looked across the river and Peter saw the temperature in her cheeks rise. "Right now I'd rather not say."

Peter nodded his acceptance of that. "Well, we both have a quest," he said, "and our wizard is Zero-One-Zero." He swept his hand before him. "Shall we to the Noose?"

16

They crossed the La Salle Street bridge, glancing over the railing into the river as they walked. Enormous chunks of ice bobbed slowly, flowing like giant blood cells through a vein.

When they reached the other side, they saw that on this side of the river the tall buildings of the Noose blocked most of the city light that bounced off the clouds. But there was still enough spill through the deep concrete canyons to see by.

Peter saw brief flashes of warmth dart from car to

ruined car. Many people were watching him and Kathryn.

She kept closer to Peter now, and he liked knowing she came to him for protection.

"Maybe some of them can help us," Kathryn said.

"No. They won't know anything. Not these people. The Noose is crawling with squatters—on the streets, in the buildings. They live here, but they aren't part of the hardware."

"I'd heard that the Noose was empty."

Peter gave her a look full of condescension and surprise that was, fortunately, hidden by the dark. "That's what the Hall says. They don't want to acknowledge the inhabitants of the Noose because then they'd have to provide services. But from what I hear, they send census guestimates into DeeCee for Fed aid."

"I didn't know that," she said quietly. Peter felt even more smug, and wallowed in it. They were now much closer to his world than hers, but even he was nervous. He'd never been in the Noose. It was a place with its own rules, rules he could translate but that were not his native tongue.

Ahead was an intersection with fires built from refuse burning on each corner. The brilliance of the heat nearly blinded Peter, who had to raise his hand to block the images. If anyone was near the fires, he couldn't make them out against the white flames.

Kathryn picked up on this and started to ask him what was up. "Shhh," he said, and fingered his gun.

Just then they heard a squeaky, high-pitched voice: "Hoi, chummers! Whatcha doing?" Looking to their right, Peter and Kathryn saw a little human, a kid, form out of the fire and walk out into the intersection.

It was hard to make out the girl's form against the bright flames, but Peter thought she wore a green leather jacket and had long, purple-dyed hair.

"She's just a child," Kathryn said with quiet horror.

"Don't you watch the news?"

"Just the financial reports."

"Exactly."

"I'd say you two are in a real rough part of town," the girl said loudly.

"I think I can handle it," Peter told her.

"Oh yeah?"

"Yeah." Peter pointed his pistol high, and Kathryn placed her hand on his arm. "Don't cramp my style," he whispered.

Behind him and Kathryn came a raking sound of metal on metal.

Lowering his gun, Peter mustered his most nonchalant voice. "Ah, sounds like a light machine gun. Mounted probably."

Peter was impressed that Kathryn didn't let off any fear.

"We're looking for Zero-One-Zero," she said.

Peter sucked in a deep draught of frustrated breath. "We shouldn't play all our cards," he said softly.

"They might know where he is," she answered. "If they do, we can cut a deal."

"I can get you to Zoze."

"Zoze?"

Peter figured it out. "Zero-One-Zero," he said smugly.

"Thank you Mr. Crime, Inc." Kathryn turned to the girl. "How much?"

"Nothing," the girl said. "Zoze pays us for bringing in clients."

Kathryn smiled, impressed and pleased that the rules were so practical. "See?"

The girl had no patience. "Hey, do you chummers want to go or not? I could be breaking stuff!"

"Yes," Peter called. "Lead on."

The girl in green led them through the streets of the old Loop. Though Peter realized someone was follow-

ing them, he decided not to look around for their tail;
it wouldn't be polite.

The girl brought them to the remains of the Carson,
Pirie, Scott building. Snowflakes floated among the
shattered display windows. Inside the building were
no lights; it looked deserted.

"This it?"

"Yup. Just go inside, they'll take care of you."

"What about you?"

The girl pointed to a camera mounted amid the in-
tricate grill work on the second floor, and Peter saw
the warmth of its electronics and a dim red light blink
on and off. "I've been logged. Zoze won't know how
much he owes me until he sets up the job. It's all on
a commission basis. Prevents me from trying to roll
the rich folks on my own." She glanced at Kathryn
and checked out her clothes, envy shining in her eyes.

"What do you do here?" Kathryn said, her voice
revealing both embarrassment and concern.

"Survive. What do you do outside?"

"The same, I guess."

"But it's easier than here."

"I bet it is, too."

"Nice clothes."

Peter looked down at the girl. She was small, but
wiry, probably as fast as a processor and able to wrig-
gle out of the tightest spots. Nonetheless, he found her
severely lacking in what it would take to survive. He'd
been a year older than she when he first hit the streets,
but he'd had the advantage of a huge body with natural
dermal armor. What chance did this gutterpunk have?
He'd give her no more than four more years. Tops.

Then he noticed a glint of silver on her temple. Was
she a decker? That would certainly give her an edge.
Decking was a valuable skill.

Kathryn looked up at him. In the dim light he saw
her face plead with him to do something.

What? Adopt the child? As if she'd let him protect her anyway.

"Come on. Let's get to your fixer."

"By the way," said the girl as they stepped toward the deserted store, "you guys looking for a decker?"

"Decker?" asked Kathryn. "One of those computer pirates?"

"Dog, what plane of existence you from, lady?"

"Maybe we will need one," said Peter. "We don't know yet, but we'll keep you in mind."

"Hey, chummer, you don't act like most trolls I know."

"How do you mean?"

"I don't know . . . How you speak. It's better."

"Thanks. I've read a lot."

"Really? That's wiz. I just read titles of files and stuff. Breena, my squeeze. She's a mage. She reads all the time. I like pictures. You ever seen a Soorat?"

"Georges Seurat?" asked Kathryn.

"Yeah, George Soorat. I love his stuff. All dots. Like primitive comp graphics."

"Did you say you're a decker? One of those computer pirates?" repeated Kathryn.

The girl placed her hands on her hips, fiesty and endearing. "Yeah, me. You got a problem with that?"

"No, she doesn't have a problem with that." Peter touched Kathryn lightly on the shoulder and turned her toward the store. "We'll be in touch. All right?"

The girl smiled. "Wiz, chummer."

They stepped into the abandoned store. The doors had been torn out years ago, and the snow floated in as Peter and Kathryn entered. When the light from outside died after their first few steps, they stopped walking.

"Now what?" Kathryn asked.

"Don't know. . . ."

A tight spot of light crashed into his eyes, and Peter held up his hands before his face.

"Yeah?" called a gruff voice. "What you want?"

"I've got a client of Zoze's here," Peter said, blinded because of the bright light. He was so nervous he wanted to break for cover, to take his gun in his hand and simply *face off* against an enemy.

"My name is Kathryn Amij. I already have a contract with Mr. Zero-One-Zero, and an emergency has come up. I'd like to have Mr. Zero-One-Zero help me in some other matters."

"It's getting late." The speaker was quite cranky.

"It's an emergency. I've got to speak to him now. People are trying to kill my companion and myself."

"Well, let me call up."

There was a brief pause. Peter heard low whispers coming from somewhere to the right and up. Maybe someone looking down on them from a balcony.

"All right. He'll see you. Hang on."

The light remained on and pointed at them. From the right came the sound of someone leaping down steps. Or maybe an escalator. It had a metal sound to it.

A few moments later a voice spoke from no more than three meters away. Peter saw a red blob about a meter and a half tall. "Drop your weapons. All of them."

Peter reached under his jacket, pulled out his pistol and dropped it to the floor.

"And you."

"I'm a CEO. Not an assassin."

Laughter. "All right." Into the spill of the light walked a dwarf. He picked up Peter's gun.

"Kill the light!" the dwarf shouted.

The spot went out, and the dwarf turned on a flashlight.

"Hi," said the dwarf, and he turned the beam under his chin so they could see him. He had a thick white beard, and the low light accentuated his deeply lined face. "The name is Changes, Miss Amij. A pleasure. And you, sir?"

"Profezzur," said Peter, deciding to keep his identity a secret.

"Very well. If you'll follow me." As the dwarf lowered the beam of light, Peter saw it glint off the barrel of a submachine gun, which hung on a strap over the dwarf's shoulder. The dwarf turned and kept the beam on the ground, allowing Peter and Kathryn to follow him to the base of an escalator. Drops and streaks of dried blood spotted the floor.

Peter thought it odd the dwarf would turn his back on them.

"Oh, I almost forgot," Changes said. "My men are watching you with low-light scopes. Needless to say. . . . Well, it's so needless I won't even say it."

They walked up the escalator, then went about ten meters forward. The dwarf stopped and said, "Might want to close your eyes." He stepped behind them and shut thick double doors. Then he pulled out a fist-sized box covered with buttons, pressed one of them, and fluorescent lights flickered on overhead. The three of them stood beside a bank of elevators.

"Better," said Changes. He turned to Peter and Kathryn, and in a tone that revealed how much he loved to explain things, he told them, "We have the most trouble with the neighbors at night. We've found that as long as we don't leave a trail of light showing them where we hang out, they usually leave us alone."

He pressed another button on the box and glanced toward the elevator. The doors of one of the elevators slid open. "After you."

17

Zero-One-Zero greeted them when they stepped off the elevator. He held his hand out to Kathryn, and she shook it. "Pleasure to meet you in person. A true pleasure."

Zoze was an obese black man. His large, round head was completely bald and as smooth as a bullet. He turned to Peter and smiled, as if they shared a secret past, better left unspoken in front of the lady. He never looked directly at Peter, but instead took furtive peeks. He seemed a man in complete control of himself—happy and devious.

"You're a man of the streets, I see," Zoze said. "Good. I like men of the streets. Come."

He waddled down the hall toward an open doorway, Peter and Kathryn following him. The dwarf brought up the rear.

Frighteningly white walls crowded a large conference room, putting the sterility of Peter's room to shame. The hard wood floor reflected the overhead lights like a mirror. The furniture, made only of chrome and glass, dissolved into the spotlessness of the area.

No dust. No objects. No stuff.

The only ornamentation in the room was a glass bowl filled with glass marbles sitting on a small glass table near the glass doors. Peter knew with a sudden flash that no one fidgeted with the marbles. They remained as they were. If they were dusted, someone was responsible for putting them all back the way they had been.

Zoze gestured to a chair at the end of the table. "If

you would, my friend, it's been reinforced to handle someone built as impressively as you."

Peter took the chair, and Kathryn took one near him. Zoze sat at the other end of the table. Peter noticed that on the table near Zoze rested a small silver box.

"Soykaf?"

Peter shook his head. Kathryn nodded.

"Changes?"

The dwarf slipped on a pair of white gloves and walked over to a cabinet built into the wall, which opened to reveal a kitchen area. He pulled a stool out from the cabinet and got busy with the coffee.

"Now," Zoze said, placing his hands in his lap, "what can I do for you? I can tell you now, Miss Amij, that the shadowrunners I hired for you have made no progress in tracking down Dr. Clarris."

"First, we would like you to step up the efforts to find Dr. Clarris." Kathryn's voice was crisp and clear.

"Oh?"

"Yes. We must find him quickly. Peter can help."

"Can he?" An amused smile cracked Zoze's round face in half.

"Yes. Second, our lives are in danger."

Zoze leaned in, pleased and curious. "Because of this search for Dr. Clarris?"

"Indirectly."

"I was asked to kill Miss Amij for the Itami gang," Peter said. "I was a member of the gang up until"— he glanced at his watch—"two hours ago."

Zoze's eyes widened. Peter couldn't tell if it was because of fear or interest. "I see." A smile formed on his face. "You wouldn't happen to be the Profezzur, would you?"

Peter nodded, embarrassed. "You've heard of me?"

"Who hasn't?" He turned to Kathryn and laughed knowingly. "And what do you want me to do about this new development?"

Peter turned to Kathryn. She looked back at him.

"We don't know," she said, turning to Zoze. "We thought you might have some ideas."

He laughed. "I see." The dwarf served Kathryn and then Zoze their coffee. "Do you have any other enemies at this point?"

"A man on my board of directors. He found out that I'd helped Clarris and that I threw the company off the trail in its search for him."

"That's bad."

"It is?"

"These two forces could well cripple you economically."

"They could?"

"Yes, indeed."

Peter was amazed at how calm the man was as he ticked off the potential pitfalls that awaited Peter and Kathryn. Peter had never thought of someone freezing up his bank accounts. The threats he'd faced had always been bullets, not electric impulses.

"The first thing we've got to do is get the money the two of you possess into accounts safe from the hands of Itami and Cell Works."

"I don't have enough money to make it worth the time," said Peter.

"You'll set up dummy accounts?" asked Kathryn. Peter suddenly felt ignored.

"Yes. We'll transfer your funds as quickly as possible. There's usually a ceiling on the amount you can withdraw in a given time frame, but we'll dump a program into your account that'll pull out the dollars the second it's officially okay to make the next withdrawal. Seconds will count on this one. It'll cost you. Twenty percent of everything withdrawn, you lose." He looked at her fixedly. "All right?"

Kathryn paused, and Peter could see her mentally clicking off the dollars she'd be handing over to Zoze. But it was either that or risk losing it all.

"Yes."

"Fine," Zoze said. His face revealed no pleasure, but Peter was certain the man was leaping for joy inside his plump body. As the fixer reached over to a small red stud on the silver box, the sleeve of his jacket caught on the tip of his coffee cup.

A bit of coffee spilled onto the glass table.

Zoze looked down at the spilled coffee and froze. An expression of silent horror crept up over his face, starting at his neck, crawling up his chin, over his cheeks, making its way over his eyes and stopping at his forehead. He looked at the coffee as if it were a thing alive—a dangerous monster that might leap off the table and kill him.

The dwarf turned from the counter and saw what was happening. Quickly grabbing a towel, he jumped off the stool and rushed over to his employer's side. With a bit of effort he reached up and wiped the spilled coffee off the table.

Zoze remained frozen, still looking down at the table with obvious terror, even after the dwarf pulled back. The dwarf stuck his head under the table, spotted a bit of a coffee smear, reached back up, and wiped off the last bit of the liquid.

As soon as the table was cleaned off, Zoze blinked once and then completed the movement of his hand toward the button on the box.

Peter and Kathryn looked at one another; Kathryn raised an eyebrow.

When Peter looked back at Zoze, he saw a keyboard made of lights appear inside the glass of the table in front of the man.

"I'm going to take care of the money first. After that, however, the two of you should consider dropping your identities and getting new names and IDs. I don't know what your long-range plans are, but if you're going to be pursuing Dr. Clarris, you'll have to stay in Chicago. The shadowrunners I have on the case have determined that, wherever Clarris is, he hasn't left the city. If you're going to be staying here, you can't be yourselves any longer.''

"I want to be me," said Kathryn.

"Kathryn Amij," said Zoze coldly, "has a contract out on her by the Itami gang. Believe me, you don't want to be her.''

"What about my company?''

Zoze stared at her as if she were a single-celled creature he'd never seen before. Then he said, "Let's take care of the money first.''

His fingers started to fly over the glass keys. The thickness of the fingers belied their practiced command of the keyboard.

"I'm going to put one of my better deckers on this. But I'll need some information, if you don't mind.'' He waited a moment, then said, "Good, he's awake. Very well, your mother's maiden name?''

The questions went on for about ten minutes. Kathryn had to pull out her pocketbook to get her account information. It was all very dry and straightforward, much like opening a bank account.

At the end of the questions, Zoze said, "We're going to put it all into an account under the name of Jesse Hayes. We have several accounts we keep open for situations like this, and that one is currently available.''

"Would that be my name if I changed it?'' Kathryn asked the question with distaste, but curiosity as well, as if warming to the idea.

Zoze laughed. "No, no. The Hayes account is temporary. Just a convenient place for shuttling the funds into. We'll have to move them quickly to another account—one we'll make in the next hour.''

He paused and pressed his hands together. "But now we come to the matter of leaving behind Kathryn. And, of course, you, Profezzur. Is that an official handle or just a nickname?''

"Nickname.''

"And you'll want to change your name as well?"

Peter had to think about it. Eddy, along with a lot of other people in the gang, knew his name. Electronic money transfers had been put into an account with his name. They knew who he was. Things would be easier if he dumped his ID and re-tagged himself.

But if he did that, if he became someone other than Peter Clarris in name as well as in form, what would remain? His whole quest for the last dozen or so years had been to return to his former identity. If his researches were sound, and he actually was going to be able to transform his body back to human, who would he be by the time it was all done?

"Peter?"

He snapped out of his reverie, Kathryn's voice drawing him like a spirit calling him from a dangerous dream.

"What?"

"Are you all right?"

"Yeah, sure. Sorry."

"Well? Do you have a decision? Are you going to re-tag?"

"Yes."

"Very well. I assume, Miss Amij, that you'll be financing this?"

She looked to Peter, then to Zoze. "Yes."

"Fine. What's your name, Profezzur?"

"Clarris. Peter Clarris."

Zoze raised his left eyebrow, delighted with the complexities of the operation that had wandered into his establishment. Peter knew that Zoze's joy came from the fact that he was in control of the situation, safe on the outside.

"All right," said Zoze when he finished typing Peter's information into the table. "And now, Miss Amij? I'll warn you now, you have the option of going to the authorities, confessing your crimes and taking the heat for them. Corporate law, as you know, is very harsh these days on the illegal transfer of intellectual property.''

"But I have enough clout to pull out of it.''

Zoze shrugged shoulders. "True. I won't use the scare tactics. Given that one of your own board members has ties with the gang and put out a contract for you, I'd say you could wangle some deal. You'd probably keep control of Cell Works, if from a new position behind the scenes. I could toggle the proper switches to help make your slide back into society easier. It might cost more than the new ID, but in the long run your life would be much easier. Because of your family ties with Cell Works, I suspect you'd remain Kathryn Amij.''

Peter looked at Kathryn as she thought the situation over. He found himself desperately wanting her to choose the new ID. She would be a fugitive along with him. She might stay with him simply because she needed somebody with her. But why should she when she could fight to get her company back?

"New name,'' she said. "New identity.''

Peter exhaled sharply.

"I may not have explained the conditions of the retag fully. Once you say yes, I will send instructions to a very talented woman who will, over the course of this night, track down and delete every trace of your existence in all electronic records. Is this what you want?''

Kathryn held her breath for a moment, then said, "Yes,'' her voice firm but quiet.

Zoze rubbed his hands, delighted beyond belief. "Wonderful, wonderful. Things are very odd now. Wonderful.'' His fingers flew over the keyboard.

It was late now, one in the morning, but only Zoze seemed to be getting sleepy. Fear of being found by the past and apprehension of the future gripped Kathryn and Peter.

When Zoze hit the return key one final time, Peter said, "Now what?"

"You tell me. People are working on trying to keep you two safe from Itami. What else do you want?"

"To find Dr. Clarris," said Kathryn.

"I already told you, my people haven't found him yet."

"Well, give us whatever information they've got," said Peter. "We'll track him down."

"All they know is that Clarris is still in Chicago. We don't know anything about the corp involved. You cut a deal without getting enough facts, Miss Amij."

"Yes." She looked down, her expression a mixture of annoyance and shame.

"Well," said Peter, "we're not going to get anywhere without one more bit of information."

Kathryn's face become emotionless. "I . . . Peter, I told you your father was working on the same research you are—the means to transform a complex organism genetically. To remove the metahuman genes."

"Yes."

"Years ago he persuaded my father that it was viable. But this year the board said there was no way to justify the cost in the face of the small return."

"Small return?" said Zoze. "Wouldn't people be desperate for that technology? How many metahumans want to be metahuman?"

"I don't know. But that wasn't the problem. The project was cut because it would be too expensive, a 'cure for the rich.' It would become a class issue, and the negative PR would have hurt us. Besides, no one is even sure if it's possible."

"I know," said Peter.

She smiled at him. "Yes. You know. You figured it out. But have you figured out the cost of doing it your way?"

He hadn't, and the question threw him. "I . . . I've

just figured out the means . . . I didn't think about manufacturing it.''

"No, of course you didn't.'' It wasn't a criticism, just a statement. Even an encouragement. "You're a theorist. I could see that in the pages I read. Just like your father. But my job, and my board's job, is getting the theories applied. And if the price point is so high that only the ultra-rich can afford it, then it becomes a dubious research project for which no one is going to want to front money.''

Peter hadn't given any thought to the "price point'' of his idea, either. Frag, it had to be astronomical. "It would involve nanotechnology,'' he said, thinking aloud, "a technology that has yet to pop off the drawing board. And magic—to get the body into a kind of suspended animation.''

Kathryn nodded. "It's not impossible, though. There are economic theorists—people who sit around and figure out how to make research and product economically viable. You didn't think of how to do it. That's all right. It's not your job.''

"But your board scrapped the research. They couldn't see a way to do it.''

"And one of those board members put out a contract to get me killed. You'll forgive me if I think their decision-making leaves a bit to be desired.''

Peter returned to her. "You said you helped my father jump contract because Cell Works wouldn't conduct the research . . .''

"Right,'' she said with an impish grin. "But someone else wanted to do the work. And they wanted your father to help them.''

"Who?''

The smile melted from her face. "I don't know. I took a chance. I took lots of chances. And I lost. They took him, and they were supposed to keep me updated. But that was two months ago. Haven't heard a thing.''

"But," said Peter, becoming excited, "we know we're looking for a corp with access to practical nanotech. Maybe just prototypes, but workable nanotech." He turned to Zoze. "Anything?"

"Don't look at me. That stuff is so new it's still in diapers. Anyone who'd know about it would have to be on the inside. And they wouldn't talk."

"Dr. Landsgate," Peter said aloud.

"What?" said Zoze.

"Dr. Richard Landsgate. He was in the same league as my father, and I know him."

Kathryn was looking at him strangely. "Peter," she said slowly, "how well did you know him?"

Her tone chilled him. "What are you telling me?"

"He . . . transformed last year."

"What? That's impossible!" Peter's mind reeled at the odds of both of them goblinizing. He remembered only too well the doctor telling him how rare goblinization had become. In 2053, most metahumans were born that way.

"He became a ghoul. No one knows why, but last year there was a sudden surge of transformations into ghouls. Maybe another cycle, like the birth cycles in 2011 and the transformations in 2021. I don't know." She touched his hand. "I'm sorry."

Peter's thoughts reeled. No one was left, all his moorings cut. Now he had only Kathryn, who he did not want to trust because of his attraction to her. "What happened to him?"

"He was teaching at Northwestern at the time. The University kept it quiet, the PR. . . . Then Landsgate ran off. Maybe he wanted to spare his family when he realized he was changing into a ghoul . . . or maybe he only craved his own kind by then. . . ."

"The bounty," Zoze said sagely.

"It's rumored he's down in the Shattergraves," said Kathryn. "The ghouls have practically owned the place since the IBM Tower went down."

"Hang on," said Zoze, and he typed out the name Landsgate while he mouthed it to himself.

"Nothing," said Zoze.

"Nothing?" Peter was incredulous. "Nothing? The man was at the top of his field."

"See for yourself." Peter got up and crossed around the table. "He's listed," Zoze said as Peter studied the screen, "but they deleted his files. He's listed simply as a ghoul. They dropped him."

Peter looked down at the screen. The letters floated in the glass. "Landsgate, Richard," he read aloud. "Goblinized, ghoul, 02-06-51."

"I don't believe it."

"Believe it. Ghouls. No one wants them around. And not just because of their nasty habits. They remind people too much of how dark a place the world is now. They'd rather cut and forget them."

Peter looked over at Kathryn. "The Shattergraves?"

"It was just a rumor."

"Best we've got though, right?"

"Um," said Zoze, with a hungry grin, "I haven't got anyone who'll go in there with you."

"That's all right."

Zoze raised his fleshy hand and placed it on Peter's arm. "Let me repeat that. I don't know anyone who would go into the Shattergraves with you. Don't be a fool. If no one else will go, you shouldn't either."

"I'm going."

Zoze looked to Kathryn.

"Peter, there are other ways," she said.

Peter looked down at Zoze. "How many of them practical?"

"Well, honestly, at this point, given the circumstances, a randomization is usually called for. I'd generally have someone other than the client go in for the action, however."

Peter thought for a moment. It occurred to him that

he didn't have to be the client. "How about this? My identity just got erased. I'm good with a gun. I've already got a handle. Take the other people off the case. I'm Kathryn's shadowrunner now. She'll pay me through you. You're my fixer, I have access to your network."

"You want him?" Zoze asked Kathryn.

She looked at Peter, annoyed. Did she think he was just trying to get money from her? "He's done a pretty good job so far."

"Done."

"The money I earn from her is applied against anything she's shelled out for me so far." He turned to her. "All right."

She eyed him, curious. Then she nodded. "So you're a shadowrunner now?"

"That's right. I'm Profezzur. By the way," he said, turning to Zoze, "most people don't think I'm very bright. I'd like to keep it that way."

"Hell, chummer, you're going into the Shattergraves. You could have fooled me."

18

Peter walked just over a dozen blocks to reach the Shattergraves, heading south on State to Jackson and then turning west. Getting closer, he saw the red glow of rats the size of dogs scuttling around in the snow searching for food. Fires built by bums burned in the upper floors of abandoned office buildings. Sometimes he saw warm-red forms looking down at him.

He knew he was almost there when he stumbled over a big hunk of ice-rimed stone. Picking it up, Peter saw that it was a jagged piece of black rock larger

than his fist. A fragment of the former IBM Tower.
Just ahead was a four-square block area of ruined
buildings where the IBM subtowers had fallen, crushing other buildings and setting off gas-line explosions
that tore up the downtown area.

Continuing down the snowy streets, Peter passed
among huge stones, the remains of huge steel girders,
and the skeletal walls of destroyed buildings. The
monumental debris created a chaotic garden of un-
moving shadows that extended far beyond his vision.

It was time to pull out his Predator.

Walking on another hundred meters, he came to two
giant stone blocks, each ten meters high, standing on
either side of Jackson Street like columns heralding
the entrance to some ancient kingdom.

He entered the Shattergraves.

Working his way carefully through the rubble, Peter
tried to head due west, thinking it would help him find
his way out again. But streets had no meaning within
the Shattergraves. Huge slabs blocked his path, and in
the darkness the snow-covered concrete melded with the
snow-covered asphalt, until everything looked like the
ruins of walls.

When he looked back, Peter couldn't make out
which way he'd just come, but his footprints still
burned hot in the cold snow. Perhaps if he found
Landsgate quickly enough, he could follow his own
prints out before the snow filled them. He moved forward slowly, gun in hand, moving it from side to side.

What was that? He halted suddenly, looking sharply
to the left.

From behind him came a soft scraping noise. He
was just turning to see when the ghoul crashed down
on him, knocking Peter to the ground and flooding his
nostrils with the stench of rotted flesh. The ghoul
gasped for air with loud breaths, its cold, torn hands
flailing at Peter's face.

Peter was so stunned that for a moment he could only take the blows.

Between blows he saw red blurs moving not far away. The words did not form in his mind, but he knew big trouble had arrived. Pulling his arm back, he snapped a tremendous punch into the chest of the ghoul in front of him. The ghoul immediately popped off Peter and landed in the snow a few steps away.

Peter leaped to his feet, but not before a dozen more ghouls had him surrounded. Some wore torn business suits; others ragged punker outfits. Not a single face was intact. The ghoul in the biker outfit had only one eye; the right half of the face of the woman in the torn evening gown showed muscle. Burns blackened their cool flesh.

They encircled Peter, crouched and ready to pounce if he made a move to escape. Their smiles were taut and maniacal—skulls enjoying a joke.

Peter still held his gun, but knew he couldn't take them all out at this range.

He made a dash for the edge of the circle. His feet slipped on the snow, but he managed to keep his balance and went crashing through the ghouls. Rotted hands to either side of him grabbed at his arms. Their touch made him want to cry out, but he ran on past them into the shadows.

He ran wildly, careening around every corner he encountered. Moments earlier a straight and narrow path had seemed the best course, now nothing made more sense than to throw himself headlong into the maze.

He slipped and fell twice, the stones under the snow scraping his skin, the snow chilling the wounds.

Deeper into the Shattergraves he ran and ran, until he could run no more. Panting wildly, he stopped and leaned against a steel girder to catch his breath.

As his respiration became more normal, Peter also became aware of a soft light shining near him.

He turned his head, too exhausted to snap into action, and saw only a fuzzy oval of white light, about two meters long, floating off the ground just ahead of him.

"Peter?" said the light.

Peter stood up straight. He recognized the voice, but could not place it.

The light floated toward him.

Within the oval Peter saw a long, bright shape that writhed slowly. The oval seemed, in fact, to be a halo emanating from the inner, glowing object.

"You've changed," said the light.

"Thomas?" Peter said, suddenly recognizing the voice.

At the moment he spoke the name, Thomas' face seemed to take form from out of the spiralling illumination at the center of the oval. Although the source of the light had something serpentine about it, the shape remained indefinite.

Thomas smiled at Peter. His face glowed from within, his expression as boyish and innocent as when Peter had last seen him. The image, frightening at first, settled into something miraculous, even beautiful.

"It is you, Peter. How are you?"

"Thomas? What happened to you?"

The head smiled bashfully. "I told you that Snake demands a lot in return for her secrets. Do you remember?"

Peter remembered something about that, talking with Thomas in his bedroom years ago, in his father's house. "Yes."

"Well, she wanted a lot from me. I wanted a lot from her. But what has happened to you? The last time I saw you, you did not have the blood of many lives on you."

Peter felt naked, as if all his secrets and shame were being laid bare before this glowing form.

"I . . . Things have been hard. Strange."

"I can well imagine. I can't think of any reason why someone with your kind nature would resort to murder."

How much did Thomas know? "What happened to you, Thomas? You left and never came back."

"I died here, Peter. I died the day I left you. I was trying to help those I could, and as I worked, I kept wondering what could make people do such a terrible thing. How could any person or group of people take it upon themselves to kill so many innocents, to cause so much grief for their survivors?"

Though Peter did not think Thomas' words referred to him, they worked their way into his chest. They lodged there and made him uncomfortable.

"The more I thought about it, the more I realized that this was what I wanted to heal. I wanted to find the disease of hatred and cure it. As I pulled the dying from the rubble, curing those I could and easing the deaths of those I could not, I thought, 'But first I must understand the disease.' The hours passed and I found myself drawing more and more upon Snake to keep up my strength. Eventually I became so weary I didn't notice when a huge wall near me gave way. I have been here ever since." Thomas looked left, then right, then, in a low whisper, said, "I can't really say coming here was the wisest decision I ever made." And then he laughed.

"So you're a ghost?"

"Yes. Mostly. But, being me, it's hard to fully grasp the implications of what I am. That's annoying, let me tell you. You think that when you die things will become clearer. I changed into this," he said and looked down at the coiling body of light, "and now all I know about myself is that I'm this."

"Did you learn what you wanted to learn?"

A dark sadness passed over the face of Thomas. "More than I would have wanted to. The ghouls of the Shattergraves have given me . . . ample behavior for study.''

"It's a ghoul I'm looking for."

Thomas looked weary. "Why, Peter?"

"He was a friend of mine. I need to find him. He might be able to help me with what I want."

"To become human?"

"Yes."

Thomas closed his eyes and said, "Don't go to the ghouls, Peter. Leave this quest behind and go back to the living."

Peter hesitated because he didn't want to upset Thomas. "Can you help me?" he asked finally. "Do you know where Dr. Landsgate is?"

"Peter, I don't want to help you do this. . . ."

"Please, Thomas."

"If you want to find him so bad, then you will find him without my help. You need only wait here a few moments longer, and I promise you that you will come face to face with Dr. Landsgate." Peter didn't like the tone of Thomas' voice. It carried a portent of doom and a weary sadness. But before Peter could examine the issue further, Thomas continued. "Peter, do you remember when we spoke many, many years ago . . . There was a girl. . . ."

"Denise," Peter said, remembering the day he realized he'd never called her back.

"Do you recall I wanted to tell you something, that day when you remembered?"

"But I was angry. And I cut you off."

Thomas seemed relieved, and the dark mood left him. "Good. You can see that. Good. Peter, there was something I wanted to tell you. There are two kinds of women. The kind that will go out with a troll and the kind that won't."

Peter thought about that. "I guess. But my problems are way past that now."

"Yes. And what about now?"

"I want to be human."

"Do you see any connection between the two is-
sues?"

"Why do you talk this way? Why don't you tell me
what you want to say?"

"Life's like that Peter. Some things you must simply live through."

Peter only had time to hear the words, and then
whirled as the ghouls came up behind him. They threw
heavy rocks into his chest and smashed them against
his head. He tried to get out of the way, but there were
too many of them, and they attacked from too many
places. They threw rocks from the ground ahead of
him. They dropped them from concrete pillars towering high overhead.

As the blows overwhelmed him, Peter looked back
to call for help from Thomas, but when he turned, all
he saw was Thomas shaking his head sadly. "Good
luck," Thomas said, but Peter was already falling into
a deep blackness.

It took him time to open his eyes, and a while longer
to realize he was hanging upside down. When he
moved, he swayed back and forth.

Holding Peter by the ankles were heavy chains
looped down from an I-beam that straddled the roofless remains of a basement. Chains bound his hands
behind his back. Dried blood caked his face.

The snow had stopped, the clouds had cleared, and
soft blue moonlight lit the roofless basement. Scraps
of metal covered the ground. Around the basement,
ghouls gathered in groups of three or five. They sat on
the floor, hunched over, feasting on corpses. His stomach clenching at the sight, Peter turned his gaze away.
He searched around for something safer—something
that might provide a means of escape, something to
fend off his feeling of helplessness.

Eventually he recognized Landsgate sitting some ten

meters off, the ghoul ensconced in a large throne made of welded metal and bones. Garbage cans roaring with fire stood on either side of the throne, the flames turning his decayed features into those of the devil himself.

Landsgate seemed lost in thought, but when he noticed that Peter was awake, he smiled, stood up, and walked over.

The feasting ghouls looked up, but when they saw that Landsgate was going to deal with the troll, they returned to their feasting. The troll was alive, and thus not very interesting.

Landsgate stepped up to Peter, and they met eye to eye. But Peter turned his face away from the ghoul, repelled by the rank smell that clung to his rotting form.

"Hello," said Landsgate, his voice thick with malice. "People usually get tossed in here by former loved ones. What are you doing here under your own juice? Are you a bounty hunter?"

Peter didn't know exactly how to begin. He had expected their reunion to be a bit more heartfelt.

He thought it best to get the improbable out in open.

"Dr. Landsgate. I'm Peter Clarris."

Landsgate looked puzzled for a moment, then he exclaimed, "Good Lord!" A smile bloomed on the ghoul's face. Deep cracks lined his lips. "I . . . I don't know what to say. I really don't. How have you been?"

Landsgate's callous humor stunned Peter. "Better," he said dryly.

"I haven't seen your father . . . in years. How is he?"

"I don't know. I haven't seen him for years either."

Landsgate leaned in and mocked concern. "Trouble at home?" he said and laughed. "Still shuffling hopelessly after your father's love?"

Peter decided to change the subject. "I came here

because I need to know who has a lead on nanotechnology.''

Landsgate suddenly looked kinder. ''And you came
to me.''

''Yes.''

He put his hand on Peter's cheek. The other man's
flesh festered from countless cuts, but Peter held back
his disgust. ''You came to me like you always used to
come to me.''

''Yes.''

Landsgate pulled his hand back and slapped Peter's
face. ''Why should I help you, you idiot?''

Despite himself, Peter felt betrayed. ''I'm looking
for him. I need your help.''

''Listen, why don't you stay for dinner before you
take off on the quest?''

''Dr. Landsgate . . . I'm . . . I think someone is
working on a way to rebuild DNA sequences in living
organisms.''

''What?''

''I think someone is combining magic and nanotechnology to make . . . to rewrite a cell, all the cells
of a body. I could be pure human again. So could
you.''

''That's impossible.''

''No.''

''No. I suppose not. I'm a ghoul. The word 'impossible' has lost its weight in the past few decades.''

''I don't understand the magic part. . . . I really
don't know if it can be done, but I think somebody is
trying to do it. And if they are, they need nanotech.
It's the only way to get to all the cells. The magic
couldn't handle all the work. No corp would ever put
the money into it.''

''A corporation is working on this?''

''I . . . think so. Yes.''

''Most of the genetic-manipulation work dried up
after the fiasco in London.''

"They're being very quiet about it."

"What do you want from me?"

"If someone is doing the work, they need the nanotech. I need a lead on anyone who might have prototypes to hand out."

"What makes you think anyone has nanotech ready? That whole line of research went down years ago."

Peter did not respond.

"All right. Some people, mostly Germans and Japanese, have been after it. But they're keeping a tight lid on it. So many bodies ruined by research just in the twenties and thirties . . ." Landsgate smiled up at Peter. "And even today. Do you know how many people from the Elevated pay to have deformed relatives brought to the Shattergraves? It's all very nasty stuff."

Landsgate turned from Peter and walked a few steps.

"God, what I would give to be human again."

"I've been working on it. Ten years now I've been trying to figure out a way. And I think I've got it."

"I haven't seen my children in two years."

Peter said nothing.

"You know, being a . . . ghoul . . . At first. It didn't seem as if it was something that had to drive me from my family and my profession. I was hospitalized, of course. Everyone knew I was transforming. And almost everyone stuck it out with me. There were the wishes. They . . . my wife . . . others . . . didn't say them out loud. But in those times when I regained consciousness during the . . . wishes hung in the air. 'If he must change, let him become something I can love.' But my eyes became painfully sensitive to sunlight. And the craving for meat. There was this thing inside my body, a new desire, and it said, 'Human flesh is what you want to eat.' It's a craving, Peter, a desire just like some people have a sweet tooth. I want the flesh of someone who was sentient. I knew what was happening before anyone else did, and I got out.

There's a price on my head, you know. Just because of my genes. Just because of what I am.

"Oh, I know. I'm making it sound light. Comparing cannibalism to a taste for sweets. But I swear, that's what it feels like. It's what my body wants. I crave it. It seems immoral to you, but to me it's just what I need to feel content."

Landsgate leaned closer, his noxious breath spilling over Peter's face.

"Why must I be the way I am, Peter?"

Peter turned away slightly, but spoke firmly. "Genetics. Some of us have 'magic' genes, genes passed on through the centuries, but active only now. My genes were for those of a troll. Yours for a ghoul."

"So this condition is natural?"

Peter stopped for a moment, confused. "I . . ."

Landsgate leaned in again, his voice soft, as if he did not want the other ghouls to hear.

"I am not an aberration. The universe dictated that there should be ghouls, and I am one. The fact that I am a ghoul is not even a condition layered *onto* me. It *is* me."

"Yes. That's one way to look at it."

The ghoul's eyes filled with tears. "How else can I look at it? I don't kill, Peter. I eat those who have died. Society says that's evil, and they shun me for it. But it is what I am. So now I kill to survive. Do I have a choice? I love surviving, Peter. You're a survivor, aren't you? You know what I mean. Here we are, thrown by the universe outside the normal bounds— and we're still alive. We're extraordinary.

"I am the way I am. If you were to succeed in finding a means to take my magic genes out of my body, I'd really be dead. You'd be killing the way the universe built my body. Countless generations of humanity carried these genes safely through the centuries and deposited them in me upon my conception. That's a hell of a responsibility to take upon yourself, Peter.

To give people the decision to alter all that history, to erase it, with a decision made within a single lifetime.''

"It's my life. I'll do as I please."

"I doubt it." Landsgate turned away, walking back to his throne, his head bent down. Speaking loudly, but to no one in particular, he said, "Take the troll. He is yours."

19

All around the roofless basement the ghouls slowly rose from their feasting, and grinned at Peter.

Peter's head still ached, but it had cleared somewhat during the conversation; he could handle the pain now. Landsgate had gone back to sit in his throne. He held his hands up over his eyes as if very weary.

The ghouls closed in around Peter.

His immediate reaction was to try to free himself with frantic motion, but his better judgment kicked in.

"Hold it," he told himself." Don't panic. Let's do this carefully. What do I have?" He paused to calculate his assets. Strength was all he could think of.

Peter calmed his breathing as best he could, then focused on the chains that bound his wrists. He gave a slow, steady pull and discovered that the links were very strong.

The ghouls moved closer.

He drew in a long breath and pulled on the chains again. He strained, pulling and pulling. The links began to stretch, but they also dug deep into his flesh. An ache spread into his wrists.

Soon he had to stop. Gasping for breath, he looked around to see the ghouls, about thirty of them, still encircling him. They cocked their heads, curious that he was still trying to escape. Knowing that he had loosened his chains somewhat, Peter shook them a bit, but still couldn't free his hands.

"Remember to breathe this time," Peter told himself. He pulled on the chains again. The links bit into his hands. Maybe they even drew blood, but he couldn't be sure.

A single link began to stretch and gave out a soft, grating scream. Peter, his eyes closed, didn't dare stop pulling. It seemed the chain would never break. Finally, intensely curious about the ghouls, he opened his eyes.

One was peering into his face, a mix of saliva and dark gruel dripping from the cannibal's mouth.

Peter screamed, and with the scream he gave one, last tremendous tug on the chains. The link snapped and released the bonds holding his right hand. He doubled over and grabbed the chain holding his ankles. Without pause he swung the chain still wrapped around his left wrist in a wide circle. The chain slammed, one after another, into the faces of the ghouls closest to him, and drops of blood splattered Peter's skin and clothes. The other ghouls instinctively jumped back.

The goriness of the situation drove Peter into a frenzy. All he wanted was to get out of the basement, out of the Shattergraves, out of the Noose. He brought his left hand up to the chain leading to the I-beam and pulled himself up hand over hand. In seconds his feet were under his head and his pace had increased. He knew, though, that, as he climbed, he would have to lift more and more of the weight of the chain still attached to his ankles and the problem nearly panicked him. What if he got stuck halfway up, unable to proceed because of the increasing weight? He shot a glance at the ghouls below and decided that he had no other choice but to keep on going.

The chain shook and Peter looked down again to

see one of the ghouls hanging onto the U-shaped length of chain close to the ground. The ghoul, a still-handsome man in a business suit, was looking up at Peter with an expression of fierce determination. Placing one hand over another, he began to climb. A quake ran through Peter's back and he increased his pace.

Below, some of the ghouls cheered and howled while others ran for the stairs up to the street level. Peter saw that they'd be able to cut him off if he didn't hurry.

He threw his left hand up over his right, then his right over his left, one hand after the other. He went as fast as he could, but slowed as he neared the I-beam; between his own weight, the weight of the ghoul, and the increasing weight of the chains he carried, it was all he could do to keep his grip.

The ghoul's hand reached up to Peter's ankle. As fear took over, Peter began to kick frantically. The ghoul swung a bit on the chain, but kept his grip, moving from the chain leading to Peter's ankles to the chain leading to the I-beam. The load lightened, and Peter felt an incredible relief. He continued up the chain and saw he was only a meter or so from the I-beam.

But the ghoul on the chain was no longer stuck beneath Peter's feet. He raced quickly up the other half of the chain and wrapped his arms around Peter's waist. As the two of them swayed wildly, Peter's hands slid a few links down the chain. The ghoul cocked his head back and tried to bite Peter, but his teeth ended up digging into Peter's lined duster instead.

Peter knew he had to put everything he had into reaching the beam. He desperately wanted to be *on* something. With three more hand-over-hands, he reached the I-beam and swung his arm over it.

Now the ghoul came in from a different angle, biting into Peter's abdomen. He ripped through Peter's shirt and pressed his teeth deep into Peter's thick flesh; the bite sent a sharp sting through Peter's body.

Peter reached down to the ghoul with his left hand and grabbed the man by the neck. The ghoul's arms flailed wildly, desperately, the rotted hands pounding at Peter's face again and again. In a quick motion he slipped his large thumb under the ghoul's chin, forced the cannibal's head up, and snapped the neck. The ghoul's body went limp, and Peter let it tumble to the basement floor below.

He allowed himself two gulping breaths, then pulled himself up onto the I-beam.

Down below, standing in front of his throne, Landsgate screamed, "Get him. Don't let him get the chains off. Get him now." But the ghouls at either end of the I-beam waited. They moved about with small steps, uncertain what to do.

Peter slipped the knots that bound his ankles and freed himself. He could try to make a break for it by charging past the ghouls, but he was certain that Landsgate had the information he wanted. He hesitated, but realized he wanted the information more than freedom.

He looked about for a way to get to Landsgate. Then he saw it. He held on to the end of the chain and stood up, balancing himself carefully on the I-beam. The ghouls at either end of the beam braced themselves. Then he turned away from Landsgate and jumped.

He sailed through the air, his duster flapping madly behind him. When the length of chain ran out, he snapped back and down toward the ground. The I-beam buckled, but held its precarious balance on the basement foundations.

Peter swung quickly down to the ground in a wide arc. The ghouls that had remained in the basement, directly under where Peter had climbed up, now stared in amazement as one hundred and fifty kilos of troll rushed at them, swinging on a length of a chain. Before they could recover from their surprise, Peter was plowing through them, heavy boots out before him, shattering the legs of several ghouls.

When his momentum slowed, he released his grip and flew off the chain toward Landsgate. He tucked and rolled through the air, then tumbled across the floor, coming to a stop only when he slammed into a garbage can roaring with fire. Jumping up, he saw Landsgate run for the stairs.

The ghouls still on the basement floor charged after him. The ghouls at street level ran for the stairs.

Peter bolted after Landsgate, taking the stairs three at a time. Getting close enough for a tackle, he threw himself bodily onto the ghoul and they rolled down the stairs. Then Peter slammed Landsgate against the wall, one arm pressed hard against his windpipe.

"Tell them to back off or you die."

"I'm no good to you dead," Landsgate wheezed.

"You're no good to me if *I'm* dead. Tell them to back off."

Landsgate hesitated, then slammed his elbow into Peter's gut. The blow caught Peter off guard, but didn't hurt.

"I don't think you understand. I'm a troll. Whatever else I am, I'm really tough. Now tell them to back off or I'll rip off your head."

Landsgate pushed again. "All right."

Peter released his choke-hold so the ghoul could be heard.

"Stop," Landsgate ordered, but the ghouls continued moving forward. "STOP!" Landsgate shouted, fear in his voice. That finally stopped them. "All right. I'll tell you. Microtech, a Swiss company. Last I heard—and this is more than a year old—they're the company into heavy nano research."

Peter ignored him. "Come on. Let's go."

"What?"

Peter lifted Landsgate by the waist. "I don't believe you. You're coming with me, and when I get what I want, I'll let you go."

"But I told you . . ."

Peter slammed the ghoul into wall next to the stairs. Landsgate's head hit the concrete with a sharp crack. "Listen. I don't trust you. I came to talk to you, and you fed me to your pariahs. Not only do I not believe you about Microtech, I don't think for a second you'd let me out of the Shattergraves. By the way, where the frag's my gun?"

Landsgate's eyes snapped open and his hand flew for the shoulder holster under his jacket. Peter slammed the hand against Landsgate's chest and the ghoul cried out in pain. "I don't want to keep doing this." Peter reached under the jacket and dug out the Predator.

"Fine. Now, the sooner we get out of here and confirm your lead, the sooner you come back home. Got it?"

Landsgate nodded.

"Great."

He lifted Landsgate again and placed the gun to the ghoul's head. He walked up the stairs. "Your boss and I are going for a walk," he said. "He'll be back in a while. BACK OFF!"

The ghouls parted, letting Peter and Landsgate pass.

For twenty minutes Landsgate led Peter through the Shattergraves. His ghouls followed and neither Peter nor Landsgate could persuade them to leave.

When the two reached the edge of the Shattergraves, Landsgate turned to Peter. "Please. Don't make me go out there. I haven't been out for two years."

"Too bad."

"Peter. For your father's sake . . . I'm a monster out there. There's a price on the head of every ghoul."

Landsgate's body trembled wildly. Peter put him

down and Landsgate dropped to all fours. He reminded Peter of a sick dog. "Please," he gasped. "Please don't make me go out there. Please." He looked up at Peter, pathetic fear in his eyes. "That's not my place. I can't face those people. This is what I know. I rule here. It's good enough. Please. For God's sake . . ."

Foam and spittle danced around the edges of Landsgate's mouth and dropped into the snow. "I'll tell you. Please, I'll tell you. Microtech. It might be . . . Microtech. But Gen . . . Geneering in France. Your best bet. That's it, Peter, please. Don't take me out. Don't make me stand alongside the living."

Peter watched the man and felt a hollow bubble form in his chest. He wanted to believe that the thing groveling on the ground before him was not Landsgate. But it was. There was no way around that. And he couldn't bear to cause the only friend of his childhood this much pain. If Landsgate was lying, Peter would just have to find another lead.

"Go," he said. "Go back, Dr. Landsgate."

Without looking up, the ghoul scrambled back toward the Shattergraves. He slipped twice, then got up on his legs and ran into the darkness.

Peter turned and walked away, stunned by the evening's events.

When he'd gone but a short way, he heard Landsgate call out to him, the voice once again firm and sardonic. "Peter!" Peter turned to look back, but saw only cold darkness. "Peter! I told you the truth! Geneering, in France. Look them up!"

20

It was full morning by the time Peter staggered back to Zoze's place. Squatters filled the streets. They'd left the warmth of the Noose's abandoned buildings and now searched for folks who'd frozen to death in the night. Such corpses might yield a knife or a bit of food in a pocket of their stiff clothes.

A few such gutterpunks eyed Peter as he made his way up State Street, his wounds dripping blood into the dirty-gray snow. He walked with a limp and clutched his right arm with his left hand. His clothes were ragged, but it was obvious they had once been fine.

He was a good mark.

But in his hands was a very large gun and in his eyes the fixed stare of a maniac. It was clear to the men and women—pure humans, orks, trolls—that he would kill if asked the time of day. They let him pass without incident.

When Peter got to the department store building and stepped inside, morning light was pouring in through the broken windows, permitting him to see the first floor clearly. All around were empty display cases, forming a kind of maze. The cases had been painted white to provide a strong contrast with the items they had once displayed. Now the white cases blended with the white floor and the bare white walls. The sight made Peter's eyes hurt.

"You look like drek!" cackled Changes from the top of the escalator.

"Is Zoze up?"

"Not yet. You kept him up pretty late last night."

"Fine. What about Kathryn? Miss Amij?"

"Zoze gave her a place to sleep in a spare room."

"Got another place for me to crash?"

"Yeah. But it's going to cost you."

"What?"

"Hey, no offense. Your lady is paying, too. It costs money to get Zoze's protection."

"He'd said he'd have a new place for us this morning."

"It's all set."

Peter crossed the floor of the escalator. "All right then. Get Zoze up. Get Kathryn up. We're getting out of here."

"Hey. I don't know. Zoze likes . . ."

Peter moved quickly up the steps of the escalator. When he reached the top, he stepped close to Changes, towering over him. "I just got back from the Shattergraves. I'm totally bagged."

The dwarf's jaw dropped. "The Shattergraves . . . that's right. You went?"

"Yeah. Now move."

"Come on."

Despite the fact that it hurt to do so, Peter paced up and down the length of the conference room until Zoze arrived.

"What's the big rush?" Zoze demanded when he opened the door, but his indignation vanished as he looked Peter up and down. His round face bore a striking resemblance to a surprised grape. "You made it."

"Yeah. And I'm really cooked. So let's get the last details down. I need some sleep. Changes said you've got a safe house for us. I'm also going to need a decker. . . ."

Kathryn walked into the room bundled in a thick green bathrobe. Before he could shut down the thoughts, Peter imagined how soft she would feel to the touch, almost as though the sweetness of pressing against her body would heal his wounds. "Peter! My God! are you all right?"

Coming to stand before him, she raised her fingertips to his face and gently touched a bloody gash under one eye.

Peter froze, nervous. The touch of her fingertips stung, but he did not flinch.

"Yes. I'm fine."

She turned and pulled her hand away, but remained beside him. Peter suddenly realized he was holding his breath, and willed himself to start breathing again. "We've got to get him healed," Kathryn said to Zoze.

"You said you wanted shadowrunners," he told her. "I can put a mage or a shaman on your team. She'll fix Profezzur up as a matter of course."

Kathryn turned back to Peter. "Are you sure you're all right?" His lust melted, replaced by a wave of gratitude for her concern.

He held his feelings in check. "Yes," was all that came out.

But their eyes met, and despite Peter's best attempts to hide from her, she locked her gaze with his. At that instant Peter suddenly saw his father's critical, judgmental eyes instead of Kathryn's. Awkward and embarrassed, he turned his eyes away.

"Where are we going?" Peter asked, seeking the safety of important matters at hand. "Where's the safe house?"

"The Byrne Projects."

Peter and Kathryn stared at one another, then at Zoze. As one they said, "The Byrne Projects?"

Zoze shrugged. "It's all I've got right now. That is, all I've got that can house a troll without attracting the attention of the neighbors. I greased somebody at the Housing Authority. I've always got a room available in the projects. It's perfect. If you wish, Miss Amij can be housed someplace better, and Profezzur can head to Byrne alone. . . . But really that's the best I can do under the circumstances.''

Peter wanted to be generous and a gentleman, insisting that Kathryn stay somewhere else, but he knew it was impractical. It'd be easier if they stayed together. Cheaper, too, and they wouldn't have to move around town to get together.

Besides, he wanted to be with her.

"No," she said. "It doesn't make sense to split up."

"But it's a metahuman housing project," Peter said, feeling safe in demonstrating his chivalry now. "A run-down, dirty, dangerous, metahuman housing project."

"The Byrne Projects are probably the best place to hide, at least for me, because it's the last place anybody would look for me."

"She's got a point," said Zoze.

Peter admired her pluck. "Fine. We still need a decker."

"And someone who can heal Peter."

"Leave that to me," Zoze said. "How about you get up to the projects and I send them up?"

"What about the girl who brought us here?" said Peter. "The girl with the purple hair?"

"Liaison," said Zoze, with surprise. "Why her?"

"She asked us to keep her in mind if we were looking for a decker."

Zoze reflected for a moment. "She's good, but she hasn't go a hot rep. It's got nothing to do with her skill—or lack of it—she's simply not a hot-dogger. She hasn't gone out and made a name for herself."

"But she's good?" asked Kathryn.

"She has fun in the Matrix and she gets by. That's what I've heard. I know I could get you better. Or I think I could. I really haven't seen her in action. But Liaison will also come cheap because she doesn't have a rep. That's important right now, with your funds limited. And, her girlfriend, Breena, is a mage. They're used to working together. That's a plus, too.''

"Contact them, then," said Peter. "See if they'll take the job. We'll get to Byrne."

"All right. Somebody will arrive later today. And I'll have Changes pack up a basket for them. They'll be armed for Bear. With Itami after you, no telling what you'll need."

Zoze supplied a driver and a Ford Totem to take them up to Byrne. The man was steady and cautious and didn't twitch at all, which made Peter miss Fast Eddy's style terribly. Turning off Old Orchard Boulevard, the driver took one of the small side streets that led into the Byrne Projects.

After all Peter's years of trying to avoid living in a metahuman project, here he was, now voluntarily taking up residence in one. A small part of him welcomed the opportunity. Up ahead he saw ork and troll children playing in the street. They threw snowballs at one another, but also tackled their opponents and slammed them into the snow-covered asphalt. It looked marvelous to Peter. This might be heavy rough-housing for pure human children, but to the powerful, solid bodies of the metahuman children it was innocent fun. Pure human kids often got quite banged up when they tried to join in on the metahuman children's games. They simply couldn't keep up, but that didn't stop some people from claiming that the metahuman youngsters were crude in their play.

Adult orks and trolls clustered in tight groups to keep watch on the children, the trolls in one circle, the orks in another.

"Here we are," said the driver, pulling up in front of one of the nine buildings that made up the projects. From his pocket he pulled out two sets of keys. "Here you go."

Peter glanced at Kathryn. She stared out the win-

dow, looking stiff and a little afraid. When Peter followed her gaze, he saw adult orks and trolls staring back at them from across the street. Even a few of the children stopped playing to watch the people sitting in the car in their projects.

"You can still go somewhere else, you know," Peter said. He tried to make it sound friendly and helpful, but it was a lie. Suddenly he didn't want Kathryn hiding in Byrne with him. He realized he was embarrassed being seen with *her* by all the metahumans around them. He thought they'd assume he'd turned his back on his kind by shacking up with a human.

But wasn't that part of Kathryn's appeal?

"No," she said firmly. "I want to be with you."

She really meant it. He was sure of that. As he continued to look at her, his self-imposed distance diminished. He cursed inwardly that his life was so complicated.

"All right."

He opened his door to get out, and Kathryn did the same.

The apartment reeked. Both Kathryn and Peter reflexively covered their noses, but it helped very little. Kathryn went to the windows and opened them, letting cold air slice through the stench.

"God, what is it?" she said. "It stinks like something's dead in here."

Peter thought the source of the smell came from the bathroom. He went in, expecting to find a decaying cat or dog in the tub. A dozen cockroaches raced down the sink's drain, but that was all he found. He located the source of the stench, however. It came from the toilet. "Down the pipes, in the basement. Something died down there and it's stinking up the pipes."

"How can people live like this?"

"Do you mean, how do they endure, or how do they let it happen?" Realizing how angry he sounded, Peter wanted to take back the words immediately. "I don't know," he put in quickly. "I don't know the answer to either question."

"Isn't this their home? Don't they want . . . ?"

"It is. But it isn't. They're all here according to how much money they make. This 'home' is defined by its poverty. No one wants to live here. Everyone wants to get out. If you're succeeding, you get out. If you're failing, you're here."

Three cockroaches scuttled in tight formation across the wall of the main room, then disappeared through a wide crack in the plaster. Kathryn first jumped, then stared at the spot where they'd gone. Without lifting her eyes from the crack, she said, "But to let things . . ."

"Kathryn, who is going to invest in something that they want to leave, that reminds them how poor they are, that they're failures?"

"Have you ever lived in place like this?" she asked softly.

"No."

"What's wrong?"

"I don't know. Just being here now . . . It makes me think somehow I should have been here earlier. I've spent so long trying to hide from these people."

"Really?"

"I just didn't want to be part of them. To be identified with them."

"But you're not one of them. Or, at least, that's not the impression I get from you. You want to be pure human again. That's what you were first. This is just— something in between."

"I don't know about that right now. I'm having my doubts. At least, right now, while I'm a troll, I AM a troll. Maybe I shouldn't try to deny that."

She looked down, thoughtful.

"What?" he asked.

"Nothing." She changed the subject with a smile. "So who are you now?"

He pulled his fake IDs from his pocket, and she did the same. "I'm Jordan Winston," he read. "Though, of course, as a shadowrunner, I've got to have a handle: Profezzur."

"I'm Sarah Brandise. How will these do against DNA and retina scans?"

"Should do just fine. They took the original scan data for our real IDs and pasted them into these."

She laughed.

"What's so funny?"

"The idea of our 'real' IDs. They're not only wiped out, but our DNA is now linked to these IDs. We aren't those people anymore. We're these people. These *are* our real IDs. We might as well never have been our previous selves."

Peter's back stiffened.

"I was just joking," she said. "Kind of." Apparently the same sensation suddenly overcame her, for she glanced at the ID, then quickly put it away. "Who are we going to be by the time all this is done?"

"Kathryn, why are you looking for my father?"

"What do you mean?"

"Why are you looking for him? You could leave town. Or you could have fought for Cell Works. You could have gotten Cell Works to continue the metahuman research. It would have taken time, but you could have done it. Why the rush? Why do you need so bad to find my father right now?"

Kathryn put her hand on her stomach and her face tightened. "Peter. My son . . . he's got the metagenes. He might well become a metahuman."

The statement startled Peter. "The chances are astronomically small. Most metahumans are born of metahuman parents today. I was a freak case. . . ."

"But the possibility is still there. I don't want that hanging over my son's life."

Peter reeled. He wandered over to a chair and sat down. It was a massive, solidly built chair, and in the midst of his confusion he found himself congratulating the CHA for at least getting the proper-sized furniture into the projects.

"Peter, what is it?"

"I don't know. You'd go through all this on the *chance*, on the nearly insignificant *chance*, that your son might become a metahuman?"

"Peter, he's my son. You make it sound as if being only a chance means it doesn't matter. Well, it does matter. To me. I want to know! I need to know he'll be all right."

"And?" He glanced sidelong at her, unable to face her.

"Look around you!" she said. She pointed at the walls, at the stained carpets. "Look at this place! This is where metahumans have to live. Look at yourself! I barely know you, but I know you haven't been very happy with your life. Spirits, you've devoted your whole existence to becoming pure human again! Why should I wish this risk upon my son?"

Peter didn't know, but deeper than ever sank the feeling that his goals were askew. He thought of Thomas telling him to leave his quest behind.

"He might become an elf. They're accepted now. There's no way today to know for sure. . . ."

"And he might not. . . ."

"He might become a troll someday," he finished.

"Of course, Peter." She sighed. "Peter, this isn't about you. It's about my son."

But since he was a troll, it was about him.

"We better get some food. Some clothes," Peter said, and stood up.

"No, wait. . . ."

"Please, Kathryn. Let's leave it for now. The whole thing just has me confused right now."

* * *

They remained silent for most of the shopping expedition, speaking only when they had to confer about what to buy, how much of it to buy, where they should but it from.

They returned to the apartment with cheap clothes that would keep them warm, food to stock the refrigerator for a week, and enough bug spray and roach traps to *believe* they could make headway against the cockroaches.

They had just set up the traps and put away the groceries when a knock sounded at the door.

21

Both Peter and Kathryn froze and looked at one another. Then Kathryn ducked around a corner and Peter pulled out a gun. Not a word was spoken, not a signal given. They moved quickly and quietly. Getting into a good team pattern, Peter thought.

"Yeah," he said from one side of the doorway.

"It's me!" It was the voice of the girl they'd met the other night.

Peter undid the bolts on the door and opened it. "Wow, big gun," she said and slipped past him into the apartment.

He could see her much better than the last time, and decided his estimates of her age had been off. She was about eighteen, but a short eighteen. She was dressed in layers, her garments all overlapped at different angles and all of different colors. It was something like a harlequin outfit, but without any sense of restraint or order. Over her shoulder was slung a backpack.

Out in the hall waited Breena, the mage, slightly taller, but only a few centimeters. Peter guessed her

age as the same as Liaison's, but her face was set and
grave and a bit angry, making her look older. She wore
a black jacket tied with a large belt, heavy black stock-
ings, and black boots. The shoulders of her jacket were
so large that they distorted her body into something
too muscular-looking for her small frame. She had
pinned silver and gold brooches to the lapel of her
jacket. Fetishes, Peter guessed, to help her with her
magic.

"Come in," Peter said, stepping aside to let Breena
enter. Then he leaned though the door and looked up
and down the hall. "We weren't followed," the mage
said. "It's all clean."

"Just making sure."

"Fine. Just don't do it at the expense of my professional pride."

During the whole exchange Breena had not looked
at Peter, but eyed the apartment instead. "Drekky
place."

"We like to think so," said Kathryn, her tone sar-
donically chipper.

Breena next eyed Kathryn up and down. "You
hanging with him?" she said, jerking her thumb at
Peter.

"Yes. For now," Kathryn said with a laugh. Peter
got a bit worried. He'd dealt with people like Breena
before. If you couldn't take their self-important strut-
ting seriously, it was better not to let them know it.

"You're rich, aren't you?"

Kathryn's amusement dissolved into the floor. "Until yesterday," she said, then added hastily, "I've still
got some money. I'll be able to pay."

"Frag, Zoze wouldn't have sent us here if you
couldn't pay. I just was curious. Your clothes, your
hair. You look rich." She wandered over to a chair
and flopped into it, slinging her legs up over the arm
rest. Closing her eyes, she looked as if about to fall

asleep. Then she stretched out and asked casually, "So what's the run?"

"She's not just hanging with me. I'm working the run, too."

"Yeah. So Zoze said. So anyway, what's the gig."

"I need you to find someone," said Kathryn.

"Who?"

"Dr. William Clarris."

Liaison and Breena looked to each other to see if either knew anything about Clarris. Both shrugged.

"He's top in his field of bioresearch. He recently worked for Cell Works. He released himself from his contract, and went to work for another company."

"So we have to find him and bring him back to Cell Works."

"No," said Peter. "We just find him. Then the job's done."

Breena raised an eyebrow. Liaison said, "Sounds great to me. What have we got?"

Kathryn said, "We know he's working for a very low-profile company doing research on a project of genetic manipulation. . . ."

"Great," said Breena.

Peter stepped forward. "The project is to prevent people with the metahuman genes from becoming metahuman."

"You're kidding," Breena said, anger in her voice.

"No."

"That's impossible," said Liaison. "Too many cells. No one can manipulate the body that way."

"You can if you've got nanotechnology."

"Doesn't exist," said Liaison.

"They're working on it. And I think this project will use the technology. I've got the name of a corp in France that might be the source of the nanotech."

"I don't believe it," said Breena.

"Why not? It's been theorized for years. . . ."

"Not the nano-whatever. This business about taking the magic out of people."

Liaison looked around sheepishly as if she wanted to avoid a fight. "Phone jack?" she said. Kathryn looked around, spotted a phoneless jack by the window, and pointed to it. Liaison crossed the room and pulled gear out of her backpack.

"It's not removing the magic from someone—," said Peter.

"Sure as hell is," Breena said, and stood. "They tried it in London, in one of the slums, and turned out babies who could barely breathe."

"That was a farce," Kathryn interjected. "It was done without authorization. . . ."

"Who cares. The kids died. Or were killed by their parents when they saw they'd produced children even more 'nightmarish' than metahumans are supposed to be. Look, chummer, I don't know what your stake is in this. You don't want to be a troll, that's your hangup. But you, lady, fragging with your unborn kid. He's got no voice in this."

Kathryn's jaw dropped.

"Astral, rich lady," Breena said, and pointed to her eyes. "I checked you both out a minute ago." Peter mentally kicked himself for not realizing what the mage was doing when she'd closed her eyes in the chair. "You've got a little aura glowing inside the big aura that's you. And the little aura doesn't know jack about your plans for him."

"He's my child."

"Fine. Whatever. Liaison?"

"Wait a minute!" Kathryn said and stalked over to Breena. "You can't just start accusing me of doing something wrong, and then drop it, just like that!"

"Sure I can."

Peter looked over at Liaison, who returned the look with a shrug.

"No you can't. You're just a child. You haven't had

to make the decisions . . . the worries that come from being a parent. . . .''

The girl jerked her arm just enough to suggest she might hit Kathryn.

"Lady, I was pregnant once. Raped at fourteen. I carried the fetus for four months before I even knew it was there. I was so hungry and cold and strung-out at the time that I didn't know the symptoms were the signs of life in me, not oncoming death. When I finally figured it out, I had to decide what to do. I mean, I'm a kid, living out on the streets. I didn't have magic then to get me through it all. Didn't even know Liaison yet. Had nothing. And I'm going to bring this baby into the *world*. When I'm out there stealing sandwiches from businessmen down in the Elevated, and I got to be able to run like Coyote just to stay alive, I'm going to be toting this belly with a baby in it? I can barely protect myself, I'm fourteen. No way I can handle another person.

"And I'm this kid that has to decide to end the life of a child? I've got to get myself scraped by some gutter slag in a basement because you rich bitches have decided that the sanctity of human life allows the Feds to outlaw abortions, but you've all got med-clinics in the corps to give you what you want!

"And you're going to stand there and tell me I don't know nothing about the hard choices? That was me getting pulled out, ruined, in that basement. Not just attached to me—but me. I was only fourteen years older than the fetus. As it was being destroyed, I'm thinking, this is what the world is doing to me. And I'm doing this to my child.''

The room fell silent. Kathryn stood half a head taller than Breena, but the girl dominated her.

"I'm sorry," Kathryn said, so softly Peter barely heard the words. She looked deep into Breena's eyes.

Breena whirled around. "Don't be. Don't be sorry

for me. Be sorry for your kid.'' She turned to Liaison. ''You ready?''

Before Liaison could answer, Kathryn cut in. ''And you're going to blame me for wanting what's best for my child. For wanting to ensure that he won't be disadvantaged because of an accident of genetics?''

''No. I'm going to fault you for being intolerant.''

''It's not my intolerance,'' Kathryn said hopelessly. ''I don't want him to suffer the intolerance of the world. I need to know he'll be all right.''

''You're playing their game. Same thing, same thing.'' Breena turned back to Liaison, but Kathryn touched her arm. The girl whirled again and held up a finger to Kathryn's face. ''Don't touch.''

Peter looked to Liaison for a gauge of how dangerous the situation had become. Her eyes showed no concern, only pain that Breena hurt so much.

''All right, let's try this one,'' said Breena tersely. ''For generations, even up to today, many men have viewed women as a kind of aberration. Men view themselves as the standard of a 'normal' human. Women are less than men, and thus less than fully human. They are objects to be owned, workers who should be paid less money.

''Now, let's say someone, undoubtedly a man, came up to you and said, 'We can fix you. We can make you a man. In fact, with the technology we possess today, we don't need women for procreation anymore. We're going to wipe the disease of women away. Finally, we can have a pure human race—a race of all men.' What would your reaction be?''

''I'm all set over here,'' Liaison said weakly.

''But that's not the same thing.''

''Yes it is. Because they'll tell you that the reason all the problems exist is because we're all so different. If men didn't feel threatened by women''—here Breena cast a disparaging glance at Peter—''or whatever, these problems wouldn't exist. We make everyone the same, no differences, no problems. By refusing, you're making things worse. And what's it matter? Man, woman, same thing. You're alive, right?''

"But we're talking about metahumans."

"Women used to be locked up because of menstruation. Men created separate places for them to go because of their menstruation. They were shunned. They were monstrous. It was considered *unnatural*. That's the key. Menstruation was something that normal people didn't do. Normal people being men.''

"That's not true. Or if it is, it was a long time ago.''

"But the patterns stay. Of course you don't know about it. They're so busy shoving facts—one fact after another—into your head at those damn schools you went to that you didn't have any chance to get context. To see how the patterns all fit into place. No perspective. You know so much stuff. But you don't know how it works! Somebody is always being defined as unnatural. But that doesn't make it so.''

Another silence fell over the room. Peter decided to seize everyone's attention before the quiet could take root and blossom into another attack on Kathryn. "Well, all right. Kathryn, I guess you might have some things to think about. Breena, you've made some good points.'' She narrowed her eyes and glared at him. "But I think we should get to work now.''

"Sounds good to me,'' said Liaison brightly. Whether she was forcing the good nature or not, Peter wasn't sure. But when she picked up her deck and carried it over to the table, everyone gave her their attention. A cord ran from the deck to the phone jack. The deck resembled his portable, but it was just the keyboard—no screen.

"Isn't it a beauty?'' Liaison said proudly. "Slapped it together myself.'' She sat down and touched a red button on the side of the deck. The button lit up. Then she picked up the jack that ran from a cord in the deck and slipped it into a plug built into her temple.

"What am I looking for?"

"A corp in France. Geneering."

"Do you know their LTG number?"

"No. Sorry."

"That's all right. I'll find it. And what am I looking for inside their data banks?"

"Information about Dr. William Clarris. Um, any research projects they're sharing with a corp in Chicago. Genetic manipulations involving nanotech. . . . It's pretty vague, I know."

"Wiz," Liaison said and shrugged. "I'll do my best. Could you spell that last name?" Peter did, and she typed it into the keyboard. "Bye." She winked at Breena, tapped a few more keys, then her body went slack, as if she'd suddenly fallen asleep.

"Strange," said Kathryn.

"Yes," said Breena. "When I close my eyes and view astral space, I see the true nature of living things. When she jacks into the Matrix, she sees false images of communication lines and three-dimensional images representing data." When Breena spoke of the Matrix, her tone changed, and it was as if she considered it an unnatural opposite to astral space. Peter thought he might call her on a bit of hypocrisy, but thought the better of it.

Peter had seen deckers at work before, and had used his stupid-troll persona to pump people for details. Although Liaison seemed oblivious to the world, he knew that right now she perceived herself to be in an immense, false, computer-generated environment called the Matrix. CPUs, datastores, datalines, all existed as three-dimensional constructs she could touch and enter.

First she floated up to the Chicago Regional Telecommunications Grid and popped through to Europe. And then she started searching for Geneering's Matrix address. And she traveled just as fast as Peter was thinking about it. Once she got into the Geneering files—*if* she got in—if she wasn't stopped by intrusion countermeasures—she'd have to start rummaging through innumerable files but she wouldn't have to read them all. Peter knew Liaison had programs that would read the data for her, scan it quickly, and give her fast reports.

Nearly a half-hour passed, and the sun's light was fading. Kathryn wandered away from the table and sat off by herself in a chair across the room. Peter continued to set out roach traps.

"Strange," Breena said, watching him. "We keep coming up with ways to kill them, and they keep changing to stay one step ahead of us. All the magic, all the tech, but cockroaches, they're still with us."

Liaison's hand suddenly came to life as she frantically slapped a red button on her deck. Her eyes popped open and she ripped the jack out of her head. "Now!" she hissed. "We're out of here now!"

22

Breena shot across the room and began to shove Liaison's gear back into her knapsack.

"What?" Kathryn and Peter asked in unison.

"Found Geneering," Liaison said in a staccato voice, grabbing the knapsack from Breena and putting the deck inside. "But the port was too obvious. Looked some more for a back door. Found it. Ran some browse programs." She went over to the window, looked outside, seemed satisfied, and crossed to the door. "Found a data file with the doc's name on it. Very cold. Looked good. I opened it and found another big file about nanotech protos being loaned out for a bioresearch job in Chicago. Before I could read it, a home-court decker showed up. He stalled me while the system launched a White Wolf. . . ."

"White Wolf?" asked Peter.

"Trace program. They're onto us," said Kathryn.

"They're in *France*," said Peter.

"But they've got a deal with a corp in town," Kathryn told him.

Peter shot a quick look around the room. So much for the cockroaches.

Then came the unmistakable sound of chopper blades in the distance.

He jumped for the window and pulled the shade back. "There's a Stallion heading this way."

"Metro?" asked Liaison.

"Yup."

"Okay. That's okay. We can avoid them."

"Wait a minute," he said. Outside he saw another chopper coming from the south. "Crusader Security is on the way, too."

"Metro will sign the job over to them," Kathryn said.

"Yeah. They're going to make a stink," said Peter. "We'd better move now."

Liaison pulled a Scorpion machine pistol from out of the backpack.

Peter opened the door, and everyone streamed from the apartment toward a stairway at the back of the building.

"We've got to get out of this area fast. I don't want a repeat of the last C raid on a project," said Peter.

"What . . . ?" said Kathryn.

"Not now," Peter said.

They hit the door to the stairs and Liaison started down. "No. Up, for now," Peter said. Liaison looked to Breena, who nodded. The sound of a door being smashed open echoed up the bare cinder-block stair-well.

Liaison led the group, then came Breena and Kath-ryn. Peter held back, making sure everyone was all right.

Suddenly he heard a child say, "Hey, what are you pinks doing here?" He looked up and saw a nine-year-old troll looking down the stairs at them. Then the child spotted the guns, and screamed as he ran off through the landing door.

From below, Peter heard several pairs of boot-clad feet running up the stairs.

"Frag," he sighed.

Liaison set herself against the central banister, her Scorpion pointed down the stairs. Kathryn stopped, but Breena said, "Come on. Just keep moving until you're near the door up there. If things hose up, just run." Then Breena took a step back and waited for the guards.

Peter tensed, the anticipation of battle warming him. Crusader was a pure humans-only crowd. And one thing Peter had learned over the years was that he loved to take down pure humans armed with guns; no other group had caused him so much pain. When he was one of them again, he would open his liberal heart and worry about the unjust treatment of anyone by anyone. But for now . . .

Liaison fired off three shots before the first guard had cleared the bend in the stairs. The first two hit the guard's black armor, doing little damage. But Liaison was targeting with each shot, raising her aim a bit on each one. The final slug ripped through the man's neck, sending him reeling back. He grabbed at the wound, and blood spurted through his fingers.

His companion stayed back beneath the stairs.

"West stairway, fourth floor," the second shouted into his mike. "Armed. Dangerous."

Nervous, the guard leaned forward and fired his HK227 submachine gun on full auto.

Liaison jumped back. The bullets chewed concrete splinters from the wall.

"Let's move it," Peter said just above the racket of the HK. "Up one flight, over to the other side of the building, and down."

The women ran up the stairs. Peter held his position to give them some time; then he squeezed off two shots before racing up after them.

By the time he hit the fifth floor, they were already halfway down the corridor.

Breena and Liaison had just passed the elevator banks when a stairwell door next to the elevators opened.

A guard looked out, and Kathryn came to a dead stop, just few steps away from the man. He looked surprised, then raised his HK227.

Peter had no idea whether or not the guard would shoot, but he called out "Hey!" before anyone had to find out. The guard pulled the trigger of his HK227 even as he turned toward Peter. Rounds bounced off the walls and pierced the flimsy doors of the surrounding apartments. Kathryn dropped to the ground. Screams filled the air.

Peter leaped to the other side of the corridor, away from the bullets, then dove to the floor. A flash of blue light filled his peripheral vision, and he thought the guard had pulled out a taser like those used by cops years earlier. Instead of feeling pain, however, he heard a gun clatter to the floor. Looking up, Peter saw the guard clutch at his face, the flesh turning to ooze and dripping down his neck. The man stood there, suspended by reflex for a moment, then collapsed and lay still.

Far down the corridor stood Breena, her hands still crackling with blue energy. Kathryn looked at the fallen man, then quickly turned away.

"Move, move!" Peter hissed and rushed over to Kathryn to help her up. "He didn't get a chance to call in. He might be the only one up here." Passing the guard, Peter scooped up the HK227.

They ran down the corridor. Just as they reached the stairwell, they heard the sound of autofire below them.

"What are they shooting at?" said Kathryn, after checking to make sure the group was still together.

"They're hitting the apartments," Peter growled, running down the stairs. Liaison and Breena rushed after him. "You three keep going!" he shouted back. "I'll draw them out and catch up to you. KEEP GO-ING!"

As the women continued past him, he heard Kathryn say with shortened breath, "I don't understand."

When he hit the fourth-floor landing, Peter slammed into the door and out into the corridor. Screams and cries filled the air. To his right and left guards were smashing open doors and firing autofire bursts. Some laughed.

"Hey!" Peter shouted. He turned to the right and shot a full clip down the length of the corridor into four guards. "Can't you pervos even aim at the right targets!"

Each of the guards caught a bullet and sprawled backward onto the hall floor. Guns firing from the left sent rounds into Peter's duster. The rounds slammed him hard, shooting new pain through the wounds he'd picked up in the Shattergraves, but his duster and natural armor kept the bullets from penetrating his flesh.

He just had to remember to get Breena to heal him.

Peter jumped back to the safety of the stairwell. He made it look like he was beating a hasty retreat, but once out of sight, he leaned back into the corridor and fired at the guards rushing in pursuit toward the stairwell. He caught the two lead guards full in the chest.

The bullets tore up their armor, and they fell back into the guards behind them.

One guard, who had been right behind the lead two, caught Peter's eye as he fell back. The man was a pure human, but he seemed to have the face of pig. For just an instant his eyes locked with Peter's, and all Peter saw in them was the most profound loathing.

He dropped the spent gun and fled down the stairs, pulling the Predator out of his holster as he ran.

Just as he was clearing the second-floor landing, he heard the landing door behind him. He tried to turn and get off a shot, but as he grabbed at the banister for support, the world around him suddenly shifted wildly. Dark shadows filled the stairwell. The stairs beneath his feet seemed to turn to rubber and he stumbled down them, crashing into the cement wall. Out the corner of his eye, he thought he saw a figure moving, now red and warm, just a shadow. His father? Billy? He looked up and saw a man with fetishes pinned to his armored chest slip back into the second-floor hallway, then close the door behind him.

Peter tried to put his hand to the floor, but missed. And missed again. And again. Finally he got up. He took a few steps toward the stairs and fell again. The walls bent in toward him. He wanted to scream out in rage, but couldn't find his voice.

A mage had done this to him. The man. Hiding now. Sustaining the spell. Waiting for the guards to come for Peter. He looked down toward the first-floor landing. An exit sign hung over the door. Maybe he could fall down the stairs and out the door.

Then what? He'd never find Breena and what's-their-names as long as his hands kept melting into his chest.

He had to take the mage out, or he was as good as dead.

Peter rolled back to the stairs and crawled up, very, very carefully. He kept his eyes shut, trying to keep out random sensory-feed. From the stairs above came the clatter of boots, guards getting closer.

He tried not to panic, but the world turned over on itself, and Peter thought he would vomit. He sent a hand toward the landing above him and dragged himself up. The doorknob was just above him. All he had to do was touch it. But it seemed so far away, as if he'd shrunk to a very small size. He glanced back down the stairs and thought he'd never been so high up before. If he fell, he knew he would never stop falling. He would fall and fall and stare at the bottom and see the impact coming forever.

His hand finally made contact with the doorknob, and he pulled it open. He fell into the hall and turned to his right. There stood the mage right next to him, looking down at Peter in surprise. Outside Peter heard the clatter of the guards' boots.

"I . . .," said Peter. But he had nothing else to say. He reached out his hand and tried to grab the magician, but the man stepped back and Peter's arm melted into the floor. Or he thought it did. He knew it was a lie. All he had to do was figure out where the image ended and reality began. Or did it matter? If he really thought his hand melted into the floor, what difference did it make if he thought it was illusion? He began to giggle. Maybe it mixed somewhere in the middle.

The door behind him opened. He rolled over and looked up at two Crusader security guards, their HKs pointed down at him. They seemed gigantic, yet like children, little boys playing by sandbox rules, but armed with real guns.

"Bye, trog," one of them said.

Then another door from along the corridor opened and Peter heard the thunderous roar of a shotgun. A spray of pellets knocked the guards against the wall.

Peter suddenly felt much better. He glanced right and saw the mage moving his arms to cast another spell, something to take out an ork with a shotgun standing in the doorway behind Peter. Peter swung his gun around. Somehow it was still miraculously in his hand, and he was able to drop the mage with two shots.

The two guards were back up now, their armor having protected them from serious damage. But before they could get off their shots, the ork fired another shell, and Peter slammed them with several more rounds, the crack of the shots firing one after another. They staggered a moment, then fell to the ground.

Peter stood up woozily and faced the ork. "Thanks."

"Just get out, quick." The ork smiled, checked the corridor, and ducked back inside.

When Peter hit the first floor, he pushed wide the exit door and rushed into the snow, at the same moment hearing a car screech around the corner of the building. It was an Ares Master van, painted black, but he knew it was a Crusader vehicle. Peter raised his gun and fired into the windshield, but the bullets merely bounced off.

The van came to a skidding halt facing him, and Peter heard the back doors open. Glancing around desperately for an escape, he saw that the door he'd just exited had locked behind him. As he turned back, ready to give the guards a final fight, he saw a fireball rushing from behind a distant dumpster straight into the rear of the van.

Breena was very good.

He hit the snow and covered his face.

The next instant came a loud explosion and a wave of heat washing over him, followed by screams. Looking up, Peter saw the snow around the van had melted away. Torn bodies lay scattered in a clean radius from the blast point, streaks of blood melting through the snow.

As he was getting up, Peter saw Liaison behind the dumpster. She signaled him to keep moving to the right, over toward a building at the project's northeast corner.

At her signal, he began to run. Even though he heard the door of the building open behind him, he knew he couldn't look back. Getting to cover was all that mattered now. It was all right, though. Liaison was taking shots at the security guards and had driven them back into the building.

Peter ducked behind a dumpster for a quick glance back, then a few seconds later he was around the corner of the building, breathing hard. The area was clear, probably because the explosion and machine gun fire had sent everyone running for cover.

Breena, Liaison, and Kathryn rounded the other side of the building at a run. Peter thought Breena looked as though the effort was almost too much for her; the fireball had knocked the wind out of her. "Frag, that was lucky," she mumbled. "A mage in that van."

"Plan?" asked Peter.

"Car. Go," answered Liaison.

"Where'd you park?"

"Down there." She gestured down the street.

"Great," he said and the four took off at a run once more.

One of the guards spotted them just as they reached the car, a gray Ford Americar. He pulled up his gun and fired. Bullets splashed through the snow and raced up to Peter just as he slipped into the back seat. The car, re-tooled for moments like this, bounced the bullets off its body panels. Liaison put the car in gear and shot down the road.

"How is everyone?" asked Peter.

Breena was breathing heavily, but said, "Fine."

"Fine," said Liaison.

He felt Kathryn tightly crammed against his right. The heat of the action and the warmth of her body twisted in him like an aphrodisiac. He looked at her closely. Her eyes were like glass, her breathing deep and steady. "You all right?"

"Uh-huh," she said.

"All right," said Peter, pulling himself up to a more dignified position. "Let's hit the Crusader headquarters."

"What do you mean, hit the Crusader headquarters?" demanded Breena, suddenly alert.

"I mean, the clue we need to find Clarris is in that building."

"Yeah," said Liaison. "They'll have a record of the phone call that came in to send the guards after us. It'll give us the name of the corp, the address—at least a telecom code. Crusader keeps all contact data in cold storage. I've tried getting in before." Driving madly down the street, she turned to look briefly at Breena. "If we want it, we make a house call."

"We've got two elements working for us," Peter said. "A lot of their men are out of the base and looking for us. . . ."

"Exactly!" said Breena testily.

"And second, Crusader's not going to expect us to show up in their own back yard."

"Makes sense to me," said Liaison. Breena gave her a look that said she was no more than a child and should wait a few more years before offering opinions.

"The place is built like a fortress," said Breena. "The tower guards are armed with MAG-5 machine guns. They're just ready and waiting for somebody to try what you're suggesting. They've planned for it."

Peter punched the ceiling of the car with his fist.

"Hey, watch the merchandise!" shouted Liaison.

"Breena, listen, we don't have a choice. The closest link we've got is in France, and Liaison got bounced out of it. That's it. Our only other lead is in the Crusader building. It *had* to be the Chicago company that called them in. If you can think of something else, great, but I can't."

Kathryn looked up at Peter with a bit of a smile, then nodded her head proudly.

Breena thought about it for a moment. "Yes. But it sounds really stupid."

"It is stupid, Breena," said Liaison. "That's the fun part. Being smart enough to live through something really stupid."

"So we need a plan, right?" said Kathryn. Peter glanced at her. She seemed to be getting into it.

"Yes," he said.

Kathryn and Breena looked at him. Liaison glanced at him in the rear-view mirror. "Well, Profezzur, you got the idea. You come up with a plan."

Peter nodded and smiled at her through the mirror. "Null perspiration, chummer," he said, recalling a phrase from the streets, and Breena laughed.

23

By the time they got to the lower end of the Northside, dark clouds had rolled in over Chicago and snow had begun to fall again.

Liaison pulled the armored Americar into an alley a few blocks from the Crusader complex, then she and Breena went around to the trunk and opened it.

Peter turned to Kathryn. "You going to be all right?"

"Me? All I have to do is guard Breena. Are you going to be all right?"

"I don't know." And he laughed a full, joyous laugh. "You know, I don't know." Freeing himself from the Itami gang made him giddy. He felt his life finally on track, reaching a culmination.

"You are a very strange man."

Breena slammed her fist against the window to get their attention. "Show time!" she called out.

Peter opened the door and got out. Breena slipped by him to take a seat in the car, then closed her eyes. "You going to check it out astrally?" Peter asked.

"Nope," she said, eyes closed. "I know they've got a ward up, and if I try to investigate, all I'll do is risk tripping it. Your shag should get by their astral security because it doesn't depend on an astral search. It's insane, and I don't like it, but if we want to catch them off guard, this might do it. They might also have an elemental on guard. But we took down two magicians at Byrne—there's a good chance one of them summoned the elemental. If so, the elemental is gone now. So, you and Liaison are going in cold."

Liaison rolled her eyes a bit to suggest that Breena just worried too much. Then Peter watched Breena as she relaxed her breathing and began to raise her hands. Small, blue sparks popped off her flesh, the sparks increasing in number until they blocked her hands from view.

Liaison stepped up and pulled on Peter's arm, indicating that he should get out of the way. When he stepped aside, Liaison leaned into the car. Breena opened her eyes and smiled at her. "Goodbye," she said, and the two of them opened their mouths slightly and kissed.

They held the kiss as Breena touched Liaison's cheeks, the blue sparks flowing from her hands and drifting over Liaison's flesh. As the sparks passed over Liaison, that part of her body vanished from sight. Breena closed her eyes again. Soon she was kissing empty air.

The blue sparks floated down around Liaison's waist, down her legs, until she had completely disappeared.

Peter guessed Liaison had pulled away when Breena

closed her mouth. She stared out the front window with a contented and dazed smile.

"Here," said Liaison, her voice floating out of thin air. A gun appeared on Breena's lap. "That's for you, Kathryn," she said. "Keep her safe. Oh, and see that small box on her hip?"

Kathryn nodded.

"That's her talkie with me. Push the button there—right. When I give the signal, it's time. Got it."

"Yes."

The voice addressed Peter again. "Ready?"

Peter saw a flicker of Liaison's form when he turned to where the voice had come from. "I can see you. I mean, I saw you, just for an instant."

"It's just an illusion spell. You know I'm here, so the illusion isn't that strong for you. It'll hold against everyone else. Or it should." She paused, then added, "But we won't know until we get there. Ready?"

"Sure."

"Give me your gun."

He pulled the Predator from its holster, and held it out. Peter felt Liaison's hand take it, then let go. The moment he did, the gun vanished from sight.

"What have you got?" he asked.

"I took an Uzi from the trunk."

"You don't fool around."

"Nope. Zoze armed us for Bear. Ready?"

He took off his holster, but kept the lined duster. "Let's go."

As they walked out of the alley, Peter said, "Does she have to kiss you to do the magic?"

Liaison laughed. "No. It just gives her a rush. I don't know. I guess you have to be there." After a pause, she asked, "Are you sure they're not going to connect you with the fight at Byrne?"

"Positive. Trust me. To these guys all trolls look alike."

* * *

Peter screamed.

He shouted.

He staggered and danced down the street.

When he was thirty meters from the Crusader head-quarters, he laughed and yelled, "Bear! I wish I could find me some soft-fleshed faggots, three or four of 'em to make it fair, to give me a good fight! I can't stand the soft folk anymore. All mushy and wet when you cut 'em!"

A thick wall of brick topped with wire surrounded the complex. At the center of the compound was a smooth, sterile-looking building three stories high. It reminded him of people, smooth people, pure humans, needing everything clean and featureless and as boring as death. He noticed several narrow slits for gunners built into a stone facade on the roof of the building.

He laughed again.

A spotlight snapped on from a tower at the corner of the compound. The spot quickly found him, washing over him and creating a glowing disk three meters in diameter.

Peter stopped and stared down at the ground, as if confused by the light. Then he knelt and touched the ground, carefully, like a drunken scientist suddenly fascinated by a flower.

"Hey, drekhead!" someone from the tower shouted. "Slot it!"

Peter looked up and around, looking for angels that surrounded him. He staggered toward the tower from which the light shone. The spotlight followed him, making Peter stop in his tracks to look down again. He took two steps forward. The light followed. He took three steps to the right. He was a child who has just discovered his shadow.

"Looks like you're having fun," said Liaison from just outside the edge of the light.

"I AM!" he screamed. "Cause I hate soft, stupid flesh!"

He danced around the street, leading the light on a merry chase, stopping suddenly sometimes, trying to confuse it.

"SLOT IT OUT OF HERE NOW!" The voice boomed from a loudspeaker.

"Who is that?" Peter yelled.

"LEAVE THE AREA!"

"Are you a softie? You got that soft flesh I love to squoosh?"

A few guards poked their heads over the top of the wall.

"Can I scrag him?" one shouted.

"NO!" came the loudspeaker voice.

Another voice shouted, "We're going to have enough trouble with Byrne. Let him buzz off."

Peter pointed at one of the men on the wall. "Are you a *coward?* Are you? You a coward? Come on! Come down and fight me!"

The men scowled at him, but didn't budge.

"Fraggin' cowards. Afraid to take on a troll unless you can do it by shooting me down with your fancy guns. You fraggers! I'll take four of you at once. That's right. Four of you."

The men looked at one another.

"Five!" Peter shouted. "I'll show you fraggin' wastes of carbon who should be running things. Or are you too busy pulling on each other back there?"

The heads dropped down behind the wall. There was a moment of loud arguing, and then the gate unlocked.

"Bye," said Liaison.

As the gate opened, it revealed eight guards. Three of them held rifles pointed at Peter.

"Hey!" said Peter, laughing and raising his arms. One of the men, apparently the leader, smiled at Peter.

He held a tape recorder up in front of him. "You want to fight?"

"Yeah!"

"You sure you want to fight?"

"Sure I'm sure, drekbrain."

"Just because it's fun, right?"

"Right. 'Course, I won't mind mashing your soft little pink heads into little pink pudding. But that's just me."

The leader switched off the tape recorder and handed it to one of the men with a rifle. "No weapons. Just hand to hand."

"Sure. Whatever." Thank the spirits, Peter thought.

The leader nodded to two of the men without rifles. They walked up to Peter and frisked him. They were good at their job. "Clean," one said, finally.

"All right," said the leader, drawing something out of his pocket. "Five on one. Right?"

"Right."

"Great."

Peter saw each of the men place studded knuckles on his hands. "Hey, wait a minute. . . ."

"Say what, chummer?"

"You get those."

"Yeah?"

"I don't get nothing."

"Right, and you're not going to get nothing. You don't want this to be to easy, do you?"

"What do you mean?" Peter said, stalling for time. He was almost certain, but not positive, he could still take the guards on. But maybe if he kept them talking long enough, Liaison would be back out with the data and he could skip the whole thing.

"I mean, you're a big strong troll. We're just puny 'softs,' right?"

"Right. But . . ."

They were on him with a quick rush.

Though Peter moved quickly, his opponents worked

well as a team, cutting off a possible dodge to either side. A pain sliced at his shoulder, and in that instant he remembered Breena hadn't healed him yet. A sudden dread passed through him.

He moved to the right and shoved himself forward, hoping to bowl over the guard that charged toward him.

He and the guard crashed into each other, but Peter had mass on his side. He hurled himself into the man and slammed him down onto the snow-covered pavement.

Peter tried to keep his feet free of the man, but tripped and stepped into the guard's groin. The man howled, and Peter stumbled low to the ground for a few steps.

In that time the other guards had gathered around him and were slamming their fists into his back. He tried to twist away from the blows, but he ran short of maneuvering room and the guards nailed several punches into his spine. A sharp pain ran up and down his back, and for a moment he couldn't see.

Their studded knuckles weren't just metal. They also had some kind of electrical shock. Peter had never seen anything like them before. His vision cleared just as he slammed into the ground. He brought up his hands to block his fall, but his palms slid across the snow and his face crashed into the pavement. He rolled over quickly, but the guards came in fast to batter his abdomen and face with swift kicks. The damage was light, but Peter knew it would take its toll. Was this really the best plan available?

He swung his arms wide (like making angels in the snow, he thought crazily) and smashed the ankles of the guards with his fists. They fell onto the street with loud grunts. While they rolled on the ground, Peter scrambled up. Lifting his head, he came face to face with the first guard he'd knocked over, who was also just getting up.

The guard swung his fist up again, but this time Peter blocked the blow with one hand and punched the man in the jaw with the other. The guard staggered back several meters and fell onto his back.

Peter whirled around to face off against the rest of the guards. He'd taken his blows, but now he felt in the spirit of the occasion. Even his pain had dissipated, dispelled by a rush of adrenaline.

The guards got to their feet, but then stood swaying a bit. Peter balled his hands into fists. A warm pleasure ran through his thoughts. He knew he could take the fraggers who'd shot up Byrne, and take them up close.

"Peter. There's a problem," Liaison said softly to his right.

"You're not fragging kidding," Peter screamed. He jumped a bit, and the guards took it as fear. They stood a bit straighter.

Peter grunted. He pulled back slightly, cutting around to the right to keep Liaison out of earshot of the guards. He moved slowly enough that they didn't chase him.

"There's no way into the building. The door is locked and has a combo lock on it. There's no way to pick it with all the guards walking around the compound. They won't see me, but they'll see the exposed electronics when I pull the face plate off."

Peter grunted again. "Just wait!" he shouted at the guards. Then he added softly, "For someone to go inside."

"I did. Almost everyone outside the building is watching the fight, though some of them are still watching the perimeter. Everyone inside is probably watching the fight over cameras."

Peter glanced up at the walls of the compound. Guards stood on the gunnery platforms and watched the proceedings through barbed wire.

"And I don't think we've got time for someone to get bored and wander back into the building."

The sound of chopper blades filled the air. Peter looked up and saw a Stallion flying in from the north. Probably the one from Byrne returning after the search.

"Right!" Peter screamed. "I'll show you pervos just like my brother showed you up in Byrne."

The guards all lowered their fists.

"What are you doing?" Liaison whispered harshly.

"What?" demanded Peter of the guards.

The leader raised his hand and pointed at Peter. "Your brother was at Byrne?"

"You bet. He wasted a half dozen of you pervos!"

The two guards by the door raised their rifles. Peter braced himself for the impact of the bullet. The leader shouted, "Wait! You! Get your hands up."

"What?" Peter said stupidly.

"Get your hands up, you trog!"

Peter raised his hands. "Aren't we going to fight?"

"No. Where's your brother now?"

Peter laughed. "I'm not going to tell you that. He's my . . ."

"Shut up! Where is he?"

"I told you, I'm not going to tell you. Come on," he said, and lowered his hands and balled them into fists. "Let's fight."

Each of the guards with rifles fired at the ground by Peter's feet.

"Hey!"

"Tell me now."

"BRING HIM INSIDE. WE'LL STRAP HIM."

"Get your hands back up, and move in through the gate."

Peter did.

24

They led him at gunpoint to the door of the building, where the leader punched in the keypad combination. The man blocked Peter's view, but he hoped Liaison could see it.

The door opened and Peter entered. With luck Liaison also made it through with the group.

The men in the building glared at him with cold expressions.

They led him into a small room with unpainted cinder-block walls. In the middle of the room was a large chair equipped with thick straps. On a table to the left rested several machines that Peter couldn't identify.

Second, third, and fourth thoughts about the wisdom of his plan began to fill Peter's mind.

"Sit down."

With feigned confusion, Peter asked, "Why?"

"Spirits! You are stupid, aren't you? Do it because I said so!"

"But why . . . ?"

One of the guards slammed the butt of his rifle into Peter's back. Peter's spine was getting quite sore. He decided to comply, and hoped to stall in the chair.

Once he was seated, several guards set about wrapping the straps around his wrists and ankles, his waist and his neck. Peter thought of the hospital, and for an instant he thought of the guards as the orderly.

Helplessness seeped through his body.

"Give me the box," said the leader.

One of the guards pulled a rotting wooden box off the table. A hand crank rose from its top, and two cables coiled out from something that looked like a generator.

"This one is a bit old-fashioned, but we've found it does wonders for trogs like you." One guard wrapped a cable around Peter's neck just above the strap, another wrapped the second cable around his right wrist. The bare cables felt cold and smooth against his skin.

Peter realized they had tied him to a primitive taser.

The leader held the box in his right hand and took the handle of the crank in his left, then began to turn the crank very slowly. Peter watched the magnets in the generator also move very slowly, and as they moved around he felt a tingle at his wrist and around his neck. His neck and arm muscles felt warm and frozen and prickly. It was gentle, but threatening.

He didn't want the torture to go on.

"Aren't you going to ask me questions?"

"Not yet. First I want to hurt you, like your brother hurt my men."

"It wasn't me that hurt them." He felt an edge of pleading in his voice, and was ashamed of it.

"And I wasn't one of the guys who got hurt. It doesn't matter."

Something in the man's words got caught in Peter's mind, and for an instant he thought about Thomas. But before he could pursue the notion, the leader turned the handle quickly around. Peter's back arched as the jolt shot through his spine. His fingers spread out and became so taut that he thought they might snap off his hand. His neck strained at the strap holding him down. He realized he was choking himself, but could not control his actions.

All he could hear was the whirring of the rusted hand crank and the sound of his own choked breath.

The leader stopped.

"Pretty impressive for low tech, huh?"

Peter gasped for air, unable to answer. "Please . . ."

The crank turned again, and once more Peter felt his body straining against his bonds. He imagined the muscles in his neck bulging out through his flesh, bloated and ruined.

The leader relented once more. Peter went slack in the chair.

"Now, what did we just learn? You don't speak unless I ask you a question. Got it?"

Peter wanted to answer, but it was as if his face were too far away to make his mouth work.

"One more lesson . . ."

Once more the crank turned. This time his arm began to shake uncontrollably. When the cranking stopped, his muscles did not. The arm kept shaking and shaking.

"When I ask you something, you answer. Got it?"

"Y . . . y . . . yes," Peter stuttered out. It took immense effort to speak the words. He didn't know how they expected him to answer their questions like this. A thought worked its way back through his head. Maybe they didn't expect him to. Maybe they could punish him more for failing.

"Now, where is your brother?"

He knew he shouldn't just answer, he had to stall for Liaison. But if he kept lying . . . ?

The door opened.

Thank Bear, he thought. A reprieve. A moment of distraction.

With great effort he turned his face toward the newcomer.

Pig-face.

The man's face was harsh and determined and weary. He smiled as he looked to the other men in the room. A true sadness passed among the assembly, a silent respect for their fallen comrades.

Peter thought for sure he was dead now.

He felt something press against his boot.

He glanced down. The strap around his left ankle slowly slid out of its buckle.

Liaison.

He started to breathe comfortably.

"I hear you've got the brother of the troll."

"That's right," said the leader.

Pig-face stepped forward.

Peter felt Liaison working on the other ankle strap.

"All right, you," Pig-face began, but stopped short.

Peter turned his head away from Pig-face.

"Wait a minute. . . ."

Pig-face grabbed Peter's head with both his hands and jerked Peter's face toward him. The motion came abruptly, and it felt as if the man had snapped the muscles of Peter's neck. His neck shook uncontrollably, feeling as though it would never stop. He wanted to cry out, but he could not control his tongue.

"This is the trog."

"What?"

"This is the same troll. This is HIM! Same duster, same trog face. Same broken horn. This isn't his brother. This *is* the bastard."

In one quick motion Pig-face had his pistol out and the barrel pointed at Peter's head.

"Good bye, trog."

A spray of autofire appeared out of thin air, riddling Pig-face's chest with red blotches.

"You're up, Prof," Liaison screamed. His Predator also appeared from thin air and landed on his lap. He realized that in the last few moments Liaison had freed his left hand.

The guards, startled by the invisible assailant, gawked stupidly for a moment before pulling out their guns and looking around. None of them noticed the gun in Peter's lap.

The guards fired in the direction of the shots, but, of course, Liaison had scrambled over to the other side of the room by that time.

Peter grabbed the gun and began to fire just as Liaison cut a line of lead across the chests of the guards. The guards returned fire. Peter, still trapped by the neck, waist, and one arm, had no way to dodge. Three slugs hit him in the chest and knocked the air out of him. For a moment he was aware only of the sound of a great deal of gunfire.

When he looked up, all the guards were on the ground, some dead, some dying.

"Come on," Liaison said. She worked the strap around his neck and waist, while Peter clumsily took the strap off his right wrist. Liaison kept saying over and over again, "Breena, Breena, Breena," in a soft, reverent, and hopeful voice.

An alarm bell rang.

"Frag!" she shouted.

"It's all right," Peter said, still so winded from the shots that he had absolutely no idea what was going on, let alone whether everything was all right or not. "My chest," he wheezed.

"Oh, that does look bad," said Liaison.

"Good. I'll try to keep that in mind."

"Ready?"

"No. Let's go."

"Open the door for me. I'll duck across the hall."

Peter opened the door, but kept behind it. He waited a beat, then stuck his head out and took pot shots at guards coming up from the front of the building. The guards turned their guns on him, then moved up the hall when Peter ducked back into the room. As they advanced, Liaison opened fire, catching them all off guard. She cut them down, all the while shouting, "Now! Now!"

Peter rushed out of the torture room and down the hall. He knew Liaison ran alongside him, because every few moments a spray of bullets appeared from mid-air and slammed guards against the corridor walls.

They reached the front door. "It's locked," she said. A key pad identical to the one outside was on the wall to the left of the door. "Frag!"

"Did you see the combination when we came in?"

"What?"

"Did you see the combination when we came in? Did you see the combination?"

"Yeah? So?"

"Try it."

"What?"

"Try it. It might be the same."

He felt her shove her Uzi into his right hand. The hand was still numb, but he could control his muscles again. He turned and fired the gun down the hall, pinning the remaining guards in doorways.

"Nothing," said Liaison.

"What?"

"Nothing, Prof. What the frag is the point of having two locks with the same combo?"

"Never mind." He dropped his pistol and raked the face plate off the wall with his left hand. "Fry it. We don't have to worry about setting off any alarms."

Some guards grabbed the opportunity created by Peter's cease-fire. Bullets flew down the hall and slammed around the doorway. Liaison gave out a scream, and a splash of blood spattered the wall.

"Damn," Peter said under his breath. "You all right?"

"Not for much longer."

Peter turned his back to the guards and raised his duster to block Liaison from the shots of the guards. He twisted his body to shoot the Uzi down the corridor.

He glanced at the lock, where he could see the wires moving around as if alive. "Frag, that hurt," she gasped.

"Almost home. Almost home."

"Oh, that's right." Liaison shouted into the talkie. "Kathryn! Now, Kathryn! Let's go!"

The guards had maneuvered into better positions, and were firing one shot after another into Peter's back. He felt himself dangerously close to passing out.

He looked down again and saw Liaison appear. She placed one wire against another. The door opened. "YES!"

They ran out through the door toward the closed gate, bullets from the guard tower ripping up the ground around them. A few rounds caught Liaison in the thigh, and she stumbled to the ground.

Peter stopped and ran back for her. She was clutching her wound, and saying, "Oh, Breena. Please, please, don't let me die." He dropped the Uzi, picked her up in his massive arms, and continued to run for the gate.

Getting closer, he eyeballed his chances. The gate was solid metal and set on wheels. The car wouldn't be able to break through it. He'd have to get over it on his own.

He began to pick up speed, running madly for the gate. Desperately ignoring the pain that racked his body, he forced himself to think only of getting over the gate, getting into the car, driving away, seeing Kathyrn. . . . Thinking of anything but the present moment. He shifted Liaison's limp body to his left arm. Though he hurt bad, his massive troll muscles supported her slight frame.

He got to the wall and leaped as high as he could. As he jumped he heard the squeal of the car stopping outside the wall.

His chest slammed against the metal of the gate. His right hand grabbed instinctively for the wire just above his head, and the barbs dug deep into his palm. He bit his lip against the pain and, with one arm, dragged himself up onto the gate. He wasn't sure he was going to make it.

"What the frag is happening?" Liaison said in a daze.

From the other side he heard Kathryn shout, "I don't know how," and Breena screamed, "Just do it!"

Machine gun fire cut through the night air from the street side of the wall. A fireball rose from the base of the wall and shot through the night straight into the guard tower. The searchlight exploded and the guards were thrown to the ground far below.

Peter got himself to the top of the gate and ripped the wire out of his way. He pulled Liaison onto his lap. The Americar was just under him now, Kathryn firing an Uzi at another guard tower while Breena stood leaning against the hood.

Just as he was balancing himself to jump to the ground, a thick spray of bullets caught him in the back and knocked him off his feet. As he fell, all Peter could think of was keeping Liaison safe. He held her out in his arm to keep from crushing her when he hit the ground.

The sidewalk arrived sooner than he expected it to. At first he thought his spine had snapped in two, then realized it was no more than immense pain. With one final effort of will, he got up from the ground and onto his feet.

"What happened to her?" Breena demanded, as Peter put Liaison in the car.

"Not now," he shouted. "Let's go!"

Kathryn ran around to the front passenger seat. Peter pushed Liaison further over along the passenger side and climbed in behind her.

When he looked back, Breena was standing motionless, red and orange sparks glowing all around her hands.

"If you blow yourself on a spell, we're not going anywhere."

"If they can catch us, it doesn't matter how soon we leave."

She opened her eyes and stared up into the sky. Peter followed her gaze and saw the chopper rising up from behind the wall. Breena raised her hands and flung a fireball at it. The ball sped through the air, then slammed into the craft's cabin.

A terrible explosion tore through the chopper. The blast threw the guards out into the air, their uniforms in flames. A second explosion cut through the engine, sending shards of metal flying in all directions.

Breena got into the car and slammed the door shut. "That felt fragging good," she said to no one in particular, then kicked the car into drive.

As they rushed away Peter saw the gate open and a Westwind, a SAAB Dynamit, and a Leyland-Rover van come out after them.

"We've got company."

"Put Liaison on the floor and pull down the seat."

Peter obeyed, though doing so was difficult because of his size. When he got the seat down, he saw that it opened into the trunk. His jaw dropped when he saw the mobile arsenal stored within it; grenades, launchers, light machine guns.

"I don't know how to use half this stuff," he called up to Breena.

She pushed the gas pedal down hard to gain distance.

"I think the Vindicator minigun is your speed, buckeroo. Pass a box of grenades up to Red, here."

Peter fished out the box and passed it to Kathryn. "What are you doing with a Vindicator in the car?" he said. "Can you even use this thing?"

"Zoze said we might need it, so I took it."

He handed the box to Kathryn, who took it carefully. "All right. What do I do?" she asked.

"First, relax. Thirty years ago you didn't know how to use a credstick to buy a business suit. You learn as you go."

"I'm only twenty-eight," she mumbled.

Bullets from the cars behind them slammed into the rear window. Some bounced off. Others exploded.

"Oh, frag!" exclaimed Breena.

Peter pulled up the Vindicator and saw that the belt snaked its way into a full box sitting in the trunk. Other cables led to a heavy battery belt with a red rocker switch on one of the battery packs. He thumbed it. The mass of metal in his arms began to vibrate and hum as the six heavy barrels at its front started turning. The dull hum quickly grew in pitch as the barrels picked up speed. He barely heard Breena instructing Kathryn as he tried to get a bead on the guards behind them. "Just pull the pins and drop them. They'll race up and go off. We don't need to be accurate, we just want to give them a very, very good scare. Hang on, though. I'm going to have to go pretty fast to get the timing to work out."

She drove the car down the entrance ramp to I-94. The instant she completed the turn, Breena slammed down on the gas, steadily pushing the speed from 130, to 140, to 150 kilometers per hour. The guards pursued. More explosive shells hit the rear window, creating a web of running fissures.

"Now you fragging pikers! NOW!"

Peter maneuvered the weapon out the left window, hooked his fingernail on the trigger, and fired the machine gun at the Leyland-Rover van, which led the pack behind them. The minigun roared, spitting bullets as fast as the barrels could rotate. Peter quickly lost control of the weapon and let up on the trigger. Some of the bullets hit their target, but most sprayed harmlessly away as the gun jumped in his grip. The van swerved a bit, but stayed hard on their tail.

Explosions suddenly blossomed behind their car, one after another. Turning to look at Kathryn, Peter saw her pulling pins and dropping grenades with the speed of an old-fashioned corn-shucker looking for a bonus.

He turned back and opened fire on the van again, leaning further out and bracing the butt of the weapon against his shoulder. Again, the minigun roared, and again he quickly lost control of it. This time, though, what little accuracy he had must have inspired some fear in the drivers behind them. The pursuing Westwind and Dynamit began maneuvering to use the van as a shield.

Suddenly one of Kathryn's grenades exploded beneath the Leyland-Rover. It began to swerve wildly, first one way, then the other, before it careened over the guard rail and smashed onto the highway.

The vibration of the minigun tearing into his shoulder, Peter managed to rake the gun's spray over the armored grill of the Dynamit. He crisscrossed the fire back and forth. On the sixth pass his bullets dug through the vehicle's armor, penetrating the engine block. The car came to an abrupt stop, down from 150 in an instant, just as the Westwind hit the base of the ramp behind it.

The Westwind tried to swerve, but smashed into the back of the Dynamit, sending them both off the shoulder into a shallow sewage ditch.

"Yes!" Peter cried. "YES! YES! YES!"

Kathryn laughed and cried, her head rocking up and down.

Peter slid back into the car. He turned Liaison over on the floor and reached down to check her pulse.

She had one. That was good enough for now.

And then he passed out.

25

The first thing Peter saw when he woke up on his back was a huge painting of people in a park. It filled the wall before him. It was a strange painting, but before he could figure out what made it so, his attention was drawn to Breena, who knelt on the floor beside him. A light green *something* sparkled over her entire body. Her hands rested on his shoulder. She seemed to be in a trance.

He noticed immediately that he felt much better than he had . . .

When . . . ?

When he was in the car.

It all came back to him. He turned his head and saw Kathryn asleep on a couch. He had never seen her look so gentle before. Until now she always seemed to have a kind of war mask on, beautiful, but defensive—even when frightened. Now . . . Not more attractive—just another part of her.

He glanced around the room. It seemed like a living room, but he thought it might once have been an office. Paintings hung everywhere. Near the baseboards. Near the ceiling. Some on the ceiling. Pictures of colored squares. Pictures of minotaurs done in a cyberware motif. Wild colors in broad strokes covered the walls beneath the paintings. Colors everywhere. Undoubtedly it was Liaison's handiwork. It had the same untamed palette as her clothes.

His gaze was drawn back first to Breena, who remained still and peaceful, and then to the painting in front of him.

He'd never seen it before, but he liked it. But he also didn't like it.

What was it?

A couple walking together, dressed in old-fashioned clothing. A man sat on the grass smoking a pipe. A monkey on a leash. Many people, all enjoying a day in a park. Kind of. Their bodies were too stiff.

He realized that the painting wasn't made with strokes. Something else. Dots.

"Like it?"

Liaison stood in the doorway. She wore an over-sized blue shirt that hung down to her knees. Smears of red and green paint covered it.

"Where are we?"

"Our place. Breena's and mine. In the Noose."

"How'd you get me here?"

"Well, I didn't do it. I was out. But apparently you were just conscious enough for them to guide you up the stairs."

"I don't remember."

"You were nearly dead."

"Oh." He glanced at Breena. "Is she . . . ?"

"She's fine. She'll be at it a few more minutes. But she'll be out of it all day tomorrow. You were really hurting."

"Did you get an address?"

"You bet." She crossed the room and knelt down on his other side. He found her very cute. "A place called ABTech on the Westside. We checked the listing, didn't find it anywhere. I went into the Matrix for a cursory check. Nothing. I'll go in-depth tomorrow."

She smiled down at him. "So. What do you think of the place?"

"It's colorful."

"You think so? I was thinking about trying to make it a bit brighter."

He stared at her. He decided she wasn't kidding.

"You like the picture?" she said and gestured to the painting in front of him.

"Yes."

"It's an original. I got it from the Art Institute."

"You what?"

"Well, I didn't get it. It's from the Art Institute. A slag I knew, he got it from a friend, who stole it from an accountant, who stole it from a partner, who grabbed it out of the Institute when they shut it down after the IBM Tower collapsed. It's my favorite painting."

Peter looked at it again. "There's something about it . . ."

"The dots. It's the dots." She got up and walked over to it. "Soorat, Georges Soorat, the guy who painted it, he made up this technique called pointillism. Breena looked that up for me. It's all these dots, and they make up the picture. No lines. Nothing's whole. Except the whole thing. He's like a science-fiction painter. Or, I think he is, anyway, because he made paintings like computer graphics before there were computers. Which is wiz, if you think about it."

He gave her a blank look.

"You know. Pixels of light, making up the whole picture. See, he used only the pure colors, red, blue, green. You can see purple back there, but there's no purple in it. From a distance the red and the blue dots mix to look like another color. Really clever. It's like old, flat televisions. And once I saw a thing called a comic book. Same idea. Dots mixing up to look like a whole."

The more Peter looked at the painting, the more stiff and lifeless the people in it seemed to be. But he decided not to mention that to Liaison.

"What's it called?"

"*Sunday Afternoon on the Grand Jetty*. Or something like that. Anyway, it's the pictures that matter. At least, that's what matters to me. See, he painted this at the end of the nineteenth century, when tech was just getting cut. And he wanted to make up a kind of painting that, you know, had that idea. Like guns with interchangeable parts. A painting made up of dots of pure color.'' She beamed at it.

"Like DNA.''

"Yeah, I guess.'' She sounded doubtful at first, and then jumped. "Yes. Like DNA. Right. We're these small dots of chromosotes, or whatever, and we're a whole thing also.''

"Chromosomes.''

"Right.''

She looked at him with a sly smile. "Are you really a professor?''

"No.'' They both turned back to the painting. "Liaison,'' he said after a pause, "what do you think of the whole painting?''

"The whole painting?''

"Yes. Not how it's made, or the little dots. But that woman there, with the umbrella . . . What do you think of her.''

"I never . . .''

"I mean . . . what do you think of how she seems as a person?''

"I don't know. I always thought of her as dots. She doesn't seem like a real person.''

Breena lifted her hands and the glow subsided. Liaison hopped over to her and gave her a big hug.

"How are you?'' she asked.

"Very tired.''

"Bed?'' Liaison suggested with a mischievous grin.

"Sleep,'' Breena answered flatly. "Help me up.''

When she was on her feet, Breena's stance was like a tired old woman's. "Thank you for healing me,'' Peter said.

"Part of the job.''

"Right.'' Did she ever let her guard down?

"We don't have any more beds, so you have to sleep on the floor," Liaison told him. "All right?"

"Sure."

"There are some blankets over there."

"Great."

"All right. Good night."

"Good night, Liaison. Good night, Breena."

"Good night."

The two women passed through a doorway, and then the lights in the room went out. Peter reached into his pocket and found the three My Cure chips. He crawled across the floor and tucked them behind a potted plant, then moved back to the center of the room.

Even though he could no longer see the painting in the dark, his eyes sought out the spot where it hung. At first he imagined the little dots floating off the canvas and smothering him in his sleep, but then finally his exhaustion took him off to blessed oblivion.

It was Kathryn's voice that woke him while it was still dark. "Hello," she said, more like a question than a statement. He was too groggy to answer immediately, and so she said it again. She sounded fearful.

"Kathryn?"

"Who is that?"

"Peter."

"Oh, Peter." She said his name again, this time with a strong note of relief. "Where are we?"

"Breena and Liaison's place. In the Noose. An old office building, I think."

"Right. Right. I remember now." She sighed. "I'm not used to this. This moving around so much." He heard her shift on the couch. "Do you do this a lot? Living like this?"

He thought about it. His life was actually more frenetic now than it had ever been. He said so. "But, to tell you the truth,'' he added, "ever since I became a troll, at fifteen, my life has been consistently hectic."

"Not mine. The only move I made was when I was three and my grandfather took Cell Works from Amsterdam to Chicago. I was practically raised in Cell Works. The entire organization was like an extended family. I traveled, for business, but it wasn't like this. Everything was tied to my family, to Cell Works. I knew my place in the corporation, how I fit into the world. Not like today at all. Today is a whole new system. The whole plan was to live out my life within Cell Works. Safe. Good. I mean, a few hours ago I might have died. I was terrified."

"Me, too."

"Really?"

Her surprise flattered him, in an obviously male kind of way. He crawled over to the couch and sat beside it. She smelled of roses and other exotic scents. "Well, there were all these people shooting at me. Shooting at me and *hitting* me. Yeah. I was scared. But it's different. This was probably your first time in something like this. . . ."

"Yes," she said and laughed.

"I got beat up my first month out on the streets. I'm a bit more used it."

"You lived on streets?"

"Yeah."

"I'd die. I'd die."

"No you wouldn't. You'd figure out what you had to do to survive, and you'd do it."

"No, Peter. No. You and Breena and Liaison. You know how to survive. Me? I was raised in a corporation. The key was stability. Long-term profits carefully measured against the short term. Spontaneity was all right, as long as it was planned and kept under control." She laughed and Peter joined in. "So, what happens now?"

"Well, Liaison got an address of an ABT. She'll

check it out in the Matrix tomorrow. I should go stake it out. Breena will probably rest, and you'll probably stay here, too. You're pregnant, and the last thing you need is to make a habit of getting involved in gun battles.''

"True." They sat silently for a moment. "So what was your favorite story?" she asked suddenly.

"What?"

"The Wizard of Oz? The Odyssey? All the stories I loved as a kid were about people in strange places, taking risks. Now I'm finally living it, and I don't know how all those people could stand it.''

"I was partial to *Alice in Wonderland.*"

"I never read that one." She leaned in closer. "I did see the simsense, though."

"They made a simsense of *Alice in Wonderland?*"

"Sure. They make simsenses of anything."

"I never tried them."

"Really?"

"I . . . I've spent my whole life trying to get my body back. The idea of living out an experience through a recording of someone else's nervous system . . . It's too much to bear.''

"Well, the Alice simsense had this great part where you fall down the White Rabbit's hole. It was so frightening. You just *rushed* toward the ground. All you could see was the ground getting closer and closer. . . . And the fear . . . Whoever they got to feel that fall . . . She was terrified and I was terrified.''

Something about the description struck Peter as wrong, but he couldn't remember the original text, so he dropped it.

"Kathryn," he began hesitantly, then curiosity drove him on, "if Cell Works was your family . . ." He paused, hoping she would pick up the thread of the conversation. She didn't. "Leaving just seems . . ."

"I need this for my baby, Peter. I need to know he'll be all right. Cell Works wouldn't sponsor the research. I needed to know what was going on, and I needed to know it now. The more my child grows, the more cells to be transformed. If someone was doing the work, I wanted to know about it. Your father was going to be my tie to the cure.''

"But all this for an unborn child . . .''

"He's not just an unborn child, Peter. He's the son of the man I wanted to marry.''

"Yes. I heard he died. I'm sorry.''

"Yes,'' she laughed harshly. "A car accident. A stupid, stupid, stupid, stupid car accident. We can do so much, but we can't always prevent cars from spinning out of control. We can't save a man every time. We can't always save the person we love the most.''
He reached his clumsy hand out in the darkness and touched the warmth of her arm. She pulled back at first, but settled down and let him slide his fingers up to her shoulder.

When she spoke again, her voice had become quiet. "You see, I want my son to be born, this son, this child, this part of John. I want him to live, and I want him to live a good life. I need to know that he's going to be all right. I want to protect him. And I know Breena thinks that makes me terrible, but I . . .'' She sighed. "I just don't want to lose him, too. I need something to be set.'' She laughed slightly. "Actually, I want everything to be set. But now I don't know. I've given up everything I had. Everything I had to offer my son, I gave it all up to keep him safe in another way.''

"You'll manage. You're tough.''

"No. I'm only tough where I know the rules. Like in the corp world.'' She pulled away and he thought she must have buried her face in her hands. "What have I done to my life? To my son?'' She began to cry. Peter sat quietly. After a while, she sniffed, her tears ended for now. "I'm sorry,'' she said.

"Shhh. No. Shhh. You have nothing to apologize for. I think we both need some sleep, though."

She sniffled again. "Yes."

"You going to be all right?"

"Yes." She stretched out on the couch. "Yes, I just need some sleep."

He waited for a moment, and when she seemed settled, he said, "Good night."

"Good night, Peter. You don't seem like a killer, you know." He remained quiet, uncertain how to respond. "I mean, I thought you were one way—you had that gun pointed at me, after all—but there's something else to you."

"I'm sorry about that."

"You were doing your job, right?"

A shame filled him. He'd become so used to his job that only now did it strike him as odd that he had held a stranger hostage at gunpoint. "Yeah. Time for a new job."

"Good."

He watched her roll over on the couch, then made his way back to his blankets and closed his eyes.

He dreamed of Alice, and of her fall, but when he awoke, he could not remember the details.

26

In the morning, Peter and Kathryn said very little to one another, but a gentleness arced in the air between them. Liaison, who was preparing a breakfast of soycakes and baco, hummed odd songs that Peter could not place. Eventually he decided she was just making them up as she went along. Breena remained quiet and aloof.

* * *

The ABTech building, which Peter located on the city's Westside, resembled a large warehouse more than a research facility. When no one entered or left the building during the first few hours of his morning surveillance, Peter wondered if ABTech had given Crusader a false billing address.

It was not until just after noon that he finally saw someone, a woman, leaving through a small gateway at the south side of the building. She was an ork. Dressed in a once-attractive winter coat now outdated, she had obviously made a poor woman's attempt to dress up.

Because nothing else had caught his eye all day, Peter decided to follow her to see if it just might lead him to something interesting. He didn't expect much, though; he assumed she was a low-paid gofer sent out for lunch.

Like most orks, she was stocky, the reason Peter was so rarely attracted to ork women. They had neither the delightful height and muscle of troll women nor the delicate fragility of pure humans. To him, ork females always floated between the extremes of his desires.

He found this particular ork endearing, however. Though he saw most of the pure human shoppers along the walks of the posh merchant area pull away at the sight of her, she did her best to maintain an air of pride. She clutched her old coat about her and held her chin high.

As the ork passed, one woman pulled her daughter off the sidewalk. Then she stood there staring indignantly after her, as if the ork woman had come to this neighborhood solely for the purpose of frightening her daughter.

The little girl also stared after the ork with intense curiosity. The woman drew the child close and comforted her, though she showed not the slightest need for comforting.

Peter opted for social invisibility.

The ork woman turned north and walked toward the Congress line Rail station.

"Well, so much for the lunch theory," thought Peter. He crossed the street quickly to make sure he didn't miss the train the woman would take. Following her up the stairs to the platform, he noticed that she clutched the handrail with a firm grip, as if she had trouble walking. Then he saw her step had a bit of a wobble.

When they reached the platform and were waiting for the train to arrive, Peter also noticed that the woman's belly bulged a bit. The winter coat had hidden the fact from across the street, but now her pregnancy was obvious.

Looking up at her face again, he found that she was looking back at him. He gave her an embarrassed smile, which she returned. Then both looked away.

That would make sense, he thought. Maybe she didn't work for ABTech. Maybe she was a volunteer in some program of theirs.

"Stop it," he told himself. "You're just guessing now. Stop guessing."

The train rolled into the Rail stop. Peter entered a car behind the one into which the ork had stepped. He then worked his way up to the front of the car and watched the ork woman through the windowed door between the cars. Though her car was crowded, he saw the pure humans trying to step away or hold themselves apart from the woman.

The train rode east for some twenty minutes. At the Logan Square stop, she got off. Peter gave her plenty of lead to keep from arousing her suspicions.

They left the station. As she headed north and continued walking for another ten blocks, Peter remembered that an ork ghetto lay in that direction.

It was immediately obvious the moment he entered the ghetto. On one side of the street the orks on the street paid him little heed. The instant Peter crossed the street, suddenly every ork down the length of the block checked him for a piece. He hadn't done anything yet, so they didn't bother him. But two mothers sent their children to follow him, probably to make sure he didn't cause any trouble.

Peter acted as if he didn't notice them, and continued following the woman until they reached a rundown high-rise. The ork passed through a massive set of glass double doors, then checked her mailbox. After pulling out her mail, she unlocked the inner door, then disappeared into the shadows.

Peter followed her into the building. Checking the mailboxes, he saw that she'd opened Wilson 5-G.

Glancing around, he saw no one. Even his tails were gone.

He stepped up to the lobby door and pulled out a thin strip of metal. Sliding it between the lock and the frame, he worked it for a few moments. The lock clicked and Peter pulled the door open and was about to step through when he heard the building's outer door open behind him. He'd been wrong about the kids who'd been tailing him. They hadn't lost interest—they'd called for help.

27

Facing off with him at this moment were five members of an ork street gang. They were checking him out, the look in their eyes pretty serious. All wore black leather jackets that showed a variety of red patches. He guessed their average age to be about six-teen.

"What you doing, chummer?" one of the boys asked.

"Visiting a friend." Peter forced a smile.

"I don't think you got no friends around here."

"Mr. Donner." Peter had seen the name on a box. "He just buzzed me up."

The boy glanced at the mailbox. "Anybody can read, chummer. How 'bout you move your trog ass back out into the street and drag it back to whatever subway tunnel you crawled out of?"

"Sorry. I have work to do."

Peter stepped through the door, but before he could close it, the kids were on the door.

They grabbed hold of the metal frame and pulled it open even as Peter tried to pull it shut. As the metal began to buckle and the glass cracked at the edges, Peter let go. The gangers sprawled backward, falling on top of one another in the vestibule.

Peter made a dash for the stairs.

And then stopped.

He hadn't come here to have ork gangers chase him through the building. He needed to find out why the Wilson woman was at ABTech, not bring a brawl to her door. Besides, he was growing weary of fighting.

He turned toward the youths, who rushed up to him, then came to a sliding stop on the smooth stone floor. Uncertain of whether to claim victory or pummel him, they took the middle road of gaping at him in curios-ity.

The lead ganger's face was broad, with two thick fangs growing from his lower gums. His eyes were a bright blue. Breathing rapidly, he seemed to have no intention of giving up his adrenaline rush just because Peter had stopped.

Peter raised his hands in a palms-out gesture of

peace. "Listen. I'm here on a job. I've got to talk to someone."

"Buzz off. I told you before and I'll tell you again—Slot it out of here."

"I'm not going to hurt anybody," Peter began, but then the ork slammed his fist into Peter's gut, making him double over.

In his dazed state Peter heard the sound of half a dozen switchblades flicking open.

Still doubled over, he raised his face. "Listen. I've had a rough week. . . ."

"I don't give a frag what you had, trog. We asked you to leave nice, now we'll toss you."

". . . and I'm not as patient as I was five days ago. Listen. I'm going up whether you like it or not. . . ."

The ganger kicked him in the face. Peter fell over backward onto the second step. The other orks did not laugh. They simply stood ready to back their friend.

Peter should have been able to dodge both blows, yet the kid had nailed him twice. He knew the damage was more to his pride than his body.

"I'm a shadowrunner and I will slice you children up into ork treats if you don't back off."

This got a response. The punks moved back, though the leader not as far as the others. "Stuff it, chummer. All the more reason to make sure you leave."

Peter jumped to his feet. The kids jumped back.

"Don't you scan it, *chummer?* I use an HK to take down anyone who gets in my way. This is my fragging *job!*" He stepped forward, hoping to drive them out of the lobby with pure bravado. The kids moved backward again, matching him step for step. "Getting through people is what I DO! Now back off, or I'll just take you out."

"Chill," the leader said, and rallied his gang. The other orks stopped moving back, and the leader addressed Peter. "Think about this, green mountain. You're on my home ground. Possibly threatening my

people. You just showed up in a place you don't belong. No one asked you to come. I'm asking you to
leave, and all you can think of is to threaten me? Don't
you scan it? You threatened us the minute you showed
your trog face around here. I don't care if you carve
me, 'cause I got no choice.''

Peter was ready this time. He saw the young ork's
neck muscles twitch ever so slightly. As the kid was
bringing his knife up, Peter slapped the punk's wrist,
lightly, then swung his own fist up into the kid's chest.

The ork slammed into one of the gang members
behind him, and the two of them went down to the
floor. The remaining three orks spread out around Peter, everyone waiting for someone else to make the
first move.

Then Peter whirled, punched, and kicked. He took
the gangers down one after another. He treated them
as gently as he could, but he was a troll and they were
orks. The things he did would have snapped the bones
of any pure human.

By the time the three orks were down, the leader
and the other kid he'd first brought down were back
on their feet. The leader rushed Peter, attempting to
knock him over. Peter caught the boy in his arms as
the two of them slammed into the wall. He jabbed his
fist into the ork's stomach twice, then let him go. The
kid fell to floor and wheezed for breath. Though his
companion almost retreated in fear, he rallied enough
to thrust his knife toward Peter.

Peter grabbed the ganger's arm and flipped him to
the ground. He then walked through the group and
gave a final kick to each gang member's abdomen.

While they were busy groaning, Peter had calmed
down. It sobered him to suddenly realize that he had
triumphantly trashed a bunch of teenagers who were
doing nothing more than protecting a woman who
would undoubtedly not want to talk to him.

"I'm an idiot,' he said out loud.

One of the kids groaned again, but none got up. Peter took the stairs to the fifth floor two at a time to get the biz over with as quickly as possible.

He knocked on the door of apartment 5G.

"Just a moment," called out a woman's voice. Then he heard a bolt turn and the door opened. The ork woman looked at him for a moment, then her eyes widened as she recognized him from the Rail platform. She shook her head, as if to deny the whole situation, and tried to shut the door.

Peter put his hand on the door and pushed it open. "Mrs. Wilson. Mrs. Wilson. Please. I need to talk to you for a moment."

She started to scream.

Peter gave a hard shove to the door and knocked it off its hinges. The woman tried to run, but Peter reached out with one long arm to grab her and clamp a hand over her mouth.

He glanced around the room. Cracks ran though the fake dark wood of the tables and chairs, but an effort had been made to keep the style consistent. The wallpaper was brown and white. The shades drawn. The whole place was somber and dark.

Two little ork children stepped into the room from the kitchen—two girls. One held a doll shaped like a pink pure-human baby in her hands. She had pink bows in her coarse, stiff hair. For a moment they stared with incomprehension at their mother and the troll who held her, then fear formed in their eyes. The girl with the doll, the younger of the two, began to cry.

"Shhh," said Peter. Now he was upset and panicked. He felt the situation rushing out of control, and it dawned on him that he'd never done anything like this before. He'd just beat up a bunch of teenagers, now he was roughing up mothers.

He let the woman go. She ran to her daughters, gathering them close to her. The three orks stared at Peter, certain he wanted to kill them all.

"Please," said the mother, "Please, just let them go. . . . They're so young."

"I'm not going to hurt anyone. . . ."

The younger daughter began to cry more loudly.

"I just need to ask you some questions . . ."

The mother met Peter's eyes. She stood, curious, ignoring her children for the moment. Her tone was flat. "About what?"

"ABTech Enterprises . . ."

"Get out!" she shrieked. "Get out.. Get out! Get out!"

"I just . . ."

"Please, please, leave. I can't talk about that." She was near tears.

Peter took a step closer. The woman pushed her daughters behind her. "You can speak. . . . I won't tell anyone what you say."

"If you have any decency in you, you will leave," said the woman. Then she gasped, looking beyond Peter to the door.

Peter spun around, expecting to see the ork gangers. Instead, he found a lone middle-aged ork in the doorway. The ork looked back and forth between the broken door and the troll. Then his face turned to anger. "What's going on here?"

"This man . . . ," began the wife.

"I need to talk to your wife about something. . . ."

"The hell you do. . . ."

"Mark," the wife said pleadingly.

The husband stalked into the room. Peter noticed immediately that the ork was strong—probably a street fighter as a kid, maybe a dock worker today. He looked drunk.

"The hell you do," the man repeated absently. "What the frag are you doing here?"

"I have to ask your wife some questions."

"He wants to know about ABTech."

The man's eyes suddenly narrowed. He clenched his

hands into fists. When he spoke again, his voice was low but full of menace. "Get the frag out of here now."

"I can't leave until I . . ."

"Get the frag out of here NOW!"

"What does your wife do at ABTech?"

Peter had just gotten the question out when he saw that at least a half-dozen orks had come out into the hallway. Two of them were kids from the lobby. Others were neighbors drawn by the shouting. The latter had donned housecoats and bathrobes.

Wrong, wrong, wrong, thought Peter.

But instead of rallying the orks to his aid, Wilson began shouting at the assembled gawkers and demanded they go away. The orks were at first surprised. But when his ranting continued unabated, they gave up and left.

Furious now, the man turned his attention back to Peter. He stomped up to him, the words hissing out of his mouth, as if he didn't want his neighbors to know more than they already did. "I don't know who you are or what you want. But get out of here now. And I don't want to hear another word from you about that place."

He stepped aside to let Peter pass.

"I'm not leaving until . . ."

The ork swung his fist up into Peter's chin, sending a sharp pain through his head and neck. Peter stumbled backward and tripped over an end table. He is strong, Peter thought. He is capable.

The ork confirmed the street-fighter theory when he rushed at Peter and kicked him in the face before Peter had a chance to surrender. The shoe smashed into his right cheek and left a burning sensation.

"Frag," said Peter aloud, and swung his arm out and tripped the man.

With a thud the ork fell to the ground. Peter scrambled up and leaped on top of the ork, his massive frame

crashing down on the other man's chest. The ork gave out a tremendous gasp, then brought his knee up into Peter's groin. The pain sliced through Peter again and again as the ork struggled to get out from under. But Peter slammed his right fist into the man's head.

"Stop it," screamed the wife. "Please, both of you, stop it." Peter had forgotten the others in the room. Now, with the wife's pleas interrupting the fight, he also heard the girls, both of them crying now.

Distracted for the briefest moment, Peter had let down his guard, giving the ork a chance to swing his hand into Peter's kidney. Peter made a mental correction: the guy was *really* strong. Without thinking about it, Peter rolled off the ork, clutching his injured side. The ork scrambled up from under him, but he was holding his face above the eye; Peter's previous punch had drawn blood.

The ork dropped his body toward Peter, hoping to catch Peter's face and neck beneath his knees. Peter rolled out of the way, then swung his right arm behind him. The punch slammed into the ork's face, and he crashed to the ground.

The woman rushed to her husband's side, placing herself between the ork and Peter. She raised a hand to Peter. "Please. What do you want to know?"

"NO!" screamed the ork, and he jumped to his feet and past his wife. He rushed and tackled Peter. The two men slammed into a couch, flipped over it, and sprawled onto the floor.

Peter, desperate to stay in control, shot his hand out and slammed the ork's face down into the ground, then grabbed the man's right arm and twisted it around his back. The ork screamed out in agony.

"No, no!" the wife shouted. "Please stop!"

"Shut up," the husband growled, his voice strained. By now, the girls had stopped crying and had run up to Peter and were pounding him on the back. Peter ignored them.

Pushing up on the ork's arm, Peter told the woman, "Talk, or I'll snap it off."

"Yes," she said, with a helpless wave of her hand.

"No. Don't," insisted the husband.

"What were you doing at ABTech?"

"I . . . I'm a subject in an experiment."

"They pay you?"

"Stop!" The husband was desperate now. He struggled wildly and jerked his arm into a worse position.

"Yes," she said hesitantly, as if something remained unsaid.

"What are they working on?"

"I don't know."

"Well, what are they doing to you?"

"I don't know."

"You don't know?" said Peter, clearly surprised. "You don't know what they're doing to you?"

"It's not me. It's the child."

Peter didn't understand. "What?"

"We needed the money. . . ."

"Laurie!"

"We needed the money . . . ," she repeated, as if Peter would understand. "The children needed food. We couldn't feed Suzie and Anne. . . ."

"I don't . . ."

"The child!" the woman screamed at him. "I sold them my baby!" She placed her hands on her round belly.

"They're experimenting on your unborn child?" he asked. The idea so numbed him that he dropped his hands limply, freeing the husband. Wilson wriggled out from under Peter and immediately got to his knees and began slamming his fists into Peter's shoulders. But the fight was out of the ork now and his blows were ineffectual. Peter's eyes met his. Tears ran down the husband's face.

He stopped hitting Peter. The two continued to stare at each other.

"I'm sorry. . . ."

"Leave," the man said simply. "Please leave."

"Yes."

Peter stood up. He turned to the woman. "I . . . ," he began, but what could he say?

"What?" the woman asked flatly, ready for the whole affair to be over.

"Your child? What will happen . . . ?"

"Aborted. Some of them are born. Others aborted. Mine will be aborted. But they all belong to ABTech. One girl, a human, Julie something, tried to run away to Seattle. They said they got her."

"Others?"

"Others! You don't think I'm the only one, you Mr. Fancy-Dressed, do you?"

"No . . . I . . ."

"Get out. You got what you wanted. Our shame is yours now. Now get out."

"Yes."

Peter walked to the door, his movements stiff, partly from the day's fights, and partly because his mind could not digest what he'd just learned. At the door he looked back.

The family was on the floor, huddled together. The older girl stroked the back of her father's neck. "It's all right, daddy. It's all right, daddy. We're all right, daddy."

He found a back exit and cut briskly through an alley and into the street. A final glance back at the building showed him a crowd of orks gathered around the front door.

Then something caught his attention out the corner of his eye. Standing next to a lamppost was Fast Eddy, twitching visibly as he tried hard to look casual. He was watching the crowd and the building, obviously waiting for Peter to appear.

Then Eddy spotted Peter gazing at him. Fast Eddy's face twitched crazily and he took off down the street.

28

Without giving a thought to the crowd milling around the building, Peter rushed after Eddy. He cut across the street to keep out of the way of the orks, but a few stood in his way. He pushed them out of his path as gently as he could.

"Watch it!" one shouted, but no one followed him.

Eddy was a full block ahead of him now. He ran like an epileptic on adrenaline boosters; his arms flailed, and he stumbled twice looking over his shoulder at Peter. Yet somehow he rolled on at an amazing pace, possessed by some unidentified demon of motion.

Peter knew he had to catch Eddy, that he had to find out how much Eddy knew. Had Eddy tailed him to ABTech? Did he know the location of Liaison and Breena's place?

Eddy ducked down one street, then another. Peter almost lost him twice, but only almost. Too many times Eddy's body failed him, and he got stuck hopping up and down in place. When Peter finally caught up to his old friend, Eddy was just turning a corner. No one was around.

Peter didn't tackle Eddy, as he had originally planned, but scooped him up and carried him off into an alley. He dropped Eddy behind a dumpster, then knelt down and wrapped his right hand around Eddy's neck.

"Hello, pal."

"Hi, Prof. How's it how's it how's it going?"

"Oh. Just great. A lot of people want to kill me."

"And that slot you picked . . . ?"

Peter tightened his grip on Eddy's neck. "Eddy, I let you talk that way before because I had no idea who you were talking about. I don't think you did, either. You were just talking about 'women,' your idea of women, not at all connected to a real person. Now you're talking about a real person. Unplug it."

"You got it, Prof." He smiled his winning smile, which was now worn and ragged.

Peter released the pressure, but kept his finger against Eddy's neck.

"You were looking for me?"

"Yeah. Listen, Peter, I'm really sorry. Really sorry. Really sorry. That was a bad call I made. I shouldn't have done that to you. To you."

Peter was immediately suspicious. "Why the sudden change of heart?"

"What? You don't think I can, you know, can, you know, think I did something wrong and feel bad about it?"

"No."

"You're right. All right, right. There's something something something else. I'm out, Peter. They dumped me. I'm dead. I'm as dead as you. I wanted to, you know know, team up like old times. You know . . ."

"No."

"Please, Peter." Eddy looked away, but Peter could see the tears shining in his eyes. "I'm really I'm really a mess. My hand, Peter"—he raised the hand Peter had snapped. A blood-soaked rag covered it. "They wouldn't spring for the magic. Magic. I'm really messed up."

Peter sighed. "Eddy, I don't trust you."

"You don't trust me? You're the one who out of the ether decides not to geek the . . . sorry . . . her, and you can't trust me? You started this. This. Didn't

I get you get you into the gang? Didn't I help you get the stuff you needed?''

Peter knew Eddy was manipulating him, but had to acknowledge the man had a point.

"Yeah. You did.''

"Yeah. I did.''

"Don't push it.''

"All right.''

"What do you want, Eddy?''

"To be the same as before. The way we used to be. We don't need the gang. We can knock over the small stuff. Have enough to live on. You and me. Get enough money to get my hand fixed. What do you say?''

"No, Eddy. I don't want that.''

"Why? Because of her?''

"Partially because of her. Partially because . . . I don't know. I want out of that now.''

Eddy barked out a laugh. "You're going straight?''

"I could!''

"Right! Hey, wait a minute! She read read read your stuff. Your troll stuff. You going to be human again?''

Peter didn't know how to answer. "Yeah. I might. I almost might be.''

"You're so lucky. I'd love to get fixed. You know, you're a troll and all, but you got . . . It works. It works. Me. What? I'm a mess. I can't do anything. I'd do anything to be cured.'' Peter stared at his friend sadly. Repairing neural damage was as difficult as genetic manipulation. Still cutting-edge, still experimental.

"All right. I'll get your hand fixed. That's it.''

They stood up and started to walk down the alley. "So, did you find that guy you were looking for?''

"None of your business, Eddy.''

"Yeah. Sure.''

* * *

"Who the frag's this?" Breena asked when Peter returned with Eddy.

"A chummer. He's in trouble."

Kathryn rose from a table where she was reading Peter's file on one of Liaison's portables. "This is the man who betrayed you."

"Hi," Eddy said, insipidly.

"I don't understand," Breena said insistently. "Who is this guy? Why is he here?"

"He needs help. I owe him."

"I don't. You! Get the frag out!"

"Look, his hand is busted up pretty bad. Please. I'll pay. Fix it."

She opened her mouth to speak, then closed it, staring hard at Peter for what seemed like a long time. She'd weighed it out. "All right."

Hours later, while Eddy slept on the living room couch, the four of them held council over soup and bread in the kitchen.

"I dug up some stuff from the Matrix," said Liaison. "ABTech Enterprises is buried under a sea of data. Nobody seems to know its history or what it does. The scoop I'm giving you I put together with pieces from here and there.

"It's a privately held company that's a subsidiary of Biogene Technologies, a biotech firm in Seattle. Biogene had some problems with Aztechnology a few years back. . . ."

"Aztechnology!" Peter and Kathryn exclaimed in unison.

"Relax," Liaison continued. "Since then things have cooled down. I don't think Aztechnology is involved with the Chicago company at all. But at the time it was bad enough because Biogene was weak. A company called Yamatetsu gobbled it up. Apparently they liked what they bought, but the property was too hot to handle because of the Aztechnology hose-up. Yamatetsu melted Biogene down electronically and set it out into the data streams.

"I think they decided to hide some of the Biogene resources and research in the UCAS proper, so Aztechnology wouldn't get involved with it. They called it ABTech Enterprises."

"That would make sense," said Kathryn. Then she put her hand over her mouth in surprise. When she pulled her hand away, she said, "Of course. It makes sense now. Two years ago somebody hit Aztechnology in Seattle to steal something hot. *Very* hot. No one knew who did it, or what they took, but now . . . It was Biogene Technologies, and they were probably going for some sort of recombinate DNA research."

"They must have pooled their own work with the data they got from Aztechnology," Peter put in, "and then worked on it here in Chicago for the last two years."

"Maybe they've got it by now," said Kathryn.

"Well, if they don't, they're very close." Peter then told them what he'd just learned in the ork ghetto.

When he was through speaking, the others remained silent for several minutes. Kathryn stood up and walked over to the sink, her back to the group.

"This is drek," said Breena. "Can't believe they're trying to take the magic out."

"Well, that might not be the way they're going to do it," Peter said weakly. "My theory . . ."

Breena's dark eyes flared as she leaned toward Peter. "You know, I'm just now realizing how selfish you are. You want to stop being a troll? Fine. But do you have any idea how many people you're dragging down with you?" She imitated him. "My theory does not rip the magic out of a person. . . ."

"Well, it doesn't. It just . . . It blocks the magic. It shuts down the genes that produce metahuman characteristics. It's not a recombinate process. That's too—unwieldy. All the work on metagenes along the lines of splicing and bonding has turned sour. It's too unpredictable.''

"So what's your trick, darling?" Breena asked coldy.

"It's ingenious, actually," said Kathryn, turning around. Her eyes were cold and hard. Distant. "He doesn't want to alter the genes themselves. He wants to prevent the environment, the new element of magic in the environment, from activating the metahuman genes.''

"And you want to shut the magical environment out from the DNA.''

"Exactly," said Kathryn. "He's going to sidestep the recombinate process. It's like keeping someone out of the sun. If you're not exposed to the sun, your skin doesn't darken.''

"Right."

"Genes already have molecular 'controllers' for different possible reactions of the DNA to the environment. Peter . . . Profezzur, wants to turn those controllers back on as if the magic wasn't in the environment.''

"Wiz," said Liaison, excited more with the detail than the implications.

"And everybody will be pasty-white," said Liaison.

"What?" asked Kathryn.

"If everyone stays out of the sun, then everyone is pasty-white," explained Peter. "Right?"

Breena nodded. "So you could take away my ability to do magic.''

"I don't know that it will work. And I don't think I could do it without you wanting me to.''

"Tox!"

"Listen!" Peter pointed a massive finger at Breena. "I changed. I know what it's like. I didn't get something extra. I used to be part of society. I had a *place*. I knew where I was, where I *belonged*. You cannot begrudge me my desire to get that back! I'm not what I was.'' He pronounced the last words with particular emphasis. ''You cannot begrudge my desire.''

''No,'' she said softly. ''You are a troll. You know this, Profezzur. No one could have figured out everything you have and not see the truth. You are a troll. Magic is back, and you are a creature of fantasy . . .''

''Don't try to make it sound wondrous!''

''It is! The world is getting jolted out of its complacency. Slowly, but it's happening. All the rules are flipped. Which gives us a chance to write new rules, and the new rules might be better.''

''And in the meantime, I'm . . .'' He could hear the self-pity about to come out of him, and hated himself for it. ''Never mind. It may seem wondrous to you. But to me it's already mundane. It's just me, stuck in the wrong body.''

''You sure talk good for a troll,'' said Liaison, an impressed look in her eyes.

''Thanks,'' said Peter drily.

''Next step?'' Breena said, changing the topic abruptly.

Peter looked around the room. ''We've got to get into ABTech, see what they've got. See if they can help me. See if they can work the operation for Kathryn. See if Dr. Clarris is there.''

''Even if they can, they're not going to let her in.''

''That's the next step. If they can do it, we'll sneak her in. We'll disguise her or something. Whatever. We'll make it happen.''

''Not without getting in there and casing the joint.''

''That would help. But we don't have to do it that way.''

''What do you mean?''

''We know that they take women into the lab and

work on them. Liaison, could you get into their records and set it up so that Kathryn was already on their list? She could simply show up, get the operation, and walk back out again.''

''That's good,'' said Breena, duly impressed. ''That's so ridiculously unexpected. You seem to have found your niche.''

''Well,'' said Liaison, ''I don't want to short-sell my abilities, but operations conducted from only the Matrix make me nervous. It's always better to have someone on-site. And I think we should case the place first. That way, we don't hit any surprises.'' She put her hand on Kathryn's. ''Sending you in there alone, with no research. I don't like that.''

''Going in astrally is out. With the drek you describe going on in that place, any magic around AB-Tech is going to be totally slotted up. No mage in his right mind would hang out there. The etheric media has to be awfully distorted by the kind of experiments they're doing. Going in astrally would be like asking for a nightmare.''

Peter realized that he'd avoided looking at Kathryn since things had become tense with Breena. When he did glance over, he saw her lost in thought. It looked as if she'd checked out of the conversation some time back. What was she thinking? ''I should go in first. To check it out,'' he said.

''Sounds good to me. You know the stuff better than the rest of us. You can go mingle and find out what's what.''

''Wait a minute. I meant I'd be invisible or something. Like you did for Liaison.''

''Still looking for that kiss?'' laughed Liaison.

Breena ignored her. ''That won't make it worth the time. We'll dress you up and send you in to talk to these folks. Leez, can you get back into Geneering, and this time just rifle through the employee records?'

"Sure, null sweat."

"Do you speak French?"

"No," Peter said, confused.

"All right. Leez? Picture, ID codes, and such. Get me someone over there from North America."

"Click."

"Breena, I hate to burn your screen, but I'm a *troll*. I *know* there are no trolls in the industrial sciences. I looked for them. There's no way I'm going to pass for someone who belongs to ABTech."

"Oh, yes you will. What you are forgetting, Profezzur, is that magic exists. It's in me, it's in you. And with it we can do wonders with your image."

"We'll need more muscle," said Liaison.

"I don't want to do it," Kathryn said.

"What?" Now it was Breena and Peter talking almost in unison.

"It's off. I don't want to go in. I don't want to . . ." She looked ill and stumbled out of the kitchen down the hall. Peter got up and followed her, but stopped abruptly when she went through a door marked Women. After a moment he heard the sounds of retching. Liaison had come out into the hall. She was standing by the kitchen, concern etched on her face. Peter waited another moment, then pushed the bathroom door open.

It was a typical office bathroom, large, filled with sinks and stalls, the same as the one he'd used at the other end of the apartment, but this one had rose-colored tiles. He saw Kathryn kneeling on the floor of the first stall. He grabbed a wad of paper towels from a countertop on the way to the stall. She was breathing heavily, her hands pressed against the rose-colored metal of the stall. He leaned down and let her see the handful of towels. She was startled for a moment, but then took them and cleaned her face.

She tried to get up. Peter took her arm, carefully, and helped her.

"Thank you," she said, her gaze averted.

"Are you all right?"

"I just . . . Sometimes I don't feel well."

"You're pregnant."

"There's that." She laughed harshly, and added, "But sometimes I don't make myself feel too well." Peter felt uncomfortable, as if he'd stumbled onto a private conversation she often had with herself. He backed away, getting ready to leave. "Why do you think those women do that?" she said.

"Sell the fetuses?"

"Yes."

"I . . . I think they think they have no choice."

Kathryn nodded. "I had choices. I was still going to sell my baby. Breena's right."

Peter was confused. "No. You . . ."

"Yes. I gave in." She balled her hand into a fist and slammed it into the wall of the stall. Her jaw was clenched tightly and her eyes shone with a thin film of moisture. "I can't . . ." she said, and gasped for air. "I can't believe myself. It's like . . . I was using my son . . ."

Peter didn't know what she meant. She saw his confusion, and smiled a malevolent smile that carried and revealed pain. She raised her arms to him. The images of the holos at her house flashed into his mind. "When I was a girl I starved myself. Anorexia. Anorexia nervosa, for the pros." Peter tried to keep his memory of the holos from showing on his face. "I was a control freak with the stamina of a teenager. Ever hear of it?"

"Eating disorder," Peter said flatly.

"Yes," she said harshly, "but oh, so much, much more. To see the problem in terms of eating is to simply scratch the surface. That's the symptom. The disease . . . The disease . . . The disease is control. To master the one thing in your life you have control of. Your body. There was so much *wrong* happening in my life then . . . My mother—" She cut herself off and changed the subject. "People think, even I did, it was about weight, about beauty. It isn't."

She began to pace back and forth across the tiled floor. "It's about saying, 'I will control what I eat, what I look like, how I behave. The world is swirling around me, out of control, but I have this. I am master of my physical form." She stopped and rested her hands against a sink, looked at her face in the mirror. Her voice became raspy, unearthly. "You can die of control. You can master your body so well you just die. Perfect control. Nothing left to go wrong."

She brought her palms up to her face and slapped herself. Peter took two quick steps toward her, but Kathryn held her hands out, stopping him. Her flesh burned red where she had struck herself.

"You know what I want to do?" She didn't wait for a reply. "I want to abort the baby. I want to get rid of it." Her chin began to tremble. "I want to forget John, too. I just want it all forgotten." She stepped back and leaned against the wall. "I mean, look at me. Am I a mother?"

She looked terrible. Peter didn't want to answer.

"Don't tell me. Because it doesn't matter what you say." She wiped the backs of her hands against her eyes to dry them. "Because I'm not going to abort my son. That's too easy. That's the coward's way out. For me. For me right now. That'd be shedding weight to *feel* like I was in control. I'm not fourteen, I'm not Breena living without money on the streets. I want *this* baby. I *want* John's son. I let myself get out of control with John, and I want to keep the lack of control with our son." She touched her hands to her belly. "I wanted the best for him. The best isn't perfection. The best is him." She closed her eyes and breathed deeply. "Peter?"

"Kathryn?"

Her eyes still closed, she said, "How long does it

take to feel all right? I've never felt all right. Most people don't know it, but I don't feel all right.''

"I don't know. I don't feel too good myself. I'm a troll.''

She opened her eyes and smiled at him. ''That's right. You are. But don't count yourself out yet." She closed her eyes again. "Does it take a lifetime? Or do we just never feel all right? Do some of us just muddle through?''

"I think some of us muddle. You don't seem like a muddler, though.''

"Control, Peter. Control. It cuts both ways." She rubbed her right hand against her forehead. "Control. Spirits! How am I going to get my company back? Now that I've given up my quest, going back to a nice place to work and a nice home seems like a damned good idea.''

The door to the bathroom slammed open. Breena stood in the doorway, her face a tight mask of indignation. "Prof? Your friend? Your chummer? Your pal? He's gone.''

29

Breena said, "Oh, I knew . . ." under her breath as she led Peter down the hall to the front door. She shouted over her shoulder, "Leez, stay with the Red.''

No lights lit the deserted halls. Feeling his way along the corridor, Peter pressed one hand against the wall. He moved slowly, because old filing cabinets and shattered computer monitors littered the floor, and all were cool and the same temperature.

"Wait," said Breena. From her pocket she pulled a ring that emitted light, then slipped it on a finger.

He heard quick footsteps echo up from the stairwell. "Come on."

They ran for the stairs. When they reached the landing, Peter looked down the center of the well and saw Eddy's trembling warm-red hand sliding along the banister.

"Eddy, come back here. What are you doing?"

Eddy didn't answer, but kept moving.

Peter bounded down the stairs, with Breena close behind. Realizing he didn't have his gun, he was glad. At this point he'd have felt obliged to shoot Eddy down, something he didn't really want to do.

When Peter got to the first floor, he saw Eddy run through the lobby toward the front door.

"Eddy! Stop or I'll shoot!" he shouted.

Still running, Eddy called back. "No, Peter, don't. You don't understand."

Brenna came up alongside Peter, her breathing ragged and loud. "Where's your gun?"

"Don't have it on me."

She faltered and lost her stride. "Son of a fragging insect."

Peter ran on.

Eddy had just reached the building's outer doors. A red glow grew behind Peter. When he looked back, Breena was forming a fireball in her hands, the heat of the object nearly blinding him. For one instant he thought about leaping in front of it to save Eddy. But then he remembered that the man just couldn't be trusted.

He dove for the ground.

The shadows in the lobby slid quickly across the walls as the fireball rushed toward the doorway. Sensing danger, Eddy glanced over his shoulder, his mouth forming into a twisted, terrified O. He jumped through the doorway out onto the sidewalk, just as the fireball slammed into the metal frame of the doors and exploded. Shattering into bits of fire, it flew in all directions.

Peter heard Eddy scream. He scrambled up and saw his friend on the ground, rolling desperately back and forth in the snow, his pants and the back of his jacket on fire.

Peter rushed through the lobby. Eddy's screams grew in intensity, and now he was clawing at his hair and his face, frantically trying to beat out the flames.

Suddenly Peter saw red bodies rush toward Eddy from out of the darkness of the street. At first he thought they might be ghouls or scavengers, but then saw they were only mobmen dressed in dark overcoats. One man spotted Peter and their eyes met. The hood smiled, just slightly, and drew an Uzi III from under his jacket.

Peter stopped running, slid for a meter or so along the smooth, marble floor, and then ran back into the lobby. Bullets raced along the wall behind him. He only caught a glimpse of the other hood, who had whipped off his overcoat and was using it to beat out the flames on Eddy.

He saw Breena rush toward him, her face set and furious. He dove at her, catching her in the crook of his right arm as he fell to the ground. Bullets smashed into the ground all around them. Peter twisted and rolled to put himself between the mobster and Breena. Two bullets smacked into his shoulder, sending a dull pain spreading through him. Breena's ring lay on the floor, illuminating them clearly. Peter reached out and grabbed it, plunging the lobby into darkness.

Outside he heard some shouting in Japanese, and caught the words "now," "orders," and "later." He looked toward the doors and saw that the mobman had left.

"Get your fragging arm off of me," Breena said with a coldness that frightened Peter. He rolled over and ran toward the doorway, leaving the ring with her.

Outside he saw the two hoods shoving Eddy into a sleek black Westwind.

"Son of a—"

Peter crouched and scuttled off toward the car, using the burnt-out bodies of other cars for cover. He was just across the street when the Westwind began to accelerate. Peter made a dash for it, running up behind and jumping onto the top. He heard muffled shouts of surprise from within the car as the impact of his body on the roof rocked it from one side to the other.

Peter swung his fist and smashed it through the windshield. As the Westwind swerved wildly, he grabbed the roof edge and clung to it tightly.

Eddy shouted, "Peter, Peter, don't . . . don't do it. It's clear, it's clear!"

Then four bullets punched their way through the left side of the Westwind's roof. Peter immediately rolled over the bullet holes and watched with nervous excitement as four more bullets shot out in the spot where he had just been.

Peter glanced around and saw that they were approaching the Michigan Avenue bridge over the Chicago River.

He rolled back over to the left and smashed his fist through the driver's door window. The Westwind once again swerved wildly, this time grinding up against the bridge's cement guard rail.

Peter wiggled his hand around trying to contact the head, neck, or shoulders of the driver. Suddenly he felt his nails dig into the man's face. The driver screamed, and the car accelerated. It careened toward the left side of the bridge, rushing into the guard rail at a tremendous speed.

Peter flew off the car and into the air over the river. The car flipped over the railing and followed.

He had nothing to which he might compare the sensation. He felt weightless, for he could not feel his body pressing against anything, but at the same time he was being drawn to the cold, ice-filled river below. He was Alice falling down the rabbit hole. He remembered it now. Alice didn't rush down the hole, she took her time. She looked at things along the way. She didn't focus on the certain destruction waiting for her below. It was enough for her to be falling. The result was inevitable. She didn't panic about it.

It was a strange thought to be having at this moment.

Then he plunged into the icy water, the sounds of the world muffling into a dull roar. The water rushed by him as Peter dropped deeper and deeper. Within seconds he could see nothing.

A panic coiled around his body. Which way was up? He twisted around, only now aware that he hadn't held his breath as he plunged into the water.

He let his whole body relax, the weight of his skin, his clothes, his shoes dragging him down. He discovered that what he had thought was up was really off to one side. He turned himself so his feet pointed down.

Then he started swimming up, keeping his head as a guide.

His lungs burned. He wanted desperately to take in a breath of air. With difficulty he forced his mouth to stay shut.

Only a little more, he told himself. Only a little more. But he had no idea how much further it would be. He had no idea how deep he had sunk. He could see no light ahead of him.

His arms strained. Just a little more.

How much little more?

Don't give up.

He couldn't stand not breathing anymore. He just wanted to take in big gulps of air, to breathe and never stop breathing.

He pleaded with himself not to try to breathe—not just yet. Just a little bit more. That's all he wanted. Just a little bit further and he could finally breathe.

Before he knew he'd arrived, his hands broke the surface of the water. His head followed, and he gulped down one quick breath of air after another. Thick slabs of ice floated around him and bumped against his body, but he didn't mind.

"Peter!" Eddy cried.

Bullets splashed into the water around Peter. He gulped down some more air and dove underwater again to escape another round of bullets slashing through the water. He turned and swam in the direction from which they'd come.

Peter had gone perhaps ten meters when his hand bumped into a body.

He surfaced and came face to face with one of the mobsters. The man's teeth chattered as he tried to bring his gun around to Peter, but Peter punched him in the jaw. It was enough to send the hood into shock. He slipped down into the water.

The gun fell onto the slab of ice. Peter grabbed it.

"Peter," he heard Eddy gasp. Peter looked around and saw Eddy floating with just his face out of the water. When he exhaled, small streams of water blew out of his mouth.

Peter swam over to Eddy. He saw that his friend's face was horribly burned; good flesh torn and scorched. His eyes were glazed over. He continued calling for Peter as if the two of them were still far away from each other.

Peter dragged Eddy through the river with his left arm, and kept the gun in his right hand in case anyone else was around to cause them trouble.

When he reached the south side of the river, he pushed Eddy up onto the cement walkway, and then dragged himself up.

"Eddy? Eddy?"

Eddy began to shake violently, then his eyes opened. They stood out in strong contrast to the charred black skin of his face. Peter could see thin silver wires, now revealed to the world.

"Come on," Peter said. He shoved the gun into the top of his pants and leaned down to pick Eddy up. "We got to get to Breena."

"No."

"Shhh."

"No, Peter. Peter. Peter. I'm all messed messed up. I don't want to live no more."

"Quiet." Peter lifted Eddy and carried him toward the stairs.

"No. No. I'm all messed up. I'm tired. But I fixed it. I told them you geeked the slot." He laughed and coughed water up. "Sorry."

"Shhh."

"You geeked geeked her. I didn't tell about your friends. I just said I knew knew knew where the lab-coat was. They they said if I found found him, they'd get me fixed."

"Fixed?"

"They got an operation now. They can fix fix fix my nerves. I can get fixed."

"Eddy. They . . . No. We can't do that yet. We don't know how half the brain works. They lied to you."

Eddy turned his face away from Peter.

"Don't worry about it. Breena will fix you. You'll be as good—"

Eddy's voice cracked as he spoke. "No. No. I wish I were like you. You."

"What are you talking about? I'm a troll."

"But you know things. You made things happen. I'm just used used."

"I didn't make anything happen."

"Yes. Yes you did. You said you wanted to find out how to to be human. Human. And you did. The suit said you did. I heard her. You did it, Peter." Peter held Eddy a bit closer. "All these things happened to to to me. To me. I didn't know why. You know why. You got it all figured out.''

"No. No I don't," Peter whispered.

"Peter, I can't stand being alive anymore. Please please kill me.''

Peter stared down at Eddy in amazement. "No!"

"But I razzed you. Twice. I can't even trust myself. I'll do anything anything to feel like I'm in control. I can't stand stand it. I want to die.''

"I don't want you to.''

"I got to tell you something.''

"All right.''

"But first, you got to tell me . . . Are you angry angry angry about going with the mob? I mean, I know you want to go straight now. Do you wish it never happened?''

Peter thought of the ork family. "It got me through my life. It got me to here, and now I can do something else.''

"So?''

"So I don't regret it.''

Eddy moved his hand around and placed it on Peter's chest. With an enormous effort he turned toward Peter. "Good. Good. Peter, remember those cops on the lake? When we first met?'' Peter nodded. "I set that up.''

Peter stopped walking.

"I set that up. I wanted to work with you. You had something. I could see it. But I knew you'd get chewed up without help. I wanted to help you. And and and you did your research, right? That's good, right?''

Peter found his mind was a blank slate, clean of all ideas and comprehension. "I don't know what to say, Eddy.''

"Say you'll you'll you'll remember me for how I helped you, not how I turned turned turned on you.''

And before Peter knew it, Eddy had slipped his hand

down to the gun, grabbed it, and brought it up to his chin.

"No!" Peter screamed.

Eddy pulled the trigger.

30

Kathryn rose up from her seat on the couch when Peter stepped through the apartment door. First she looked him up and down, then she looked into his face. "What happened?" Her concern made him want to cry.

He was afraid to talk about it. "Um, where are Breena and Liaison?"

"Packing. They say we've got to get out of here right away."

"No. We don't." A chill settled into him as he stood in the doorway. He began to shake.

"You've got to get out of those clothes."

As she headed toward the bathroom to get some towels, Breena entered carrying a well-worn vinyl knapsack. "Recognize this code?" she asked, and pointed to the display on the telecom.

"You don't have to leave."

"DO YOU RECOGNIZE THE NUMBER?"

He stepped over to the telecom and looked down. The display listed a telecom code and the time the call had been made. Peter recognized the number as the code of The Crew. The call had been made about thirty minutes ago.

"Yeah."

"Whose number?"

"My former boss. In the Itami gang."

"He knows where we are," said Breena tonelessly.

"No. Eddy didn't tell him."

"How do you know that?"

"I spoke with him."

"Oh, and then you let the little rat go again?"

"He killed himself." Peter realized that Kathryn was in the doorway, holding a stack of towels. He calmed himself and continued. "He's dead. The hoods are dead. All he told them was where Clarris was. He didn't tell them about you, me. He told them Kathryn was dead. He just wanted to get back on their good side, so he gave them information he didn't think would hurt me."

"I'm sorry," said Kathryn. He kept his gaze away from her.

Breena wasn't having any of it. "And you believed him?"

He took a fierce step forward, towering over her. "Yes. I believed him. Now, if you want to run, that's fine. But there's no need. He didn't reveal anything about this place. I'm sure of it."

Liaison had come in and was standing next to Kathryn.

"What's up?"

"The Prof's friend told the Itami gang where Clarris is." She turned to Peter. "I assume that means they want him, too. And they'll go get him."

"Look," said Liaison, wandering into the center of the room, and turning around to address everyone, "I know I'm pretty slow on some of this human interaction stuff, but could you guys humor me for a minute?"

Peter couldn't help but smile. "What?"

"Kathryn," she said, her tone somewhat exasperated, "you just said before you don't need to find this lab-coat. You don't want the operation after all. Still true?"

Kathryn nodded.

"And Profezzur, I never did figure what you were getting out of this, but do you need him?"

Peter thought of the My Cure chips sitting behind the plant. "I'd like to see him, yes."

Breena threw up her arms. "Like . . . !"

Liaison raised her hands and silenced her lover. "How important is it to you?"

Peter thought of Eddy dead in his arms, now buried in the Chicago River. And Thomas, dead in the Shattergraves. Landsgate a ghoul. Jenkins. Jenkins. Jenkins. So many people dead already. His need to show his father his work paled against the lives lost. And yet so many years of work . . . Even his father was obsessed with it, willing to break his contract with Cell Works just so he could keep searching for a way to stop people from being born metahuman. Did Peter need to see that man?

His gaze lighted upon Kathryn's face. So beautiful, strong. Slotted up, but still wonderful. "No." He surprised himself. It wasn't just because he'd found a friend in Kathryn or because of the grief for those who had fallen, but everything. The sum total of his life thus far. Looking back on it, it seemed more than enough to stand on its own. "No," he said again, and laughed. He felt tears welling up in his eyes and suppressed them. "No, I don't need to see him." A lightness filled his chest. He looked at Kathryn. Her smile grew slowly, full of pride and pleasure.

"Then what's it matter what the Itami gang is up to? We're done. It's all over."

Peter felt a slow snake of relief work its way up his spine. Could it be over? Was he finally released to wander through life without the past clinging to his shoulders?

"No," said Kathryn. "Not quite. There's one more thing. I don't want him for the operation. That I've resolved. But I want my position at Cell Works back. Itami wants Dr. Clarris so Garner can bring him back as a prize. I want him for the same reason.''

"Oh," said Liaison, her face slack for a moment. Then she smiled with clear understanding. *"So ka. Let's do it.''*

"Wait a minute, Kathryn. There are some problems," said Peter. "First, Garner dug up data on you, and then so did Itami. It won't be enough for you to get Clarris. The gang will turn everything over to the board. They'll bleed you.''

"Then I'll need something to prevent them from doing that.''

Peter stroked his chin. "Oh, that'll be tough. Wait a minute! The reason they've got you is because they've got records of you helping Clarris escape and then hiring your own shadowrunners to find him.''

"Yes.''

"But Garner is their stress point at Cell Works. If we get data on him—specifically, get his ties with the gang, then all the data cancels out. We blackmail them on that end. They flash their LEDs, we flash ours. I'm sure Liaison could help us in such a venture.'' Liaison blushed.

"Maybe," said Breena, starting to pace, slowly getting drawn into the logistics, "But if Red here really did help the doc escape—I assume the doc knows this?''

"Yes. We discussed it in detail.''

"When he's dragged in to Cell Works, whether you get him or Itami, he's going to download and send you packing.''

"Unless," said Peter, "he had a reason to lie.''

Kathryn nodded slowly. "Yes.''

"What would that be?" Breena asked.

Peter shook a finger at Kathryn, suddenly very excited. "He was probably as surprised that he didn't end up at Fuchi as you were, right?''

"Yes.''

"And this was all a plan. He was supposed to be able to keep in contact with you." Kathryn nodded. "He probably hasn't had the opportunity at ABTech, but if you were to make contact with him, he'd listen."

"Yes. I think so."

Peter rhythmically clapped his hands together. "All right. I think I've got a plan."

"Are you going to be drunk again?" asked Liaison with a smile. Apparently she'd liked that shag at Crusader.

"No. A very sober scientist. Just like Breena suggested earlier." He walked over to Kathryn and took the towels from her. "Liaison, you work with Kathryn tonight. You two track down every bit of electronic data that Garner might have lying around. Stuff at the office, on his home computer, anything you can deck into. And you get that personal information for Breena's spell. And Breena, can you do an astral check on ABT?" She gave him a look. "If you think you should."

"Won't do me any good. If they're slotting around with fetuses inside of grieving women, the background count there won't let me see a fragging thing, that I'm sure of. But I can get the spell set," said Breena. "What about you?"

"Me?" said Peter, walking off to the bathroom to dry off. "I'm going to make a special present for Dr. Clarris."

Liaison jacked into the Matrix, armed with the Cell Works passwords and data about Garner that Kathryn had given her. They giggled like schoolgirls as they ripped through his private and illegal dealings. Then Liaison was off to France to dig up ID on a tall scientist from Geneering.

Breena gathered her supplies, then called Zoze for some transport and some slick shadowrunners. When her tasks were complete, she went to sleep. She wanted to be well-rested when the time came to cast the spell.

Peter borrowed Breena's portable and slipped in a My Cure disk and spent the night typing. The work made him giddy, and every once in a while his laughter was louder than Kathryn's and Liaison's.

He felt a hand against his face, and he thought for a moment it was his father.

When he looked up, it was Kathryn smiling down at him.

"Morning," she said.

"Morning," he said.

"You don't have to do this, you know."

"Exactly. That's the wonder of it."

She laughed.

He pulled himself off the floor, very sore and stiff. "How'd you two make out?"

"Wonderfully. I can see why Itami picked Garner. He's ambitious enough to be everywhere, but clumsy enough to be controllable."

"And the letter?"

"Just finished sending it."

Breena sat on the floor behind him, pouring some powder from a leather pouch into a silver bowl. "I did an astral check on ABTech when I woke up. It's just as I thought. The place is crawling with horror. I ducked back without even going into the place. If they got mages, they're a dark bunch."

Liaison sat on the couch, legs tucked under her. "I was just in the Matrix a minute ago. No word yet of anything gone haywire at ABTech." She held out a small walkie-talkie. "Here. You can use this to contact me if you need me in there."

"Will you have to drop the illusion if the run gets hosed? I've heard about the astral link between the spell-caster and the spell. . . ."

"I'd rather keep you under disguise," said Breena. "And in that place—there's no way they'd trace the link at first. It's like trying to see inside of Lake Michigan. As long as you're out of there fast when the shooting starts, everything will be all right. Well, Binky, ready to be pure human?"

Peter glanced at Kathryn and found her looking at him. He wasn't sure, but he thought he saw disappointment in her eyes, as if she didn't want to see him as anything but a troll. "Yes, I'm ready. Let's do it."

Breena picked up a color fax print with the image of a man's face on it. Thomas Waxman. She pressed her fingers into the silver bowl and then raked the powder over the fax. Then she held her fingers above the fax, which she kept horizontal with the ground to keep the powder on the paper, and spoke a few words so softly that Peter could not hear them.

Electricity formed around her fingers. The powder jumped off the fax and up to her fingers, then back and forth between the paper and Breena's hand.

The light dazzled Peter. He thought of his plunge off the bridge and of falling through life. He saw the magic before him in a different light than he had before. Before it had been a tool, a strange tool, but no more than a tool.

Now he realized he didn't really know at all what it had to offer. How did it really mix with the way the body was built? Cutting himself off from the magic of the world was an option, but too easy.

As he watched the light grow brighter around Breena's hand, he thought of the cells in her fingers, the DNA within the cells, the magic genes along the DNA. Genes that let her tap into the way of the world in a manner forgotten for a very long time, if, indeed, magic had ever existed before. The magic let her connect directly with the world. Magic was not a tool. It was the thing that joined flesh to the air, and through the air to the powder. And to everything.

The differences between objects, people, broke down. And then the differences were built back up. Not through power over each other, but through the individual patterns drawn on identical templates.

The powder gathered in the light and floated around her hand. She turned to Peter and said, "Bend down."

He did so, and she gently touched her fingertips to his face.

The sensation startled him.

He closed his eyes, for he thought he might laugh or cry. He did neither, fearing either one might ruin the magic.

In his dazed state all Peter could think was "Of course!" as if a secret truth had been revealed to him, the exact nature of which stayed in a corner of his mind, just out of reach and full comprehension.

He felt Breena pull away from him, but the sensations stayed. The odd feeling passed down his neck, along his chest, and down his legs.

And then Breena cried out.

Peter opened his eyes and looked down at her. She sat doubled over on the floor. Liaison rushed to her side and put her arms around Breena's shoulders. "There, there," she said, and kissed Breena's forehead.

"What? What is it?" asked Peter.

"There's a blacklash sometimes," said Liaison. "Spells don't always work right."

He turned toward a mirror that hung on the wall. He still saw himself, but the image of another person flickered over him. The second man was more than two meters tall and had receding sandy blond hair. He wore a very classy suit.

The image was handsome. But Peter didn't think it was him. The troll in the mirror—that was him.

"It keeps flickering. Didn't it work?"

"I see it, too," said Kathryn.

"Same as the invisibility," Liaison said quietly, still holding Breena. "You know what the truth is, so the illusion doesn't hold. Profezzur's not really different. How we see him has changed. But it should work just fine for people who have no reason to be suspicious. It'll even fool cameras. It just took a lot out of Breena."

"Will she be all right?"

"I think so. It's always hard to tell. But you better go. She's going to have to keep focusing on the spell to keep it going. It's going to drain her. . . ."

"Maybe we should cancel . . . Wait until . . . ," said Peter.

"No," said Liaison. "This is one of the risks. Breena told me all about it. It happens. You can't get this close to magic without things snapping out of your control. You either accept the lack of control, or you get out of the biz.

"Go," Liaison said. "Go now."

31

Peter walked quickly up Michigan Avenue. Lacking his troll body to scare off potential muggers, he kept his head up and tried to move with confidence, thinking that if he could look confident, the world would think he had reason to be. Maybe that did the trick, for no one bothered him. But Peter found the whole experience very strange. For so long he'd worn his metahuman flesh as a badge of anger and strength. Now, he felt exposed, naked, and weak, not because of how he saw himself, but because of how he thought the world saw him.

Crossing the bridge over the Chicago River, he pulled the three chips out of his pocket. One was labeled "My Cure," one "P. Clarris," and the third, "CW." He took My Cure and crushed it between his thumb and forefinger, then dropped the pieces over the side of the bridge. P. Clarris he put in his right breast pocket, CW in the left. His father would get one of those two chips.

The area just past the bridge was run-down, but people with SINs worked it. All around him secretaries and suits were arriving in buses they had taken from their homes further north.

Women glanced at him. Men sized him up.

It had been so long since Peter had been noticed with anything but an undercurrent of suspicion or a strong hint of fear that he didn't know how to react. He glanced away, afraid. Would he reveal that he wasn't really pure human? Would they see his fear, his social awkwardness? There had been a safety in being ignored. Before he could afford to be angry at everyone on the street, because no one paid attention to him, or, at least, no one behaved as if they did. And then, as a member of the Itami gang, Peter had been able to vent his frustration with the ultimate fury. He joined the game of death and killed on command. He turned everyone into meat, just as the world had done to him.

Now he was part of the world of pure humans again. An attractive woman caught his eye, giving him a half-smile as she walked on by.

Was it really so simple?

Up ahead, he spotted a beat-up Bulldog Step-Van, brown with scratches that revealed silver. He stepped up to it and knocked on the side door. "Hello?" shouted an amused voice.

"Zoze sent me," said Peter.

The door slid open and Peter came face to face with the barrel of a shotgun. "Hoi, chummer," said a vatjob with a metal right arm. "Alone?"

Peter kept his face expressionless. "Yup."

The vatjob put the gun down and smiled. "Come on in." Peter climbed in and the Bulldog sagged to the right. The boy looked at him curiously, but smiled.

At the back of the van was a woman with rigger jacks in her temple. "Morning," she said wearily, making her way up to the front of the Bulldog. As the rigger took the driver's seat and jacked in, Peter was surprised to see that despite the van's worn exterior, the controls were quite fancy. Settling back into her seat, the rigger rested her hands on the wheel, even though she would not be using either the wheel or the gas pedal to move the van. Her thoughts would do all the work. The engine started up and the Bulldog took off for the Westside.

"Here's our number," said the vatjob, pointing to a radio built into the wall. Peter set his wristcom so he could punch it up with a single button. "We're gonna need code names. I'll let you pick." The boy exuded a youthful enthusiasm that charmed Peter.

Peter said, "You're Anderson. I'm Duckling. Got it?"

The boy laughed. "Duckling? Okay."

The van parked a few blocks down from the ABTech building, and Peter went on foot to knock at the nondescript steel door. Nothing happened, so he tried again, this time pounding on the door.

A few seconds later he heard metal scrape against metal and then the door opened, revealing a man in grease-covered gray overalls. The man looked like something out of a car repair shop, not a biotech factory.

"Yeah?" the man said, annoyed but disinterested in Peter.

"I'm Thomas Waxman. I'm here for a tour of the ABTech plant."

"Oh, sure," the man said brightly. "Come on in." He held the door open so that Peter could step inside. The next moment someone was smacking Peter behind the knees with a thick piece of metal, making him collapse to the floor. Only an hour as a pure human, he thought, and I've already given up my guard.

"Frag, this guy's limbs are tough," said a voice behind him.

Peter rolled over with a grimace, expressing more pain than he actually felt. The grease monkey and two guards with Predators stood over him. One of the guards held a crowbar in one hand.

"Do you mind telling me what this is about?"

"SHUT UP!" said the grease monkey. He leaned down and rummaged through Peter's pockets, pulling out the fake IDs and passport Liaison had made up for him.

"I have an appointment. My people . . ."

"I said shut up."

The grease monkey looked at the picture ID, then to Peter, then the ID, then to Peter. Fear crept up Peter's spine. Did the guard know something? Maybe it wasn't possible, for whatever reason, that Waxman could be in Chicago. What if the guard knew that? Would the illusion begin to waver as the guard's knowledge fought with the magic?

"Hmmm," was all the grease monkey said. "Run them through." He handed the documents to the guard with the crowbar.

Peter knew that the fake IDs wouldn't withstand top security checks. The plan called for the e-mail letter to anchor visual inspection of the IDs.

"What the frag is going on here!" Peter shouted.

The grease monkey turned to him, his face full of violence. The guard with the IDs stopped, too. "Don't give me the macho crap. When I report back to Geneering about how you rough up their employees, I think they'll take a dim view of the whole project. Drek, this is why I left this country!"

Inside he smiled. This was kind of fun.

The grease monkey's face softened, and he looked at Peter curiously. "Geneering," Peter said. "We're lending you the nanotech. We sent you a letter. My visit was announced."

Without taking his eyes off Peter, the grease monkey said to the guard with the IDs, "Take these to Doc Tumbolt. Get him to confirm this guy."

The guard left. Peter started to rise. "Can I get up now?"

"No."

Tumbolt was out of breath when he arrived. "Dr. Waxman!" he exclaimed. "Spirits!" He reached down and helped Peter up. "Please forgive . . . I don't know what to . . ." He handed Peter the stack of fake IDs, and Peter put them away. "We had no idea. . . . That is, no one noticed the letter. It must have passed by . . . We would have made arrangements to meet you. . . ."

"Which we would have refused, for security reasons, of course," said Peter.

"Speaking of security, how did you find this place, doc?"

Tumbolt raised a finger to scold the grease monkey, but Peter shrugged to show he took no offense.

"After all, we went to great lengths to make sure you didn't know where the nanotech was going."

"And you didn't think we'd follow up the shipping route and make sure we knew where the prototypes were at all times?" He turned to Tumbolt. "I'll be direct, since your guards seem to prefer that tactic.

We were content to let things run your way until someone broke into our files earlier this week." He turned back to the guards. "Now we know that isn't your fault. And actually, the main purpose of this trip is to ease the minds of my company's management. They just want to know that everything is proceeding along well."

"We send you weekly reports—," Tumbolt began.

"Yes, yes. But we decided it was time for an on-site inspection. Now I don't know who did it, but someone from ABTech wrote back saying it would be all right. I can contact my people and ask them to dig up the letter."

"Not now. You must be exhausted. Come, would you like to rest for a while? I can get a room for you."

"No, actually, I'd like to begin the tour right away."

"Of course."

Tumbolt shot a brief glare at the grease monkey, then let Peter through a dirty door that led to a sterile white corridor. The guards remained quiet as Peter and Tumbolt left, and Peter knew that the grease monkey would check ABTech's outgoing e-mail long before he could fake his call tur   ope.

Tumbolt led Peter to an elevator that led deep underground. When they stepped out, he found himself looking through a huge pane of glass into a large room filled with operating tables, each contained within a plastic bubble.

"Where are the patients?"

"We often power-down the operating facilities. Nothing is wrong."

"Doctor Tumbolt, we've heard you recently brought Dr. Clarris on board. . . ."

Tumbolt lifted one eyebrow in surprise and awe. "You people do have good sources."

Peter nodded. ''I didn't want to talk about it in front of the men upstairs, but my real reason for being here is to discuss Clarris' theories in the context of our nanotech research.'' He leaned in, sharing a valuable secret, taking Tumbolt into his confidence. ''I'm sure you understand.''

Tumbolt smiled back, honored. ''Of course. This way.''

They walked down a long corridor. A huge human with red cybereyes and a targeting system cable leading from his right temple to the gun in his holster eyed Peter carefully as they passed.

After they had gone by, Peter commented, ''Rather coarse security.''

''Not our doing. Our parent company in Seattle sent them to us after you were raided and our contracted security firm failed to catch the intruders.''

''Hmmm.''

Tumbolt pushed open a door into a conference room. ''Is Clarris here?''

From behind Tumbolt Peter saw two women and a man writing out strange symbols on a chalkboard. They wore jewelry like Breena's.

Mages. Peter held his breath. If they checked him astrally, they'd see through the illusion.

The three glanced briefly over their shoulders for a moment, shook their heads, and went back to work. Tumbolt shut the door.

''That's the damnedest part of the operation,'' he said, leading Peter down another hall. ''I'm too old to understand it. I don't *want* to understand it.''

''I see.''

''Oh, I don't mean I ignore it,'' Tumbolt said quickly. ''I mean, I know what they're up to. We've worked it so the process utilizes magic. The nanotechs go in and clamp down on the metahuman generepressors. But the only way we can get the nanotechs to identify the right genes is with magic. It's a kind of magical dye. They have to build a small spell lock—a little silver star—for the fetus. Horribly expensive. They're still trying to figure out how to get the material and labor costs down. Between the costs of the nanotechs and the magic, it's an economic nightmare. A cure for the rich.'' He laughed. ''And right now it is. But someday . . . someday we'll have that price point down, by spirits.''

Tumbolt pushed open the doors to the cafeteria. ''Look! There he is,'' Dr. Tumbolt said happily. Peter's back stiffened. His father sat alone at a table.

Peter and Tumbolt crossed the cafeteria, and as they approached, Peter saw that his father looked very, very old. He held a plastic fork in one bony hand, chewing his salad with a mechanical rhythm. And yet, Peter saw, the eyes were unchanged. They held their vague stare and soaked up every detail. Peter remembered waking fourteen years ago to find his father looking down on him. Always looking down. Even now, Peter still couldn't determine exactly what it was his father looked at. He seemed to be looking at Peter, but his focus could have been on someone to the right or someone far behind Peter. It was as if Peter's father was unwilling to commit. Or to let the world in on what he chose to see. A secret. A protection from the evil eye.

''Dr. Clarris,'' said Tumbolt, ''I'd like to introduce Thomas Waxman. Dr. Waxman, William Clarris.''

Peter's father looked up from his food and grinned. The smile chilled Peter, for it bore no resemblance to anything in nature. It was practiced. ''A pleasure to meet you,'' said his father.

''The same,'' said Peter. He was torn in two directions—one, to stay with the plan, and two, to blurt out his real identity to his father. He got lost for a moment looking into his father's eyes—it had been so long since he'd seen him. Half his life. The P. Clarris chip seemed to burn hot through the pocket of his jacket. "I did it, dad," he thought. "I did the impossible."

Peter shook himself out of these ruminations. "Dr. Tumbolt," he said, "if you would excuse us. Please." His father gazed on with apparently disinterested serenity. Tumbolt looked hurt. "Please. A matter of some delicacy." Tumbolt actually pouted, then waddled away toward the cafeteria counter without another word.

Glancing at the chairs at his father's table, Peter realized that none of them would support his weight. "Could we go somewhere private to talk?"

Without the slightest change of expression, his father said, "What's this about?" He seemed neither pleased nor upset.

"Please. It's very important. I have a message from . . . Kathryn."

William Clarris blinked twice, as if Peter had complimented his shoes, then carefully placed the fork on the table. "All right. My room will do."

They left the cafeteria and took a corridor that turned into a hall lined with doors on either side. Peter noticed that each door had a name on it. When they reached the one marked "Clarris," his father produced a card key and opened it. "Please," he said, and gestured for Peter to enter. Then his father followed him in, closing the door behind them.

32

A bed, a desk, a computer system, a rack of chips. Nothing on the walls, nothing to tie to the past. Or even the present. Like father, like son. Peter wanted to say, "Dad, we've got to stop this," but instead he said, "Dr. Clarris. I'm in the employ of Ms. Amij. She hired me to get a message to you."

"Yes," his father said plainly, "I thought . . . I wondered if she would ever find me. The plan . . . didn't work out," and again he smiled that joyless smile.

"Well, I did find you. And she wants you to leave with me now."

His father's eyes narrowed, just slightly. "What?"

"Your life is in danger here. We have reason to believe that another faction is on its way to get you."

The slightest bit of anger flared up in his father's eyes. "Does *everyone* know where I am?"

Peter suddenly felt frightened, on the spot, fearful of his father's wrath, even though his father didn't know who he was. "There have been complications. But the simple truth is that many people want to get you."

"The mercenaries from Seattle. They're here because of you . . . ," his father said.

"And because of the other faction. And because of you. Now, if you don't mind—"

"No. No, I'm not going." Peter noticed that his father's hand was shaking. He stepped over to the desk and sat down in the chair.

"Da . . . Dr. Clarris. I don't think . . ." Peter was momentarily at a loss for words. "There are professional killers coming to extract you," he said. "If you don't come with me, I—"

"They brought in magicians and bodyguards—I don't know if you've seen them, but they look quite professional. I'm staying."

"You are an employee of Ms. Amij's."

"Her company refuses to approve the research in which I'm interested. I'm staying here."

Peter froze for only half a beat. "Is it going well?"

"What?"

"The research. Is it going well?"

Peter's father blinked at him. He became carefully guarded once more. "Well enough. It's a start."

"Impressive facilities."

"Yes."

"I understand you have test subjects."

His father stared at him for a moment, still apparently indifferent. "Yes. We have test subjects."

"Lucky that you could get volunteers."

"What . . . ? What are you getting at?"

Peter realized that he was coming dangerously close to blowing the whole run. And yet, he wanted to know who he was dealing with. Those women . . . He reached into his jacket and pulled out the chip labeled "CW."

"What's that?" his father asked.

"A bribe, just in case you didn't want to come. I'll show it to you in a minute. This metahuman research is very important to you."

"Yes."

"Yes?"

"Yes. It's very important. I have my reasons."

"Reasons?"

"Yes, reasons!" His father was quite cross now.

"A son? You had a son, yes?"

His father stared at him. "Yes. I had a son. If you know that, why are we playing this game?"

"What happened to him?"

"What business—"

"What happened to him? After he became a troll, what happened to him?"

His father looked down. "I don't . . . He died. . . . I don't know."

"So why the work? Why the pursuit of the metagene cure?"

His father looked up, eyes cold, a fury behind them. "No one should have to go through what I did. What he did."

"And what was that?"

"Who do you think you are?"

"A man who brings you an offer from Ms. Amij for you to run your own project at Cell Works." He held up the chip between his thumb and forefinger. "This stolen research document will put you on a new track."

"I'm already on a track."

"But how is it going? Don't you at least want to see what this chip has to offer?"

His father leaned forward, just a little, a cat waiting to pounce on a piece of fuzz. "Maybe."

"But before I give you the chip, you have to answer me a question. Why? Why get rid of metahumans?"

"I don't want to 'get rid' of metahumans—I want to give the people the choice of how they will be. Some control of their destiny."

"So Peter could have controlled his destiny."

"Yes." The word came out like a footstep on a creaky floorboard.

"And if he hadn't become a troll, if it could have been changed, what would have been his destiny?

"A career in academics. Applied sciences. Whatever he wanted. He could have done something."

"And as a troll he couldn't."

"Of course not."

"How did you know?"

"What?"

"How did you know? How did you know what he could and couldn't do?"

"He was a troll."

"So, even though you don't want to 'get rid' of metahumans, everyone would be better off if they didn't exist."

His father paused. "I suppose."

Wrong answer, thought Peter. "Here." He placed the chip on the table. It was a copy of My Cure, but one altered by a night's work of careful errors. Bril-

liant errors. Four of them, all very subtle, so subtle
that they would lead anyone off the right path and into
years of wasted work. His father picked up the chip
and placed it in his computer. Peter turned around
and placed his finger against the chip in his right
breast pocket, the P. Clarris chip, the last remaining
copy of his work. He applied firm pressure and felt
the chip shatter between his finger and his chest. The
pressure against his chest as the chip shattered carried reverberations into his heart. He turned back to
his father and said, "Look it over. You'll get to use
all of it if you go back to Cell Works."

Peter took a position against a wall and stood patiently as his father scrolled through the document.
He couldn't help but compare how his father read the
text against the way Kathryn had. Kathryn was *alive*
when she read, she leaned in, engaged. His father
seemed devoid of energy, all life focused from his
eyes, which sucked in the light from the screen and
gave nothing back.

At the end of two hours, William Clarris was still
reading when an explosion rocked the walls.

"They're here," said Peter.

His father whirled around, confused. "What?"

"The other faction who's looking for you . . . some
mobsters, actually, they're here. Now. Are you coming?"

His father looked back at the screen hungrily.
"This is good," he said. "Very good. This is an
approach I've never seen before."

"Do you want it?"

His father nodded. "Yes. Yes, I'll come with
you." He shut down the computer and took the chip.

A sadness and happiness passed through Peter.
Happy because the plan was working, which meant
Kathryn might get Cell Works back. Sadness because
his father was gone. All that remained was a man, a
fearful, hateful man with whom Peter knew he could

not afford any connection. He would fall through life without a dream of his father during the plummet. Would that be all right? Yes. Maybe.

They rushed out into the corridor and turned left back toward the cafeteria. Speakers blared a toneless message: "Attention. Attention. The facility has been infiltrated. Report immediately to your designated secure station." Peter reached out his arm and kept a tight grip on his father's lab coat. They reached a stairwell, and Peter opened the door. From upstairs came the sound of gunfire.

"New plan," Peter said absently. Peter thought there might be a back entrance for the kitchen, something used for supplies and food. He moved toward the cafeteria, half-carrying his father as he went. He forced his way through the crowd also trying to get out and to the shelters. By the time they entered the cafeteria, Peter and his father were far ahead of the pack. They moved quickly across the empty eating area to the kitchen, getting about halfway across the room when the door slammed open behind them.

Coming through the cafeteria doors were the street samurai Peter had seen earlier, followed by a woman in a scarlet suit. Pinned to the lapels of the jacket were spell fetishes. The mage looked at Peter and her gaze turned glassy. "Waste him!" she said as her eyes snapped back into focus.

"Get down!" the samurai shouted to Peter's father as he brought up his AK-97 toward Peter.

Peter knocked his father to the right and dove for cover behind some tables to the left. As he skittered across the floor, three slugs pounded the ground beside him.

He pulled his Predator from the holster at his lower back, then kicked over a table to use for cover. Raising his head to get a shot on the samurai, Peter spotted the muscular warrior working his way closer.

Where was the mage? He glanced to the right and
spotted a wall of gray ooze rolling across the floor
toward him. For a moment he froze. He'd never seen
such a thing.

He tried to jump out of the way as it rushed up to
him, but his confusion made him panic and stumble
to the floor. The bulk of the ooze splashed off to the
right, but a few drops hit Peter's legs and ate into his
skin. Peter writhed on the ground and bit his lips in
agony as the material of his pants and shoes melted
into his flesh. Corrosive fumes billowed up around
him, the acid splashing onto the floor, the wall, and
the plastic tables and chairs.

Breathing heavily, Peter scrambled up and ran for
his father, his legs aching with sharp pain. They could
still make it out, but it would be tough. Limping
along, he took wild shots at the samurai and the
mage, keeping them down for cover. "Come on,"
Peter said, scooping an arm around his father and
rushing toward the kitchen. His father's stone face
finally broke and revealed terror. The situation was
that bad.

Peter glanced back. The mage, exhausted from the
spell, was kneeling on the ground, holding her head.
He hoped she'd be out for the fight.

Still making for the kitchen, Peter and his father
were rounding a corner when they slammed into a
massive weight. It was the samurai, and all three of
them tumbled to the ground. Before Peter could get
his bearings, the samurai was slamming his fist into
the acid-melted flesh of Peter's right shin. The pain
was so great Peter nearly blacked out.

The samurai stared hard at Peter, for the briefest
moment sizing up the situation, then, with a smile,
he raised his hand again, this time driving his open
palm into Peter's face, slamming Peter's head into the
tiled wall. A headache bubbled up from his spine and
filled his skull. Out the corner of his eye he saw the

white flash of his father's lab coat as the old man tried
to crawl away.

The samurai slammed Peter in the face again. Peter
realized he was quickly losing the ability to feel the
blows. The samurai coiled back for another punch.
He smiled again, and three long blades emerged from
the edge of the man's fist, turning his hand into a
living weapon. The samurai jabbed that hand toward
Peter, and the blades rushed closer. Peter, struggling
to remain conscious, thrust his hand up and knocked
the blow aside. Then came a strange sensation as
something seemed to slip away from his body. The
samurai's eyes grew wide. Suddenly there was a troll
beneath him. Breena must have let the spell down.

Peter smiled, as if they were going to share a moment of adversarial admiration, then reached out, and
pulled the samurai's body close. Peter opened his
mouth wide and chomped down on the samurai's
shoulder. His massive teeth drove deep into the other
man's flesh, and warm blood filled Peter's mouth.

The samurai screamed loudly, right into Peter's ear.
Peter bit down harder.

He released the bite, and the samurai fell back,
clutching his shoulder.

Peter grabbed his Predator from the floor and
dragged his father into the kitchen. His father was
staring at him in terror. Peter imagined what he must
look like: his terrible troll face, the mouth and lips
smeared with blood. The shock he'd given his father
made him giddy.

The sound of gunfire came thick now. He knew the
Itami gang had come in, armed to the teeth, but were
not expecting the shadowrunners from Seattle to be
guarding the place. All he had to do was get out while
both sides fired away at each other.

The samurai slammed into Peter's back, sending
both of them crashing into a rack of pots and pans.
The metal cookware clattered against the floor and

caused a terrible ringing in Peter's head. His body was in worse shape than he thought.

The samurai had picked up a meat cleaver off the floor with his left hand. He moved his arms in some kind of martial arts gesture, the cleaver in one hand, the cyberware blades sticking out of his flesh in the other. Peter raised his hand to shoot, and realized his gun was gone again.

He scrambled up, thinking desperately that he needed a plan, anything to get him through the next five minutes of his life. A thick wave of heat rose off a grease-filled pan. He turned away. . . .

And then turned back and grabbed the pan. The samurai rushed him, a bull in a rage.

The heat of the handle burned him, but Peter put his focus on the motion. He swung the pan and splashed the hot grease onto the punctured flesh of the bite he'd made in the samurai's shoulder.

The samurai screamed and dropped to his knees.

His father was on the ground, stunned. As Peter approached, he raised his arms and tried to fend Peter off. Peter reached down, picked his father up, and carried him under his arm. The weight strained him, but he had no time for discussion.

He couldn't spot his gun amid all the kitchenware, and decided to press on without it. Seeing a door that led out of the kitchen, Peter ran up and opened it. Just as he did, a ball of flame smashed into the wall beside him. The mage was back. He didn't turn to look, but instead ran up the stairs beyond the door.

He moved as quickly as his painful legs and the burden of his father's weight would let him. He just wanted distance. Distance from the mage. Distance from the Itami forces, the mercs. He just wanted out.

He ran up two landings, then opened a door into a corridor and stepped into it.

For a moment all was quiet.

Then three mobsters turned the corner down the

hall. They spotted him and raised their guns to fire. Peter rushed down the corridor, holding his father in front of him. Bullets slammed into his back and numbed him. He slipped around a corner and fell against a wall.

"Come on," he said to his father, spotting a freight elevator down the hall. "Just a little more to go."

"This is madness," his father said.

"Yup," answered Peter.

He heard the hoods running down the hall behind them. He got up, dragging his father along with him. At the elevator he slammed the button, but the hoods were rounding the corner. "Give us the labcoat!" one of them shouted.

The elevator door opened. Peter let his body fall into the car, and he dragged his father to the floor with him. Bullets crashed into the elevator's door-frame, then there was silence followed by the sound of running feet. Peter reached up and jabbed the button for street level. Please, he thought, please please please shut.

The doors closed. The sound of pounding came from the door, and then the elevator rose. A moment later the doors opened. They stepped out into a loading area in an alley.

Peter keyed the Bulldog's number.

"This is Anderson."

"Anderson," Peter wheezed, "This is Duckling. You ready?"

"Let's do it."

Peter rushed down the alley toward the street, still half-carrying, half-dragging his father. As Peter hit the sidewalk, the mobsters opened fire from cars parked across the street. The bullets cut through the air around him. As much as possible Peter tried to shield his father's small frame with his own massive body.

Then suddenly one of the cars flashed into a ball of flame. Bits of metal ripped through their pursuers, sending them sprawling to the ground with massive lacerations.

Peter heard a squeal of tires down the street. The Bulldog rushed toward the building, the rigger in the driver's seat. The boy leaned out the passenger window with a grenade launcher. He got off another shot, the grenade turning another car into a flaming wreck. The Bulldog squealed to a stop and the side door slid open.

Peter grabbed the doorjamb for support and shoved his father into the van. He was about to follow when he heard the building's steel door open. He turned and saw the grease monkey, armed with a tripod-mounted Valiant machine gun set in the doorway, open fire. The bullets cut deep into his right side and he spun around and slammed into the Bulldog.

Grease monkey continued to fire, grinding the bullets into Peter's chest. Peter couldn't feel his limbs anymore and knew he'd never be able to climb into the van on his own. He didn't have to. A strong pair of hands reached out from the van door and pulled him in.

Peter sprawled on the floor. The van door shut, and he felt the aggressive motion of the vehicle streaking down the street.

A few minutes passed and then Peter felt someone, the boy, lean over him.

"Oh, frag," he said after a cursory examination.

"Clarris?" Peter gasped. "Is Clarris here?"

"The package in the lab coat? Yeah, he's here."

"Get him to Amij."

"We got it, chummer, but when I saw those mob boys arrive, I really didn't think you'd make it. Now we'll get you back to Breena and she'll . . ."

Peter never heard the rest. His eyes had closed and he lost track of the world around him. It was all right now; he knew that much at least. His body felt warm and strong around him, a part of him. He no longer longed for a future time. What he had right now was enough.

BEING

be-ing (bē'ĭng), *n.* **1.** Existence, as opposed to non-existence. **2.** Conscious existence; life <the aim of our *being*>. **3.** Mortal existence; lifetime. **4.** Substance or nature <of such a *being* as to arouse love>. **5.** Something that exists <inanimate *being*>. **6.** A living thing. **7.** Human being; person.

33

Peter looked like a troll again.

He was pleased as all hell that he did. Living or dying, this was the form he wanted. Pain, pleasure, it was all his. The boundless loneliness he'd felt all his life, the constant search for someone or something to fill his emptiness, came snapping back in on him, and suddenly he felt his desires and wants bounded by his own flesh, his troll flesh. "Much more manageable," he thought. What was it Thomas had said to him in the Shattergraves? He'd asked a question. Something about whether Peter could make any connection between how some women might be attracted to him and others not, and his own search to be human again?

Yes, he saw it. Some men will think themselves men, and others will not.

The chopper buzzed in low over The Elevated. The silver and glass buildings were wondrous, no doubt about it, and he pondered how Kathryn could ever have believed she didn't already live in Oz.

He looked at her, sitting next to the pilot, her green suit cleaned and pressed. He could see her putting her corp mask back on her face. She spotted him watching her, smiled, and then the mask was on.

His father sat behind him, equally indifferent to the

architecture outside or to the troll beside him. Peter had insisted they keep his identity a secret from his father. He didn't want to give his father an opportunity to judge him ever again. Cowardly, perhaps, but why suffer any more than he had?

Peter had overheard a conversation William Clarris had had with Kathryn, and knew that his father cared only about getting back to the lab, getting locked up behind the safety of those sterile white walls. He would say whatever she wanted if he could continue his work. Peter's father would have just enough money to finish out his life spinning wheels on Peter's false data.

The chopper descended and the pilot brought it down to a clean landing. Just outside the helipad Peter saw several Cell Works security agents, a few Cell Works suits, and Billy, flanked by two of his thugs. He'd known Billy would be at the meeting, but seeing him still took his breath away. Peter was nervous, more nervous even than when he'd been about to meet his father. The copter doors opened, letting Kathryn, Peter, and his father climb out. Peter ducked down very low and moved methodically away from the blades. He took up a position slightly behind Kathryn, as if he were her bodyguard.

A white-haired man, one of the Cell Works suits, stepped forward. "Ms. Amij, wonderful to see you again." They shook hands. "We were quite concerned."

"You had reason to be," she said, and the Cell Works suits laughed politely. Kathryn looked at Peter, giving a tiny roll with her eyes. "But it is good to see you again, Mr. Serveno. How is your daughter's cough?"

"Much better now. Thank you, Ms. Amij."

Her gaze turned to Billy, and Peter stepped forward, taking a position between them. The blades had come to a stop now, and their normal tone of conversation

could be heard by everyone. A cold wind sliced across the roof. "Hello, Billy," Peter said.

Billy kept his eyes away from Peter. "Profezzur."

Peter decided to get right to business. "Billy Shaw, Ms. Amij. Ms. Amij, Billy Shaw."

"I've heard a lot about you," said Kathryn.

"Yeah, yeah. What's the deal."

"The same as we sent you yesterday, sir. Your stock stays. I stay. I run the company, as I should. I make a profit, you make more money. You stay off of P . . . Profezzur's back." Billy shifted, trying to figure out a new angle. "You've read the package we sent you. That's the deal." Her tone made it clear the matter was non-negotiable.

"And Garner?"

"He's yours. We've got his sanctioned confession on tape and locked away. If we release it, corp court will authorize a complete audit and investigation into everything you've ever bought, touched, or looked at. You played big time without paying percentages to the right people."

Billy turned slowly to Peter, then smiled. "I like her. You're going to do good for yourself." He turned back to Kathryn and put out his hand. "Deal."

Kathryn took it. "Deal."

Billy turned back to Peter. "I don't know if you did the right thing, but you stuck to it. And for that I admire you."

"Thanks, Billy." Peter felt his throat tighten. "See you around."

Billy made a gun with his fingers and pointed it at Peter. "Better not." Then he laughed and said, "Take care." He walked off toward one of two elevators, along with his men and some of the Cell Works security. Peter longed to spend just a few more minutes with Billy, but the doors of the elevator opened, he got in, and was gone.

Kathryn turned to Serveno. "Get Dr. Clarris set up

downstairs, please. He has a valuable document that he wishes to begin studying right away.'' Peter looked down at the ground. He could imagine nothing more terrible than sending his father on a wild research goose chase at the end of his life. But it was the only way to prevent him from actually completing the research. Short of killing him, that is, which of course Peter could not do.

Serveno, Peter's father, and the remaining guards boarded a second elevator and also left the roof.

Peter glanced at the elf chopper pilot, who sat oblivious in the cockpit, listening to music on headphones. He looked back to Kathryn, and she stepped up to him. ''Well,'' said Peter.

''Well.''

''You're good at this. This whole bargaining thing. Being a boss. Asking about the guy's kid. That was good.''

She twisted her hips slightly, girlish, amused and annoyed that he could name all her tricks. ''It was. I am good at this.''

''But you also handled yourself pretty well in a fight. Wanna go be a shadowrunner with me?''

''No.'' She smiled. ''No. I'm here. This is what I want. Nice, steady order.'' She glanced away, then back at him. ''How about you? What are you going to do? Want a job?''

Peter exhaled a large breath. He wasn't sure if she was kidding. ''That an actual offer?''

''You do good work. You're a good person. Yes, it's an offer. My staff would be confused for a bit, but they'd get used it. I'm the boss. I can make them get used to things.''

He smiled, flattered. Warm. ''I'll take that under consideration. But I was also thinking about going up to Byrne. Setting up some sort of tutoring program. Maybe . . . I don't know. Trying to get the place cleaned up.''

"You'll need a job either way. You could give away the huge salary I'll pay you to any cause you want. Buy a lot of data chips. Paint. Whatever."

"Hardball, eh? I'll think about it. Really."

"All right."

They stood silent for a moment, enjoying the sight of each other's eyes.

"Um," Peter said, his voice high-pitched for a moment. He paused again and watched a swirl of snow cut over the roof and drop off the side of the building. "Could I take you to dinner some time?"

Kathryn smiled coyly and then crooked her finger. Uncertain, he leaned down, and she gave him a peck on the cheek. He stood up, again, very happy. "Yes. Yes, you may."

"You're serious about the job?"

"Yes, again."

"All right. I've gotta go now. After I find a new place, I'll give you a call in a couple of days."

"Yes, you will," she laughed.

He turned and crossed the roof to the helipad and climbed into the chopper. Kathryn looked at him through the glass. She waved and Peter waved back.

The elf turned and said, "Where to, chummer?"

Peter thought about it and realized he hadn't a clue where to go next. "Could we just cruise around for a while?"

"You got it."

The elf flicked a switch and the blades started up. Kathryn waited on the roof as the chopper lifted into the sky. She and Peter waved to one another once more, then she entered the building.

Peter settled into the seat as comfortably as he could. He looked down at the snow-covered buildings of the city. They seemed to rise and fall like the waves of a stormy sea frozen for one moment. So much to see, Peter thought. So much to fall into.

"Tell you what," Peter shouted to the elf. "I'm

going to take a nap. We got enough fuel for an hour?''
The elf checked a gauge and nodded. ''All right. Wake
me up in an hour, and I'll have a destination.''

"*So ka.*"

Peter closed his eyes, the steady thrum of the blades
comforting him. He'd sleep, and when he woke up,
he'd have a plan. Or he'd make one up on the spot.
But what mattered was that when next he opened his
eyes, he'd still be a troll. Thank goodness.

MAGICAL ADVENTURES

MAGICAL REALMS

☐ **KING OF THE SCEPTER'D ISLE—A Fantasy Novel by Michael Greatex Coney.** Fang, the most courageous of the Gnomes, joins forces with King Arthur and the beautiful Dedo Nyneve to manipulate history in a final confrontation of wills and worlds. "Spirited, zestful . . . truly magical." —*Booklist* (450426—$4.50)

☐ **SUNDER, ECLIPSE AND SEED—A Fantasy Novel by Elyse Guttenberg.** Even as Calyx struggles with her new-found power of prophecy, her skills are tested when the evil Edishu seeks to conquer Calyx and her people through their own dreams. (450469—$4.95)

☐ **WIZARD'S MOLE—A Fantasy Novel by Brad Strickland.** Can the politics of magic and the magic of advertising defeat the Great Dark One's bid for ultimate power? (450566—$4.50)

☐ **MOONWISE by Greer Ilene Gilman.** It was Ariane and Sylvie's own creation, a wondrous imaginary realm—until the power of magic became terrifyingly real. (450949—$4.95)

☐ **THE LAST UNICORN by Peter S. Beagle.** One of the most beloved tales in the annals of fantasy—the spellbinding saga of a creature out of legend on a quest beyond time. (450523—$6.95)

☐ **A FINE AND PRIVATE PLACE by Peter S. Beagle.** Illustrated by Darrell Sweet. Michael and Laura discovered that death did not have to be an end, but could be a beginning. A soul-stirring, witty and deeply moving fantasy of the heart's desire on both sides of the dark divide. (450965—$9.00)

If you and/or a friend would like to receive the *ROC Advance*, a bimonthly newsletter featuring all the newest and hottest ROC books and authors, on a complimentary basis, please fill out this form and return it to:

ROC Books/Penguin USA
375 Hudson Street
New York, NY 10014

Your Address
Name _____
Street _____ Apt. # _____
City _____ State _____ Zip _____

Friend's Address
Name _____
Street _____ Apt. # _____
City _____ State _____ Zip _____